I0609662

ARMOR BRIGADE

ARMOR BRIGADE
BOOK 1

TOBY NEIGHBORS

Armor Brigade

Copyright © 2023 by Toby Neighbors

ISBN: 978-1-952260-52-0 eBook

978-1-952260-53-7 Paperback

Mythic Adventure Publishing, LLC

Idaho, USA

ALSO BY TOBY NEIGHBORS

My Lady Sorceress

The Man With No Hands

ARC Angel

Battle ARC

Broken Crucible

Hidden Kingdom

War INC

Carthage Prime

Cronus Team

Skandia Seven

Mercurial

Magnificus Prime

Incursio

Merlin Appears

Runners

Survivors

Infiltrators

Resistance

Conquest

Occupation

Extraction

The Signal

Battle Orders

Base Of Fire

Hard Site

Recall

Evade

Assault

Space Fever

PROLOGUE

"WHAT A BUNCH OF PATHETIC, soft, ugly, worthless human beings," the drill instructor shouted. "I'd just as soon wipe my backside with the lot of you. I did not enter this man's army to work miracles, but that's what I've been tasked with doing. Of the thirty recruits in this class, only half of you will make it through basic training. And I know that there's plenty of you snowflake liberal pansies who would jump at the chance to be washed out. But that's not how this works. You fail basic training; you repeat basic training. You have been called by your country to defend our great planet, and I will make battle troopers of you if it is the last thing I do. Is that clear?"

"Yes, Drill Sergeant!" the recruits shouted.

"You're right about that," he grumbled. "What's your name, slimeball?"

The drill instructor was standing in front of a chubby, terrified-looking man with pale skin.

"Quincy McMasters," the man said.

"How old are you, McMasters?"

"Twenty-five."

"Twenty-five what, recruit?" the drill instructor screamed in Quincy's face.

"Twenty-five years old, Drill Sergeant."

"At least you have a few brain cells in that oversized head, McMasters. You look like a marshmallow. Do you like to eat, son?"

"Yes, Drill Sergeant."

"When was the last time you did a sit-up, McMasters? Or ran a mile?"

"I don't really know, Drill Sergeant," Quincy said softly.

"Speak up, recruit!"

"I don't know, Drill Sergeant!"

"You will know after today. I can guarantee you that."

He walked over to a huge black man with bulging muscles. He had thick eyebrows, a square chin, and a broad smile on his face.

"What are you smiling about, recruit?" the drill instructor asked.

"Looking forward to showing you what I can do, Drill Sergeant!" the man replied.

"You look like a damn cartoon character," the drill instructor declared. "You think those muscles are going to help you, but I'm guessing not. You'll drop before you've run a mile."

"No, Drill Sergeant!"

"What's your name, muscle man?"

"Henry Dyson, Drill Sergeant."

"My name is Sergeant Garth Reed. But you will call me Drill Sergeant. You will wake up when I tell you, do what I tell you, eat what I give you, and sleep when I tell you. Nothing in the next three months will be your decision. You can turn that part of your brain off if you're smart enough to have one. It's my job to make you into killing machines. When I'm done with you, you'll run all day straight into the face of danger without thinking twice, and when all is said and done, you'll ask for more."

He paced in front of the group. It was all men. They were dressed in camouflaged pants, white T-shirts, and boots that laced up over their ankles. Their heads and faces were recently shaven. The drill instructor moved to a younger recruit in the middle of the platoon.

"What's your name, recruit?"

"Cosmo Frost, Drill Sergeant!"

"Where are you from, Cosmo?"

"Saint Stevens, west side, Drill Sergeant."

"You're about to have the worst three months of your life, Frost," the drill instructor shouted. He was so close to Cosmo that their noses nearly touched. "Can you comprehend that, recruit? Do you have anything rattling around inside your head that can accept the words that I'm saying?"

"Yes, Drill Sergeant!"

"Very good, Frost. I read your file. You were on your way off world when the call to duty came. And here you are. Did you have big plans, Frost?"

"I was going to school on Triton, Drill Sergeant."

"How about that. A college boy. Maybe there's hope for you, Frost. But let me be absolutely clear. The only hope you have of surviving the next two years is by taking heed of every detail of everything I teach you. I'm going to make you a trained killing machine, a deadly warrior, and a useful member of this military. But make no mistake: while you will be a lethal force, recruit, you will be dead if you don't take every minute of this training seriously. Can you do that, Frost?"

"Yes, Drill Sergeant," Cosmo replied.

"We shall see. Let's start with a short run. About face! Let's begin, recruits. Follow me!"

He started jogging and the platoon followed behind him. The sun was in their eyes as it sank toward the western horizon. The first day of their military training was almost over, but the hardship had only just begun.

CHAPTER 1

IT WAS FINALLY HERE! The day Cosmo had been waiting for all summer, maybe all his life. His bags were packed, his interstellar transport ticket was purchased, and he already had a dorm assignment. He was going off world for the first time. He knew his mother was going to miss him, but she had struggled to provide for him as a single parent. In many ways, her life would be easier with him gone. And eventually, he would get a good job and help her financially.

He threw off his blanket and got a shower. His mother was waiting when he came walking out of his little nook in their tiny apartment. It wasn't really a bedroom, just a wide section of the hallway that led to the bathroom. She had hung a curtain for him there when he turned fourteen. He came out smiling, and she did her best to match his excitement.

"You've got your ticket?" she asked.

"On my PIP," he said, holding up his portable information pad.

"And you'll message me?"

"As soon as we arrive," he told her. "Pictures too. I promise."

"Oh..." She was still smiling, but there were tears in her eyes. "I'm going to miss you so much."

"I'll be back in three years," he said. "You'll hardly even know I'm gone."

"I'm so proud of you," she said, embracing him.

"Thanks, Mom."

"Take care of Allura and message me. You don't have to write every day, but at least once a week."

"I'll write so much you'll want to block my number," he said, kissing her on the cheek.

"Your dad would be proud. Now go change the world."

"Yes," he said with a wide smile.

He left their apartment with his duffel bag stuffed with clothes and a tiny suitcase his mother had saved up to buy. It was secondhand, but Cosmo didn't care. The hard case had the slate computer he'd earned by taking advanced courses in high school. He wasn't a brainiac, but schoolwork and studying weren't difficult for him. He didn't play a lot of sports like most of his classmates, and he didn't need to party every weekend. And then there was Allura. Cosmo did well in school, but Allura was an academic superstar. They had started dating nearly two years ago, and they both applied to universities on Triton Four. Cosmo was accepted into the Brookings School for Business Studies. Allura had a full scholarship to the Triton Technology Institute. Everything is in our favor, he thought as he rode the elevator down from the eighteenth floor of his building.

Sure, the elevator smelled like someone had relieved themselves in it. And his home world, Fiona Grand, was at war with the Ma'Tis, but that was far away in the coastal areas. The crustacean invasion, as most people called it, had been raging his entire life. Scenes of the fighting were shown daily on the news programs, but most people believed that the government was using the war as a way to solidify their emergency powers. Not that Cosmo worried about any of that. He had two small scholarships and a generous grant that allowed him to study on Triton. And he was going on an adventure with Allura Presley. What could be better than that?

He saw her as he approached. She was already on the sidewalk outside her building. It was nicer than his own. Everything about her was nicer, which was what made it so hard to believe that she actually liked him. Cosmo felt like he had won the galactic lottery. When she smiled at him, it felt like fireworks were exploding inside him.

"Are you ready for this?" she asked as he approached.

He leaned over, kissed her cheek, and whispered, "I've been ready for this my whole life."

"Let's go," she said.

"How's your parents?"

"Fine," she replied as they started for the spaceport. "Kara starts school next week, and Beau will be starting quarterback this year. I doubt they'll even realize I'm gone."

"That's not true," Cosmo said. "Your dad made me promise on pain of death that I would look out for you."

"He was teasing."

"He loves you," Cosmo insisted.

"The real question is how was your mom?"

"She teared up, but she'll be okay. I promised to message her at least once a week."

They stopped at the hover-bus pickup area. It came gliding along a minute later. They stepped on, waved their PIPs at the automated ticket reader, and found seats together. There was a video display above their heads, but they ignored it. The prime minister was giving another speech, but Cosmo wasn't planning to be around long enough for anything the government on Fiona Grand did to affect him. He was on the cusp of becoming an intergalactic traveler, his future was bright, and he had the most beautiful girl in the sector sitting right beside him.

The hover-bus took them to the central terminal of the city. It was packed with people catching flights and speed trains to all parts of the planet. No one had traveled by boat since the Ma'Tis invasion. The aliens were water people, although they raided inland deeper and deeper all the time. There were also shuttles up to the orbital station that was protected by the Galactic Fleet. The Ma'Tis weren't the galaxy's only space-faring species that humans had to worry about. Of course, none of that was on Cosmo's mind as they waited in line to board the shuttle that would take them up to the space vessel that would carry them to the Triton system.

Security was tight, but they passed with no issues after being scanned for weapons. It wasn't until they reached the gate to board their shuttle that things fell apart.

"Oh, I'm sorry sir, but you can't board," the attendant working the gate told Cosmo.

"What? I've got my ticket, right here," he said.

"What's wrong?" Allura asked the woman.

"I'll have to get a supervisor," the attendant said.

"No way," Cosmo said. "This can't be happening."

"It's a mistake. We'll work it out," Allura said.

She was always calm, but then she hadn't lived through the tragedy he had. Nor had her life been plagued by setbacks the way his had been. Everything came easy for Allura. Not that Cosmo was jealous or resentful, but his life was haunted by bad luck. It was one of the reasons he was looking forward to leaving Fiona Grand. He hoped that perhaps his life would turn out better if he could just get away for a while.

"They're not going to let me board, and I'll have to get a new ticket," he complained. "It'll be days before another ship is going to Triton if I can even get a seat on it. I'll miss orientation."

"Stop it," she said. "You don't know that anything bad is going to happen."

He wanted to believe her, but when he saw the security officer approaching with the gate attendant and her supervisor, he felt a cloud of dread settle over him.

"Can I see your identification?" the supervisor asked.

Cosmo handed over his state-issued ID, while Allura asked, "Is there a problem?"

"No problem," the supervisor said. "I take it the two of you haven't seen the news this morning."

"What news?" Allura asked.

"There's been a big push by the Ma'Tis. They've reached the Vassburg metro area."

"But that's four hundred kilometers inland," Allura said.

Cosmo had no idea how she knew that. He could picture Vassburg in his mind. It was a major city, but he had no idea how far it was from the coast. It was just the kind of thing that Allura knew.

"Yes, well," the supervisor said, "Prime Minister Ketel has issued a stay on all males between the ages of eighteen and twenty-five. I'm afraid you can't leave the planet, young man."

"A stay?" Allura said. "But that can't be right."

"I'm afraid it is," the security officer said. "They're reinstituting the draft. It's for the common good."

"But I..." Cosmo tried to explain. "I'm supposed to go to university on Triton Four."

"We're sorry," the supervisor said. "But the PM issued an executive order at eight o'clock this morning. It went into effect immediately. You are welcome to board the shuttle, Ms. Presley. But I'm afraid we have to ask you to return home, Mr. Frost."

Cosmo stepped back. He was afraid he was going to be sick.

"This isn't fair," Allura said. "He's got a ticket and scholarships too. You can't keep him from going."

"It's not up to us," the security guard said. "We have to follow the law."

"But it just can't be," Allura said.

"I'm afraid it is," the supervisor said. "We'll give the two of you a moment to decide what you want to do, Ms. Presley. But you'll need to board in the next few minutes, or you'll miss your flight up to the orbital space dock."

"You have to go," Cosmo said, fighting back the tears he felt stinging his eyes.

"No, I'm not leaving you," Allura said.

"You have to," he insisted. "You miss this flight, and you'll miss the start of classes. They might even revoke your scholarship."

"I don't care," she said.

"Allura, if they take your scholarship, your parents will be so angry. They can't afford to send you there. It's over a hundred thousand credits each quarter. You have to go."

"What about you?"

"I'll follow. I'll find a way," he said, but without conviction.

"If they're drafting people into the military..." she said, afraid to finish the sentence.

"I know," Cosmo said.

"I can't," she said, suddenly very emotional. The tears came hard and fast. "I can't leave without you."

"Yes, you can," Cosmo told her. "Just go to school. It's the right thing to do. I'll catch up once they clear me to leave. There has to be a way to appeal the stay."

"You promise you're coming?" she asked.

"I promise," he told her. "You go. I'll message you as soon as I find out what's going on."

She nodded and wiped the tears from her eyes. "I love you, Cos."

"I love you too."

They kissed, but neither of them felt good about it. Allura turned away fast, but he saw more tears. The gate attendant scanned her PIP and Allura disappeared into the tunnel that led to the shuttle. Cosmo watched her go, then slumped into a seat next to the wide window that showed the aircraft lifting off. He held his duffel bag to his chest and tried not to cry as the shuttle he was supposed to be on lifted into the air and flew away. Cosmo felt like a part of his heart had left him, and he didn't think he could recover.

CHAPTER 2

ALLURA DROPPED into the high-backed seat and fastened her safety harness. She had purposely left the seat to her right vacant. That was Cosmo's seat. He deserved that seat. He worked hard for it—so hard. School had come easy for her. She had no trouble understanding the materials, and it only took hearing the information or reading it one time and she could recall it all. Her mind was like a sponge, and she could call up information faster than a supercomputer. But none of that would help her get through orientation without Cosmo.

They had met at school. He was handsome and popular with the teachers, but there was a sadness to him as well. His father had died when he was little—just seven years old. A raid by the Ma'Tis had damaged the tracks of the west coast Mag-Lift speed rail. No one knew until it was too late. The derailment had killed seven hundred people. Cosmo's father, Joshua James Frost, was one of them. Cosmo's mother had never recovered from her grief. She was a sweet lady, and she treated Allura like her own daughter, but as the shuttle lifted off, Allura wondered if she was going to be like Cosmo's mother.

Her sadness wasn't lifted by the incredible sight of passing through Fiona Grand's upper atmosphere, nor the brilliance of the stars from orbit. When the ship docked with the space station, she shuffled off with the other passengers, but she couldn't help but feel robbed. Cosmo would have been so thrilled. They were supposed to be starting a new phase of their life together. No one understood her like Cosmo did. In school she excelled academically but had trouble connecting with the other students who saw public education as more of a social event than a time to learn. She had friends, of course, but unlike her brother Beau, who was a popular, athletic star, she was more interested in learning than in hanging out or keeping up with who was dating who.

She walked across the concourse carrying her luggage. Unlike Cosmo, she had a matching set of luggage with little wheels to make moving the bulky, hard-case containers easier. She had a big suitcase and a small one, along with a travel bag full of her essentials. After checking onto the big transport headed for the Triton system, she found the private cabin, secured her luggage, and then had a good cry. She messaged Cosmo on her PIP, then sat on her bunk wishing he was there with her.

Ship announcements were made as they began to depart from orbit. The transport would accelerate for several hours before it could make the jump into hyperspace. The entire trip would last three days. She had no idea how she was supposed to deal with her loneliness. It was tempting to message her parents, but she knew what they would say: Don't worry. Just take care of your business and be safe. Maybe it's for the best. How could being abandoned by the one person in the entire galaxy who understood her and was always there for her be for the best? It didn't compute. Allura liked things neat and clear, not ambiguous, and uncertain. But her parents had always just tolerated Cosmo. They thought he was too introspective, and even though she didn't like to think ill of her own parents, she knew they didn't like that he was poor. What they didn't know was that Cosmo had been so strong and compassionate with her that Allura didn't suffer by her parents' lack of attention. She was the smart, capable firstborn. Their attention was given to their popular son and their needy younger daughter. Without Cosmo in her life, Allura would have struggled through school. And she wasn't sure that she could manage life all on her own.

It took much longer for messages to connect to the planetary network from outer space. Personal correspondence was not a priority in space communications. And the farther the transport got from Fiona Grand, the longer it took for his reply to her message to reach her. The message she got back from Cosmo was upbeat, but she didn't believe a word of it. Miss you and see you soon. Have a great trip. He was obviously upset, and she should have been there to help him. Guilt came crashing in on top of her own misery.

She read the message and cried again. Finally, after getting through the grief of leaving home alone without her boyfriend, she made her way to the dining section of the ship where frozen meals were served on biodegradable trays. She heated one, picked at the bland food, and returned to her cabin with a package of cookies from a vending machine. The days passed in a blur. She slept a lot. Tried to read a book but failed. And eventually she looked into the history of the Ma'Tis invasion, watching documentaries on her PIP while she wondered what Cosmo was doing back at home.

CHAPTER 3

"NO!" his mother declared when she came home from work and found him in his usual spot by the window. "No, you're supposed to be on your way to Triton."

"They wouldn't let me on the shuttle," he said.

"The damn politicians!" his mother complained. "They can't do this to us. Surely, you can appeal. You've been accepted and the school is expecting you."

He knew all that, of course, and had already looked into the appeal process. After standing in line at the local government office for over an hour, he was given a form to fill out and told that the appeal board was about six months behind. He had left without bothering with the form. He called his government representative but got a recording instead of talking to a real person. Worse still, before he even got home, he got a call from an automated message service informing him that he had been drafted.

"Appeals take at least six months," he told her. "I already looked into it."

"Oh, sweetheart, I'm so, so sorry."

"That's not the worst of it," he said.

"Don't," she said as she collapsed into the old loveseat that was across from his chair. "I don't want to hear that."

"Two days," he said.

"No," she argued.

"Fort Randal. I can catch a bus at the local recruiting office."

"You signed up?" she asked.

"Drafted," he told her. "I'm in the first wave."

There was a lot of cussing. Cosmo's mother didn't normally use such language, but she was furious. He pulled out the bottle of whiskey she kept in the back of the pantry. His mother wasn't a drinker, but she couldn't always afford medicine. The whiskey had been a gift from her boss at the cleaning agency where she worked ten hours a day, five, sometimes six days a week and barely made enough to keep them in the tiny apartment. She used the whiskey when she got a cold, and she only took a sip when her nerves were shot. Cosmo poured her some into a coffee mug.

"Drink this," he said. "Look at the bright side: I'll be getting paid."

"Are you out of your mind?" she whispered as the sip of whiskey she had taken burned her throat and made her wince.

"I don't have a choice," Cosmo said.

"What does Allura say about it? She can't possibly be okay with you going off to war."

"She's on her way to Triton."

"She left without you?"

"Of course she did," Cosmo said.

His fear and disappointment had been replaced with resolution. There was no way to escape his fate. He couldn't run away. Even if he knew of someone who could get him off world, he had nowhere to go, no means to make a living. Fiona Grand was his home. If he was being called to defend her, then he would do what he had to do.

"I made sure of it," he continued. "She has a bright future."

"So—do—you," his mother insisted.

"The law is the law," Cosmo argued. "If I don't report I'll be arrested. It's just for two years, and who knows, I might not even be part of the fighting. There are a lot of jobs in the military other than fighting."

They talked late into the night, both of them taking turns fuming over the injustice of it all. The next morning his mother went to work despite a raging headache. That was the tradeoff for the booze she had ingested. Just one mug less than halfway full had been enough to give her a terrible hangover.

Cosmo went to the military recruiting office. He wasn't the only person to arrive with questions. He found out that he would be sent to Fort Randal outside Lucasville for intake and basic training. After that, he would be assigned to whatever school his commanding officers decided was best, and depending on what specialty he was given, he would serve the remaining time on his two-year enlistment as needed. It wasn't much of a reassurance, but there was hope that he might not see any fighting. Not that Cosmo was afraid of a fight. He had fended off school bullies and held his ground when challenged by the rougher kids in his building. But he wasn't a child anymore, and the military wasn't like a schoolyard.

The Ma'Tis had suddenly become much more aggressive. He went back and looked at the archived news stories regarding the war over the last six months. Normally, the Ma'Tis, which looked like giant versions of crabs, complete with hard exoskeletons and massive pincers, only sent raiding parties inland. They were amphibious creatures who had taken over Fiona Grand's oceans. Even the most advanced underwater vehicles were no match for the aliens. But on land, the humans had held their own. The once populous coastal cities were all abandoned, and the military kept roving bands of fighters near the shoreline. But over the past two months, the Ma'Tis had formed an army and unleashed a new weapon. The scientists called them bio-bots: tiny organic machines that were the size of a human cell. They could force their way into a person's body, disrupt the circulatory and nervous systems, and take control of their host. No one with exposure to the bio-bots lived more than a few hours, but those infected had caused serious harm to the defensive forces along the coast.

It was a scary development and Cosmo wasn't looking forward to the idea of fighting the Ma'Tis. There were plenty of newsreels, along with popular movies of heroic humans taking down the towering, crustacean aliens. But Cosmo didn't see himself as a warrior. He was just a regular guy. How much difference could he make against the alien threat?

The next morning he kissed his mother goodbye for the second time that week. She didn't hold back her tears. When she hugged him, she squeezed hard and then told him to take care of himself.

"And message me," she said.

"I'm not sure how often I'll have access to my PIP," he said. "From what I've read online, bootcamp is pretty austere."

"Just let me know something," she insisted. "However and whenever you can."

"I will, I promise."

He left, walked to the recruiting station, and joined almost twenty other new recruits who had been drafted. Most were older than he was. Three other boys were fresh out of high school, and the others were all in their twenties. No one talked. There was a feeling of anger among them. No one liked being forced to do something. The government on Fiona Grand hadn't implemented a draft since the Global Cooperation Treaty nearly a century earlier. Cosmo spent the last few hours of his personal time texting a message to Allura.

I'm not sure when you'll get this, he wrote. I was drafted in the first round. No surprise. I got the notification after spending all morning trying to get an appeal hearing on the PM's executive order. But the appeal board is six months behind, and the local officials weren't taking calls. So I'm in the military. Actually, I'm waiting to take a bus to the intake facility near Lucasville. Basic training lasts three months, and when I finish that I'll be assigned to a specialty training. Hopefully, I'll be able to send you more info on that down the road. The recruiter here in town told me they'll take my PIP right after we start basic training. So don't worry if you don't hear from me for a while. I'll message you as soon as I can.

I can't believe how much I miss you. I hope you're having fun for the both of us. You should almost be to Triton Four by now. Send me pictures. I want to see your dorm room and what the campus looks like. I know this stupid draft has thrown a wrench into our plans, but I did learn that military service comes with a college funding plan. Maybe I can get back into business school and catch up when this stint in the military is over?

One more thing: I know you don't want to hear this, and I didn't want to write it, but we have to be honest. There's a chance I won't make it. Even if I do, two years is a long time. I'll always love you, no matter what. But I don't want you to wait for me. You'll be in a new school with lots of new people. I want you to enjoy yourself. Go out, have fun. If you meet someone new, I'll understand. I want you to be happy. Know that you made me happy and that I'm holding what we had close to my heart.

It was sappy, and she wasn't the type who loved romantic comedies or expected him to make a big fuss for Valentine's Day or anniversaries, but he didn't know what else to say. His future had been ripped away from him. There was no way to know when or if they would ever see each other again. He was resigned to his fate and resolved to find a way to get through the next two years. No matter what they threw at him, he only had to make it two years. He could do that. Nothing in life was risk free. He could drop dead from a brain aneurysm, or the bus to basic training could fall off a bridge. The risk he could live with; it was the uncertainty of what he'd be doing that ate away at him.

When the bus arrived, they scanned their PIPs and climbed aboard. As the vehicle glided away from the recruiting station he turned and looked back at the city, wondering if he would ever see it again.

CHAPTER 4

FORT RANDAL WAS MUCH SMALLER than Cosmo expected. It was one building with rows of tents behind it, built on a low hill and ringed by mountains. When the hover-bus stopped, Cosmo and his fellow recruits were led into the main building.

"Welcome to Fort Randal," a man in uniform told them. "Today, you'll be given health and fitness tests along with everything you'll need for training. Let's begin."

Cosmo was used to being told what to do and where to go. The public education system on Fiona Grand was strictly regimented. He fell into line and was taken straight into a hallway that led to a medical facility.

"Name!" a gruff looking soldier in desert fatigues with a medical band around his upper arm said as he stepped into the first of a series of small rooms.

"Cosmo Frost."

"Frost, Cosmo, you are officially checked in," the man said without looking up. His total attention was on the computer slate he was using to find each recruit's name and check them in. "Take off your clothes and put them in this bag."

The soldier put a sticker onto a big plastic bag with a zipping tab at the top. Then he held it out to Cosmo.

"PIP too, jewelry, wallet, all personal items. Even your shoes."

Cosmo felt insecure. He had played sports in school and changed clothes in a locker room, but it wasn't the same as being ordered to strip in front of a total stranger. But he hadn't expected basic training to be easy or fun. He did as he was told.

"Now drink this," the trooper told him.

"What is it?"

The question obviously made the medical attendant angry. He stood up, his face twisting with rage.

"Don't ask questions! If that was a boot full of piss, you would drink it and say, 'Thank you, sir!' I don't have time to coddle you, Frost. Do what you're told and keep your mouth shut. Is that understood?"

"Yes," Cosmo said.

"Yes, what?"

"Yes, sir?"

"Is that a question, Frost?"

"No, I'm sorry."

"You will say 'yes, sir' when addressing a superior officer. Now drink that dye and move on to the next station."

"Yes, sir," Cosmo managed.

He drank the thick, syrupy liquid, which was slightly sweet but had a bitter aftertaste. He tossed the empty paper cup into the trash and walked through the next doorway to find himself in a barber's room. There were two chairs. The man who had gone in ahead of Cosmo was in one seat with a towel around his waist. The barber was shaving the man's head. The other barber handed Cosmo a towel.

"Wrap this around your waist," he ordered, "and sit down."

Cosmo wrapped the towel around himself and took his seat in the other chair. The barber switched on his shaving device. Cosmo's thick, wavy hair fell in chunks. The haircut only took a minute, and then the barber brushed the loose hair from his neck and shoulders.

"Off you go," the barber said.

"Thanks," Cosmo managed as he got to his feet.

"Don't thank me, kid. I'm just doing my job," the barber said with a frown.

The look on the man's face filled Cosmo with a sense of foreboding. In the next room he found showers in tiny stalls. The water was lukewarm. He was ordered to wash up in just three minutes. Afterwards he was sent into an exam room with the same towel around his waist. A medical tech walked around him, looking at his body. If Cosmo had felt embarrassed before, he was mortified as he was rated like an animal at a sale.

"Arms up," the med tech ordered.

"What are you looking for?"

"Any signs of abnormalities," the tech ordered. He sounded bored and had zero sympathy for Cosmo. "Birth marks, skeletal deformation, muscle tone, skin disease. Go ahead and take off your towel."

"Is that really necessary?" Cosmo asked.

"You don't want to be close quarters with someone who's got a communicable disease, kid. Those most often show up on the genitals. We check everyone."

Cosmo felt a mix of shame and outrage as he unwrapped the towel, but the exam only lasted a few seconds.

"In the next room is a whole-body, three-dimensional imaging scanner. Go in, stand on the mark, and let your hands hang down. Once that's done, you'll be given clothes."

"Okay," Cosmo said, thinking it was the best news he had heard since he arrived at the base.

"Good luck, recruit. Next!" the medical tech shouted.

Cosmo went into the next room. There was a large machine on one side. On the floor was an X painted with spray paint. Cosmo went over and stood on the X. The machine started up all on its own. A ring from the ceiling slowly lowered as what looked like a camera spun around and around. When the ring reached the floor, it reversed course and went back up. The entire scan took just a couple of minutes.

Cosmo left the scanning room and found himself in what looked like a locker room. There were stacks of clothes: green T-shirts, gray sweatpants, socks, underwear, even athletic shoes. Everything was divided by sizes. Cosmo got what he needed and got dressed as quickly as possible. The other recruits were being called out of the room, some before they even finished getting dressed.

"Frost, Cosmo!" shouted a trooper who stood by the door with a computer slate.

Already dressed and feeling much more comfortable, Cosmo hurried over to the man.

"I'm Cosmo."

"You're with Dr. Banner. Room six."

He pointed down a hallway. There were lots of doors on just one side of the hallway, and each one was marked with a number. Cosmo found number six and opened the door. Inside, there were two chairs. One was already taken by a woman in a white coat with a computer slate. She was tapping on the device and nodded to the empty chair.

"Have a seat, Frost," the woman said.

She reminded Cosmo of a teacher. She had that same bored, yet authoritative tone to her voice. He sat down.

"Your scans look clean," Dr. Banner said. "Any history of disease in your family?"

"Not that I know of," Cosmo replied.

"Any prior surgeries?"

"No."

"What about mental issues?" the doctor asked. "Anyone in your family diagnosed with a mental disorder or hospitalized for emotional issues?"

"No, but I don't really have much family. It's just me and my mom."

The doctor looked up at him. Cosmo thought that maybe her expression softened a little. Perhaps, he thought, there was a touch of compassion in her gaze.

"How do you feel about being drafted?" she asked.

Cosmo shrugged. "I'm not happy about it," he replied. "But I'm not depressed if that's what you're asking."

"Your chart says you were accepted into university on Triton. How do you feel about not being able to attend?"

"It sucks," he said.

She tapped away on her pad.

"Would you consider yourself a patriot, Recruit Frost?"

"I guess so," he said.

"How do you feel about the Ma'Tis?"

"Not good. But if I'm honest, I don't think about them very much."

"Have you ever been in trouble with law enforcement, even if it didn't result in an arrest?"

"No," Cosmo said. "Never."

"How do you feel about authority?"

He shrugged. "I don't feel anything about it."

"What if you're ordered to do something you are uncomfortable with? Will you follow those orders?"

"I'm here to do what I'm told for the next two years," Cosmo said.

Dr. Banner smiled as she tapped on her screen. "You'll be okay, Frost. Do what your instructors tell you and you'll be fine."

"Is that all?"

"Yes," she told him. "Go join the others in the room with the red door."

"The red door?"

"Yes, at the end of this hallway."

Cosmo got up and left the tiny exam room. He felt as though he was being rushed through the intake process. The people around him didn't really care if he was fit or crazy, as long as he would follow orders. There were so many thoughts bouncing around inside his head. In all his life he had never considered joining the military. On Fiona Grand, soldiers were called troopers. It was a respectable profession, but not one that Cosmo had dreamed about. He found the room with the red door and went inside.

There were other men in the room. Most were older. Two benches were set next to the walls. Cosmo took his place on one and slowly the room filled up.

"What's your name?" a husky boy with a few whiskers on his chin and neck asked as he sat down beside Cosmo.

"Cos. What's yours?"

"Quincy," the husky boy said. "What were you doing before the draft?"

"I was on my way off world," Cosmo said. "Business school on Triton. You?"

"My family owns a bakery. We sell to all the big shops."

"And now you're a trooper," Cosmo told him. "You excited about that?"

"Hell no," Quincy said. "I had a life back home. A girlfriend, money—even had my own hover-car. Now look at me."

"It's just for two years," Cosmo said, trying to stay positive.

"If you can survive two years," Quincy argued. "We're all just cannon fodder. You've seen the news reports. Do you really want to fight the Ma'Tis? I don't. I want to go home."

Cosmo did too, but he knew thinking that way would only make things more difficult. He was in the military and there was no way to get out of his two years of service. He didn't like it, but no one was asking him to like it. The law said he had to serve and so that's what he would do.

After a full hour of waiting and nervous talking, the door at the far end of the room opened. A man with a wide-brimmed hat stood in the opening. He had desert fatigues. The sleeves of his shirt were rolled up to his elbows, revealing muscular forearms with faded tattoos. The ends of his pants were tucked into the top of his boots which laced up. He wore a canvas belt with a pistol in a covered holster on one hip.

"All right, on your feet," the man said, his voice a growl. "You're in the army now, and you will act like it. Follow me."

He turned on his heel and led the way out through what looked like an indoor training facility. He walked fast as the recruits followed in an unorganized bunch. A set of double doors led to a wide area that Cosmo would later learn was called a parade ground. The man in the uniform spread everyone out in two neat rows.

"You are in the army now, and you will damn-sure act like it!" the man said. "I have been assigned to turn you from soft, slow, ugly, pathetic civilians into army troopers. Looking around, you may think that is an impossible task. I would be inclined to agree with you. But I'm a drill sergeant in the finest military in this galaxy. Nothing is impossible once I set my mind to complete it. Over the next four weeks, you will learn how to function in the army. It's what we call basic alpha—the first phase of your training. It will be physically chal-lenging, and not everyone will succeed. But you will all give me one hundred percent of your effort, or I will make your life so miserable that not even your mamas back home will want anything to do with you. Now, when I ask you a question, you will respond with the phrase 'Yes, Drill Sergeant.' Let's try that all together now. Is that clear?"

"Yes, Drill Sergeant," the group said. It was a mix of voices, some enthusiastic, others with a defeated tone, and no real unity.

"How pathetic," the drill sergeant said. "Everything in the army is done together, with passionate enthusiasm. You don't say it, you shout it, in cadence, all together. Try again. Go!"

"Yes, Drill Sergeant!" the platoon replied. It was louder, but still mingled.

"We have a long way to go," the drill sergeant said. "We will start every day in this position. Get used to it. Feet together, back straight, shoulders relaxed but not hunched, eyes straight ahead. This is called standing at attention. You will practice it while I make my inspection. If you do a poor job or lose focus, you will be called out and given additional motivation to do things the army way. Is that clear?"

"Yes, Drill Sergeant."

"Mmmmm," he said in a deep, gruff rumble. "There's hope for you pukes yet. That was almost an acceptable response. When I say fall in, you will assume this same assembly and stand at attention until you are given further orders. We'll practice this all day until we get it right, recruits. This is the military way. This is my way. And you will bend to my will, or I will break you down. Is that clear?"

"Yes, Drill Sergeant!"

CHAPTER 5

ALLURA HAD TAKEN a hover-cab from the airport to the Triton Technology Institute. She had seen videos of Newton City, but actually being there was still a shock. Millions of people living in towering high rises gave the metropolis a truly three-dimensional feel. There were thick lanes of traffic at various heights and flowing through the neatly organized city.

The TTI was a single building that consisted of hundreds of labs, auditoriums, classrooms, offices, and recreational space. Housing was shared with several other universities including the elite Paragon University, the Crispin College of Design, the Ellsberry Philosophical and Theological Seminary, and the Brookings School for Business Studies. Each university was built to reflect the studies carried out within, and all were built around the student center—a huge tower that housed over twelve thousand students. Allura pushed her luggage along a wide sidewalk. The grounds between the skyscrapers were neatly landscaped. She joined thousands of other freshmen who were set to attend classes in just a few days.

A booth was set up at the entrance to the student center. A group of student volunteers were checking the new students in. When Allura got to the front of the line, a handsome upperclassman glanced up at her.

"Hi there. What's your name?"

"Allura Presley," she replied.

"From?"

"Fiona Grand."

"What school are you attending?"

"TTI."

"Oh, there you are," he said, looking up and giving her a flirtatious wink. "Lucky you, private pod on the forty-seventh floor. I'm pushing your security codes to your PIP. Welcome to Newton, Allura Presley."

"Thanks," she replied, feeling her cheeks flush.

In her mind she was thinking of Cosmo. It didn't seem fair that she was on Triton, checking into her dorm, and looking forward to classes. It was all new, and the city was amazing. Everything was big, new, and clean. It was nothing like Fiona Grand, which was considered a frontier planet on the edge of what had become contested space. Triton was deep in humanity's territory, and the entire planet was occupied. The oceans were dotted with floating cities. The continents were carefully divided between nature preserves and ingeniously designed cities. With a population of over forty billion people, there wasn't much room for an invasion by the Ma'Tis.

Somewhere far away, Cosmo was enduring who knew what in the military. He had no choice in the matter, but she had every choice. She rode up an elevator that was packed with new students. Every few floors the lift stopped to let a few off. She was one of three students left when the elevator finally reached the forty-eighth floor. Pushing her luggage and thankful for the wheels on her two big bags, she exited the lift and found herself in a long, curving corridor. Her scholarship provided her with a private pod. It wasn't exactly a room as most people thought of them. She found the door number that was assigned to her and punched in the security code. Inside was a loft bed with a desk below it. She had a tiny closet, a wall entertainment display, and a window that looked out toward the TTI building. It was tiny—barely larger than a storage closet, but it was her new home. She should have been thrilled, but when she sat down in the desk chair, she couldn't hold back the tears.

On her PIP there was a message from her parents and several from the university welcoming her, reminding her of the orientation schedule, and giving dozens of social options for her free time over the week before classes were to start. But there was nothing from Cosmo. She desperately wanted to hear back from him. On the voyage through the galaxy, she had written him dozens of messages. She knew that interstellar messages took time to deliver, but the truth was she missed him terribly and felt guilty that he was at home preparing to fight for the freedom of their planet while she was off on Triton deciding between the new student mixers being offered. The handsome boy who checked her in was nice, but she had no interest in fooling around with other guys. She had known pretty early in their relationship that she had found her soulmate. There was plenty of physical attraction between them, but more importantly, they were best friends. And no matter what Cosmo thought about things, she wasn't going to quit on them.

She didn't arrive at her decision quickly. She unpacked her bags and logged onto her school's network servers. It was almost time for dinner, and then her floor had a scheduled get-together in the common room. She ate in the cafeteria on the third floor. The meal was the best she had eaten since leaving Fiona Grand, but she wasn't hungry. An idea had been poking around the edges of her mind. When she went back to her pod, she used her PIP to investigate a little further.

Triton was a center of commerce, technology, education, and as it turned out, home of the Galactic Military Air Training Academy. Fiona Grand, like most other planets, sent pilots to the ATA for training. As she browsed the site, a chat box popped up. Her heart was pounding as she typed in an inquiry.

Can a person train for a planet-specific air/space force?

The response was almost instantaneous. Yes, what planet would you be interested in serving?

Allura's fingers shook as she typed back: Fiona Grand.

The response was a link to two tracks of study. One for pilots, which was a two-year program. That didn't help her at all, she thought. There was no sense in joining the military if she wouldn't be out of training before Cosmo's term of service ended.

That left the second option: a ten-week bombardier course. If she qualified, she could be trained and, on her way, back to Fiona Grand in just three months. She decided to skip the party and spent her evening researching the ATA.

CHAPTER 6

THEY RAN. There was seemingly no point to it. The trail was dirt and wound through the foothills, up and down. The platoon, which was what Drill Sergeant Reed called them, had spread out to a long straggle. Cosmo didn't enjoy running, but he wasn't in bad shape. Still, his legs burned, and his lungs ached as he jogged along. The drill sergeant set a slow pace that Cosmo had no trouble keeping up with at first, but the terrain was difficult. The path was just wide enough for two people. Quincy quickly fell behind. Cosmo started to drop back with him, but then the larger man, Henry Dyson, came up beside Cosmo.

"Don't do it," he said. "He ain't gonna make it."

"It's the first day," Cosmo replied.

"That's right, and this here's a test—you mark my words."

"A test?"

"Yeah, man. They gonna divide us up soon. Some people are gonna be grunts in the infantry. They give them fools a rifle and helmet, but they just targets for the aliens to shoot at."

"And the rest?" Cosmo asked.

The big man shrugged his shoulders. "They got different jobs, but the one you want is mech pilot. They only got so many of them big, armored machines, but if you gotta fight a Ma'Tis, that's what you want to be in."

"And you think me sticking with Quincy will hurt my chances?"

"Yeah, that's what I'm saying. You do you, bro, but just remember, they watching you all the time. And there's a reason they're drafting people now. They need bodies. You don't want to be just another body between the aliens and whatever they're trying to take."

"How come you know so much about it?" Cosmo asked.

"My family is military all the way back to my great granddad."

"But not you?"

"I got a scholarship to play ball. Been chasing the dream until now. Minor leagues, but I had prospects."

"I was on my way to Triton to go to business school."

"Yeah, I knew you was smart. That's what they want. Half this platoon won't get through basic on their first try, even if they lower the standards. And your chances of getting into the armored divisions is almost nil if you can't pass the PT test on the first try."

Cosmo looked back over his shoulder. They were jogging up a hill. Only nine of the recruits were still in any kind of formation. Quincy was way back and walking. Cosmo could see the baker's red face even from a distance.

"It's cool that he's your friend," Henry said. "But if you want to survive then you need to be the best of the best."

"Mech pilot," Cosmo said.

"Yeah, that's right. We can make it too. Forget about college, man. It'll be waiting on ya when this is over. You focus on the training like it was your lifelong dream. Then maybe, just maybe we get into the armored division. Then we go from being expendable to being essential. That's what you want. Make yourself so valuable that they won't throw your life away."

Cosmo nodded and focused on his running. What Dyson said made sense. The bigger man was pretty smart. Cosmo had always been the type to look out for others. He was friendly and didn't really stand out in a crowd. But maybe his thoughts about life were wrong. He could do better, try harder. The first step was to stop moping over what he had lost and start focusing on whatever the army put in front of him.

"All right," Cosmo said. "I can do that."

"My man," Dyson said. "Let's do it."

They didn't push the pace, but they slowly caught up with Sergeant Reed and the half dozen other recruits keeping pace with the drill instructor. The run was only five kilometers, but over the hilly terrain it felt like more. And Cosmo was tired when they finished.

"Stretch, gentlemen," Sergeant Reed barked. "Slow and steady. Don't pop a tendon but work out the kinks. You'll thank me tomorrow."

Dyson, being an athlete, knew how to take care of his body. Cosmo followed his lead. When the last of the stragglers finally reached the base again, they were given dinner. It was hardy fare, grilled chicken, mashed potatoes, a variety of vegetables, and fruit punch.

"Don't overdo it," Dyson told Cosmo. "Stick to protein and vegetables at night. Don't guzzle that punch either."

"But don't I need carbs if we're going to be working out so hard?"

"You need carbs in the morning, protein, and fiber at night. Trust me, you'll sleep better."

Cosmo followed his new friend's advice. Most of the other recruits were devouring the food. They were all famished from the stress of the long day, but he could also tell the results of their choices. He felt satiated but not stuffed. Many of the other recruits seemed on the verge of passing out.

They went out to the rows of tents, and each man was assigned a place to rest. Inside the tents was a sleeping bag and a little kit with toiletries. The bathroom facilities were all outdoors. The showers were in clusters, the toilets in portable latrines. A trough substituted for a sink. Cosmo couldn't imagine a more difficult case of roughing it, but he didn't complain. After the platoon had showered for the night, they were given their final instructions.

"I want each of you to take the time this evening to write home," Sergeant Reed ordered. "Inside your tents you'll find your PIPs. Tell your families and your sweethearts that you have arrived and are well. But also let them know that you will not have access to your portable information pad. After tonight, you will not have anything other than your basic kit, a change of clothes, and your sleeping bag. Don't waste your time. Write your message and get to sleep. Mornings come early around here."

Cosmo took a few moments to convey the messages to his mother and to Allura. He knew the message could take two or three weeks to arrive on Triton. But he sent the message and hoped that it found its way to her sooner rather than later.

Getting to sleep wasn't easy. He was exhausted, but also keenly aware that he was lying on the ground. The sleeping bag was insulated, and the temperature was falling, but it wasn't the cold that kept him awake. Fear, frustration, and the feeling of rocks poking into his back made sleep hard to come by.

It was still dark and a full two hours before dawn when a group of troopers rushed through the rows of tents, waking the recruits. It wasn't just Cosmo's platoon either. There were other platoons in training, though from the looks of things some had been there for a while. As the troopers shouted for the recruits to get up, Cosmo crawled out of his sleeping bag, pulled on his shoes, and hurried out of his tiny tent. He was one of the first members of his platoon up. The stragglers were being screamed at, and eventually a few had to be dragged from their beds. Dyson's tent was next to Cosmo's, and the big man just shook his head as they waited for orders.

"Red Platoon," Sergeant Reed bellowed. "Fall in behind me."

The group shuffled over, most of the recruits complaining as they went. Cosmo and Dyson hurried. They wanted to prove their intentions even if they weren't able to keep up with everything the drill instructor had planned. They walked through the darkness. It wasn't a march because they hadn't learned to march yet, but it was what would become their morning march, followed by the early-morning exercise. Sit-ups, push-ups, leg raises, squats, and pull-ups. It wasn't just grueling; it was on the verge of sadistic. Sergeant Reed heckled and belittled the group at every opportunity. Cosmo was glad that he had taken Dyson's advice the day before. He wasn't the strongest or the most fit but did the exercises well enough to avoid the drill sergeant's wrath.

When the morning PT ended, they had breakfast. Eggs, bacon, sausage, and ham were all served on large pans. The recruits ate hardily. Dyson skipped to the end of the line where there was a pot of oatmeal, some bananas, and some apples.

"Carb up," he told Cosmo. "That other stuff won't last. Those guys will be puking on the next run."

Turning away from the eggs and bacon was difficult. There were fluffy biscuits too, and gravy. It all looked so good, while the oatmeal looked bland. But Cosmo didn't think it would hurt to skip the heavy, grease-laden food. He had oatmeal and an apple. After breakfast they marched. It took a few days to get it right. Anyone who stepped out of line or fell out of step was sent running. And Dyson was right. Many of the recruits looked sick, and a few couldn't keep their breakfast down.

The entire middle of the day was spent learning how to come to attention or shift into at-ease positions. Cosmo's back ached from standing straight for hours on end. Lunch was sandwiches. The afternoon consisted of more marching, more learning. The evening was spent running. There was just enough time for showers before they ate dinner. Cosmo was so tired that he was ready to crawl into his tent and go right to sleep, but before he could, Sergeant Reed dropped another bomb on them.

"No platoon in the field sleeps without someone standing watch," he said in his grumbling voice. "You will all take turns on two-hour shifts. Who volunteers to go first?"

Cosmo raised his hand. It took all the willpower he possessed, and he wasn't trying to impress anyone. He simply wanted to get the duty over with as quickly as possible. In his mind, it was better to get one six-hour stretch of sleep rather than have his rest interrupted.

"Frost, Dyson, Pike, Saunders, you have first watch," the sergeant ordered. He then assigned four recruits to second, third, and fourth watches. Half the platoon would cover watch on alternating nights. While the others went to bed, Cosmo and Dyson were sent to one end of Red Platoon's row of tents. Saunders and Pike were sent to the other end.

"You stay on your feet," Sergeant Reed ordered. "You do not go to sleep, or you will regret it for the rest of your short lives. Is that clear?"

"Yes, Drill Sergeant," Dyson and Cosmo said in perfect unison.

He left them standing side by side in the dark.

"Two hours," Dyson said. "That's not too bad."

"It's not good either," Cosmo said. "I'm so tired I could cry."

"Yeah, we're still adjusting," the bigger man said. "When I first got in the league I was overwhelmed too. I mean I always took playing ball serious, but that was nothing compared to the pros. Guys spent every waking minute in the weightroom or studying film. Practice was like a relief from the pressure. But you adjust to it. We'll get used to this too."

"I hope you're right," Cosmo said. "If you hadn't warned me about the food, I'd probably have passed out already."

"Nah, you're good. But those little things make a difference, eh?"

"Yes, so thanks, man. I really appreciate it."

"No sweat, no sweat. That's how I roll. Besides, it's easier to walk the path when you've got a friend by your side, you know. A cord of three strands is not easily broken."

They stood staring out into the darkness and talked. Occasionally they walked around just to keep their legs from cramping. But for the most part, the two-hour watch passed quickly. When Cosmo finally crawled into his sleeping bag, he couldn't feel the rocks or hear the canvas flapping against the tent poles. He closed his eyes and immediately fell asleep.

CHAPTER 7

ALLURA WOKE UP FEELING UNCERTAIN. She had gone to sleep thinking about the audacious plan of joining the ATA. It would mean throwing away her scholarship, and she knew there were hundreds of applicants who would have done anything to take her place. Classes were starting in just four days. If she quit, what would her parents think? They wouldn't be pleased, that was certain. But it was her life. She could get her degree and go to work at a large tech company or help launch a start-up. Both options were a sure way to prosperity, but without Cosmo they seemed completely worthless. Better, it had seemed the night before, to join the fight. She couldn't protect him, but maybe she could help in the war effort in a very real and practical way.

Of course, in the clear light of day her arguments for leaving school seemed weak and even frightening. A bombardier rode in a ship and used advanced mathematics to drop various types of bombs onto enemy locations. It was anything but safe. The same job could be done via computers with drones, but the Ma'Tis had scrambling tech that made the computer-fired bombs unreliable. They also had anti-aircraft weapons that could shoot the bombers down. They didn't use airships, and there was quite a bit of conjecture about how the sea creatures got into space to begin with, but that didn't really matter.

What was essential, however, was the risk involved in such a daring plan.

And if she joined the ATA, she might not get into school again down the road. Most of the best schools communicated about applicants. There was a very real possibility that if she angered the admissions department at Triton Technology Institute, they might blacklist her with other prestigious universities. She could be throwing her future away, even if she lived long enough to return to school.

So she got dressed and went to orientation. She listened to the professors, many of them world renowned for their breakthroughs in all sorts of fields—from mapping brainwave patterns to predict behavior, to advanced AI drone bots that were used in all sorts of dangerous jobs, and even simple tech like speeding up PIP operating systems. The faculty at TTI were famous across the galaxy. They gave lectures on the exciting research they were carrying out, and spoke about how if the students worked hard, they too could have a positive impact on the galaxy. It should have been exciting and inspiring. She saw it on the faces of her classmates. Allura wasn't intimidated by the prospects of rubbing shoulders with the most intelligent members of her peer group, but she was worried about Cosmo. Common sense told her that being so consumed with a boy was more than a little silly. Yet she couldn't deny her feelings for him. And Allura wanted more than a marriage of convenience. She knew it wasn't uncommon for people to marry and divorce several times throughout their lives. But she didn't want that. She wanted romance and excitement in her life. She wanted a partner that she could depend on—and one that she could look forward to waking up next to every single day. Which was exactly how she felt about Cosmo. So she skipped lunch and went to the ATA recruiting center.

"Welcome," a woman with long blonde hair pulled back into a tight braid said as Allura walked into the recruiter's small office. "How can I help you today?"

"I want to know more about becoming a bombardier," Allura said.

"Well," the woman said with a bright smile. "It's one of the most exciting jobs in the air/space forces. What planet are you from?"

"Fiona Grand," Allura told her.

"A frontline world," the blonde woman said with surprise. "I have to say we don't see many people from contested space here on Triton."

"I'm here to go to school," Allura said. "But the fighting has gotten bad back home. I'm wondering if I can help somehow."

"Well, not everyone is accepted into the bombardier program. It's a math-intensive course, and it takes a good eye and steady hand. If you qualify, it's a great way to get into the service and gain valuable combat experience. Would you be interested in a military career?"

"I don't know," Allura said. "To be honest, I've never really thought about it."

"Why don't you take the ASVAB test. That will tell us what you qualify for. Then we can dig a little deeper into what track would be best for you."

"What's the ASVAB test?"

"Oh, that's our Armed Services Vocational Aptitude Battery. It's pretty standard stuff."

"How long does it take?"

"Most candidates complete it in just under an hour," the blonde officer said.

It took Allura half an hour to complete the test, and the look on the officer's face told her that the results were favorable. While the woman read the results, Allura looked at her uniform. It was crisp and clean, without a wrinkle anywhere. The royal blue pants with a black stripe fit the woman's figure perfectly, and the white shirt with dark shoulder boards looked tailor made. Everything about the woman spoke of professionalism, but there was also a touch of glamour. Allura could see herself in uniform, and she liked the thought of it. She couldn't help but smile as she imagined what Cosmo would say if he could see her in a uniform like the recruiting officer wore.

"Wow, I'm impressed, Allura. You got top marks on the ASVAB," the blonde woman said. "You qualify for pilot training and that's no small feat. You could join the ATA and become an officer in the Space Force. I'd love to show you what's involved in that career track."

"I'm really only interested in getting back to Fiona Grand," Allura said. "The bombardier role would do that, right? Ten weeks of study, then I could transfer to the FGAF?"

"Yes," the blond woman said. "You know your stuff. We have basic training, of course, but it runs simultaneously with your vocational track. You'll enlist, which is a four-year commitment, but your training will be paid for. You'll do it all here on Triton. Then, once you complete your training, you can apply for transfer to any world where there is fighting. Fiona Grand is currently taking all the bombardiers they can get. Is that what you want to do?"

"I don't know," Allura said.

"You seem pretty certain," the officer said. "And I can tell you, there's nothing more rewarding than military service."

"I'd be walking away from my formal education," Allura said. "Giving up my scholarship."

"And you're worried about losing that opportunity," the woman said with a nod. "I completely understand. What university are you set to attend?"

"TTI," Allura said.

The woman smiled, "I should have guessed from your results on the ASVAB. Look, we have a great relationship with the admission department over there. I can make a call, get you cleared for service, and an almost guaranteed spot in school down the road. A four-year enlistment comes with the Airman Education Initiative, which will pay eighty percent of your school fees. And in most cases the university will cover the other twenty percent in appreciation for your service. You wouldn't be giving up higher education. In fact, with your test scores, you could apply to officer training once you've got at least two years of service. In most cases, you can get a degree while you serve. There's no downside here. I've got a bombardier training program that launches in two weeks."

"If I sign up, I'll have to drop out of school. Then I'll have no place to live," Allura pointed out.

"We can take you on an emergency intake," the officer explained. "The facilities are here in Newton, but you probably already know that. You'd go into temporary housing, and you can begin your basic training immediately, then go on to bombardier school once it launches in two weeks."

"That would solve one problem," Allura said. "But four years is a bigger commitment than I expected."

"It's standard military enrollment for enlisted personnel. Two years is usually reserved for draftees."

Allura nodded, trying to keep her face impassive. She felt so conflicted. One part of her wanted to sign on the dotted line. She would do anything to help Cosmo. But another part of her thought it was crazy to give up her scholarship and be committed to the air/space force for two years longer than Cosmo.

"I'll have to think about it," she finally said.

"Of course, you've got some time. Just let me know how I can help. The Air Training Academy would love to have you in our ranks."

"Thank you," Allura said.

The ride back to school was difficult, and the afternoon lectures were pure torture. The truth was, Allura wasn't passionate about school. She was good at it, but learning advanced chemistry, or electrical engineering, or getting a computer science degree wasn't her dream. It was the practical path in life. The opportunity had opened up before her, and everyone said she should jump at the chance to go to TTI. But the longer the orientation lasted, the more she knew it wasn't what she wanted to do with her life. The idea of joining the military had never occurred to her, but she couldn't deny that the thought of making a difference was appealing. And the recruiter had shown her a path forward full of potential and possibilities.

That night there was a party for all new students in the basement ballroom of the student center. Allura forced herself to go. She had to know what she was giving up if she enlisted. But nothing in her high school life had prepared her for a college party on Triton. There was a band—not just a nameless, local group—but the Jupiter Blitz. She had listened to their ballad "Forever Lost in Your Arms" about a thousand times when she was in junior high school. The band rocked out on a stage at one end of the long, rectangular ballroom; drinks were given out free on the other end. Everything from kegs of beer to spiked punch was being served, along with Jell-O shots and pot gummies. Allura saw people dancing, people getting sick, people making out, and people like herself just hovering along the edges trying to take it all in.

"Hey! I was hoping you'd come," a boy said as he approached.

It took Allura a moment to remember him. He was the student volunteer who had checked her in the day before.

"Oh, hi," she said.

"You're Allura, right?" the guy said.

He wasn't alone. There were a few other guys with him. Two of them looked totally baked. Their vacant stare and dilated pupils were dead giveaways. She smelled beer on the breath of the boy who spoke to her.

"I'm Crypto," he said. "We go by our online names here, mostly. But Allura is pretty cool."

"It's nice to meet you," she said, extending her hand.

He looked at it and laughed. "What planet are you from?" he asked. "Let's party!"

The next thing Allura knew he had had moved beside her, had his hand around her waist, and was pulling her toward the back of the ballroom.

"What are you doing?" Allura asked.

"Getting you a drink, babe. We need to loosen you up. You're a college girl now. Partying is just part of the scene. These are the best years of our lives. We have to live it up."

"I'm not here to party," Allura said. "I have a boyfriend."

The guys with Crypto all laughed. He looked at her. "But he's not here, is he? So what he doesn't know won't hurt him. Look, there are two kinds of students here: those that know how to have a good time, and those that burn out fast. You can't handle the workload without blowing off some steam. That's why no one bats an eye when we have a raging kegger, right boys?"

They all shouted. Crypto's hand slid lower, and Allura pushed him away. "No, this isn't for me."

"Hey, where are you going?" the boy called, but he didn't chase after her.

Suddenly the music was too loud, and there were too many people in the ballroom. Allura felt like she couldn't breathe. She had to push her way through the throng to reach the corridor that led to the elevators. And then she rode up to her pod and packed her bags.

CHAPTER 8

THE FIRST FOUR days of basic training were exactly the same. The only thing that changed was the food they were served. It was hot and dry in the mountains, and Cosmo only had enough time for his body to work out the soreness of the constant training when they were introduced to the obstacle course. They were taken up onto a hill. The trail split there and went in opposite directions. At the bottom of the hill, wrapping around it, were the obstacles.

"This is the basic course," Drill Sergeant Reed exclaimed with pride. "You will all be judged on this circuit. Today, we'll go down and run each obstacle bit by bit. Over the next three weeks you will run this course every day, and if you can complete the course within five minutes, you'll move on to the second phase of your basic training."

"What happens if we can't?" Quincy asked.

He was by far the most vocally miserable recruit and had drawn several other poor performers into his circle of friends. Cosmo was glad not to be one of them. Not all the people around Quincy were overweight or even out of shape. Arnie Potts was maybe the most physically gifted member of Red Platoon. But he hated authority and couldn't take being told what to do.

"If you fail," Sergeant Reed snarled, "you repeat the first four weeks of your training. So don't fail. Here we go."

He jogged down the hill and we followed. At the bottom of the hill the trail turned and led directly to a two-and-a-half-meter vertical wall.

"Dyson, Potts, you will scale the wall and stay on top to help the others," Sergeant Reed shouted.

"Good luck," Cosmo told Dyson.

"No sweat," the big man replied.

He dashed off, jumped for the top of the wall, and levered himself up. Arnie Potts followed, but with less enthusiasm. They both sat straddling the ten-centimeter plank on top and waited for the others to follow. Cosmo was near the front of the line. He ran, jumped, and easily grabbed the upper plank. His feet scrambled on the wooden planks as he levered himself up.

"My man!" Dyson said with a huge smile.

Cosmo flung his legs over the opposite side and dropped easily to the ground. Some of the other recruits had more trouble. Reaching the top wasn't difficult. Cosmo stood at almost exactly two meters tall, and he could reach up and grab the top of the wall without jumping. But pulling oneself up to the top was taxing. And some of the recruits carried significantly more weight than the others. They struggled until Dyson or Potts pulled them over. Cosmo wondered if they would ever be able to do it on their own. They had three weeks to accomplish that task, or they would be stuck repeating the first four weeks of basic training until they could.

The second obstacle was a very low series of barbed wires spread between two short poles. The ground beneath was soft, almost muddy. The recruits were forced onto their bellies to scramble underneath the wires. If a person raised their head too much, they were reminded by the barbs which gouged into their flesh. Staying low wasn't natural. The dirt that wasn't moist puffed up into Cosmo's face. Still, he crawled through without too much trouble.

Third up was a series of ropes. There were enough for five recruits at a time to swing over a pool of water that had collected under them. It seemed simple enough. Dyson ran forward, jumped for the rope, and swung way across the watery obstacle. But when he let go of the rope, he came down off balance and fell back, landing on his rear with a splash.

When Cosmo swung over, he put his feet down on the far side without letting go of the rope. But just like his friend, Cosmo's momentum at that point was going the wrong direction, and he was off balance.

"It ain't as easy as it looks," Dyson called.

Cosmo lifted his feet, swung back across the wide puddle, then forward again before managing to drop right at the edge of the water. It took him a second to steady himself, and then he trotted away from the obstacle.

"You got lucky, bro," Dyson said.

"Tell me about it," Cosmo replied.

"Use your core, you lazy, half-witted idiots!" Sergeant Reed barked. "The point is not to fall in the water. You fall in during testing, you start over."

It took a while for the platoon to get across. Some jumped for the rope but couldn't get a grip. The puddle of water wasn't deep, but it was dirty. Everyone who fell into it smelled like sewage. Sergeant Reed took the entire platoon around and made them do the rope swing again and again. By his third attempt, Cosmo had the technique down, even though his hands burned from slipping on the rope.

The fourth obstacle was a simple balance beam, only it was ten meters from one end to the other. Once again there were five of them set several meters apart and running parallel to the trail so that several recruits could cross them at once. If you fell, you had to go back and start from the beginning. What should have been an easy obstacle was made more difficult by fatigue. And those who had fallen into the water had heavy shoes still squishing out the dirty liquid with every step.

The final obstacle was a rope net that led over a five-meter-high wall. The rope wasn't taut. It sagged and moved as the recruits climbed up. The hardest part was getting over the top. Cosmo had trouble lifting his leg high enough to swing it over, and when he did, getting a solid footing on the other side was difficult. After climbing over the net obstacle, they still had to run up the hill again to complete the course. It became a regular part of their training. They lifted weights, marched, practiced standing at attention—learning the chain of command, saluting superiors—and marched some more. After lunch each day, they ran the obstacle course over and over, and then they marched some more. In the evenings they did calisthenics, ran through the hills, and finished their day standing watch. It was a grueling, physical gauntlet, and Sergeant Reed was a merciless instructor. He gave no praise for doing something right but hounded anyone doing things wrong. And the only relief was physical injury. Cosmo heard some of the recruits planning ways to break an ankle, or hoping they could tear a tendon. Any injury with a long recovery time was an automatic failure. Those that failed basic training were sent on to do the scut work no one wanted without rank and on the lowest pay grade. A group of unranked soldiers pumped out the portable latrines, took care of the garbage on the base, and spent hours washing everything from the dishes after chow time to the main building on base.

There were offices on the upper floors of the main structure, and quarters for the personnel stationed there. The recruits slept out in the flimsy tents no matter the weather. Cosmo was grateful to be there at the end of summer and beginning of fall. Winter would be cold, wet, and extremely miserable, especially the outdoor showers. But life was beginning to take on a rhythm on the little base. And Cosmo could see the changes in his own body. He wasn't getting bigger, but he was getting harder. Muscles were taking shape, and the little bit of fat he had was quickly burned away. Food was fuel. He knew what to eat at each mealtime and how to stay hydrated without becoming waterlogged. His feet, ankles, and knees got stronger. The soreness went away, and the runs became less stressful. Night watch was never fun, but it was manageable. And marching became second nature. Once his body adjusted, the days blurred together. His fear shifted from failing the obstacle course at the end of the four weeks to failing his friends and even disappointing Drill Sergeant Reed. He hadn't wanted to join the military, yet he found himself becoming an army trooper and actually looking forward to the next phase of his training.

CHAPTER 9

ALLURA SIGNED up for bombardier school the day following the big party. The blonde recruiter, whose name was Faleska Janovich, contacted the admissions office at TTI. They had Allura's spot at the school filled within an hour. Faleska took Allura to the Air Training Academy. It was in a group of old buildings near a spaceport on the edge of Newton City. There were actual runways for old aircraft that were used to help train pilots. Once she was checked in, Allura was put in a tiny room reserved for visitors to the school. She had her days to herself but was given access to the physical requirements needed to pass the basic training portion of her schooling, which she was even able to do before her schooling began. She also cut her hair very short. It wasn't buzzed, but the sides and back were kept short according to ATA regulations.

She was given uniforms which she was in charge of cleaning and ironing. She learned how to shine her shoes and make her bed according to the Air Training Academy regulations. Even though she was a new recruit, she did earn some money which was funneled into a bank with branches on Fiona Grand. The hardest part of her new career choice was informing her parents. She sent them a lengthy message and was in no hurry to hear back from them. The two weeks leading to the start of bombardier training were a bit lonely, but she felt empowered at having taken her future into her own hands. She messaged Cosmo too, but when his message reached her, she realized that he wouldn't get a chance to see her news for some time—maybe not even until his basic training was over. She wondered how he would take the news and spent a lot of late nights worrying about him.

When her classes started, she was moved with the other recruits to a shared barracks. There were males and females going through the training. Most, like Allura, were from worlds where alien conflict was taking place. Many were already in the air forces of their respective planets. Collectively, humanity had a space force which each planet contributed to, but each world had its own military as well. In some sectors, planets were hotly contested between species. Allura found herself right at home with her fellow bombardiers who were both intelligent and serious about the program. And while they all shared sleeping quarters, there were separate bathroom facilities, and the trainees were respectful of one another. It was nothing like the university dorms where she had seen coeds mingling in every area of their school housing, including the bathrooms.

Their commanding officer for the duration of the program was Lieutenant Phoenix, a dark-skinned woman with short hair and burn scars on one arm. She had been a bombardier on Skoos Primär before the Ma'Tis had pushed the human populations back into the ice caps. Eventually the colonies there were abandoned, and Lieutenant Phoenix was wounded as she helped with the evacuations.

The training program was in two separate phases. The first was academic. The trainees learned about the different types of ordnance that could be used, how to calculate amounts of explosive power, and how atmospheric conditions affected each type of bomb. Allura excelled in the classroom. She understood the lessons and could not only remember them, but quickly put the material into practice. The simulation training was more difficult. Each bomb in their arsenal fell differently. The Ma'Tis used powerful computer-aided jamming technology that interfered with guided missiles and sent warheads with propulsion off course. The only reliable way to hit the aliens from the air was by using bombs that were pulled down with gravity. Each planet was different. Allura learned how to calculate gravity, momentum, wind speed, and even the moisture in the air. What might normally be done by computer was left to the bombardiers to do by hand. Allura could do the math, but there was also a natural feel to dropping bombs that had to be learned through experience. Her first trip up in a bomber was an eye-opening experience.

"You will go up, make a run, then a second," Lieutenant Phoenix explained. "You should make your calculations, but you also need to see the real-world applications."

Allura was in the second group going up. Six trainees in a stripped-down bomber. The excitement was palpable. Allura didn't regret giving up her university education one bit. No number of parties could come close to the adrenaline rush she felt as she climbed on board the aircraft for her first bombing run. Acing tests, completing advanced courses in school, even being at the top of her class didn't compare with what she felt as she strapped into the aircraft.

"Ever been on one of these before?" Vivian asked.

She was only a few years older than Allura, who was the youngest trainee, and an airman first class. She had black hair and wide cheek bones that made her seem exotic in Allura's estimation. They had become fast friends.

"A shuttle," Allura replied.

"I mean an old-fashioned airplane," Vivian said. "This one is older than both of us combined."

"I haven't flown much," Allura said, her heart pounding as the aircraft lifted off in a vertical launch using repulsor engines.

"It's different," Vivian said. "No artificial gravity. No motion dampers. It's all very utilitarian. You feel everything."

"Oh," Allura said.

"I mean, it's good," Vivian continued. "You want that feeling, as if you're part of the aircraft. It helps."

"You've gone on bombing runs before?"

"I was a loader," Vivian said. "Making sure the right ordnance was dialed up. You have to learn to move with the movement of the aircraft."

It didn't take long for the aircraft to hit turbulence. The entire vessel shook. Allura wasn't frightened, but she was beginning to understand just how utilitarian the bombers were. And despite the fact that it was only a training run—the first of what she guessed would be of many—she felt a thrill with every bump and shimmy the aircraft made. It was as if the danger and ruggedness of the run was waking up a part of her she never knew existed before. And she loved it.

"We're on approach to target," the pilot's voice announced. "Trainee one to the launch bay. I repeat, trainee one, please check into the launch bay."

"That's me," Vivian said. "Wish me luck."

"Good luck," Allura said.

The launch bay was in the middle of the bomber. It was a big, wide aircraft with motorized racks that dropped the bombs. On training runs, the bombs were weight-adjustable, target-marking devices. They couldn't replicate the shape of most bombs, but they could be set up to act like most conventional warheads.

Allura and the other trainees were wearing headsets so they could hear one another over the roar of the aircraft's engines. They could also hear the chatter between the pilots and the bombardier.

"Bombardier One is locked in," Vivian said. "Permission to open bomb bay doors."

"Permission granted, Bombardier One. We are approaching target at fifteen hundred meters altitude. Air speed is two-seven-niner. Wind is from the east at eight KPH."

Vivian repeated the information. The different sections of the bomber were sealed so that opening the bomb bay doors didn't affect the cabin pressure in the cargo area where the trainees waited for their turn to drop real ordnance from an aircraft. Allura had done the job in a simulator dozens of times, but nothing compared to actually dropping something from a moving aircraft at a target fifteen hundred meters below.

"I've got the target in my sights," Vivian said. "Permission to release, Tango One?"

"Permission given. Fire away," the pilot said.

There was a pause and Allura could visualize what was happening. The targeting device in the bomb launch bay was in fact an optical scope. The only technology the bombardier had was a hand-held, analogue stopwatch. Vivian would have already measured the speed, the time it would take her bomb to reach the ground, and approximately when she should release it.

"Tango One is away!" Vivian said. She almost shouted the words; her voice was brimming with excitement.

Allura felt the aircraft turn suddenly. They tilted to the side and the force of gravity pulled her back against the side of her seat which was made of hard polymer and padded with a thin layer of foam.

"Circling around, Bombardier One," the pilot declared. "Prepare for your second drop."

There were times when a single bombing run would empty an aircraft's entire load of warheads. There were other instances where the bombing needed to be very precise, and a bombardier might work for hours making pass after pass to hit specific targets. But training would be rather straightforward. The idea was to drop a bomb onto the designated target area as close to center as each trainee could manage. The weight-adjustable target markers would bury themselves into the ground like darts on a board. Each drop would be measured and recorded, along with the calculations each bombardier made before taking the shot. It was an analytics-heavy program, which suited Allura just fine. She would pore over the numbers—not just her own, but those of all the trainees. Her mind was like a sponge for that type of information. And she was excited about the prospect of putting her new skills to the test.

After Vivian's second run, another trainee took her place. Then it was finally Allura's turn. She was bombardier three. Every centimeter of her body tingled as she made her way forward. There was an internal stairway that led down to the bomb bay section of the aircraft. She passed Terry Franks on the way. He looked miserable.

"How was it?" Allura shouted at him, trying to be heard over the roar of the aircraft.

"Lousy," he said. "It's like trying to hit a target the size of a pinhead from a moving platform... impossible."

He continued up the stairs and Allura descended. The bomb bay launch space was just a stool on a slightly elevated walkway. She sat down, connected the tether lines to her jumpsuit, which was really impact safety coveralls. She put on the headset and checked the controls.

"Bombardier Three is locked in," Allura said.

"Just in time, Bombardier Three, we are approaching target," the pilot said.

"Permission to open bomb bay doors?"

"Permission granted," the pilot replied.

Allura worked a large, red lever back and forth. Panels on the belly of the aircraft slowly opened. The target center was on an island just twenty kilometers from Newton City, in one of the big freshwater lakes. She could see it ahead of them, but it looked small. In an open area on one side of the island was the target zone. It looked like a giant bullseye. The center was red, with a blue ring around it, followed by yellow, green, and orange rings.

The pilot gave Allura the airspeed, altitude, and wind readings. Her control panel was really just an old-fashioned slate. She scribbled her equation and then started her stopwatch. There were only nine seconds until she needed to drop her first bomb.

"Target acquired," Allura said. "Permission to release Tango Five."

"Permission granted," the pilot said. "Good luck, Bombardier Three."

Allura's entire body tingled. She knew her equations were right, but she couldn't control every variable. The pilots were supposed to fly over the island on the same heading each time, but no one was perfect. Allura wouldn't have minded having the exactness of a computer to launch the bombs, but she knew that wouldn't be nearly as much fun. And even though she was practicing the art of war and felt a twinge of guilt at being so excited, she focused on the task at hand. She took hold of the firing lever. One pull would release her bomb, pushing it forward again would load the next one into place.

With one eye on her stopwatch and one on the target they were flying over, she tugged back on the firing lever. "Tango Five is away," she said, her heart pounding as she watched the big, bullet-shaped practice round drop into empty space beneath the aircraft. She leaned forward, expecting to watch it fall to the target, but the aircraft banked, making a wide turn to circle for the second pass.

It was a little anticlimactic. She wanted to know how her first-ever bombing run had gone, but there was no time and no indication. The practice round wouldn't explode, and the pilots who had a better view of things than she did, wouldn't give her any feedback. The aircraft looped around and headed for the island again. From the pocket of her jumpsuit, Allura pulled out a pair of compact binoculars. They were what Lieutenant Phoenix called "good glass," meaning they were well made on the inside. The lenses were highly polished and clear. She held them up to her eyes to see the island. Her marker was there, but outside the target area. There wasn't time to really study her first shot. The pilot was reading off the information she needed. Allura felt rushed as she did her equations and checked the stopwatch. Everything was happening so fast. Perhaps looking to see how her first bomb had landed was a mistake. She fired her second shot in a rush, and then waited for the aircraft to level out before disconnecting and starting back toward the cabin where the other trainees were waiting.

When she got to her seat and put her headphones on, Vivian gave her a wink.

"How was it?" Vivian asked.

"Amazing," Allura said. "I just wish I knew how I did."

"Normally you'll have a spotter," Vivian said. "I did that for a while too."

"It's so exciting," Allura said. "I can't imagine how it will be doing it for real."

"It gets crazy," Vivian said. "The Ma'Tis shoot back. Not every bomber returns to base."

Allura nodded, once more feeling guilty for her enthusiasm. She had never been touched by war. Her parents were both civilians, and no one in their extended family fought in the war. But she couldn't help but think of Cosmo. She would be high above the fighting, and he would be in the thick of things. Still, she felt like she was doing something important, and there was both a tangible effect and data-rich feedback to her actions. Something about being a bombardier fit Allura like a glove, and she might never have known about it if not for the sudden, unexpected turn of events on Fiona Grand that had separated her from Cosmo at the last possible moment. She wasn't grateful, but she was excited about the future. And she wondered if the man she loved felt the same way.

CHAPTER 10

"TODAY, GENTLEMEN," Sergeant Reed said, sounding almost like a regular human being, "we will be doing practice runs on the obstacle course. Each one of you will be timed. Your task is to complete the course as if you were being graded officially. The time to beat is five minutes."

There were only eighteen men left in Red Platoon. Quincy and most of his cohort had found ways to injure themselves. Anyone who couldn't get physical clearance to continue training was immediately removed from the platoon. Where they went or what they did exactly Cosmo didn't know and didn't want to find out. Over the three weeks since he had arrived at Fort Randal, his training had succeeded in narrowing his focus to one solitary goal. He wanted to be the best in the platoon. It didn't matter that he was drafted. It didn't matter that all they did every day was physical training and marching. He wanted to be excellent in everything he was asked to do. Weakness was abhorrent, as was cutting corners or finding ways to get out of one's duty. All that mattered was becoming the lethal killing machine that Drill Sergeant Reed had promised they would become if they gave themselves over to his instruction.

"Bet you a turn at night watch I can finish the course faster than you," Dyson bragged.

"Maybe," Cosmo replied. "If you don't fall off the rope swing again."

"So, is that a bet?" Dyson asked.

"You're on," Cosmo told him.

They had to wait their turn. Sergeant Reed was joined by five other troopers of varying rank, each with a stopwatch and a set of binoculars. The platoon members were spaced out one minute apart. When it was Cosmo's turn, he took off down the hill, but not at a full sprint. He didn't want to get careless and twist an ankle. Besides, after having worked on the course for the last two weeks, he knew that it paid to have gas in his tank for the sprint up the hill.

He reached the bottom of the hill and sprinted toward the vertical wall. He jumped, used his momentum to reach the top and flip his body around. He landed, bending his knees to absorb the shock—just as Sergeant Reed had taught them—and took off to the wire crawl. The ground had recently been soaked, leaving the recruits to crawl through the mud. Cosmo dove forward, his hardened muscles absorbing the fall and sending him sliding forward. He kept his head down and worked quickly through the obstacle. When he got to the far side, there was mud caking the front of his clothes and weighing him down. Still, his hands were a bit slick and slid down on the rope as he swung across the stinking pit, but he had no trouble flinging himself forward and landing on his feet. He dashed across the balance beams and then climbed the net rope.

They had learned to flip over the top rather than climb over. It was a bit like doing a summersault, and Cosmo was determined to get down fast. He made the flip, bounced down to the bottom without getting his feet tangled in the net, and sprinted up the far side of the hill.

He ran all the way back to where the platoon was waiting. One of the troopers marked his time and he bent over, hands on his knees, sucking wind. In his mind he was thinking about the mistakes he had made. His slip on the rope swing was the worst. It could have cost him dearly if he had fallen. And his muddy boots were difficult to manage on the balance beam. He calculated that he could shave off ten seconds by correcting those two issues. When Dyson joined him a moment later, he looked angry. The smell from the rope swing was impossible to miss.

"Looks like you fell again," Cosmo said without looking up at his friend.

"The damn rope was muddy," Dyson growled. "I probably still beat your time."

"We'll see," Cosmo said, standing up straight and putting his hands on his stubbly head. He looked at his friend for the first time since they finished the course. "You hurt?"

"Hell no," Dyson said. "I want a rematch."

"Fall in Red Platoon, and can that chatter," Sergeant Reed shouted. "That was the sloppiest bit of PT I've ever seen. Half of you wouldn't pass if this was the test."

He read off their times. Dyson had competed the course in five minutes, thirty-eight seconds, which was remarkable considering he had to go back to the beginning of the course after falling into the water on the rope swing. Cosmo's time was four minutes, fifty-six seconds.

"You did it bro," Dyson said.

"Don't get cocky, Frost!" Sergeant Reed demanded after giving Cosmo his time. "Four seconds isn't much of a margin of error."

"Yes, Drill Sergeant!" Cosmo shouted.

Still, he felt good. Only six of the recruits had finished the course in the required time limit. Cosmo wasn't the fastest, but he was pretty close. The best time was four minutes, fifty-two seconds. And he planned to get faster before the week's end.

That night they had Salisbury steak, roasted potatoes, and corn on the cob. Cosmo ate his fill but stuck to Dyson's eating plan. He stayed away from the carbs and sugar at night. The banana pudding with vanilla wafers looked delicious, but he refrained. With the limited number of recruits, they were standing one-hour watch shifts every other night. But Cosmo was relieved of his turn by Dyson.

"The next time I'll beat you," he warned.

"The next time I won't bet you," Cosmo said.

"Oh, so that's how you gonna be," Dyson said. "Not even gonna give me a chance to win my hour back."

"That's right," Cosmo said. "You gotta know when to walk away."

He slept easy that night until the rain started. It was the first time it had rained since basic training had started. The simple A-frame tent held up to the soaking, and the canvas material did a good job of keeping the water from soaking through. Still, the moisture seemed to fill the air, and when Cosmo woke up just before the air horn sounded the next morning, everything was a muddy mess.

The rain continued off and on for the next three days. There were times when it felt heavy, but they continued their training. They marched in downpours and through deep puddles. They ran with their clothes and shoes soaked and heavy. At night, as they stood watch, the rain chilled them. Worst of all, they were kept from practicing on the obstacle course for half of the week that remained. When it cleared, they threw themselves into the final preparations, focusing a large part of their afternoon time running the obstacle course. It was as much about technique as it was speed. Each of the five stations had something to master—a little secret to help the recruits get through the course in as little time as possible. By the end of the week, Cosmo could feel the pressure. He could lift weights, keep pace on long runs through the mountains, and do everything required of him. But if he slipped or failed the obstacle course in any way, it would ruin his hopes of staying with Dyson and making it to the elite armored division. Cosmo didn't know much about the military he had been drafted into other than how to do as he was ordered and what the enlisted ranks were, but he had decided that if he was going to fight the Ma'Tis, he wanted to be essential, not expendable.

"Today's the day," Sergeant Reed growled. "We'll be skipping our morning activities and going straight to the test. If you pass, you get a ticket to phase two of basic training. If you fail, you stay here another four weeks and do it all over again. And believe me, gentlemen, you don't want to fail. So get ready. You only get one shot at this."

"Any advice?" Cosmo asked his friend as they warmed up with a jog out to the obstacle course.

"Yeah, don't screw this up," Dyson said with a broad smile.

Just like before, they had staggered start times. The testing was informal. Nothing was a surprise. Cosmo finished the course with no problems and was confident he had passed. Dyson was the fastest in the platoon and hadn't fallen on the rope swing since their practice a week prior. In fact, everyone from Red Platoon except for Tad Grissom passed. Tad took a nasty fall on the balance beam and broke his arm. He would be sent off to a medical facility while the remaining members of Red Platoon followed Sergeant Reed into the main building to find a banquet waiting for them.

"Eat up, recruits," he said. "We'll be heading to Lois Operating Station on the coastal plateau in exactly one hour. Once you finish eating, gather your kit and meet me here."

The meal was all the pizza they could eat. It was the first junk food they had enjoyed since basic training began. There were sodas too, and a salad which went untouched.

"This would be better with beer," Dyson said.

"They probably don't want you getting drunk on the way to the second phase of training," Cosmo said. "You ever hear of Lois OS?"

"Nope," he said, shoving half a slice of pizza into his mouth. "I guess we'll find out all about it soon enough."

And they did. A transport picked them up from Fort Randal and took them to a series of portable buildings on a wide plateau that over-looked the ocean. The sun was low when they arrived, but it glistened off the deep blue water.

"Don't fall in love," Sergeant Reed grumbled. "The seas no longer belong to humans."

"Have you fought the Ma'Tis, Sarge?" Dyson asked.

"You bet your ass, Dyson. They're nasty bugs, but they can be killed. And with the PM's new draft, we'll finally have the personnel to push them back into the ocean where they belong."

"Is it dangerous being this close to the shore?" Cosmo asked.

"Lois is one of a dozen observation stations," Reed said. "Sooner or later the bastards will come crawling up on the beach, and when that happens the FG Army will be here to punch them right in the mouth."

He led the group into a portable building that was their home for the next two months. Bunks were already assigned. Lockers had fatigues instead of just PT sweats. They spent the next day learning new skills. They made their bunks with military precision. Learned how to iron their fatigues, roll their sleeves, polish their boots, and tuck their pantlegs. There were still long runs and plenty of calisthenics, but also weapons training.

The rifle of choice in fighting the Ma'Tis was the XJ7 loaded with heavy penetrators. They each received a rifle, and Sergeant Reed taught them to take it apart, piece by piece.

"In the field, maintaining your weapons is your second-highest priority," Reed explained.

"What's the first, Sarge?" Matteo Von'Gola asked.

"Not getting killed!" Reed barked. "Now pay attention."

The XJ7 was a tactical rifle with an optical scope. It had semi-auto, three-, five-, and ten-round burst fire settings. The magazine held forty rounds of finger-length, soft lead bullets sheathed in a tungsten jacket with a reinforced-armor piercing tip. The bullet's center was hollow, to allow for compression on impact, and loaded with explosive material that was meant to punch the round through two inches of solid steel.

"It still won't penetrate a bug's shell," Reed said. The Ma'Tis were called various things: crabs, bugs, sea monsters, crawlers, and crusties —the last because of their exoskeletons, which were incredibly strong. "A solid hit will knock one backward. Remember, they have six legs, which makes them hard to take down. Always aim for the joints where they are the most vulnerable."

They put the guns back together, then took them apart again. They did this for three days until the task could be done blindfolded, and Cosmo could name every part of the weapon. Finally, they were ready to take the guns out to the shooting range. Starting on their bellies, the rifles propped on little sandbags and pulled snug against their shoulders.

"Take your time," Reed said as he walked behind us. "This weapon must become as familiar to you as your own reflection. Every rifle has its own nuances. Learn them."

They fired single rounds at targets twenty meters down range. It wasn't easy. The recoil was powerful. The bullets didn't use gun powder, but explosive gel. The stock had built in struts to make the recoil less difficult on the user, but it felt to Cosmo like he was trying to control a tiny explosion. The point wasn't comfort, but sustained accuracy. Their fatigue shirts had foam pads on the shoulder of their dominant hand to help protect from bruising, but Cosmo still had a tender place on his shoulder and dark bruise for the next week.

They would get handguns too, but their first objective was to master the XJ7. They started each day with a ten-kilometer run and spent the evening learning close combat. Throughout history, soldiers had learned to fight one another. That was no longer needed. Instead, Cosmo's platoon learned the art of Ku Jit So, which was a fast-moving martial art, usually practiced with a bladed weapon and meant to keep the practitioner alive in close quarters with the Ma'Tis, and even pry open a gap between a bug's exoskeleton and inflict damage.

"One trooper against a bug will not usually end well for that human," Reed barked as we practiced moving, jumping, and climbing on Ma'Tis dummies in one of the training facilities. "Best to always keep moving. Stay clear of the big claw and get behind the ugly bastards if you can."

The Ma'Tis had wide shells on their backs. They could fold their arms and legs in and disappear under the protection of their thick back shells, almost like turtles. But the area between the top of the shell and their heads was vulnerable to a knife blade. Most Ma'Tis stood close to three meters tall, but with a run and jump the recruits could catch the top edge of the alien shell, pull themselves up, and stab into the soft bits of their neck.

Two weeks into training, Cosmo was shooting standing up and hitting ninety percent bullseyes on the shooting range, with targets at seventy meters. It was the best percentage in the platoon, which was down to just fifteen recruits with a couple more guys getting pulled after injuries. They added in steep, rocky climbs to their PT and got regular checkups and scans. They were given supplements to aid their physical performance and began learning to use different weapons and explosives.

"The Ma'Tis have two primary weapons," Reed extolled as they stood around a holographic projection table. The image of a large, crab-like creature appeared. It had one massive claw and a laser weapon strapped to its smaller claw arm. "This laser weapon is effective up to seventy meters. The closer you are the more effective it is. Of course, they can crush you to death with either claw should they manage to grab onto you. That big claw can decapitate a grown man in less time than it takes to shell a peanut.

"But the real danger is this." He tapped a button and a throbbing blob spilled out of the Ma'Tis warrior's shell. It formed around the alien's feet like mercury, combining and moving with a life of its own. "This is their manufactured, biological, self-replicating, autonomous substance. The eggheads call 'em bio-bots. They're part machine, part living entity. The best way to describe them is to liken them to cells, similar to what make up our own bodies. The Ma'Tis have cells too— each one a microscopic factory that can carry out work, send messages, and self-replicate. The aliens took that biological building block and swapped out the instructions. Their bio-bots are in fact trillions of microscopic killing machines. Their sole purpose is to infiltrate the enemy. The only way to resist them is to keep them from getting to us, which is why the armored units seal off completely. You see this glob dripping from one of these SOBs, you don't fight it; you run like hell. They will penetrate your body and kill you from the inside out, but not before taking control of your nervous system and turning you against your fellow troopers."

"How the hell are we supposed to fight that?" Dyson said.

"Fire," Reed explained. "Intense heat is the only way to kill them. But they move pretty fast, and they can spread out, reassemble, and cover any terrain. The good news is they don't last long. A few hours and their systems mutate and break down. But this is what has given the Ma'Tis the ability to push inland. We don't think they can mass produce it yet, or maybe it takes time to grow the substance. We aren't sure. But if they can come up with more, we're in trouble. It's one of the reasons you're here. We have to quadruple our fighting force fast if we're going to hold them off.

"To that end, you will learn to use tripod-mounted flame projectors and thermobaric grenades. The air force is producing old-fashioned napalm, and the eggheads are adapting our armor to be more heat resistant. Today, you will begin learning these advanced weapons and tactics."

"Point me in the right direction, Sarge," Dyson said.

"Assemble on range eight in fifteen minutes. Dyson, you can help me carry the gear."

Cosmo and another recruit named Dominic Elijah Lowenthal, but who everyone called Del, joined in. They pulled heavy crates on tiny castor wheels out to the shooting range. It wasn't set up like a gun range, but had burned-out structures spread across a rugged, rocky field. Sergeant Reed opened a crate and pulled out a cylindrical object.

"This is a thermobaric grenade," he said. "Allow me to demonstrate."

He rammed the object against his thigh, which crumpled the bottom. Cosmo heard a soft hissing sound. Reed threw the device. It landed fifteen meters away, and suddenly flames shot up from the ground and rolled out in a wave. The platoon felt the heat and stepped back as black smoke billowed up into the sky.

Reed picked up another of the devices. "These are simple weapons," he explained. "Gas is released from one section to the other when you activate it by hitting the bottom side. The upper chamber fills, mixing with the gas from the lower chamber until the pressure inside bursts the cap. When the gas comes into contact with oxygen, it burns. These are simple, effective weapons. Drop one of these on the bio-bots and they'll die or run and hide at any rate. But they are not to be used in close quarters. The fire cannot be directed, gentlemen. Set this off too close and you will get cooked. *¿Comprender?*"

"Yes, Drill Sergeant," they all said in perfect unison.

"Now, let's set something on fire," he growled with a smile on his rugged face.

CHAPTER 11

ALLURA HAD MISSED the target on both of her shots, but so had every other trainee on that first practice run. Over the days and weeks that followed, they spent hours training on simulators and more time in lectures. They memorized different explosive devices—their effective ranges, best altitude deployment, and what forces affected their flight path. They studied weather patterns at different altitudes, practiced safety drills, and learned how to survive if their bomber was shot down over water or land. It was like drinking water from a firehose, and Allura was loving every minute of it. Unlike school, where so much of what she was taught was theory, everything she learned in her bombardier training was practical.

After six weeks of mainly classroom and simulator training, the focus changed to include more practice runs in actual bombers of varying classes. And on top of it, they were given half a day's leave on a Saturday. The entire group of trainees went out for a meal together. They discovered a Latin cantina just off campus. Some of the older trainees drank margaritas, but Allura, Vivian, and Celeste didn't join in. They shared a meal with the others, then caught public transport to a shopping center where they stocked up on toiletries, makeup, hair products, and even a few souvenirs.

"Where are you from, Celeste?" Allura asked as they settled at a coffee shop with outdoor seating near the ATA campus.

"Terra Turro," she said. "In the Nyjar system."

"What's it like?" Vivian asked.

"Hot, dry, crowded," Celeste said. "And beautiful. It's not like this. We don't live in cities like this. We are connected to the land."

"What do the Ma'Tis want with a world that is hot and dry?" Allura asked.

"Nothing. We fight the Moshee, and the Akumba."

"I haven't heard of them," Vivian said, stirring her drink with a tiny straw.

"They aren't found outside the Nyjar system yet," Celeste said. "The Moshee come from the gas giant, Terra Rafa. They raid for hard minerals. And the Akumba live underground on Terra Turro, and Terra Yova. They ride the asteroids and drop out of the sky, burrow deep underground. We have been fighting them a long time."

"They sound dangerous," Vivian said.

"The Akumba grow very large," Celeste explained. "Their carcasses are rich with minerals that the Moshee want. We are stuck between them."

"Sounds brutal," Allura said.

"It is, but that is why we fight," Celeste said. "To protect our people, our way of life."

"I never thought about fighting," Allura said. "Not until my boyfriend was drafted. We were literally at the spaceport about to board a shuttle off world and the prime minister halted all travel for males between the ages of eighteen and twenty-five."

"Are you serious?" Vivian said. "That's terrible."

"I thought so too. But now... well... I wouldn't be here otherwise."

They drank their coffee and talked about the training program, their fellow trainees, and what the plan was for after graduation.

"We've only got four more weeks of training," Celeste said. "Then I am going home."

"What's it like on Fiona Grand?" Vivian asked Allura.

"It's good," she said. "Clean air. Not so crowded as this. But there's still plenty to do if you live in one of the bigger cities."

"What's the fighting like?" Vivian asked.

"Until recently it was mainly skirmishes and raids. At least that's how the newscasters described it."

"Now they are making a push inland," Celeste said. "It is not uncommon."

"How do you know so much about the Ma'Tis?" Vivian asked her. "They haven't even invaded your world."

"I study my enemies," Celeste said. "All of them. We are warriors; we must know who we fight and how to defeat them."

Allura took the advice to heart. As their training progressed, she studied about the Ma'Tis in her spare time. She kept several books on her PIP and read about the aliens she would be fighting on the long training flights as she waited her turn to drop bombs on targets. There was so much to learn. The Ma'Tis were from a yet undiscovered star system. Their world was obviously much like those that humanity craved: liquid water, areas of dry land, oxygenated oceans. The Ma'Tis were formidable creatures. They breathed using gills like a fish, only they could seal off their gills when they came out of the water and survive on land for days at a time before needing to submerge and breathe again. They were incredibly strong too, easily lifting three times their body weight. Underwater they could do even more.

The first planet the aliens had invaded was Iconium, in the Aegean system. Iconium was eighty-five percent oceans. The only continents were at the poles, and islands dotted the wide seas. Humanity had been there for well over a century when the aliens arrived. They dropped through the atmosphere and into the oceans where they disappeared for almost forty years. When they reappeared, they conquered island after island, driving the human inhabitants off. At first it was believed that the huge, crab-like aliens ate humans. It wasn't until dissected bodies washed up on the shores that it became clear that the Ma'Tis only took bodies to study them.

Diplomacy with the aliens was an utter failure. The aliens communicated with squeals and chattering with claws and mandibles. Even the best AI systems couldn't decipher patterns in their speech, if it could be called that. Most xeno-biologists believed the aliens used a combination of pheromones, audible sounds, and even telepathy to communicate. Their antennae could detect vibrations in the air and water. They worked in unison to build large, underwater communes, fed on sea creatures, and raided on land to drive back humanity. They were also known to attack sea vessels. The oceans belonged to the Ma'Tis, and humanity even getting close was cause for battle.

What alarmed Allura was that in almost every case of long-term invasion, the Ma'Tis pattern of raids and skirmishes eventually turned into strategic attacks on vital settlements and stripping of resources. Those first few worlds the Ma'Tis had invaded were eventually lost to the aliens. And since most of their actions took place below the waves, there was still a lot that humanity didn't know about them. The most pressing was how they traveled through space at all. Their vessels, if they could be called that, didn't give off any radiological or electromagnetic signatures. They were called seedpods by the scientists who studied the Ma'Tis, because like a nut, they carried the aliens through space only to crack open when they fell into the oceans where they released the Ma'Tis to carry out their own colonization projects.

Of more concern to Allura were the weapons used by the Ma'Tis —specifically the ground-to-air missiles they used. Unlike the lasers carried by the Ma'Tis warriors, their air defense often consisted of hard projectiles that were small enough to go unnoticed by radar systems—or at the very least would show as a cloud, making evasion difficult for pilots. The projectiles were launched using rail-type weapons that literally flung the projectiles into the air. There was no propulsion to the objects, just momentum from their launch. They didn't use laser guidance and didn't alter their flightpaths to track down airships. Instead, like a volley of arrows, the Ma'Tis relied on volume to bring down the ships tasked with dropping fire from the sky.

One of the biggest mysteries about the aliens was the electronic interference field, or EIF they projected. No one knew where it came from or even how it worked, but anything that approached had either its electronic systems scrambled, or in the case of missiles, its guidance systems usurped altogether. Some people believed the aliens created a mental co-op, a projection of their telepathy that created a synergistic covering to protect them from air attacks. Humans, desperate to use any tactic against the Ma'Tis, had reverted to ancient strategies. Aircraft were stripped of non-essential electronics. Pilots learned to fly using visual flight rules, navigating using visual markers rather than radar or computer-assisted navigation, which put the flight ceiling much lower than most aircraft were capable of attaining. And bombs were simply dropped, allowing gravity and weather conditions to propel the warheads down onto the enemy positions. But bombardiers were required to reliably hit targets on the ground without computer assistance, and being on the bottom of an aircraft was dangerous when the enemy was firing projectiles up at the aircraft.

The class of trainees was improving on their practice runs. They could almost all hit bullseyes on stationary targets in calm weather conditions with no evasive maneuvers from the bombers. But the Ma'Tis knew this danger and rarely stayed out in the open. They used local weather conditions to help shield them from danger. Bad weather made visual flight rules incredibly difficult. It also impacted bombardment trajectories in unexpected ways. Hitting a target from a thousand meters up in swirling winds was incredibly difficult. It required a mix of knowledge and skill that few bombardiers lived long enough to perfect. The biggest danger was the need to fly low. From ten thousand meters, the bombers were safe from the Ma'Tis projectiles, but hitting an enemy target from that height was nearly impossible. The bombs would almost all meander off course and were just as likely to hit friendly positions as the enemy forces. The only way to increase the bombardment accuracy was to fly lower. The worse the weather, the lower the bomber needed to fly. Some missions required the aircraft to drop as low as a few hundred meters, which left them incredibly vulnerable to both ground-to-air defenses and the unpredictable weather.

The bombardier trainees made runs at targets in canyons and on steep hillsides. They practiced in all weather conditions, even at night. Allura was the smartest person in her class, but Celeste was the most naturally gifted bombardier. As graduation loomed, Allura was connected with the air/space forces on Fiona Grand who were thrilled to be getting her. Upon graduation, she would be flown from Triton back to FG and stationed on Hawkstone Air Base in the Kiebble mountains nearly a thousand kilometers from Saint Stevens where she grew up.

She typed the wheres and whens in a message to Cosmo. She

could contact her family when she was back on Fiona Grand and settled in at the air base. But she still had no word from Cosmo other than the message he had sent at the start of his basic training. All she could hope for was to make contact when she was back on FG and fighting the same enemy he was.

CHAPTER 12

"THIS IS YOUR MACS," the officer said. He stood at the front of a classroom. Cosmo and the remaining members of Red Platoon were only a few weeks away from completing their basic training. "That stands for military account and communication system."

It was a flexible, heavy-duty PIP with enhanced features for combat.

"On it, you will see your basic information. This device is not a toy, it's a tool. It gives you access to the Fiona Grand military network. We don't use the MACS to watch movies or send messages to your sweethearts. It is a streamlined communication system that is connected to your vital info, current military assignment, and veteran services such as the FGA Credit Union where you can access your pay."

A hand immediately went up. Cosmo didn't have to look over his shoulder to know that it was Frankie Voss. He had been an accountant for a small firm before being drafted. At every opportunity he had asked about their pay, and he finally got the answers he was looking for.

"Sir, may I ask what our pay is?" Voss asked.

"Recruits earn a thousand credits a week. Once you have been promoted to E-2 you will receive the standard pay for that rank."

"A thousand?" Voss asked, sounding more upset than Cosmo had ever heard him.

"Each week," the officer giving the lecture said. "Now, once you log into the system you should each see the specific field of service you have been selected for. At the end of your training, you'll have instructions on where to go and what to do next. You'll want to keep your MACS with you at all times. Any questions?"

There were none and the lecture ended. They were all adjusted to military life by that point of their training. And it wasn't hard to guess where most of them would serve. A few members of Red Platoon would be assigned to the corps of engineers, or artillery platoons, while most would be assigned to infantry. The draft wasn't instituted to fill out the logistics or administrative posts. The army needed warm bodies to hold the line against the Ma'Tis, and that was the job of the infantry. They would join existing platoons assigned to dig in and hold defensive positions against the Ma'Tis or between the oceans and direct routes to important civilian settlements. But Cosmo was hoping for a different assignment. He looked over at Dyson, who gave him a reassuring nod.

Cosmo tapped on the screen, inputting his name and military identification number. The screen showed a connection to the Fiona Grand military network. His MACS had only a few icons: a message center, an app for making video calls, a calendar, a GPS navigational app, and a link to the FGA Credit Union. It was tempting to tap the banking app to see how much money the government had taken from his meager pay in taxes and fees, but he could do that math in his head. What he was really interested in—what they were all anxious to find out—was whether they had been selected for the armored division. Cosmo tapped the messages icon and saw a list of messages, but the one he was interested in was labeled: All Army Activities Message —Assignment Memorandum.

He tapped the message, then scanned it. It felt strange, like time had slowed down. He could feel his heart thumping, and there was a dull roar in his ears. And until he saw the words Armored Division, he couldn't breathe. But they were there, his assignment to the only truly offensive segment of the Fiona Grand Army. He looked over at Dyson who was still reading his memo.

"Well?" Cosmo asked him.

Dyson held up a finger and kept reading. Cosmo could see his lips moving slightly as he read the message. Then he grinned as he looked over at his friend.

"Did you get in?" Cosmo asked.

"Armored, baby!" Dyson said. "You?"

"Same," Cosmo replied, feeling a sense of relief. Tension had been mounting as they progressed through basic training. He did his best on every skill they were taught, all the while hoping he would make it to the armored division, but fearing he would fall short. Or worse still, that Dyson would make it and he wouldn't. The two had become close during their training, and whatever their assignment, they hoped to stay together after graduating from basic.

"You guys are nuts," Frankie said.

"All right, Red Platoon, time to move," Sergeant Reed said. "Don't get soft on me just because you're moving on soon. I expect each and every one of you to be the best damn troopers wherever you go next. To that end, let's hit the range. Fall in platoon."

They lined up and marched out to the gun range. They were down to pistol drills, having already qualified on the other weapons they would be expected to use. Everyone was in a good mood, and it carried over to dinner that evening.

"Two more weeks," Dyson said. "Then the real fun begins."

"How long is mech school?" Todd Butler asked. He was the only other member of Red Platoon to get into the armored division.

"Four weeks," Cosmo explained. He and Dyson had already studied everything they could about the armored division. "One week of operational instructions and three weeks of practical."

"That ain't bad," Butler said. "But I'm tired of running sims and field exercises. I want to fight the Ma'Tis."

"You were a clerk in a men's clothing store," Dyson told him, "And now you want to fight aliens."

"I didn't know what I was missing," Butler said.

"No doubt," Cosmo agreed. "I'm ready too."

"We moving from the minor leagues to the big show, boys. It's about to get real."

Frankie Voss slid over to where the guys were sitting. "What are you guys gonna do with your salary surplus?"

"Our what?" Butler asked.

"You know, man, the money we've been paid for the last three months."

They hadn't actually competed all three months of their basic training, but they understood what he meant. Cosmo had checked his account with the credit union. His weekly pay of one thousand credits was reduced to just six hundred seventy-five after taxes and fees. But that added up to nice little nest egg that would be over eight thousand credits once they finished basic training.

"It ain't much," Dyson said.

"Tell me about it," Frankie complained. "I lost over seventy-five percent of my personal income from what I was making before they drafted us. Still, you should be thinking about what to do with that money. Don't just waste it."

"It's earning interest in the credit union, right?" Butler asked.

Frankie snorted. "Are you really that stupid? Interest on saving accounts is well below the yearly inflation rate. If you do nothing with your money, it shrinks. Didn't they teach you that in school?"

"Public education," Cosmo pointed out, "didn't cover personal finances."

"No kidding," Butler said. He was only a year older than Cosmo, while Frankie Voss was twenty-three years old with a bachelor's in accounting.

"Take a look at the mutual funds," Frankie said. "They're a safe bet and will get you over the inflation bump. If you want to take on a little more risk, I can recommend some stocks to look into."

"What's in it for you?" Dyson asked.

"Nothing," he replied. "I mean, we're all in this together, right? We might as well benefit. We aren't getting paid much, but we've got free housing and meals. A little discipline with our finances could really get us ahead when this is all over."

"What assignment did you get?" Butler asked him.

"Artillery," he said, clearly not happy. "I guess they didn't need any more engineers."

"You want to build bridges?" Dyson asked.

"I'd rather not get shot at," Voss replied. "Or have my head ripped off. I didn't sign up for any of this."

"Yet here you are," Butler said.

"Thanks, captain obvious," Voss said. "I'm just saying you should do something with your money, that's all."

"I'll be sending most of mine back home to help my mother," Cosmo said.

"Damn, that's pretty selfless, bro," Dyson said.

"She raised me by herself," Cosmo replied.

"Your dad run off?" Butler asked.

"No, he was killed in an accident," Cosmo said. He didn't bother explaining that the Ma'Tis were responsible. He had never felt the need to avenge his father's death, even though he knew that the aliens had ultimately been responsible. The accident had occurred when he was very young, and he hadn't given the aliens much thought growing up. They were far away, and while his father wasn't forgotten, he wasn't really part of Cosmo's life either. But since being drafted and confronted with the reality of the Ma'Tis on Fiona Grand, he had felt a deep-seated, simmering anger that longed to be let loose. Perhaps it was why he had thrown himself into the training so completely.

"I'm sorry to hear that," Frankie Voss said. "But we could all be killed before long. The money we're being paid isn't worth the risk, but it's all we've got."

"You'll be okay," Cosmo told him. "We'll look into the mutual funds."

"Good to hear it," Frankie replied. "At least I'll know I did some good while I was here."

They moved off to speak to another group at another table.

"Just two more weeks," Dyson said. "Then the fun begins."

They had no more personal time than before. Since moving on to the second phase of their basic training, they each got a full night's sleep and only had to stand watch twice a week. But nearly every waking hour was busy. Still, Cosmo found a few minutes before falling asleep that night to check his personal message account with his new MACS. There were nearly thirty messages from Allura.

He opened them in the order they had come. The first few were written from her voyage to the Triton system. They were melancholy, but he feasted on every word. Despite having found that he really enjoyed military life, he still missed his girlfriend. They had never been separated for so long. He wanted to take his time reading through the long list of messages, but they were so good he couldn't stop.

And then he got a message he wasn't expecting:

I don't know what you're going to think about this, but my mind is made up, she wrote. I've decided to leave TTI and join the military.

"No," Cosmo said out loud.

He wasn't the only recruit reading messages on his little bunk. Dyson was beside him, but already trying to sleep.

"What's that, bro?" Dyson asked.

"Nothing," Cosmo told him. "Sorry."

Dyson sighed and went back to sleep as Cosmo, his hands trembling, kept reading.

I'm going to become a bombardier. I've looked into it, and I think it's the best fit for me. Maybe if you had been here, school would have felt different. And I gave it a try, but it seems wrong somehow. How can I take classes and attend parties while you're out risking your life. The kids here don't get it. They're oblivious to what is really going on in the galaxy. All they care about is getting high and having a good time. But I can't just pretend that what you're doing doesn't matter. So I'm leaving school and going to the Air Training Academy here on Triton. It's where they train pilots and bombardiers, so I'll just be shifting over to their campus. I had to agree to a four-year enlistment, and I'm sorry I made that decision without you, but it feels right. The training course starts in two weeks. I'll graduate about the same time as you and then I'll be sent back to Fiona Grand. We might not be together, but I couldn't stand being worlds apart. I hope you understand. Love forever xxooo

Cosmo felt as if he had been doused with ice water. Allura was the most important person in the entire galaxy to him, even more important than his own mother. The last thing he wanted was for her to put herself at risk. He stayed up that night and read every message she had sent. When he finally finished, he felt numb. Allura wasn't just becoming a bombardier, she was loving it. It made no sense, and yet he too felt like he had found a part of himself in basic training that he didn't know was missing. As he drifted off to sleep, he realized their future was completely different from what they had planned. And even though they were both in risky positions, he couldn't help but wonder if things might be better than he had dared hope they could be.

CHAPTER 13

GRADUATION WAS A SMALL CEREMONY, but Allura got her official Fiona Grand uniform along with a bombardier's logo pin, and an ATA ring. Her shuttle for the Fiona system didn't leave until the following day. A couple of her fellow bombardiers had to leave the campus immediately for transport back to their home systems, but Vivian and Celeste insisted they go out and celebrate.

The Neon Dream was a dance club. After a big meal, they got all their gear packed for their flights the following day, then went out to continue the celebration. They had wine at a bar near the ATA campus. In her uniform no one questioned her age, and before long they were at the Neon Dream, sipping fruity cocktails and shouting over the throb of the music. Eventually, the three women got on the dance floor. They were hours away from leaving Triton and none were looking for a hookup, although they got plenty of looks and even a few free drinks from the men in the club. They danced together, just the three of them, cutting loose and acting silly after ten weeks of long lessons and even longer training flights. And the future, while exciting, was also dangerous. They would be separated across the galaxy, and while their friendship would endure, it would be lived out over long messages that took weeks to reach one another. So they danced and laughed and did their best not to think about the danger that was facing them.

"Who wants another drink?" Vivian said.

She was on the verge of drunk. "I'll get them," Allura said. Getting the drinks was her way of getting herself soda instead of liquor. She had consumed two alcoholic beverages, first at the wine bar, then at the club. They made her feel lightheaded and happy but also a little nervous. She had avoided drinking parties in high school. She wasn't afraid to break the rules; she just had a healthy respect for them. And she didn't want to do anything she might regret. Her greatest hope in leaving for home was the possibility of seeing Cosmo again. And while he had insisted that she not wait for him, getting together with anyone else wasn't something she had any interest in.

"Me, me, me," Celeste said. "I am feeling loose, and it is wonderful."

"You got the moves, girl," Vivian declared.

"I do have the moves," Celeste said. "And I feel like dancing the night away."

Allura laughed. Celeste wasn't drunk, but she was letting her hair down for the first time since their bombardier training had begun. She left her two companions and went to the bar.

"Two tequila sunrises, and one soda with lime," she ordered.

The bartender held out a device to scan her banking card. The machine beeped, a light came on green, and the man behind the bar started mixing their drinks. Allura turned back to her friends and watched them from the elevated space above the dance floor where the bar was located. There were swirling, colorful lights changing with the beat of the music. At first Allura had been intimidated by the club, but it didn't take her long to loosen up. She was making memories that she intended to keep for the rest of her life, and there was no reason not to have a little fun. She had earned it, she told herself.

"Hey! I know you," a sweaty boy with his shirt half unbuttoned declared. "I haven't seen you since the start-of-school dance. Where have you been hiding, baby?"

It was the student volunteer who had checked her into the dorm room at the TTI. She remembered that he called himself Crypto, and he seemed just as drunk and high as he had been the night of the dance. He had gotten a little too handsy that night, and she didn't want a repeat of that incident.

"Seriously?" Allura said. "I dropped out."

"So... that uniform isn't a costume?"

"No," Allura said.

"Well, hey, you look great," he said.

Allura wasn't impressed. She turned back around, waiting for her drinks. Crypto was undeterred. He cozied up to her at the bar.

"You should be a little more friendly," he said. "You wouldn't be so haughty if you knew who my father was."

"I don't know, and I don't care," Allura said as she picked up her three drinks.

"You'd be lucky to land a guy like me," he insisted.

Allura ignored him and headed back toward her friends. She made it halfway, moving carefully down the stairs with the drinks, when she felt a hand grab her shoulder. Crypto spun her around. Allura dropped the drinks as he pulled her close to him.

"Dance with me," he insisted.

"Are you crazy?" she shouted as she pushed him away.

He lost his footing and dropped onto his butt on the stairs that led up to the bar. People laughed, and Allura saw his face transform from blurry confidence to fury. She stepped back as he got to his feet. In a lunge he shoved her hard. Allura fell backward and slid across the wooden dance floor toward her friends, but Crypto wasn't finished.

"I'll show you what happens when you try to — oooppfff!"

Celeste stepped up to Crypto and slugged him hard in the stomach. He staggered back, his eyes wide with surprise. Vivian helped Allura to her feet. Crypto turned his anger onto Celeste and took a swing at her. Allura and Vivian both screamed in shock and fear, but Celeste ducked under the clumsy punch, and drove her fist straight into Crypto's groin. He bent forward in pain and Celeste grabbed his upper arms, threw her hip into him, and flipped him over her body and onto the dance floor. He hit his head and crashed hard.

"That's enough!" one of the club's bouncers said.

"He put hands on my friend," Celeste said.

"I know, which is why I'm not hauling you ladies out. But this guy has friends. You better move on."

"Friends?" Allura asked.

The bouncer pointed to a group of sullen-looking college boys at a booth in the back.

"His father is an investor too," the bouncer said. "Gives his kid anything he wants. You don't need that kind of grief in your life."

"We're leaving," Vivian told him.

"Good idea," he told them. "Good luck. I did a stint in the Space Corps. Never met any fly ladies as fine as the three of you, though."

They left feeling pretty good about themselves.

"Where did you learn to fight like that?" Vivian said when they were outside the club and walking back toward the ATA campus.

"My father taught me. I had brothers," Celeste said. "They didn't take it easy on me."

"Well you saved my bacon," Allura said. "I didn't mean to knock him down."

"You shouldn't have to worry about some creep getting rough with you," Vivian said.

"But you should be ready if they do," Celeste said. "When you get home, take some self-defense courses. Bad things happen to people who are unprepared."

By the time they got to their quarters on campus, the three young women were exhausted. They fell asleep easily and woke up feeling the effects of the night before. Allura wasn't hung over, but she had a bruise on her left hip from when she fell on the dance floor, and her neck was stiff. Still, the other two girls had it worse. Both looked sick as they stumbled to the showers. After cleaning up, they shared a hover-cab to the spaceport where they were finally forced to say their goodbyes.

"You will be safe," Celeste said. "And message me."

"We will," Vivian insisted.

"You be careful, too," Allura told her.

They hugged, each one with tears in their eyes.

"We'll plan a reunion," Vivian said.

"Just say when and where," Allura said.

"You have to come to Terra Turro," Celeste said.

"It's a deal," Vivian said. "Next year, we'll plan it and make it a girls' vacation."

They split up. Allura had an official Air/Space Force bag with her new uniforms inside, but also her luggage full of her civilian clothing. After checking in with the gate attendant, she was allowed onto the transport. It was a big space vessel. The FG Air/Space Force didn't pay for a private cabin. She had three days in a little pod—just a seat with a short privacy wall. She could recline her seat and extend a footrest for sleeping, but it wasn't the same as having a bed. Not that Allura cared. She was going home, and it felt good. She had accomplished something, was earning a salary, and was prepared to make a difference. Whatever came her way, she thought she would be ready for it.

She was wrong.

CHAPTER 14

HIS MOTHER SHOWED up for graduation. Cosmo hadn't expected to see her or anyone that he knew. There were eight platoons graduating. When the day arrived, the newly promoted privates dressed in their formal uniforms and marched out to the parade ground together. A small set of bleachers had been erected, and music played from a loudspeaker. The sun was shining, cool breeze from the ocean wafted up over the plateau, and brightly colored banners fluttered overhead. It was a perfect day in Cosmo's mind.

"Well, despite all evidence to the contrary, you managed to become troopers in the FG Army," Drill Sergeant Reed declared to the men of Red Platoon who were lined up outside their barracks, waiting their turn to march to the parade ground for the graduation ceremony. "I will say this just one time, so listen up. I am damn proud of all of you."

Cosmo couldn't help but smile. He was at attention, his feet together, his back straight, his gaze straight ahead, but his lips curled up into a smile.

"What the hell are you grinning about, Frost?" Reed bellowed. "You think you've accomplished something?"

"No, Drill Sergeant!" Cosmo shouted.

"Good! Don't get cocky," the drill instructor continued. "Never forget that we are facing an aggressive alien enemy that wants each and every one of you dead. And they're getting pretty damn bold. So listen to me. Your final orders from me are this. Don't die. Fight your ass off, follow orders, be the best of the best, but don't die. You do that, and you'll earn my highest regard. Is that clear?"

"Yes, Drill Sergeant," the entire platoon shouted in unison.

"Outstanding. Red Platoon, about face! Forward, march!"

They set out for the parade ground where they stood in formation with the other platoons. The audience clapped for each group that arrived. Brigadier General Samuel F. Kelly stepped to a podium and gave a short speech. Cosmo listened as he stood at ease, his hands clasped behind his back. He could see the ocean in the distance. It was nearly eight kilometers from the plateau that Lois Operating Station was built on, and over a thousand kilometers below them. The view was spectacular, and Cosmo allowed himself to enjoy the moment. He only wished that Allura could be there to see it. His plan had been to get a degree simply because that seemed to be the logical next step, and his teachers had worked so hard to help him get the scholarships and grants needed to attend university. But as he stood listening to General Kelly, he realized that he didn't regret getting drafted after all. Being a soldier wasn't just something he had accomplished; he was good at it and enjoyed most everything about it. Basic training had been difficult at first, but once his body adjusted to the rigors, he felt at home with the rigid command structure, the brotherhood of his fellow recruits, and the singular focus of all their training.

General Kelly wrapped up his remarks, and Colonel Allison Evenrue read out the names of each recruit. They came to attention as their drill sergeants pinned on the awards each had earned. There were ribbons for basic training graduation, general marksmanship, and unique insignias for each division that the recruits were moving into. When Cosmo's name was called, among the general polite applause from the spectators was a familiar whistle. His mother had used it to get his attention when he was little. As Drill Sergeant Reed pined the row of ribbons onto his chest, it took all his willpower not to look into the stands.

"Sounds like you've got a visitor, Frost," Reed said as the Colonel read out the next name over the loudspeaker. He extended his hand, and Cosmo shook it, feeling a bit odd to do something so familiar with his drill instructor.

"Yes, Drill Sergeant," Cosmo said softly. "That's my mother."

"Sounds like she's proud of you," he said with a nod.

"Yes, Drill Sergeant. Thank you, sir."

Reed stepped back and saluted. Cosmo returned the salute and felt his face flush. He wasn't embarrassed, but he felt a sense of pride in himself that he had never experienced before. Sergeant Reed went to get ready for the next name from Red Platoon that would be called out by the Colonel, and Cosmo glanced into the stands. He saw his mother. She was standing up, waving. He smiled and it felt good.

"We have special accomplishment metals to award," Colonel Evenrue said once all the names had been called for graduating. "If I call your name, please come forward to the podium."

A series of names from each of the other platoons was called—no more than three.

"From Red Platoon, Private Henry Edward Dyson and Cosmo Logan Frost," the Colonel read out.

Cosmo was shocked, but Dyson was already moving forward. Cosmo quickly fell in behind his big friend. They lined up and once more the Colonel called out awards.

"For the Platoon Leadership Award, Henry Edward Dyson," the Colonel said.

Sergeant Reed stepped forward and pinned a little silver device next to the ribbons on the big man's chest. They shook hands.

A few moments later the Colonel called out Cosmo's name.

"Earning the highest marksmanship scores of this graduating class is Cosmo Logan Frost," the Colonel said. "He is also the recipient of Red Platoon's Distinguished Graduate Award."

The crowd clapped, his mother whistled, and Drill Sergeant Reed pinned two medals onto his chest. Pictures were taken, and then the ceremony ended. The crowd came out onto the parade grounds, and before he knew it, Cosmo's mother was there.

"Oh, my gosh, Cos, I can't believe how good you look," she said.

"Thank you," he managed as she squeezed him hard. "And your medals."

"I had no idea," he said.

"Highest marksmanship scores of the entire class," his mother continued. "Oh, honey, I'm so proud of you."

"Thanks, Mom."

Drill Sergeant Reed appeared beside them, and he extended a hand to her.

"You must be Mrs. Frost," he said.

"Call me Nicole," she said, shaking Reed's hand.

"You should be proud," he said. "Frost is an excellent trooper. One of the best I've ever trained."

"I am proud," she said.

"Some people have natural talent for what we do," Reed said. "Private Frost is one of them."

"Thank you, Drill Sergeant," Cosmo said.

"I have about a thousand questions," his mother said.

"Then I'll leave you to it," Reed said. "I'll see you both at the banquet."

Cosmo was just about to respond when the music on the loudspeaker was replaced by a blaring Klaxon. His mother looked frightened. The alarm was loud and jarring. Cosmo looked around, but it didn't take long to recognize the source of the alarm. Out of the ocean, figures were moving.

"Drill Sergeant, look!" Cosmo said, pointing.

"I see them," Reed said. "Get your mother to the shuttle, Frost. Meet us at the armory. It looks like we've got one more thing to do today."

"Yes, Drill Sergeant!" Cosmo said loudly. "This way, Mom."

"What's happening?" she asked.

"The Ma'Tis are here," Cosmo said, as he led her to a row of hover-buses. "Get on board and do whatever you're told. I'll contact you as soon as it's safe."

"Cosmo," she said, tears flooding her eyes.

"Don't worry, Mom. I'll be fine."

"You better be," she said, getting onto the bus. "I got a message from Allura."

"She wrote me too," he said. "Who would have thought it?"

"I'm proud of you," she called out. "Proud of you both."

He waved goodbye, then turned and ran for the armory to join his platoon in his first real battle.

CHAPTER 15

"JUST LIKE WE TRAINED," Sergeant Reed barked. "You know the drill. Let's go, people. Time to show the bugs who they're dealing with."

Cosmo grabbed a rifle, slung it over his shoulder, and started stuffing ammunition magazines into the stretchy loops on a utility belt he had pulled around the tail of his dress uniform jacket.

"Frost, hold on a second," Reed said. "Take this."

He handed Cosmo a heavy, high-caliber rifle. It had bi-pod legs secured to the barrel and a big scope mounted on the rail. The end of the barrel widened near the muzzle, and the thick stock had two compression coils to lessen the recoil on the shooter.

"I just got orders," the Sergeant said, his gruff voice a growl. "We're going to hold the main admin building. That's the tall one for those of you who can't read the signage. I'm talking to you, Butler."

"I can read, Sarge," Todd Butler exclaimed, "Just not very fast."

Sergeant Reed ignored him. "Dyson, you're Frost's spotter. I want the two of you up on the roof. Butler, you're on door duty with Voss and McNaire. We are on comms channel foxtrot two niner. Get into position and don't do anything unless you hear from me, is that understood?"

"Yes, Drill Sergeant," they all replied.

"This is not a sim, gentlemen. This is the real thing. Those bugs get close, we're going to show them the way straight to hell. Stay cool, follow my orders, and remember your training. Let's move."

Cosmo picked up a box of long-range ammunition. It was in a metal container with a handle. The ammo was even heavier than the big rifle. The entire platoon donned battle helmets and armored vests, which they pulled on over their dress uniform jackets and their new ribbons from graduation. Dyson picked up a spotter's scope case, and they hurried off together toward the admin building. Despite the weight of two rifles and an extra ammo can, Cosmo wasn't even out of breath when he reached the admin building. It was the tallest structure—a large, square tower with narrow windows. Butler and Voss were already at the doors.

"Welcome to the big show," Butler said. "Save some for us, Frost."

"He'll do no such thing," Dyson said. "Best marksman in the whole damn class. We're going to show the crabs it ain't safe on land."

"Fine by me," Voss added. "Good luck."

They ran through the lobby. Army buildings weren't constructed to impress anyone. The words *utilitarian* and *spartan* were used when describing most of them. The admin building at Lois Operating Station was no different. The lobby was a small room with some plastic chairs near a window into a receptionist's office. Cosmo and Dyson hurried through the lobby to an elevator where Sergeant Reed was waiting for them.

"Straight up to the roof," he said. "There's a stairwell on the top floor. Get up there and tell me everything you see happening on that beach."

"Yes, Drill Sergeant," Cosmo said as the elevator doors opened.

"General Kelly wants snipers on every building. You're call sign Red One, make me proud."

They stepped into the elevator and Reed gave them a reassuring nod. The doors closed and Dyson looked at his friend.

"Red One, that's what I'm talking about, baby!"

"Yeah, no pressure," Cosmo said.

"You got this, man," Dyson assured him. "No different than the gun range."

"Except it's moving targets that shoot back," Cosmo said.

"They ain't got nothing can hit us from that far out," Dyson said.

The elevator doors opened, and they stepped into a narrow hall. There were two offices on their right, on the land side of the building. One door was on the left, with General Kelly's name printed on it.

"The big dog gets the big office on the top floor," Dyson said.

"With the ocean view," Cosmo added.

"I could get used to that every day."

At the end of the hall was a utility door. It was painted dull gray, with the words Rooftop Access stenciled across it. They pushed through, found a set of metal stairs going up, and made their way onto the roof. It was a beautiful autumn day. The sun was shining above them, the cool ocean breeze wafted up, and from the land side of the plateau there were trees with golden leaves showing. But on the ocean side, the sight was spoiled by hundreds of bodies moving out of the surf and joining hundreds more on the dark sands of the beach.

"Damn," Dyson said. "That's a lot of aliens."

"Too many," Cosmo said, setting the sniper rifle onto the air exchange unit near the corner of the building. "That's no raiding party."

"An invasion force," Dyson said.

"Part of it," Cosmo said. "They wouldn't send their entire army to shore right where we happen to have a base."

"Man, I hope you're wrong," Dyson said as he extended the legs of the tripod built onto the sniper scope.

Cosmo set up the bi-pod legs on the sniper rifle and looked through the scope. He had to adjust the focus. The Ma'Tis came into view. The sight of them was hard to accept. They looked so different, so menacing. It was impossible not to feel animosity for the strange creatures. They walked sideways on four of their six appendages. The last two they held up like arms. One had a small pincer with a laser weapon strapped to the claw. The other pincer was massive, an oversized, serrated claw that narrowed to a point. Cosmo felt a shiver run down his back.

"Laser distance is funny," Dyson said. "The reading keeps changing."

"Give me a wind reading," Cosmo said. "At this range, we have to factor in everything."

"On it," Dyson said.

He pulled a little device from the spotter's case and powered it on. The contraption read the wind conditions, the humidity in the air, and their altitude. He read off the information to Cosmo.

"Got it," the younger man said, making a few more adjustments on his scope.

Meanwhile, on the main com-link channel, General Kelly's voice could be heard. "Snipers, report in. Over."

"Yellow One, I'm in position and ready to fire, sir. Over."

Cosmo recognized the voice, but it sounded older. There was only a skeleton crew of veterans at Lois Operating Station. It was built on the plateau with a beautiful reason as a way to show off the Army's brightest and best new recruits. But almost all the personnel stationed there were either recruit instructors or support staff. There were no regular units stationed on the big hill overlooking the ocean, no armored platoons or artillery divisions. But Cosmo thought the voice of Yellow One was the grizzled range master who supervised their shooting instruction, sometimes helping Sergeant Reed.

"Orange One is ready, sir. Over," another voice said.

"Blue One is good to go, sir. Over."

"Green One is in position, sir. Over."

Most of the other buildings were arched platoon barracks. But the armory was a regular-shaped structure, as was the chow hall, the laundry facility, and the garage for the various vehicles that were kept at the base. Cosmo glanced over his shoulder, saw the shuttles heading inland, and felt a bit of relief knowing his mother was being carried to safety. He started loading rounds into the sniper rifle.

"Red One is ready, sir," he said. "Over."

"All right, people. This is no drill," General Kelly said over the com-link. "We've got reports coming in of invasion forces launching all along the eastern seaboard. That's why we've upped our forces. This is war, people. And it won't be won by what we do here, but that doesn't mean we're going to let the crabbies have our base. Snipers, you are cleared to open fire. I want controlled shots. We aren't going to stop them with the first volley, but I want them to see their own dead as they come on beach. Make it happen. Kelly out."

The sniper rifle held eight rounds. The bullets were sixty-caliber, armor-piercing bullets that were nearly as long as Cosmo's hand from palm to fingertip. He checked the weapon's recoil damper, then flipped off the safety latch.

"Here we go," Cosmo said to Dyson.

"Start with that big ugly bastard in front of the others," Dyson said.

Cosmo saw the alien his friend was talking about it. It did seem larger than the others, with a crimson shell that had white streaks. Cosmo centered the scope's crosshairs on the creature's head, just above the shell. He took a breath, then slowly released it as his finger settled on the trigger. With his breath half expelled, he stopped breathing to steady his aim and gently stroked the trigger. The rifle boomed, jerking back into this shoulder. He immediately worked the lever that ejected the spent shell and loaded another into the chamber.

There was a pause as they waited for the bullet which was traveling well over the speed of sound to cross the eight kilometers. The high-powered projectile took two and a half seconds to reach the crab. Cosmo and Dyson were both looking through their scopes when the bullet hit. Black blood sprayed out in a fine mist, as the top of the alien's head flew straight up into the air. Its legs curled and the body toppled onto the ground.

"That's a hit!" Dyson said. "Damn, good shooting, brother!"

At the same time that Dyson was celebrating, the other snipers began to shoot. Cosmo focused on his next target. He felt a sense of relief that his aim had been true, as well as a surge of exaltation at seeing the enemy fall. But there were more coming out of the water with every surging wave of the ocean. He quickly fired again.

The Ma'Tis seemed unfazed by the losses. Not that there were a lot. Many of the shots were off target. Cosmo's second shot glanced over the front of one alien's shell and impacted another. Neither of the aliens was seriously injured by the large-caliber bullet.

"Unbelievable," Dyson said.

"They're tough," Cosmo said.

The Ma'Tis looked like crabs, but they weren't all exactly the same. Some were wider than others, with tiny heads that barely protruded from their shells. Others had long lower legs and shorter arms. Some even had eight appendages. No matter the shape of the aliens, they were armored with thick, nearly impenetrable exoskeletons. The only weaknesses were the face and joints. It wouldn't do much good to disable one leg when there were five more to keep the alien moving. On the other hand, some of the crabs had tiny heads. They looked like there was nothing but eyes peeking up from between the shells.

Cosmo didn't get into a hurry. He took careful aim and fired slowly. The third shot also hit the shell, just clipping it before bouncing the bullet straight into his target's face. Blood and brains flew out as the alien dropped onto its back with its legs curling in death.

"Good shot," Dyson said. "Damn, it's hard to just watch."

"We can alternate," Cosmo said. "Give my shoulder a rest."

"You're the sharpshooter," Dyson said.

"Not by much," Cosmo said, before taking another shot. "And this is what Sergeant Reed would call a target-rich environment."

"All right, yeah," Dyson said. "One load each?"

"Sounds good to me."

Cosmo finished out his eight-round load with five kills. Then he moved over to trade places with Dyson, who got busy loading in eight more bullets. Before he could finish, the ocean seemed to surge forward.

"What is that?" Cosmo asked.

"I don't know," Dyson said.

As they watched, a huge structure rose up out of the water. It was massive—at least a hundred meters wide—and mounted on treads that churned through the soft sand of the surf. It didn't take a ballistics expert to recognize the laser cannons mounted on the massive vehicle.

"Drill sergeant..." Cosmo said.

"I see it, Frost," Reed growled.

"What should we do?"

"Keep doing what you're ordered to do," the gruff drill instructor replied. "That's all we can do."

"Snipers, hold your fire," General Kelly's voice sounded in their com-links. "All units, go to ground and converge on my location. We have air support inbound. I repeat, go to ground, and meet at rally point alpha."

"Time to go," Cosmo said as he snatched up the spotting scope and the kit it came in.

"Damn, I didn't even get a shot in," Dyson said.

"Looks like you'll get a chance soon enough," Cosmo replied.

The big man slung the sniper rifle over a shoulder, snatched up the ammo can, and followed Cosmo back to the stairs. They didn't want to wait for the elevator. The admin building was only five stories, so they hustled down the stairs.

"Red Platoon, fall back to the admin main doors," Reed said. "I repeat, meet at the—"

A strange sound cut the drill sergeant off mid-sentence. It was almost like the sound water makes when dripped onto a hot skillet. Cosmo and Dyson weren't the only troopers in the building stairwell when it happened. The entire structure shook for a second, then light and dust rained down from above.

"Holy hell! What was that?" Yorik Kravinski shouted.

"They targeted the building," Cosmo said. "The upper floors are gone."

"Move! Move!" Dyson shouted.

They sprinted down the stairs and burst out into the building's small lobby. Twelve members of Red Platoon, plus Sergeant Reed.

"Where's Gallop and Kreed?" Voss asked.

"They were on their way down," someone replied.

"In the elevator," Reed grumbled. "They aren't responding, and we don't have time to dig them out. Follow me, Red Platoon."

"They're dead?" Voss asked.

"Think about it later," Dyson told him with a gentle shove. "We're out of here."

"They're dead," Voss said.

The admin building wasn't the only structure hit. The chow hall was gone. A laser blast had hit the wide structure dead center, and the outer walls had crumbled in. The roof of the laundry was on fire. And the upper two stories of the admin building had been vaporized. Cosmo couldn't help but look up as he ran along with his platoon mates. If he had hesitated, even for a few seconds, he would have been killed. The thought made his heart pound and his stomach twist.

He was just about to look away from the ragged top of the admin structure when he spotted an aircraft in the distance.

"What's that?" he asked, pointing at the aircraft.

"Looks old," Dyson said.

"Not old, just old-fashioned," Sergeant Reed said. "That's the Air Force bombers. Let's hope they can take that big vehicle down before it turns the hill into molten rock and us with it."

Cosmo looked up again. Air Force bombers? Was it possible? he wondered. Could Allura be on that plane? There was no way to know. All he could hope for was that he might live long enough to find out. But if the bomber failed, he didn't think there was much hope for the rest of them.

CHAPTER 16

ALLURA HAD COME DOWN from orbit on a commercial shuttle. She had caught a ride on an FGAF transport to Hawkstone Air Base. Her commanding officer was a cold-looking woman named Captain Debora Lansing. Allura reported to her office as soon as she got off the transport.

"I read your file," Captain Lansing said. "I appreciate your willingness to join the fight, but this isn't like the Air Training Academy. I want you on spotter duty until further notice."

"Excuse me, Captain?" Allura asked.

"You heard me, Airman Presley. Lives are at stake here."

"I'm a bombardier," Allura argued. "Anyone can spot. I trained to—"

"To what? To drop bombs on enemy targets from two thousand meters up? That's useless here, Airman," the captain responded angrily. "You've run sims. Great. You've hit targets on Triton. That's wonderful. But this is the real world, Presley. The enemy shoots back. We miss our targets, people die."

"I'm aware of that, Captain," Allura argued. "That's why you need me."

"What's the gravity here on Fiona Grand, Airman?"

"One point two eight two seven three one on the Newtonian scale, Captain," Allura said.

"And if you're traveling at four hundred eighteen nautical kilometers per hour, with a distance to target of one hundred fifty-seven kilometers, how long should you wait to fire?"

"I would need altitude, and wind speed to make the assessment."

"Five hundred meters," Captain Lansing said. "Wind speed is fourteen meters her hour at your tail."

Allura was calculating in her mind. She preferred having a slate to work out the mathematics, but she didn't have that luxury if she was going to impress her commanding officer.

"What's our payload?"

"Napalm canisters and bunker busters."

"I would fire the BBs in four minutes, eighteen seconds. The napalm could be dropped earlier—five minutes and two seconds."

Captain Lansing frowned. "You know your equations, that's good. But you don't know combat. All my bombardiers have combat runs, Presley. I'm not putting precious lives in your hands until you do."

"Yes, ma'am," Allura said, trying not to let her anger show.

"This isn't a popularity contest," Lansing admonished her. "And we don't keep tabs on who does what in Condor. We work together and get the job done. Nothing else matters."

"I understand," Allura said.

"Good, because we've been called up. You're in Delta Six. Your bombardier is Tony Mackinsey. We call him T-Mac. Drop your gear and get suited up. We're on the move, Airman."

Allura saluted. "Yes ma'am."

She left her bags, which were in the captain's outer office, and rushed into the hangar. The bombers were already out on the flight line. One of the maintenance personnel, an older man with a thick mustache was pushing a fuel pump on a big dolly across the open hangar.

"Where's Delta Six?" Allura asked.

"They're all prepping for takeoff," he said pointing.

"Which one is Delta Six?"

"The last one in the row," the older man said.

"Thanks," Allura shouted, already running.

The bombers were turned sideways on the long landing strip. They had repulsor engines that could lift them straight up into the air, but also thruster engines and wheels. When the Air Force returned to the archaic aircraft designs, they had built them with versatility in mind. The loading doors were open and small forklifts were loading bombs into the aircraft. Allura ran up the ramp of Delta Six and reported to the pilots by putting on a helmet with a built-in headset. She powered the wireless com-link on and spoke clearly.

"Airman Allura Presley requesting permission to come aboard as spotter."

"Permission granted, Presley," the pilot said. "You're just in time."

Allura moved from the cargo section where the bombs were in long tracks that fed them into the opening at the bottom of the ship. She took a narrow set of stairs down to the catwalk above the lower hull where the bomb bay doors were located. There was a man on the stool by the controls. He had senior airman stripes on his coveralls and didn't bother turning around as she approached.

"You the rookie from ATA?" he asked.

"Yes," Allura said.

"Great. Go get strapped in. We'll be taking off shortly."

"What's our target?" Allura asked.

"The bugs are making a push inland, that's all I know," he said. "But we'll find out more soon enough. You ever spot before?"

"No," Allura said. "I'm a bombardier."

"You've got moxie, I'll give you that," he said. "But you don't earn that title in training. Once you've hit an enemy target you can call yourself a bombardier."

Allura wanted to argue. She wanted to know if he had trained on Triton. She knew most bombardiers hadn't. They were mostly trained on the job after serving as spotters. But she didn't want to make waves. The truth was she hadn't flown a real combat mission, and while she chafed at being benched for her first, she was also extremely nervous. She had only been back on Fiona Grand for a few hours and had gone straight in to report to her commanding officer. Less than ten minutes after that, she was flying her first mission. It seemed much too fast, but she wasn't in training anymore.

"All right," Allura said. "Anything I need to know?"

"Just tell me what happens," he said. "We'll come in low and fast. I need eyes on the target after we've gone past."

"Got it," she replied.

The walk back up from the bomb bay and around to the spotter's capsule under the nose of the aircraft seemed long. She knew it wasn't. And the aircraft was built for combat, not training exercises. Allura had to turn backward and climb down a ladder built into the wall of a narrow chute that led down to the spotter's capsule. Inside was a single seat attached to the aircraft's frame at the top. Below her was a round, transparent bubble. She swung over to the seat and strapped in.

"Spotter in position," she announced.

"Copy spotter. Let's make sure you have full rotation," the pilot replied.

Allura hit the switch to power up her seat's rotator. The seat immediately lowered further into the capsule. There was a little knob on the arm of her seat. She turned it to her right and the seat rotated. She could see the rear hatch as it rose up into the closed position. On the landing strip, the bomb loaders were headed back to the hangar. She turned the knob the opposite direction and her seat rotated the other way. She let it go a full three hundred sixty degrees, then reported in.

"Spotter has full rotation," she said.

"Outstanding. All right crew, tighten up those seatbelts. We lift off in thirty seconds."

Allura heard the air traffic on her helmet headset. The other bombers were taking off. She watched them rise up into the air, slow and steady, before engaging thrusters and flying away from the airbase.

"Good luck, Condor," Captain Lansing's voice came through the headset. "Godspeed."

Delta Six lifted off with no problem despite being loaded to maximum weight capacity. The bomber was a long, cigar-shaped aircraft with wide wings. The landscape shrunk beneath Allura, who discovered that being in the spotter's capsule wasn't a bad place to travel. The seat was a little stiff, but the view was unparalleled.

They flew for over an hour, eventually circling out over the ocean. It was beautiful, but Allura couldn't help but wonder what horrors lurked beneath the emerald waves. Eventually, the pilot's commands broke into her private musings about the aliens who lived in the deep places of the oceans.

"T-Mac, we are one hundred kilometers from the target area," the pilot said. "Descending to five hundred meters. Flight speed is four hundred knots. Wind is eighteen kilometers per hour south by east."

"Roger that," the bombardier said. "Rook, tell me when you see the target."

"Copy," Allura said, pulling a pair of large, high-powered binoculars from a pouch built into the side of her seat.

"T-Mac, I'll pass wide, then circle to line up the drop," the pilot said. "Let's go ahead and open bomb bay doors."

"Opening bomb bay doors," the bombardier said.

Allura felt the ship shudder as the doors opened back past her capsule. She could have turned to see them open, but she was looking ahead, not behind the ship. In the distance was a brown haze, which she took for the shoreline.

"I'm getting word that there's some kind of big gun ships coming out of the water at various locations," the pilot said. "We geared for that, T-Mac?"

"I've got two bunker busters," he replied. "Should send the bugs straight to hell."

"Good to hear it. Keep them ready. Spotter, can you make out the enemy yet?"

Allura was looking through the binoculars. The shore was still a haze, but she could tell there was movement on land.

"Negative," she replied. "We're too far out."

"Roger that," the pilot said. "We'll get closer."

Allura was still looking through the binoculars when she saw the big alien vehicle. It was at the edge of the shoreline where the waves were breaking against it. At first, she had thought it was a boulder or rocky outcropping. But as the aircraft streaked forward, the massive vehicle came into view.

"Target in sight," Allura said, her heart suddenly crashing hard inside her chest. "It's huge."

"What about the crabs?" T-Mac asked. "Can you see them?"

"They're everywhere," she said. "I don't see any part of the shoreline that isn't crawling with them."

"It's the invasion everyone's been talking about," the pilot said. "I'll bring you in right over that thing down there."

"Copy that," T-Mac said. "Calculating the drop."

"Sir, if I may," Allura said. "I think I see something on the target. It could be laser cannons."

"What are they pointing at?" the pilot asked.

"It's hard to say for certain, but I think they're pointed inland. If you go right over top of it, and it isn't completely destroyed by the bunker busters..."

"She's got a point, T-Mac," the pilot said.

"What's the dimensions on that thing?" the bombardier asked.

"Impossible to say for certain," Allura replied. "But it's definitely wider side to side than front to back."

"I'll take a bigger target any day of the week, Jimmy," T-Mac said.

"Roger that, coming around on heading four three one. Slowing to three hundred knots. You'll have a decent cross breeze, T-Mac."

"No sweat, dialing up the BBs now."

Allura felt the aircraft turn. For the next few minutes, it wound around in the sky, moving closer to shore, and flying toward the huge Ma'Tis vehicle. Smoke from targets on a hill above the shore was visible. Fortunately, the wind was blowing it inland and not out over the beaches, where the crabs were moving slowly inland.

"There are thousands of them," T-Mac said. "I've never seen so many."

"They aren't kidding around," the pilot said. "You're free to fire at will."

"Copy that," the bombardier said. "I've got the target in sight. Preparing BB one for drop on my count. Three, two, one... she's away!"

Allura had already swiveled her seat around so that she was facing the rear of the aircraft. She had both hands on the binoculars but kept them in her lap. Her safety straps were pulled so tight she could barely breathe, but she wished they were tighter. She felt exposed in the spotter capsule. Sweat was beading on her forehead as the bomb dropped from the open bay doors.

"You want to toss a couple of those napalm canisters on the shore-line?" the pilot asked.

"Negative Jimmy. The smoke might obscure that giant ship."

"Hit!" Allura called out. "Impact on the left end of that thing."

She held the binoculars up and looked as the aircraft banked for another bombing run. "It's down but not out. Looks like the BB went straight through and detonated underneath it."

"Can she still fire?" T-Mac asked.

"There were several undamaged cannons on the far end. I think they're swiveling upward.

"Better not risk another flyover," T-Mac warned.

"We'll come in from straight out," the pilot said. "Should be able to bank away once you release the payload. Everybody hang on to some-thing. Things are going to get bumpy."

Allura shoved the binoculars into the pouch and held onto her seat. The bomber went racing toward the shore. She heard the back and forth as T-Mac prepared his payload. As soon as it was released, the aircraft banked away. Allura rotated her seat and fought the g-forces trying to pull her in the wrong direction and keep her from seeing the outcome.

The bomb sailed through the air. It was propelled by the momentum of the aircraft and driven down by the insatiable force of gravity. Allura leaned forward, every muscle in her body straining to hold her in position to see what happened next. And it was completely worth it. The bomb didn't just damage the alien vehicle, as the first one had. It exploded and in doing so, set off a series of explosions within the ship itself. As Allura watched, one end blew apart, engulfed in flames. Then just as quickly, three more blasts ripped the vessel apart.

"Direct hit, direct hit!" Allura cried over the bomber's comm system. "The whole thing just blew up."

"Great work, T-Mac," the pilot said.

"Let's clean up the mess," the bombardier said. "Permission to drop the napalm."

"Granted. Fire at will."

Bombs weren't fired, Allura thought. They were dropped. But it didn't matter. As she watched, canisters of napalm fell through the air.

The thin-skinned bombs were filled with chemicals that burned hot once the small warhead exploded. Fire raged from the bombs in long, orange clouds of death. Smoke billowed, and the masses of crab-like aliens went into a frenzy. The ocean water was super-heated into steam which joined the billowing smoke. The beach was chaos.

"We've got plenty of ordnance left," T-Mac said. "Bring us around again."

"On our way," the pilot responded.

The enemy was thick on the strip of land between the water and the rolling sand dunes. Some took cover, hoping to avoid the burning bombs dropped on them from above. Allura had no need to spot for them. They couldn't miss the enemy which was spread out in a long line up and down the beach on either side of their ruined cannon vehicle.

But the smoke and carnage also hid the Ma'Tis response to the bomber. And maybe their luck in hitting the enemy so far had made the pilot sloppy. Allura never knew; she didn't get the chance to ask him. As he brought the aircraft around for another bombing run, hundreds of projectiles were launched from the ground. Perhaps if she had been looking through her binoculars, she might have seen how they fired the pointed stakes. They were made from what looked like coral from the oceans and were as long as her forearm from elbow to fingertip. The volley came flying up and just missed her capsule under the nose of the aircraft.

The rest of the ship wasn't as fortunate. The stakes punched through the fuselage. Some hit the wings, others hit the body of the aircraft. The landing gear was wrecked, the thrusters damaged. Worst of all, T-Mac was injured in the barrage. The aircraft suddenly veered inland.

"Mayday, mayday, mayday," a different voice shouted. "The pilot's hit. We're losing fuel. Delta Six is going down. I repeat, Delta Six is going down."

CHAPTER 17

GENERAL KELLY HAD ARRAYED the platoons of newly graduated troopers along the edge of the hilltop. Below them, the ground fell away steeply in jagged, rocky cliffs. They weren't completely vertical, but Cosmo thought that climbing up them would be incredibly difficult.

"Range, Frost?" Sergeant Reed asked.

"Hard to say, Sarge," Cosmo replied. "The laser range finder is giving me fits. Maybe three klicks. Maybe more."

Behind them the base was in ruins. Every building had been targeted by the big alien vehicles' cannons. But the Air Force bomber had taken it out, and General Kelly had ordered everyone to the crest of the hill.

"I want everyone to stay cool," Sergeant Reed ordered. "We don't fire until the General gives the order. Make sure your weapons are ready."

"Wish we had some grenades," Voss said.

"Looks like that bomber is coming back around to make another pass," Dyson said.

"Let's just hope they don't get too close," Butler replied.

Cosmo watched as the bomber disappeared into the smoke from the previous run and he wondered once again if it was possible that

Allura was on the aircraft. He hadn't heard from her, but that didn't mean she was there. Still, he hoped she was still light years away. Fear was breathing down his neck, and it was taking all the discipline he had learned over the previous three months to hold himself together. There were thousands of Ma'Tis on the beach. They had crawled over the sand dunes and were approaching the gentle slope of the wide hill he was perched on. There had been eight graduating platoons stationed at the Lois Army Base. Almost all of them were draftees. The tiny number of support staff wasn't enough to really turn the tide in a battle with so many alien warriors bearing down on them. If the platoons fell apart, Cosmo knew he would die.

That was the thought in his mind when the bomber came rushing out of the clouds of smoke. At first it seemed the dark, dense smoke was clinging to the aircraft. Then he realized it was hit and going down.

"Oh, no!" Voss shouted.

The aircraft banked hard and flew over their heads, barely higher than the hill they were perched on.

"What happened?" Butler asked.

"Enemy fire," Sergeant Reed said. "It's up to us now, Red Platoon. You've been preparing for this. Now's our chance to turn the tide. Once those crusty bastards start climbing, General Kelly will give the order to fire on them. We've got the advantage of high ground and good cover. Remember your training and we'll be fine."

Cosmo couldn't help but wonder if the troopers from Red Platoon who had been riding down in the elevator when the building was hit had been thinking they would be fine. If Dyson had suggested they wait for the elevator, Cosmo wouldn't have argued, and they'd both be dead too. He shivered as fear ran an ice-cold fingernail down the nape of his neck.

"Sniper teams, report in. Over," General Kelly ordered.

Dyson unslung the sniper rifle and handed it back to Cosmo, who was waiting to hear from the other teams. No one replied for a few seconds. Then to his relief, the gruff range master replied, "Yellow One, ready. Over."

"Red One, ready. Over," Cosmo said.

"Orange One is in position, but I lost my spotter," a nervous voice said. "But I don't think I need one at this range, sir... Over."

"All snipers open fire," General Kelly ordered. "Target the leaders. Let's hold them back as long as we can."

Cosmo checked the breach. The sniper rifle was ready to fire. They were laying on their bellies, so he folded his free hand under his chin, took aim, and fired. The bullet hit a Ma'Tis warrior in the head. It dropped, and Cosmo was on to another.

He fired his eight rounds quickly. The shots weren't simple, but they weren't as difficult as before. He could easily aim and fire without having to adjust and wait to see the result of the shot. The heavy sniper rifle kicked into his shoulder, which was already aching. When he finished his eight shots, he handed the rifle to Dyson, who reloaded and fired away.

Not every shot killed the enemy, but even a missed shot did damage as the Ma'Tis drew nearer in their unorganized crowd. Dyson finished his eight shots and handed the heavy rifle back to Cosmo. He pressed the big bullets into the loading slot on the bottom of the weapon. When he got all eight rounds loaded, he worked the bolt to load a round into the breach.

"There," Butler said. "Take out that big one."

Through the scope, Cosmo could see the alien's black eyes. They were like obscene nodules on either side of its broad, flat head. He took a shallow breath, held it, and stroked the trigger. The rifle, which he held firm against his shoulder before shooting, still kicked hard. It was like getting punched with every shot. But Cosmo wasn't thinking about the recoil or the pain he was feeling. The long sniper bullet went straight through the alien's head and hit the crab behind him. The second crab was knocked back by the impact of the bullet, which didn't penetrate his shell.

"Great shot," Butler cried.

But the slow-moving aliens were gaining ground. Behind them, a rumble sounded as the bomber crashed. It hadn't nosed dived into the ground, but the landing hadn't been easy either. When Cosmo handed the rifle to Dyson he looked back. There was no smoke rising, which was a good thing, but he could see the wreckage far out in the distance where the plain sloped away from the plateau.

"Think anyone made it?" Voss asked.

"I hope so," Cosmo replied.

"Let's stay focused," Reed said. "Let the fly boys worry about themselves right now. We can't help them, and they can't help us."

"All platoons," General Kelly announced. "Prepare to open fire on my command."

The first of the aliens were reaching the ground that rose up in craggy cliffs. They were still a kilometer away, and a thousand meters was a long shot, but with the angle and the need to push the aliens back, Cosmo wasn't surprised by the order. Nor was he unhappy to switch from the big sniper rifle to the more comfortable XJ7 tactical weapon he was used to.

"Stay cool," Reed ordered. "Keep tabs on your ammunition. Semi-auto fire. Aim before each shot. Just like we trained. This is no different."

It felt completely different. Runners had been sent to the armory to gather as many rounds as possible. There were a few rotating-barrel, belt-fed machine guns ready to be set up five hundred meters back from the crest of the hill. Meanwhile, boxes of ammunition had been carried out to the line of troopers who had stacks of rifle magazines beside them on the hilltop. It didn't seem like they could possibly run out of ammunition, but Cosmo dreaded the thought that maybe they would. Even after the bombing run and the sniper fire, there were thousands more Ma'Tis. He hadn't seen them releasing bio-bots, but it was only a matter of time.

The armory had been hit before the grenades had been brought out. That left only their guns, which were effective at five hundred meters, and probably would do well with the platoon shooting down on the enemy. But Cosmo hated to think about what would happen when the crabs got close enough that their own laser weapons were effective.

"Platoons take aim," General Kelly said. "Fire on my command... now!"

The various platoons, including Red Platoon, opened up with their tactical rifles. The soft lead rounds were filled with secondary explosive charges that pushed the fragmented metal past the shells of the Ma'Tis. The troopers were trained to target the softer areas of the shell where their bullets would make the most damage. A Ma'Tis warrior with a cracked shell felt the pain of that wound but could go on fighting. To disable the aliens, or better yet kill them, the bullet had to penetrate their exoskeleton. The bullets rained down. Many missed. Cosmo knew this from the rocky shrapnel kicked up in the air as the bullets smashed into the rock before reaching the enemy. But the crabs were hit too. They presented a smaller target from above, but their shells were softer near the top too. Dozens were killed in the initial barrage. Cosmo, like most of the other troopers, fired quickly and emptied his first magazine within moments of the order to shoot. And as he reloaded his XJ7, he looked up.

"They're going to flank us," he said to Dyson.

"That was fast."

"You can say that again," Cosmo replied. "There's just so many of them."

"Just do your job," Sergeant Reed growled. "General Kelly will deal with the enemy and give us orders to take them out when the time is right."

He sounded almost bored. The veteran soldier was busy blasting away. His shots were almost like a metronome, one shot every two seconds. Cosmo focused on the crabs climbing the hill, and he joined in the slaughter. The crustacean aliens had no trouble climbing the rugged cliffs. They seemed even more agile and certainly faster, when climbing than when walking on a flat surface. Hundreds died, many falling back and knocking those behind them down the hill. The battle had become a bitter, ugly drudgery. Some of the aliens shot back, but they were out of range. It was like they were flashing colorful lights toward the troopers on the hilltop, hoping they would somehow frighten the humans away.

Cosmo did his best to imitate the unflappable drill sergeant. He loaded his rifle, fired his forty rounds in a methodical, passionless way, then reloaded and did it again. Beside him, Dyson was doing the same thing. Part of Cosmo wanted to get up and run away. Even though it seemed they had stopped the alien advance, he knew that many more were coming up from the sides of the hill. Sooner or later they would appear, and the fighting would grow more dangerous.

Sweat and dust mingled. The blood pounded in Cosmo's ears,

which were ringing despite the hearing protection from his battle helmet. Dust hovered over the hillside. Below, the wounded aliens wailed and screamed. It was the most awful, blood-curdling noise that Cosmo had ever heard. His dress uniform was wrinkled, stained, and dirty. His finger grew tired from pulling the trigger over and over again. When he popped out an empty magazine, he flexed his hand for a moment before grabbing another and ramming it home.

"This is some crazy shit right here," Dyson said. "It's like they ain't even scared of dying."

"Maybe they're not," Cosmo said. "Maybe they think it's noble or something."

"Like I said, crazy," Dyson replied.

"White platoon, Blue platoon, and Red Platoon, fall back to the secondary placement on my command," General Kelly said. "Prepare to take up cover positions as we fall back."

"Why we falling back?" Dyson said. "The crabs ain't even close."

"They're coming in from the side," Cosmo said.

"Red platoon!" Sergeant Reed bellowed. "Gather as much ammo as you can carry. Prepare to move out."

"All right," Dyson said. "But I must have killed a hundred of them creepy crawlies."

"It ain't over till they're all dead," Butler replied.

"And there's still thousands more," Voss added.

"Fall back," General Kelly said, his voice carrying through the com-links over the report of the tactical rifles and the screams of the wounded aliens. "White, blue, red, fall back to cover positions now."

"You heard the man, and you know the plan," Reed shouted. "Let's go Red Platoon! Move! Move! Move!"

Cosmo slung his rifle, gathered as many magazines as he could, and scrambled to his feet.

"What about the sniper rifle?" Dyson shouted.

"Leave it!" Cosmo shouted back.

They ran away from the crest of the hills and around the smoking rubble of the buildings that had once been their homes, workshops, and offices. They stopped, each platoon converging on a separate machine gun location. They gathered bricks and chunks of metal from the piles of rubble that had once been buildings to make shooting nests and give them cover.

"Red Platoon, cover the right flank," General Kelly ordered. "Blue Platoon cover the left flank. White platoon, cover our rear."

"Will they surround us?" Voss shouted to Sergeant Reed.

"Depends on their objective," the drill instructor replied. "Odds are their rally point is inland somewhere."

"That mean they'll go around us?" Voss asked.

"It's possible," the Sergeant said. "If we can prove that taking us out won't be easy."

"We haven't proved that already?" Dyson asked.

"So far we're a one-trick pony," Reed said. "Now we get to show them what we're really made of."

It wasn't long before the flanking units appeared. Cosmo and Dyson were behind a mound of rubble, watching and waiting.

"How close we gonna let 'em get?" Dyson wondered.

"Draw them in and cut them down," Cosmo replied. "If we fire too soon, they'll just go around us and hit White Platoon with twice as many bugs."

A moment later the order was given and the machine gun opened fire. The air was filled with flying lead. Dyson and Cosmo kept their heads down while the machine gun blazed away. From where he lay peeking around the edge of his pile of rubble, Cosmo could see the Ma'Tis caught in the heavy, concentrated fire. Body parts were flying, hard shells shattering, blood and fluids sprayed through the air. The aliens returned fire. The laser bolts sizzled through the air and burned into the piles of rubble.

"All units, open fire! All units, open fire!" Sergeant Reed ordered over the com-link.

Cosmo leaned out one side of the mound of rubble and started shooting. Dyson leaned out the other. The cacophony was stupendous: the roar of the machine gun, the shouts of the warriors, the wails of the wounded, and the crack of bullets flying past them faster than the speed of sound, all combined in a horrible roar. It was the sound of war.

"I'm hit!"

The voice was familiar. Frankie Voss, the accountant, shouted in surprise. There were other voices too. Some calling out for help, others screaming in pain. A laser bolt skimmed the edge of Cosmo's shoulder, another slammed into a brick and kicked up a shower of rocky shrapnel that stung his face. But Cosmo didn't stop fighting. The ground was littered with Ma'Tis bodies. The aliens had to crawl over their own dead to keep fighting, which they did. But the troopers had cover and the Ma'Tis did not. Their hard-shell exteriors were tough, but at close range the XJ7 had enough punch to crack them open and drive them back.

Eventually the machine gun ran out of ammo. But by that time there were only a few Ma'Tis left standing. Cosmo, Dyson, and a few others took them out.

"Is it over?" Cosmo said.

"I think so," Dyson replied.

They turned, looking around. They could see Ma'Tis in the distance, moving inland. The ground was covered in bodies and body parts. The sun was setting, and Cosmo wondered how the world could go on like normal after the battle. It didn't seem real. Neither did the bodies of his friends. Even Sergeant Reed had been hit. In fact, the tough old drill sergeant had been shot four times. His left arm was hit in the bicep and shoulder, and his right thigh had a nasty looking laser burn. But the real damage was to his abdomen, just under the bottom of his armored vest.

"We've got medevac inbound," Colonel Allison Evenrue said over the com-link. "Gather the wounded and converge on the orange smoke."

Someone set off a billowing smoke grenade that spewed orange smoke. Dyson grabbed Sergeant Reed under his arms, and Cosmo lifted his legs. The drill instructor didn't cry out in pain, but his face was set in a rigid mask.

"Don't worry, Sarge," Dyson said. "My cousin Lonnie got hit back home. He was in way worse shape, but he's fine now."

Reed didn't reply. His eyes were open, but it was taking all his considerable strength not to cry out in pain.

"We'll take care of the platoon," Cosmo told him.

They set the drill sergeant down when they got to the rally point. It was just past where their old barracks had been. The metal building was gone. In its place was rubble and melted steel. There were already a dozen other wounded troopers on the ground. Two hovercrafts were moving toward the plateau from over the ocean. Cosmo glanced out toward the beach and saw that there were still aliens moving around. He couldn't tell if they were picking their way through the bodies or searching them. Some were even moving back into the water. All around the location that had once been a parade ground were piles of bodies. The Ma'Tis had lost by sheer number of bodies, but despite all their effort, Cosmo knew more of the aliens were marching inland. The first battle had been fierce and deadly, but it was just a drop in the bucket of what was to come.

"Let's go see about the others," Cosmo said.

"Yeah, okay," Dyson replied.

"You did good today."

"So did you, brother. We for real now."

"Army troopers."

"Blood brothers," Dyson said.

They bumped fists and searched for survivors.

CHAPTER 18

ALLURA HAD UNFASTENED her safety harness, banged her head on the side of the seat, and barely made it out of the spotting capsule before the bomber crashed. The thrusters gave out before the copilot could stop their momentum, and only a few of the repulsors worked, but they were close enough to the ground that the crash wasn't fatal to those on board.

The pilot had been hit by a projectile that bounced off the rear bulkhead and punched through his seat from behind. It severed his spine and killed him instantly. T-Mac wasn't as lucky. He was hit by three separate stakes, one through his foot, one that nearly tore off his arm, and one that shattered his hip. He was unconscious when Allura found him, but still breathing. She pulled off his helmet and unfastened his safety tethers. He was a small man, shorter than she was, and only thirty pounds heavier. She couldn't carry him out, but she did get him onto an emergency gurney with its own repulsor.

"That'll work," she said as the gurney lifted into the air. "We have to get you out of here."

She pushed him back through the aircraft, which was tilted slightly on one side. The rear hatch had been crumpled slightly, leaving a gap big enough for Allura to climb through. She pulled out the bombardier and realized that if Captain Lansing had given her what she wanted, it would be someone else pulling her wrecked body from the aircraft. She shuddered at the thought of it and moved the wounded Airman away from the aircraft.

"Hey! How'd you get out?" the copilot shouted as she circled around the ruined bomber. He was still in the cockpit.

"The cargo hatch was crumpled," she said. "You can get out that way."

"Can't," he argued. "The cockpit door's blocked. You'll have to come back in and get me out."

He was a lieutenant, and she was just an airman. She had no idea how long he had been in the Air Force, but she was certain he had been in the military longer than she had. Yet he sounded like a frightened child.

"Did you radio in?" she asked.

"Can't," he shouted. "No power."

"All right, I'm on my way," she said.

Going back into the aircraft still loaded with dozens of napalm canisters seemed like suicide, but she had to do something. It amazed her how little damage the aircraft had sustained. It was clearly wrecked and couldn't fly, but the cargo bay full of bombs hadn't been damaged. The corridor above the bomb bay doors had buckled, and there was no way to reach the cockpit from the inside. She would need heavy equipment to cut through and remove the crumpled airframe that had the pilots trapped.

She did find the emergency survival kit. Her training had not included firearms, but there was a laser pistol in the emergency survival kit along with first aid supplies and survival equipment. She lugged the kit out of the aircraft. It was the size and shape of a suitcase, but with no wheels. Breathing hard, she left most of the supplies by T-Mac after covering him with a reflective emergency blanket that was made from a thin sheet of aluminized plastic. Then she took the laser pistol to the front of the aircraft. Climbing up the outside wasn't easy, but she managed it. The windows were small. The pilots relied on their instruments, not their sight, to fly the aircraft.

"What are you doing?" the copilot said.

"Can't get you out that way," she called back. "I'm going to cut through the window."

"What?"

She held up the laser pistol, wondering how the high-strung pilot had gotten through his training. "Stand back!" she ordered.

He cowered behind his seat. Allura could see the pilot, whose eyes were open and gazing down at his instruments in a sightless stare. She felt sick to her stomach, not sure if it was from fear, revulsion, or shock —perhaps all three. She pointed the gun at the largest of the windows and set the pistol on steady beam. The battery was small and wouldn't last long. Its warning light began to flash just as she finished cutting through the plexiglass of the cockpit window. She had to help pull the copilot out through the narrow opening, but he looked relieved.

"That was..."

He was looking around. They seemed to be in the middle of nowhere. A few trees dotted the flat, grassy plain they had crashed onto. But in the distance, they could see movement, and the sounds of gunfire sounded like gentle raindrops instead of deadly instruments of war.

"Yeah, we're not safe here," Allura said, reading the fear on the copilot's face.

She was frightened too. On her first day in the actual Air/Space Force, she had flown a mission against the enemy and narrowly escaped death. The shock of it all was starting to set in.

"We should stay with the ship," the pilot said. "When help comes, this is where they'll look."

Allura knew that in many cases that was the wise thing to do, but their situation was different.

"We can't stay here," she said. "The bomber is full of heavy ordnance. It could ignite at any second."

"No," he insisted. "Those bombs are contained."

"Even if you're right, the Ma'Tis shoot lasers. And there are still thousands of them."

"What are you proposing?" the copilot asked, his voice strained with desperation.

"I think it's best if we go back to the base," Allura said.

"Are you insane? Didn't you see it from the air? The base is completely destroyed. It'll be overrun if it isn't already."

"They're fighting," she argued. "That's what we're hearing. They might need our help. Besides, we need to get T-Mac to a doctor. He's hurt pretty bad."

"You're out of your mind if you think I'm going back to that base."

"Then your only other option is to stay ahead of the enemy. The power on that gurney won't last long. We can't carry T-Mac. The only hope he has is that base."

"Then you go," the copilot said. "I'll take my chances."

He climbed down off the ship and set out across the open ground. All Allura could do was return to T-Mac and activate the gurney's repulsors. She wished she hadn't wasted the laser pistol's power freeing the copilot. Fear was threatening to suffocate her, but she knew for certain there were no settlements for well over a hundred kilometers from the coast. That meant it would take days and days to walk out and find help if she moved inland. And there was no way that T-Mac would survive that long without help. Not to mention the gurney would probably run out of power in less than an hour.

"What do you think?" she asked him, knowing he couldn't hear her, much less respond. "I know, it's a gamble, but I can't think of any other way to save you. And I'm not leaving you behind."

She set out toward the base where the fighting was heavy with only a slim chance that she might find help. Fear was making her tremble, but she had assessed her situation, made up her mind, and she refused to doubt herself. It was better to face her fears—and the enemy—head on. At the very least she might be able to get a weapon and have a chance to defend herself. And if she saw that the base was overrun by the Ma'Tis, she could always turn around and flee. But that thought was even more frightening. She didn't want to die, and she was tempted to question every decision she had ever made, but she knew that wouldn't help her survive the next few hours. She needed to focus on what was happening at that moment and on protecting her fellow bombardier. With her mind settled, she pressed on toward the fighting, in the hopes that she would find the help she needed and not the death she feared.

CHAPTER 19

GENERAL KELLY LOOKED HAGGARD. He was moving through the survivors slowly. He had a rag tied around his head with blood soaking through one side. Colonel Allison Evenrue was with him, urging the commander to go with the wounded.

"No," he grumbled. "I'll leave with the last of our troopers."

"That isn't necessary, sir," she told him.

Cosmo and Dyson had joined with Butler and Sid Nash, a tough, former policeman from Premier Point. Almost everyone in Red Platoon was either wounded or dead. The three platoons called back from the crest of the hill had taken the heaviest losses. They had gathered the wounded and helped them to the rally point, and then helped the medics get them on board the hovercraft.

"You... hey there, Trooper," General Kelly called out as he pointed at Cosmo.

The group from Red Platoon came to attention, even though they were tired and dirty. It was still intimidating to be called out by the commanding general. Cosmo was sure they had done something wrong.

"What are you doing?" the General asked.

"Sir! Getting our wounded onto the medevac transports, sir!" Cosmo replied.

"Leave that to us, marksman. I want you back on sniper duty. You won the marksman award, Private..."

"Frost, sir!" Cosmo said.

"Right, Frost, I remember now. Back on the hilltop, son. There are more aliens down there, and I want you to take the bastards out."

"Sir, yes sir!" Cosmo said.

The General moved on, but Colonel Evenrue lingered a moment.

"Do you have a rifle that will reach the aliens on the beach?" she asked.

"We left our long-range gear when we were called back," Dyson said. "But we should be able to find it."

"That's good," she said. "I want the four of you on overwatch. We don't need any more surprises. I want a three-hundred-and-sixty-degree scan of the area. Alert us immediately if you see anything moving in this direction."

"Yes, Commander," the four troopers from Red Platoon said in unison.

She dismissed them and went back to the General while Cosmo led the way back to the crest of the hill.

"What are we gonna do if we can't find the sniper rifle?" Dyson asked.

"Just keep looking until we do, I suppose," Cosmo said.

There were still two platoons on the hill with rifles ready. Those firing down on the aliens hadn't suffered the losses that the three platoons sent to stop the flankers had. Still, everyone looked like they were in shock. Their first battle had been intense. And already there was a foul odor wafting up from the dead aliens below. It was impossible to count the bodies. They were piled up on top of one another, many with missing limbs and cracked shells.

"Gotta be a few thousand of them," Dyson said.

"We're lucky they didn't overrun the camp," Nash said.

"They could have if that had been their objective," Cosmo said, pointing down at the beach that had been scorched by the Air Force napalm bombing. "It's an invasion force. They're moving inland. We only stopped a fraction of their numbers."

"It's war then," Nash said. "For real now."

"Yeah, we in it now, bro," Dyson said. "It's on."

They found the sniper rifle and spotter's kit right where they had left it. Cosmo did a quick check on the weapon while Dyson checked the ammunition can.

"We still got a few hundred rounds," he said.

"What should we do?" Butler asked.

"Keep watch, just like the Colonel ordered us to do," Cosmo said. "You can use the spotter scope. Dyson and I will take turns shooting and help you out if need be."

They were up high enough to see over the plateau. If he had been looking behind him with the scope, he would have seen the lone airman approaching with a hover gurney, but Cosmo's focus was on the beach. He got down on his stomach, brought the rifle to bear, and started scanning the beach. The ruined alien vehicle was still smoking, but he had clear view of the beach directly below the cliffs. Only a few of the crab-like aliens were moving around. Looking through his scope he could see they were wounded. Some were wandering aimlessly while others were trying to get back to the ocean, probably hoping for medical attention. Cosmo didn't know if the Ma'Tis had doctors or hospitals. But it didn't matter at that moment. He took aim, adjusted for the distance, and fired his first shot.

The big sniper rifle bucked in his hands, pounding his bruised shoulder, the report making his ears ring. He had to readjust to keep tabs on his target. The bullet took nearly three seconds to reach the alien, and to his relief it hit right at the top of the creature's shell, knocking off a chunk before crashing through the alien's wide head. He swiveled to his next target.

"You were right," Nash said. He was standing up and had the spotter's scope on its built-in tripod, the telescoping legs fully extended to give him a solid base. "I can see more of them. A lot more."

"Probably more of those tanks too," Dyson said. "We'd have been wiped out if the bombers hadn't taken that thing down."

"It still had time to destroy the base," Butler pointed out. "Richie and Kevin were in the admin center when it was hit."

"I can't believe we're the last ones standing," Nash said.

They all had minor wounds from the battle. Cosmo's face was nicked up from the grit being blown from the building debris he had taken cover behind. One shoulder was bruised from the recoil of the sniper rifle; the other had a slight burn from a laser grazing it during the battle. It was all minor, but it made the fighting real. They weren't training any longer or running simulations. They were Troopers in the Fiona Grand Army. But out of thirty recruits, half hadn't made it to graduation from basic training. And of the rest, only four were still on their feet after a single battle. Even their hardnosed drill instructor had gone down.

"Just lucky, I guess," Butler said.

"No," Cosmo said. "Not just luck. Think about it. When you're in that battle do you want to take on the hard-charging, fearless enemy, or do you choose an easy target? I'm not saying luck doesn't play a part, but we can be the guys no one wants to take on."

Dyson laughed. "My man. That's what I'm talking about."

"Yeah, I can see that," Nash said. "Make our own luck."

"We're gonna need it," Butler added.

Cosmo killed three more Ma'Tis aliens on the beach directly below the remains of Lois Operations base. They could see others moving in the surf far to either side of the wide plateau. They took turns making the nearly impossible shots. It was simple harassment, with little to show for the effort, but the survivors of Red Platoon didn't mind. Cosmo and his friends were glad to do something.

The last of the transports arrived just before sundown. Colonel Evenrue met the four men from Red Platoon as they came down from the crest of the hill.

"Good work, gentlemen," she said. "The wounded have all been taken to Hawkstone Air Base. The four of you are going straight to Fort Mammoth for Armor Division training, but I've noted your role in this battle and put all up for commendation. Thank you."

"We just did our job," Cosmo said.

"Like Sergeant Reed trained us to do," Butler added.

"It was an honor to be here with you today," she insisted.

The newly graduated battle troopers came to attention and saluted. She returned the salute, then saw them onto one of the transports. Cosmo and Dyson sat by the open door as the aircraft rose up. They saw Colonel Evenrue look around, then climb aboard the other hovercraft. She was the last person out of the ruins that had been Lois Operating Station.

Their transport banked hard. They all relaxed a little, and Cosmo looked at his friend as the light faded. Dyson looked as tired as Cosmo felt.

"That was some graduation," Dyson said.

"Yeah, the afterparty was a hell of a banger," Cosmo replied.

"You can say that again, bro. One hell of a banger."

CHAPTER 20

ALLURA STAYED with T-Mac until they reached Hawkstone. There, medical personnel rushed him away. It felt a little anticlimactic. She wondered if the pilot, who had insisted on going inland instead of helping her get T-Mac to the army base, had been picked up. She had no way of knowing.

She also had no idea where to go next. All of her belongings were in Captain Lansing's outer office. The bombardier squadron was code-named Condor. They operated out of a series of hangars on the other side of the base. Allura set out walking. There was activity all around her. Hawkstone Air Base was a busy place. She saw fighter jets, hybrid shuttles, and medical hovercraft. Massive hangars lined long runways. There was a military hospital that was fifteen stories tall, as well as administrative offices and personnel housing.

Eventually a senior airman in a hover-cart stopped and offered her a ride.

"Where you headed?" he asked.

He was a few years older than Allura, with a square jaw and bright blue eyes. His short hair was frosted yellow and contrasted with his dark eyebrows. The skin on his jaws and chin looked almost blue from the stubble. It was late in the day, and the airman needed a shave.

"Condor section," she said.

"You're in luck," he said. "Climb aboard. I'll give you a ride."

"Thanks, she said.

"Where you coming from?"

"I just flew my first mission," she said. "And survived my first emergency landing."

"Wow," he said. "I'm not sure if your luck is good or bad."

"Me either," she said.

"Lots of activity around here," he said. "Word is the bugs are pushing inland."

"I'd say that's right," Allura replied.

"First mission, huh? You a spotter?"

"I was this trip," Allura said. "I just got back from bombardier training on Triton."

"Wow, maybe you should have stayed there," he said with a grin. "My name's Higgs, short for Tad Higgins. But all my friends call me Higgs."

"Nice to meet you. I'm Allura. What do you do here?"

"Senior ordnance loader," he said. "I run a team that loads the bombers."

He drove up to a hangar with a massive bird painted on the side. The huge doors were open, and Allura could see people gathering in the back where the offices were located.

"This is you," Higgs said.

"Thanks," Allura said.

"Anytime, Allura. Don't be a stranger."

He gave her a flirtatious wink, then sped away on his hover cart. Allura felt tired and emotional. She didn't like thinking about how close she had come to dying. And the memories of T-Mac's injuries were hard to get out of her mind.

She was halfway across the hangar when Captain Lansing appeared. She was trailed by a group of men and women in flight coveralls just like the ones that Allura was wearing.

"Airmen Presley," the Captain said. "I take it T-Mac was killed?"

"No, ma'am, just wounded. He's been taken to the hospital."

"Damn," she replied. "He was one of our best. We're down to a dozen bombers and only eight bombardiers. Come with me."

Allura fell in with the group. There were three other women and four men. They were all older than Allura, and she saw the bombardier insignia on their coveralls. They walked across the tarmac to another hangar where two bombers were being loaded with bombs. The Captain took them up a set of metal stairs to a conference room with a holographic projection table and several chairs. Allura was happy to sit down. She felt exhausted and hungry, but there was no time to complain. Captain Lansing immediately joined a tele-meeting that was already underway.

"Welcome Captain Lansing," a gray-haired man said. Only his head was projected by the holographic table. Around the edges, there were several other small faces that Allura couldn't make out. "Now that we're all here, let's get started. The enemy has pushed inland. We have satellites over the eastern seaboard, but as you know, the intel they can pick up through the Ma'Tis haze is spotty at best. We believe they have at least a dozen more of the mobile artillery vehicles and probably somewhere in the neighborhood of eighty thousand troops."

The holograph changed from floating heads to a three-dimensional map. Red blobs represented the Ma'Tis forces. They were moving toward a city. Allura couldn't recognize it by sight, but it was substantial in size, with several skyscrapers towering over a well-planned, geometric city layout.

"Their target is most likely Hillsdale," the voice of the gray-haired man continued. "We've begun the evacuation, but we need to slow their advance."

"What about the bio-bots?" someone asked. "Were they used in the invasion?"

"No reports of the bio-bot weapons being deployed," the gray-haired man replied.

"They're saving them," someone else said.

"That's most likely the case," the gray-haired man said. "We're considering every option. And we have new weapons to bring online in the days ahead, but our first goal is getting the people of Hillsdale to safety. To that end, we are ordering a bombing campaign to commence immediately. Captain Lansing will send in her Condors to take out the artillery vehicles and slow the Ma'Tis advance."

"Sir," Captain Lansing said, "with that many troopers, our vessels will only get one shot at their artillery vehicles, and we'll lose probably eighty percent of our bombers and personnel in the process."

"We're aware of the risks, Captain. Your orders are to use three-ton Devastator warheads from a height of five thousand meters. That should give you enough firepower to get the job done but keep you well out of harm's way."

"Not if they bring their laser cannons to bear, sir," she replied.

"I've already ordered long-range sensors and spotters to be in the field, Captain. They'll relay the position of the weapons to your people in the air. You're to come in from behind and take out their vehicles."

"Sir, the accuracy needed to make those kinds of drops is nearly impossible," Lansing said. "And our bombers will only be able to carry four Devastators per aircraft. We'll make the effort, of course, sir, but you should be aware that the hope of success is very, very slim."

"Success will be getting the city evacuated before the enemy arrives. Anything you can do to slow them down, Captain, will be part of that success."

"We'll give them hell, sir," Captain Lansing said.

"We have no doubt. Scramble your birds and put your game plan together. You will begin your mission at 0500 hours. Keep in mind there will be civilian transports in the area around Hillsdale."

"Copy that, General. We'll be ready."

The teleconference ended, and Lansing looked up at the bombardiers. It seemed to Allura that her CO was staring right at her.

"You all heard General Yori. Questions?"

"Captain," a man to Allura's left said. "I can't make that calculation. I'd need a computer at the very least."

"Me too," a short woman sitting beside Allura said. "T-Mac could do it, possibly. Hanz or Sibel, but they're both out of commission. We just don't have the skill to drop something so big from so high."

"I'm aware of the difficulty," Captain Lansing said. "So is the General. Can any of you make that type of calculation?"

The bombardiers shifted in their seats, and Allura raised her hand before she realized that none of the others would.

"Airman Presley," Captain Lansing said. "We haven't had time to introduce you to the group. We lost over half our bombardiers in the invasion, including T-Mac who you helped out of his ship and to safety. For that, I say thank you."

The group also murmured their thanks, but they were all eyeing her skeptically.

"You can make this drop?" the captain asked.

"I can," Allura said. "We trained with heavy ordnance on Triton. HAHO drops can be tricky depending on the conditions, but it's possible. The target is big enough."

"You'll take lead position," Captain Lansing ordered. "I would prefer for you to have more real-world experience, but with the situation being what it is, we don't have that luxury. Once you make the drop and we have confirmation of its success or failure, you will pass on the equation you are using. Conditions won't be the same up and down the enemy line, but they should be close. Like the general said, as long as we can slow down the Ma'Tis, we will have succeeded. I'm also ordering the pilots to take evasive actions the moment the guns on those ships move. We can't risk losing any more of you. To that end, if your aircraft is hit, you are to evacuate immediately. I'll have fast transports standing by to pick you up. Is that clear?"

"Yes, Captain," the group replied.

"Very good. Report to your birds at 0430. Until then, you are dismissed."

The bombardiers got to their feet, but Captain Lansing gave Allura a look that told her to stick around. She lingered in the conference room as the other bombardiers left.

"You made quite a claim," the captain said, leaning against the holographic projection table and crossing her arms. "I know that ATA is a good school, but this is the real world, not a sim, not a question on a test."

"Yes, ma'am, I'm aware of that fact," Allura said.

"And you can make that kind of calculation on the fly, in your head?"

"I can," Allura said, feeling her cheeks flush. She wasn't the type to brag, and didn't really like talking about herself, but she knew she was up to the task.

"Air speed, humidity, the rotation of the planet, the differential between the wind at altitude, and the wind speed at ground level all come into play," Captain Lansing said. "My bombardiers are mostly volunteers. They've learned on the job. It isn't hard to make a low-altitude calculation when you're dropping napalm that spreads out half a kilometer from the impact zone. They aren't really equipped for this type of run."

"I can do it," Allura said. "I earned a full ride to TTI before joining the ATA. Math has always been a strong suit."

"Then I want you to teach the others," Lansing said. "They won't listen to you now, even with your ATA training. You're too young, too green, but if you make this drop and hit the target, you'll be a rockstar."

"I'll make the drop," Allura promised.

"We'll see," Lansing said. "A decent bombardier is better than a dead one. The most important thing is coming back alive."

"Yes, ma'am."

"Get some rest. There's an empty bunk shack in this hangar. Grab your gear, get some grub and some sleep. We're less than ten hours from launch time."

"Yes, Captain," Allura replied.

"And Presley, welcome to Condor."

"Thank you," Allura said, not quite sure she was happy to be there.

CHAPTER 21

THE HOVERCRAFT LANDED at Fort Mammoth in the dark. Cosmo and his companions had fallen asleep on the flight. They were all tired after a long day and their first battle, but there would be no rest for the new battle troopers.

"New recruits," a sergeant first class shouted as they climbed out of the transport. "To the line. Move! Move! Move!"

The survivors of Red Platoon weren't the only new members to the Armor Division. A few recruits from each graduating class had been assigned to the elite division. Twenty-five newly graduated battle troopers filed out and formed a line on the tarmac.

"No time for introductions," the sergeant snapped. "We have a priority mission, and you have the honors, gentlemen. Welcome to Armor Division. Follow me and we'll get you geared up."

The sergeant set out, and the new arrivals followed him. Cosmo didn't know if they were being tested, but it seemed odd that they would be given an assignment so quickly.

"They don't waste any time around here," Dyson said.

"You think this is some sort of initiation?" Cosmo asked.

"Could be," Dyson replied. "We better stay alert and ready just in case."

The sergeant led them to a room that looked like a prep area for a sporting event. There were wide lockers with names printed on each one.

"Find your locker and get changed!" the sergeant yelled. He wasn't as gruff as Drill Sergeant Reed, but he had the same sense of command. "Five minutes, gentlemen. Let's move!"

Cosmo spotted his last name and hurried over. Like the rest of the new battle troopers, he was still in his tattered, dirty, dress uniform. He pulled it off and got into a set of compression pants with a matching shirt. Next, he stepped into the lower section of body armor that was different than anything he had seen before.

"What do you think this is?" Cosmo asked Dyson as he ran his hand over the metal frame that ran down the thigh portion of the armor to a set of gears at the knee.

"Support, maybe?" Dyson replied. "That upper body army is pretty big."

It was heavy too. Part armor, part battle suit. They helped one another pull the upper section over one another, then hooked the upper and lower parts of the heavy armor together. The final bit was a helmet that sat partway down into the wide neck section of chest armor. When the helmet was put on it activated the armor, which was all connected.

"This way!" the sergeant yelled. "We are on the clock, gentlemen. No time to waste."

They walked down a corridor where they were met by technicians and divided into teams of three. Cosmo, Dyson, and Nash were put together and designated Delta Team. Each had a large device hooked to the back of their armor.

"These are line of sight communication beacons," the sergeant yelled. "Each team will be dropped behind the enemy lines. You will locate the Ma'Tis tanks. You know what they look like since one was destroyed just offshore near Lois. Your job is to communicate with the bombers coming in and relay what those laser cannons are pointing at. It's that simple. You will spread out in a single file line with at least a kilometer between each member of your team. If you can see the next man in line, you should be able to communicate. The last man in the group will convey to the bombers what the first man is seeing once the air jockeys make contact. Is that clear?"

"Yes, Sergeant," the group of armored battle troopers shouted in unison.

"Damn, I love new grunts. Let's get you armed and mounted up."

They each got a weapon. It was thick, bulky, and heavy, but the suit Cosmo wore was essentially a light mechanized suit. The metal frame built into the armor had power assists so that the bulky armor and weapon didn't feel heavy at all. With weapons in hand, they were loaded onto small drop ships.

Their battle helmets with enhanced vision allowed them to see one another inside the windowless cargo bay. Charlie team was on board with Delta, but they were on different communication frequencies.

"I guess this ain't no initiation gag," Dyson said.

"We're on lookout duty?" Nash complained. "I wouldn't have protested a meal first."

"They don't want you stinking up that new armor suit," Cosmo said.

"Well, they're gonna be disappointed," Nash replied. "I'd need a shower if that were the case."

The flight lasted nearly two hours. Charlie team was dropped first. When the ship landed again, it was well past midnight. The three new battle troopers trundled out of the ship.

"Good luck, Delta team," the pilot of the drop ship said. "See you on the flip side."

Then the Sergeant's voice spoke through their helmet's communication system. "Delta team, you are five klicks behind the enemy force. Proceed with haste until the enemy is in sight. Form up in single file formation and keep pace with that tank. You don't need to get too close and draw the enemy down on top of you. But watch out for stragglers. Report anything out of the ordinary. Get moving, gentlemen. Sergeant Ramey out."

"Great, just a casual five-K jog in full armor," Nash said. "Just what I was hoping for."

They set out together. Running was part of their lives and had been since the first day of basic training. But it only took the computer assistance software a short time to learn their movements. Less than half a kilometer after they started, the motorized gears on their legs did most of the work. It felt more like they were on an elliptical cardio machine than running cross country in full armor. Even the bulky rifle seemed light as a feather.

"This ain't so bad," Dyson said. "I could do this for a while."

"I could still use a burger," Nash said. "Maybe a shake."

"It's unbelievable," Cosmo said. "How fast do you think we're going?"

"My helmet's got a speedometer," Dyson said. "We're running six kilometers per hour."

"Let's see how fast these suits can go," Nash suggested.

They began to sprint. It took Cosmo a few moments to get the speedometer up on the view screen of his battle helmet. He had direction, speed, distance, and even weather conditions feeding right into the suit and showing right in front of his eyes. He could view the information by glancing down and see through it to the terrain they were covering. The light enhancement made everything visible in a black and white image on the view screen. Cosmo didn't know if he was seeing through the helmet or seeing a video of the outside. Perhaps when the sun came up it would be easier to learn about their new armor, but he was loving it so far.

"That's about it," Nash said. "Fifty-five klicks per hour."

"How long you think you could keep that speed up?" Dyson asked.

"Not long," Nash said.

"Maybe a minute, at most," Cosmo said.

They slowed to just twenty-five kilometers per hour. Cosmo could feel his legs moving, but there was practically no impact when his foot hit the ground, and the springing action of the armored suit made it easy to keep up the pace. And it wasn't long before the enemy came into sight.

"There they are," Dyson said. "I'll take point."

"I'll cover him. You do the talking, Frost," Nash said.

They spread out in a line with Cosmo at the rear. They had to alter course and slowed way down. It only took a casual walk to keep pace with the Ma'Tis, who moved slowly over the ground. Most were walking sideways. They were on a wide, flat prairie and seeing the enemy wasn't hard. The battle troopers spread out over six kilometers.

"I got eyes on the tank," Dyson said. "All eight barrels are pointing forward, maybe sixty degrees."

"I can hear him," Cosmo said. "We should spread out more."

"Roger that," Nash said. "I'll just stop and let him get another kilometer ahead of me."

Cosmo backtracked a little. Dyson kept talking so that Cosmo would know when he was far enough away.

"All right, Nash, I've lost Dyson's signal."

"You can stop yapping," the former cop said. "I've dated women who talked less than you."

Cosmo couldn't hear his friend's response, but he could imagine the snappy comeback. He let the other two battle troopers get farther ahead of him. When Nash was a full five kilometers ahead, Cosmo started walking again. He was worried that the terrain might change and break up their communication links, but they walked all night on what seemed to be a flat plain.

The stars were bright overhead—or maybe his helmet's low-light enhancement made them stand out. Still, Cosmo enjoyed seeing them. He was tired but not really sleepy. There was still adrenaline in his system keeping him alert. They did see stragglers, but it wasn't clear that the aliens saw them. The battle armor was heavy but not loud, and in the darkness, they moved like shadows. None of the straggling bugs were close, but things were going to change once the sun came up —which it did a few hours after the team got set into their positions.

"We've got light in the east," Cosmo said. "Tell Dyson to keep his head on a swivel."

"I can't listen to you both at the same time," Nash complained. "But in this instance, you were both giving me the same advice, so it worked out. What are we supposed to do when the crusties see us?"

Cosmo didn't answer right away. In his mind, there was only one thing they could do. Their orders were to stay in position, which meant fending off the aliens. The only question was would the Ma'Tis send forces back to take down one or two enemy soldiers? If they did, the group would be in trouble.

"Dyson says to ask you," Nash said.

"I don't think we have much choice," Cosmo said. "Better check your weapon."

"Nice," Nash said. "Way to state the obvious, bro."

"Glad I could be of service," Cosmo replied. "Besides, I'm not in charge."

"Somebody has to be," Nash said. "We elected you."

"I don't accept."

"Sure you do, Frost. Some guys are leaders. They're just born with it. There's a reason Sergeant Reed awarded you with the platoon leadership metal thingy. We all see it."

"I'm just trying to not get killed," Cosmo argued.

"Whatever, you're still in charge. Any word from the bombers?"

"Nothing yet. Anything happening up there I should know about?"

"Dyson, our fearless leader wants to know what the crabbies are up to."

There was a pause, then Nash laughed.

"They're walking," the former policeman said. "Creepy, giant bastards have been walking since they came out of the ocean. I guess they don't need rest."

"Rest is a four-letter word," Cosmo said, repeating a line he had heard often from Sergeant Reed. "We'll get all the rest we need when we're dead."

"Nice. See, I told you, a natural-born leader," Nash replied.

"Stuff it, old man."

"Who you calling old? I'm younger than Dyson."

Cosmo waited while the two older troopers argued over who was actually younger. They were both his senior by around four years at least—maybe more. Cosmo wasn't really concerned with ages. In fact, his attention was focused on a Ma'Tis alien that had stopped moving. He guessed the creature was two, maybe three kilometers to his right. It just watched them in the gray light of dawn. Cosmo glanced at his rifle. It was a large-bore laser weapon, the type that was normally mounted on ships but with a short barrel and wide, blocky foregrip. It also had some type of projectile magazine. Below the laser barrel was a second muzzle, which he assumed launched the projectiles.

"Anyone know what we're packing here?" Cosmo asked.

"Laser blaster up top?" Nash said. "Looks like spring-propelled explosive shells from the bottom. Not sure about that though. Our armor's got plenty of computer-assist tech, so it must be magnetically shielded from the aliens' disruptive haze. Not sure how it would hold up close to so many. Dyson's not complaining of any problems though."

"That's good to know," Cosmo said. "I think we're going to get a chance to try them out before long."

Another pause, then Nash spoke up. "Dyson said there's a lot of stragglers maybe a kilometer behind the main force. But they aren't concerned about him. He's still three kilometers back from their tank. He could fall back farther if he needs to. Seeing it in daylight won't be a problem."

"We should drop back as far as he's comfortable," Cosmo said. "There's no sense in getting caught in the blast zone."

"Copy that," Nash said, after relaying the idea to Dyson. "We'll stop and let them get some more distance on us."

As they waited, a faint, static-laced voice broke into Cosmo's helmet.

"Spotter team, this is Condor One, do you read? Over."

"Condor One, this is Delta team," Cosmo said. "We're in position and read you, over."

"Copy that, Delta team. Can you give us a wind speed reading down there? Over."

"Uh, it's six kilometers per hour out of the north," Cosmo said. "Do you need anything else? Over."

"Where are the Ma'Tis cannons pointing? Over."

"Sixty degrees up and directly ahead. Over."

"Copy that. We're coming in from your six. I strongly suggest you pull back. We're firing from five thousand meters. There's no telling where this heavy bomb is coming down. Over."

"Roger that. We'll pull back, Condor One. Over."

"Turning you over to our bombardier," the pilot said. "Out."

"Guys, we've been ordered back from the alien line," Cosmo told Nash.

"Roger that."

There was a pause. Cosmo turned and searched the sky but couldn't see or hear the bomber. It was still a long way off, he supposed. But when he heard Allura's voice, he nearly dropped to his knees.

"Delta team this is Talon One. What's it look like down there? Over."

For a moment Cosmo couldn't speak. He felt as if someone had grabbed him by the throat and was strangling him.

"Delta One, do you read? Over."

"Yeah, yeah, I read you," Cosmo said. "Allura?"

"Cosmo? Is that you?"

They had completely forgotten about radio etiquette.

"It's me. Oh, my gosh, Allura, I've got so much to tell you."

"Me too, me too," she said. "I miss you so much."

"I can't believe you're here. What made you join the Air Force?"

"I messaged you," she said. "I just needed to get involved. It's a really long story, Cos, but right now I need to focus on this drop. What's the humidity down there?"

"Forty-eight percent," he said. "Wind speed is the same."

"Hang on, I've got to convert KPH to nautical miles per hour."

Cosmo waited, his heart banging in his chest.

"Yo, Cos," Nash said, in a razzy tone, "you know this chick?"

"Yeah," Cosmo said.

"So what's the skinny, Frost? Don't keep us in the dark. She hot?"

"She's my girlfriend," he snapped.

"Oh," Nash said. "I thought that was just a make-believe thing you had going on."

"Shut it," Cosmo told him.

"Cos," Allura said. "What are the cannons doing?"

"Nash, update on the cannons, please," Cosmo said.

There was a slight pause. "No change."

"No change," Cosmo relayed the message. "They're still facing forward, about sixty-degree lift."

"Okay, okay," she said. "Oh, sorry. Over."

"Copy that. Over," Cosmo said.

He was dumbstruck and excited and afraid all at the same time. Slowly the bomber came into view, just a tiny dot far away. There were clouds in the sky, puffy white and lower than the bomber.

"They're way up there," Nash said.

Cosmo turned and saw his friend still three kilometers away. From where he stood, Dyson was still out of sight. And, as crazy as it sounded, Allura Presley was in an airplane. Cosmo wondered what her parents thought about her joining the Air Force. They would be furious and blame him, he knew, but he didn't really care. She was close, and for the moment, that was all that mattered in the world to Cosmo.

CHAPTER 22

ALLURA'S HEART WAS POUNDING. The excitement of making a good drop was high, but hearing Cosmo's voice after over three months apart was even more thrilling to her.

"Permission to open bomb bay doors?" she asked.

"Permission granted," the pilot replied. "Flight speed three hundred knots. I can slow down to two fifty at this altitude if that helps."

"Three hundred is fine," Allura said. She was working the numbers in her head fast, calculating the speed that the bomb would fall and the conditions it would drop into that would affect it.

"Distance to target?" she asked.

"Forty-five kilometers," the pilot replied.

"Permission to release Big Baby One?"

"Granted. Fire at will," the pilot replied.

The bomb's payload, the granulated chemical explosive, weighed two thousand, seven hundred and twenty-one kilograms. It was sheathed in nearly fifty kilos of metal and had a hundred-kilo impact detonator in the nose. It would shed the bomber's momentum by eleven percent every second after launch. The wind would shift it slightly as it fell, and they were far enough up that it would take the bomb twenty-two seconds from the time of its release until it hit the target.

"Pilot, can you bring us over a few degrees into the wind?" Allura asked. She didn't know the pilot's name. In fact, no one in the entire Condor program had been very friendly to her. She had gotten a hot meal from the chow hall on base, eaten by herself, then gotten her gear and found the sleep shack in the hangar below the conference room. It was just a bare room with a locker. She stowed her gear, put a padlock on the locker, and slept on the narrow cot, whose spring squeaked every time she moved. Not that she would have gotten any sleep if she had been in the most luxurious bed ever made. Beyond the hangar, airplanes, shuttles, and transports were lifting off and landing. And in her head were all the things she would have to do to make the drop in what seemed like an incredibly short amount of time. Allura knew that everyone in the Condor program was waiting to see if she could do what she claimed. If she missed, they would never respect her. That added pressure didn't help her sleep.

"Copy that. Adjusting three degrees," he said.

She could see the line of aliens in the distance, a dark stripe on the golden landscape. Somewhere down there was a man, her man, and that only made her hands tremble all the more. She had hoped to see Cosmo soon, to tell him of her decision and all about her training. If she missed, he would know it, and that really made her nervous. She wanted to impress him more than anyone. She had made a radical life change and had been really proud of her decision while she was at the ATA, but since coming home she had been less certain.

"Target acquired," she said. "Almost there."

The only sound in the bomb bay was the rush of wind. She was tethered to a stool and had her feet hooked under a safety bar. Her hand was on the release switch that would drop the heavy bomb, which was hanging over the open bay doors directly in front of her.

"Big Baby One... away!" she shouted as she pressed the firing button.

The bomb dropped out of the aircraft, and for a moment she could see it arching through the sky below the aircraft. Then the pilot put them into a hard turn. Gravity pushed her down and back. She was held in place by safety tethers and her feet, but she held onto the control board anyway. In her mind she was counting down the seconds.

The bomber made a looping turn and was actually traveling back away from the line of aliens. They would have to wait for the report from the ground, from Cosmo, to know if she had hit the target.

"Impact," his familiar voice said. There was a pause, and she feared that she had missed the alien vehicle. He was probably embarrassed for her; that was what was taking so long. She wanted to ask him what he was seeing. His silence was a strange kind of painful torture.

"Target destroyed, I think," Cosmo said. "There's a lot of smoke and debris down here. Over."

"We'll check it out," the pilot said.

The aircraft turned again and was flying parallel to the line of aliens marching toward Hillsdale.

"Can you see anything?" Allura asked the pilots.

"Negative, visual is impaired. Too much smoke," the pilot said. "Ground force, move in and give us a visual report. Over."

"Copy that," Cosmo said. "Delta team moving in. Over."

Allura felt a stab of guilt. What if they got killed because they were investigating her bombing run. She felt like she might be sick as the bomber circled around and got lined up for another run toward the target.

"Condor One, we have visual confirmation of the bombing," Cosmo said. "Target was destroyed, as were quite a few of the Ma'Tis. Good shooting, Talon One. Over."

"Outstanding, Delta team. Pull your people back and report to base. We are on to the next target. Condor One, out."

Allura wanted to tell Cosmo goodbye. In fact, she wanted to tell him a lot of things. She hadn't even had time to get settled since coming back to Fiona Grand. She hadn't gotten any messages from him, but then she hadn't had time to check her PIP since getting back on world. Everything had been crazy, but at least she had heard his voice. She wondered briefly what he was doing down on the ground, but the next target was only about ten kilometers down the line of alien invaders. She had to refocus on the task at hand.

"Target acquired," she said.

"Give 'em hell just like before, Talon One," the pilot said.

"Thank you," she said while her mind was busy calculating the timing of her second drop.

Everything went off without a hitch. The second bomb actually hit the Ma'Tis vehicle on one side, but the tank was completely wrecked. The high-yield warhead did short work of the alien vehicle and left a crater in the ground. The other half of the Ma'Tis craft was flipped completely upside down and managed to crush dozens of the crabs in the process. The mission was a complete success.

She transferred her formula to the other bombers who fed in the numbers and tried to replicate her success. A computer-operated bomber could have released the ordnance at the precise time. A half a second would be too late, and weather conditions from wind to humidity affected the warhead. A bombardier could have the perfect formula, but they still needed to do the math correctly. None of the others could pull it off.

When she got back to the air base, she was met by Captain Lansing.

"Great work, Presley. Unfortunately, we couldn't replicate your success."

"The formula was right on. It's just B equals—"

"No," Lansing said. "I'm not sure how you do that kind of calculating in your head. I'd need a slate and at least half an hour to work out that kind of math. The others can't pull it off. We need you back up there."

"Okay," Allura said. "When?"

"We're loading your ship now. Good luck, Airman."

Allura appreciated the respect, but she was tired too. Still, there was nothing for it but to go back to the bomb bay and get ready for another run.

CHAPTER 23

THE DEVASTATION from the bombing was incredible. Even over ten kilometers away, the ground had shaken.

"What are they doing?" Nash said. "You okay, Dyson?"

"Yeah, man," he replied. "I'm fine, but the crabs are gone, baby. That was a hell of a shot."

"What are you seeing?" Cosmo asked.

"Lots of smoke," he said.

Cosmo couldn't help but move toward his friends, who had fallen back. Nash was only a couple of kilometers from Cosmo, and Dyson was less than five.

"Did they hit the tank?" Cosmo asked. "They're asking for a report."

"Looks like it," Dyson replied.

"Target destroyed, I think. There's a lot of smoke and debris down here."

"What are they up to?" Nash asked.

"Doing a flyover," Cosmo replied.

"They won't see much," Dyson said. "There's fires burning everywhere. Even some of the crabs are burning."

"Ground force," the bomber pilot said, "Move in and give us a visual report. Over."

"Copy that," Cosmo replied. "Delta team moving in. Over. Guys, we're going to have to get closer and check it out."

"Of course we are," Nash said.

They jogged forward. A soft breeze started up, blowing the smoke away from the trio.

"Not sure we should get much closer," Nash said. "The crabs are looking for payback. I've got two groups headed this way."

"We better change their minds before Dyson gets cut off," Cosmo said.

"I'll take the group on the left," Nash said.

"Copy that. I'm on the other group," Cosmo said.

He was still three to four kilometers from the group, but his helmet had a targeting app that could zoom in just like a sniper scope. He could see a group of Ma'Tis moving toward them. He raised his rifle and pulled the trigger. Laser beams flashed from the short-barreled weapon. They didn't burn through the shells of the Ma'Tis, but they knocked them down and caused damage. Cosmo was too far out to see it clearly, but he liked his new rifle.

"This bad boy does the business," Nash said.

"Not bad at all," Cosmo replied.

"I can see it now," Dyson said. "That thing is totaled. There's nothing left but debris."

"Great!" Cosmo said. "Fall back. I'll report in."

He gave the report, hoping to hear Allura's voice again, but the pilot had taken charge. When Cosmo looked up, the bomber was turning away from their position.

"That's a wrap, fellas," Cosmo said.

"Hang on," Nash said. "What the hell is that?"

Cosmo turned around and looked back at his friend. Nash was pointing toward the group of aliens he had targeted with his rifle. There was something coming out of the aliens' shells. Cosmo couldn't see it clearly. He turned and looked at the group he had taken down with the laser rifle. There was something seeping from their shells too.

"That don't look good, boys," Nash said.

"Dyson?" Cosmo asked.

"Yeah, I see it," he said, his words coming in puffs as he ran.

"Could be bio-bots," Nash said. "It's moving this way."

"Then we move out," Cosmo said. "Nash, let's put down some cover fire. Use your grenades."

Cosmo hit a switch on the side of the bulky rifle. The display switched from a percentage of the rifle's battery power to the number twenty. He lifted the rifle and fired. It bucked slightly and made a hollow puffing sound. The projectile flew forty meters and dropped to the ground with a bang.

"It's out of range," Cosmo said.

"For me too," Nash replied. "Dyson, time to turn on the jets."

"Yeah," he said.

Cosmo was running too. He was sprinting toward his friends. The substance from the dead or dying Ma'Tis warriors had left them and was moving toward the battle troopers. It looked like water running down a recently waxed hover-car. The fluid was *flowing* across level ground. It reminded Cosmo of the mercury his chemistry teacher had shown the class in high school.

"Try the laser," Nash said.

Cosmo switched back to the laser blaster and fired away. The beams had an impact, but it was like throwing rocks in a pond. The strange substance flowed away from the bits burned up by the laser beams and reformed. Cosmo realized it would take a dozen battle troopers and thousands of shots to stop the bio-bots with laser fire.

"This isn't working," he said as he closed the distance to his friends.

"We gotta do something," Nash said.

"Command, this is Delta team, do you read me? Over," Cosmo called on the command channel of his helmet's communication system. There was no reply. "Looks like we're on our own."

"No surprise there," Nash said. "I'm getting closer. Gotta use the explosives and blast that stuff."

"Careful, Nash," Dyson said. "Don't take any chances for me, man."

Cosmo kept running. He was too far away to help Nash. And Dyson was still in danger. More groups of the alien fighters were moving toward them. They needed to be retreating from the enemy, not running toward it. But Cosmo wouldn't just stand by while his friends fought for their lives.

Their new rifles fired the grenade rounds as quickly as they could pull the triggers. Nash shot a quick volley; the explosions kicked up dirt and dust.

"It's moving fast!" Nash called out. "What the hell is this stuff?"

"Get out of there!" Cosmo shouted. "Move! There's nothing more you can do."

Nash fired again, waving his rifle wildly to try and track the bio-bots.

"They're splitting apart," he complained.

"Run!" Dyson shouted as he sprinted past Nash.

The Ma'Tis had turned their attention to the trio of battle troopers. After the shell shock of the bomb (which caused massive devastation among the alien invaders) wore off, they looked for an enemy to fight. Cosmo, Dyson, and Nash were the only people around. There were hundreds of the crab-like aliens scurrying toward them.

Nash turned and started running too, only he wasn't as fast. Their armor gave them incredible speed, but it took time to generate. And the bio-bots were faster.

Cosmo dropped to one knee, brought his rifle to his shoulder, and fired away. The laser blasts chugged from the bulky weapon, hitting the tiny, alien mass that was closing in on Nash. The concentrated laser fire was a bit like shooting at a swarm of bees.

"We need cover!" Dyson yelled.

"Not much of that out here," Cosmo replied.

"I got this," Nash said.

To Cosmo's horror, the former cop slid to a stop, spinning around, and fired his grenade launcher. It was a bold move. The bio-bots were only a few meters behind him. Still, it might have worked if he hadn't run out of ammo after the second shot.

"No!" Cosmo shouted.

The swarming mass was less than half of what it started out as, but there was more than enough to overwhelm Nash. It raced up the armor.

"Get off," Nash screamed. "Get off me."

He was spinning around, swatting at the writhing substance but to no avail. It converged on his helmet.

"They're getting in," Nash shouted.

The scream that followed made Cosmo's legs feel weak. Nash dropped to his knees, his weapon clattering to the ground, his hands on his helmet. He wailed in horror and pain, then abruptly the scream stopped. Cosmo watched his friend topple over, his body twitching. It took all his strength to stand up again. Dyson was charging toward him at a full sprint. Behind him was an army of Ma'Tis and more than one swarm of bio-bots flowing over the grassy prairie toward the two remaining battle troopers.

"Gotta go!" Dyson shouted.

"Yeah," Cosmo replied, his mouth dry, his brain foggy.

He turned and started running. Dyson passed him. The bigger man was really moving, but it only encouraged Cosmo to push himself harder. They had trained for months, and while running for their lives didn't seem courageous or dignified, they both understood the dire situation. Fortunately, once they got going, they easily outpaced the Ma'Tis. The bio-bots were faster than the towering crab aliens they came from, but they didn't have much range on their own. When Cosmo looked back over his shoulder, the bio-bots weren't chasing them. The swarms of mercury-like alien substance were returning to the Ma'Tis warriors.

"Looks like we're outrunning them," Cosmo said.

"Good," Dyson huffed.

After nearly ten minutes of running they had gotten far enough from the aliens that their communication systems could reach the satellites overhead. They called for help and were given an evacuation plan. Cosmo didn't mention Nash. They would have to explain what happened eventually, but the memory of seeing him fall and hearing his screams was too much for the young trooper. His eyes filled with tears. He knew it was something he would never forget as long, or as short, as he lived.

CHAPTER 24

THEY WERE PICKED up by a transport an hour after Nash died. They had run until help arrived and climbed onto the hovercraft exhausted.

"Just the two of you?" the pilot asked.

"Yes," Cosmo said.

"Nash didn't make it," Dyson added.

"Sorry to hear that," the pilot said, but he didn't sound surprised.

They flew up and right back over the bombing site. Normally it would have been dangerous to fly over the Ma'Tis lines, but the aliens were disorganized. Cosmo and Dyson looked down through the window. There was a huge crater, the soil blackened from the heat. The edges of the bowl-shaped indentation in the landscape were littered with debris from the tank, but there was nothing else left from the massive vehicle. It had been a perfect hit, and there were bodies piled up around the scorched earth too. The Ma'Tis died on their backs, their legs curled in like spiders and their dark blood oozing into the ground.

"They nailed the bastards," Dyson said.

"Unbelievable," Cosmo said. "There's nothing left of that tank."

"I guess that slowed down their assault."

"But they aren't going back," Cosmo pointed out. "There's still thousands of them."

The enemy lines were disjointed. Some sections had continued forward, others were spread out or even just wandering around in an aimless fashion. But there were thousands of the aliens—more than Cosmo had imagined. They were down but not out of the fight, and the sight of them made him feel small and weak.

The transport took them back to Mammoth, where they were taken into a room to remove their armor. It went into a charging rack while they were given sandwiches. Cosmo was so tired he felt like he could sleep standing up. But an officer with Captain's insignia and the same sergeant who had sent them out the night before, were ready to brief them. Sleep would have to wait.

"Tell us what happened," the sergeant said. "Don't leave anything out."

They relayed the events exactly as they had happened. Cosmo could tell that Dyson felt guilty. Nash had been trying to buy him enough time to get away from the bio-bots. They had never fought the alien swarms before. If Nash had known they wouldn't keep coming after him—that in his armor he could outrun the strange alien weapon —he would still be alive. But they hadn't known, and turning to fight had been Nash's idea. No one had told him to do it. He had sacrificed himself to save his friends, and Cosmo tried to focus on the nobility of his act, even if it had been unnecessary.

"I'd say your friend was a hero," the captain said once they had finished telling their story. "The brass might have more questions, but I think we've got everything we need here."

"Showers and sleep, in that order," the sergeant said. "You've earned it. Follow me, Troopers. I'll show you to your barracks."

They weren't the first ones back. Half the troopers sent out were already in their bunks, sleeping. Cosmo could have curled up in the corner and slept. He was physically and emotionally drained. The hot shower was nice, but he was running purely on instinct. After cleaning up, he dropped onto his assigned bunk and fell asleep before his head hit the pillow.

The next day Cosmo and the other new arrivals to the armored division were escorted to lunch and given a basic tour of Fort

Mammoth. Much of the base consisted of research and development facilities. The main areas that Cosmo and his friends needed to know were the chow hall, barracks, and PT building. After breakfast and their tour, the group was sent to building 1A for their introduction into the Armored Division of the FGA.

"Welcome," a colonel with a blue, flat-topped cap said from the podium in front of the classroom where Cosmo and the other new arrivals were gathered. "My name is Colonel Long. I'm in charge of training here at Mammoth. You've been assigned to Armor Division because you are the best of the best. We don't do second place here; we don't settle. Armor Division is the offensive branch of the army's fight with the Ma'Tis. Infantry and artillery focus on defense; we take the fight to the bugs."

There was murmured approval. Cosmo joined in, looking at Dyson. They were both ready for payback after seeing Nash killed by the Ma'Tis and their bio-bots. At the front of the class on a large video screen, the image of a mechanized combat system appeared. It looked like a skeleton with a capsule in the middle. As they watched, a pilot climbed into the MCS, locked his feet into the legs of the device, took control of the large hydraulic arms, and closed the capsule around his body.

"This is the MCS, the flagship workhorse of the Armor Division," Colonel Long said. "Only in these power-assisted suits can we fight the Ma'Tis one on one. Here, you'll learn everything about the MCS, from maintenance to combat deployment. We set the bar high, gentlemen, and you will exceed expectations, or we will ship you back to HQ for reassignment. It's that simple. Your training begins now. I want you all lined up in the hallway outside, on the double."

The entire group seemed to move in unison, hurrying from their desks toward the exit. But before they could get outside the Colonel spoke again.

"Private Dyson, Private Frost, stay a moment please."

Cosmo looked up at his friend, who had a worrisome expression in his eye. They were the only members of the group who had lost a comrade in the mission the night before. Cosmo couldn't help but feel like maybe the assignment had been a test, and he had failed it. He and Dyson came to attention in front of Colonel Long.

"Dyson, Frost, you've been requested to join Armor Brigade. You'll need to head over to R&D building six."

"Armor Brigade, sir?" Cosmo asked.

"It's an experimental unit," the Colonel said. "That's all I can tell you. You'll find out more when you arrive. Ask for Captain Swift."

"Yes, sir!" Dyson said.

They both saluted, turned on their heels and hurried out of the classroom. In the hallway, Butler waved to them.

"Hey, what's going on?" Butler asked.

"We've been reassigned," Cosmo said.

"To an experimental unit," Dyson added.

"Oh," Butler said, clearly looking relieved that he wasn't with his former platoonmates. "Is that good or bad?"

"Can't say," Cosmo said.

"See you at the barracks," Dyson added.

They bumped fists with Butler before hurrying out of the building and starting their search for Research and Development building number six.

CHAPTER 25

ALLURA MADE six bombing runs in total. She hit five out of six of the enemy tanks. The one bomb that missed the target had impacted directly in front of the massive vehicle. The blast broke apart the tank's treads before it toppled into the crater left by the impact. It wasn't destroyed, but it was out of commission.

When Condor One landed back at Hawkstone Air Base, there was a crowd waiting for it. The pilot sent word to Allura.

"Looks like you've got a welcoming party," the pilot said. "The brass is on the tarmac."

"The brass?" Allura asked. "What's going on?"

"We got word that you're in high demand. The brass wants to see you right away."

"What for?"

"What do you think, Talon One? You pretty much single handedly took the teeth out of the Ma'Tis invasion. I didn't hear the word hero, but..."

"It was a team effort," she said, feeling embarrassed as she made her way toward the cockpit of the aircraft, suddenly hesitant to leave.

"Don't be so modest," the pilot said. "Go out and take a bow. Opportunities like this don't come along very often."

"We should go together," Allura insisted.

"Can't," the pilot replied. "We've got post-flight checks, and the brass doesn't like to wait."

She left the cockpit and went out the rear hatch of the aircraft where Captain Lansing met her. Allura could tell by her superior's frown and the way her arms were crossed that she wasn't happy.

"Welcome to the circus, Airman Presley," Lansing said.

"Sorry, Captain."

"Oh, don't feel sorry for me," Lansing said. "You're going to do more for this department than I could have hoped for."

She led Allura, who was still wondering what her CO meant, around the aircraft to where a group of people were waiting. Some were there to congratulate her. She recognized her peers in the bombardier group, and there were people from the maintenance and ordnance divisions in their dark fatigues. Most were cheering for her as if she had made the winning score in a hotly contested ball game. She was aware of the success of her mission, but she still felt that the response of the crowd was over the top.

Among the throng was a group of officers in dress uniforms. They stood clapping as Lansing led Allura to them. There were several high-ranking officers in the group, one was a colonel, and another had stars on his shoulder boards. Allura came to attention before them and saluted just the way she had been taught by the military protocol video course she had taken on Triton while waiting for the bombardier classes to begin.

The officers returned her salute, and the general, whose name badge above his numerous ribbons and metals said "Saville," stuck out his hand. She shook it.

"Welcome back, Airman Presley," he said with a broad smile.

"Thank you, sir," she said.

"That was one hell of a job out there, bombardier. Outstanding."

"It was a team effort, sir," Allura said. "I was just doing my job."

"Nonsense," the General barked. "No need for false modesty. You did what no one thought possible. Five enemy vehicles destroyed. No Air Force losses. That's a huge accomplishment in and of itself, but even more importantly, your work stopped the enemy advance. They're scrambling, trying to reestablish order. The grunts on the ground will be able to hit them hard. And most importantly, you gave the civilians in Hillsdale time to evacuate. Thousands of people owe you their lives, Airman Presley. And we can't let a thing like that go to waste. That is why I am hereby promoting you to Airman First Class."

"Thank you, sir," Allura said.

"Don't thank me," he replied. "Just keep up the good work."

A female officer, who looked like a model even in her dress uniform, stepped forward. "I'm Major Reece, head of public affairs for Hawkstone Air Base. You'll be working with me for the foreseeable future."

Allura turned toward Captain Lansing, who looked like she was furious, but kept her mouth shut.

"I'm a bombardier," Allura said. "Condor Division."

"Of course you are, and soon you're going to be the face of our winter recruiting push," Reece said. "We'll clean you up and get you on the PR circuit. I've already got my team hard at work publicizing your accomplishments. It's going to be a major marketing push. I think we'll finally get some of the college-bound applicants truly interested in joining the fight."

"I don't know how much help I can be," Allura said.

"Don't worry about that," General Saville said. "That's Major Reece's job. Now let's get you settled. I'm sure that Captain Lansing has plenty to do getting the rest of Condor ready to support the army's plan to push the Ma'Tis back into the sea."

He led the group of officers away, and Lansing waved for Allura to go with them. She had no idea what lay ahead, but all she could do was follow orders and hope that she didn't do anything wrong in the process.

Someone was sent for her belongings, which consisted of her civilian clothes still in her luggage and her rucksack with the fatigues she had been issued at the Air Training Academy on Triton. She was ushered onto a hovercraft with the other officers and whisked across the base to a tall building, which she later learned was senior officer housing. There were apartments for special guests, and Allura was put into one with a lieutenant from Major Reece's PR division.

All Allura wanted to do was get a shower and then rest. Bombing runs were both physically and mentally taxing. She felt like she needed some downtime and still wanted to get her PIP back on the local networks so that she could message Cosmo. Nothing in her short life had prepared her for the stress of the bombing runs. Tests in school had come easily to her. The practice runs on Triton had been difficult, and yet they hadn't felt like a life-or-death struggle. When-ever Allura closed her eyes, she could see Senior Airman T-Mac broken and bloody, his body slumped over the bombing controls with Ma'Tis shell-shaped projectiles lodged in his body.

"I'm Tessa," the lieutenant said. "I'm going to be your liaison."

"Nice to meet you," Allura said.

She had just stepped into the apartment. It was small, with a single room living space and two tiny bedrooms. But the wall facing the city that had grown up around the air base was transparent and gave them an incredible view. Night had fallen, and there were lights below them as far as the eye could see.

"Not a bad view, eh?" Tessa said.

"It's beautiful," Allura said.

"Rank has its privileges," Tessa said. "You should put in for officer training when you can."

Somehow, Allura's bags had already been brought to the apart-ment. While Allura took a shower, Tessa prepared dinner for the two of them. Allura was hungry when she came out of her tiny room, so she was more than a little disappointed to find out that dinner was a salad.

"I use fruit juice instead of dressing," Tessa said. "And the protein flakes taste just like real nuts."

"Oh, thanks," Allura said, wishing she had something hot and satisfying. It felt as though her life had been usurped. All she had done was the job she was assigned, but apparently, she had done it too well. "Is this all we're having?" Allura said.

"Major Reece wants you in shape for the PR push. The camera adds ten kilograms, so we're on a crash diet. But give it a try. I'm sure you'll love it."

Allura didn't love her meal. It was bland and unsatisfying, but she ate it and then sat staring out the big windows at the city lights.

"How long have you been in the Air Force?" Allura asked after Tessa had rinsed their salad bowls and settled onto the little couch next to her.

"Two years," Tessa said. "I got my associate's degree in marketing online, then got a commission to join the Logistics Division. It's going to look great on my resume when I'm ready to move on."

"This is what you do?"

"Whatever Major Reece needs. She has people doing copy writing and graphic design. I'm more of a special-projects person—her go-to, especially when we have models. I was on the pageant circuit for years and did some modeling when I was fifteen."

"Oh," was all Allura could think to say.

"It's a stepping stone, really, but I'm pretty lucky," Tessa said. "Major Reece knows all the movers and shakers in fashion and marketing. I'm thinking three more years in the Air Force, then I go into the business world. If all goes well, I'll break into a larger market by thirty—maybe Bellux Prime or Sophistica Six. The ultimate goal is to end up on one of the core planets with my own marketing firm. Hey, did you know they have rejuvenation therapy on Triton that can literally turn back the clock? I'll be there one day, just you wait and see."

Allura didn't fill her handler in on the fact that she had already been to Triton. Maybe Tessa knew it and didn't care, but Allura had known girls like Tessa in high school. They were more concerned with how they looked and who they were seen with than in anything they were being taught. Tessa obviously didn't care about Allura or the fight with the Ma'Tis. She hadn't joined the Air Force to make a difference. It was, as she said, a stepping stone to what she wanted in life.

Perhaps, Allura thought, she was no different from Tessa. Allura had joined the Air Force to be close to Cosmo, even if it was just in theory. Bombardier training had seemed like a perfect mix of academic challenge and real-world impact. She could have gone to school and gotten a good paying job somewhere. It wasn't that she couldn't make a difference in the galaxy by using her talents and intellect in the private sector, but with Cosmo forced into the fight, she felt good being able to help in some small way. But that had turned into something she wasn't sure she was ready for.

"We should really get some sleep," Tessa said. "The next few days will be so busy, and we don't want you looking tired."

"Oh, okay," Allura said, thinking that she hadn't been told when to go to bed in years.

"If you need anything, just knock on my door," Tessa said.

She stood up and waited. Allura had hoped the other woman would just go on to her room, but she waited on Allura to move. It seemed surreal. Tessa was her superior in the Air Force, but Allura was a grown woman, perfectly capable of deciding when she would go to bed for the night. Tessa didn't see it that way, and Allura didn't feel like fighting. So she got to her feet and headed for her room.

"Good night," Tessa said.

"Yeah," Allura said, feeling hollow and strange. "Good night."

CHAPTER 26

COSMO AND DYSON were left waiting in a sterile room with nothing to do but wonder what was going on. They were in R&D building six. The receptionist had led them into the waiting room, but there was nothing on the walls and nothing to do in the room. They pulled out their MACS devices and checked messages. Cosmo felt a sting of disappointment that he hadn't gotten a message from Allura. He wrote to her, just a quick note, so that she would have his FGA contact info.

"Man, this waiting is getting old," Dyson said.

"Not what I expected," Cosmo said.

"We should be suiting up in Mechs and joining the fight," he said ruefully.

"You think we're in trouble?"

"I think we worked our butts off to get here. I don't know what Armor Brigade is, but it's not what I was expecting."

"Maybe it's better," Cosmo said, but without much enthusiasm.

It took nearly an hour for the door to open and someone to speak to the two young battle troopers. Cosmo was a little surprised to see the same Captain who had questioned them about their fight with the Ma'Tis the evening before.

"Private Frost, Private Dyson, welcome to Armor Brigade," the captain said. "Follow me."

Cosmo and Dyson got up quickly, slipped their MACS devices into the cargo pockets of their fatigue trousers, and followed the captain. They went through a doorway and down a short hall with small offices on either side. At the end of the hallway, the doors opened onto a large workspace. It seemed to be part laboratory and part auto garage. Cosmo's eyes were drawn to a row of large robots. They were bi-pods with wide hips and long arms. They looked like walking battleships. There were four lasers mounted near the top of each robot's upper body, one at each shoulder and one on the side of its head—if it could be called a head. Instead of faces, the robots had what looked like tri-barrel rotating guns, the centers of which were obviously cannons of some type. The robots looked rugged and dangerous.

"What are those?" Dyson asked.

"It's your new best friend," the captain said. "It's a heavy-arms vehicle for offensive combat. I call them HAVOC drones."

"Killer robots?" Dyson said. "Aren't those outlawed?"

"Autonomous robotic soldiers are indeed outlawed," the captain explained. "These aren't that. They are built to be tethered to a battle trooper and used in combat. They're a versatile, high-powered weapon. And you two are going to be the first battle troopers to lead them into combat."

"Wow," Cosmo said. "It looks... amazing."

"Wait until you see it in action," the captain explained.

"Can't be better than a Mech," Dyson said. "I don't really see the point."

The captain nodded. He picked up a remote control and activated a holo-projector that beamed a three-dimensional Mech into the air in front of them.

"The Mech units have their place in combat, but they also have shortcomings," the officer explained. He was enthusiastic. "The biggest problem with the mechanized battle trooper is its speed and the inability to fully protect the pilot. As you know, it takes months of specialized training to pilot a Mech, and then they're only really effective in certain terrain. A hill is difficult to navigate, much less a mountain or uneven ground. If heavy rain makes the ground soft, Mechs either bog down or lose their balance. And once they go down, they are extremely vulnerable."

"So how's this better?" Dyson asked. Cosmo could hear the disappointment in his friend's voice, but Cosmo could see the potential of the new creations.

"First, we don't have to train a battle trooper to walk in one," the captain said. "That saves us months of expensive training time. Second, the HAVOC is capable of advance across every type of terrain. When needed, the arms can assist in movement, giving the platform much more stability. But the real advantage is that the HAVOC is, true to its name, heavily armed. Each one is like having fortress-level weapons that are mobile. And because the user isn't pinned inside the HAVOC, it can move at greater speeds."

"How fast?" Cosmo asked.

"They can keep up with battle troopers in MAL armor," the captain said.

"What's that?" Dyson asked.

"The armor you wore yesterday," the captain explained. "It's called movement-assisted light armor—strong enough to protect you from laser fire yet light enough to get you mobile. And as everyone knows, speed in combat is the greatest asset a trooper can have."

"How does it work?" Cosmo asked.

"That's what I'm going to show you," he said. "My name is Malcom Swift. I got my masters at TTI, and my PhD at Fulcrum Robotics on Delphi Nine. I was the youngest to complete the program. And these," he waved his hand at the HAVOC drones, "are going to change this war. Let's get you both suited up, and we'll have you synced up to your HAVOC counterparts in no time."

"Hang on there," Dyson said. "This is all a bit hasty. I'm not a drone operator. I'm a battle trooper."

"Indeed you are," Swift said, "and I'm going to make you more deadly than you can imagine. Operating the HAVOC platform will become a natural part of your actions in combat. Think of it as an extension of your body, or a tool that you can use. Once you're in armor, we can start running simulations. Trust me, this is going to blow your mind."

Cosmo could see the doubt on his friend's face. But they had been in the MAL armor, and Cosmo knew it had advantages. The Mechs were the elite fighting units in the Fiona Grand Army, and he had seen movies and television shows about them for most of his life. It would take some time to think of the HAVOC as being on par with the Mechanized units.

They went to a small changing area, stripped off their fatigues, and put on the compression suits that went under the armor.

"I've made a few improvements," Captain Swift said. "The data you brought back from the field was a huge help in perfecting the MAL armor."

"The data about our friend dying," Dyson said.

He wasn't angry. Cosmo knew him well enough by that point to know the difference between his defiant attitude and actual anger, but Captain Swift didn't know that.

"I'm terribly sorry," he said. "I do that, sometimes. I get so excited about a project that I don't take other people into consideration. I am sorry about your friend. Private Nash was a hero, and his death was not in vain."

"We know," Cosmo said.

"But I added an emergency mode to the armor, which seals it off completely," Swift explained. "And, while it isn't proven yet, I added an electrical shock feature made to defeat the bio-bots. If you are ever in that situation again, you can activate the emergency mode and once the swarm is on you, hit the bio-bots with a powerful electric current. It should kill them, but if it doesn't, it should at least scramble their processing units enough to confuse them."

"How long can we stay sealed up?" Cosmo asked as he stepped into the pants portion of the suit.

"Ten minutes or so," Swift said. "But it's also possible to have an additional air supply. The rack on the back of the armor is made for interchangeable gear, depending on the mission."

"You want our helmets on too?" Dyson asked.

"Yes, absolutely," Swift said. "You'll do a full tutorial while I get the HAVOC simulation ready. I think you're going to find that the MAL armor is much more functional than Mech armor. You won't be as strong, but you'll be much faster, and the armor is much more versatile. If things go well, you'll be able to take on the Ma'Tis in almost any environment under any conditions. The Mechs can't say that."

They pulled on their helmets and activated the suits. Captain Swift brought them out to an area of the workshop where a series of wires hung from the ceiling. The officer moved around them, plugging the various wires into slots Cosmo didn't even know were there.

"These are external monitor wires," he explained. "They will help me gauge how well you perform in the simulation."

"Can't your super suits do that on their own?" Dyson said.

"I built them to collect data, yes," Swift said. "Performance, power consumption, versatility, and damage control are all hardwired in, but it has to be downloaded. This gives me instant feedback in the moment."

"But it's just a simulation," Cosmo said. "We won't really be doing anything."

"You'll be controlling simulated HAVOC drones, and that is where the gold mine of information is coming from. Along with your own vital readings. The more data I have, the better I can make the system. All right, you're ready. Go ahead and start the tutorial."

Cosmo had used the suit before and was accustomed to the visual interface. When the helmet came on, the tutorial was there, and all he had to do was activate it with a voice command.

Welcome to the MAL armor tutorial program. Let's begin with the armor itself. Made from kinetic energy-absorbing nanofibers, the outer layer of the armor is made to endure the rigors of combat. Lined in the outer layer is smart plate technology. Thousands of interlocking tiles create hard barriers to protect the user while adapting to almost any environment to also ensure total freedom of movement. The electromagnetic current used to lock and unlock the smart plate technology is also useful for attaching weapons that are made of metal components. The thin-line hydraulic assist will enhance any movement. Users will be stronger and faster than they are on their own. Finally, the MAL battle helmet is a state-of-the-art interface that will allow the user to control the HAVOC drone platform while fighting alongside it.

The tutorial lasted half an hour. After the initial introduction, they learned how to bring up the different systems in the helmet using voice commands as well as how the retinal tracking cameras inside the helmet would allow them to control various features of the HAVOC drone. Once they finished the tutorial, Captain Swift's voice filled their helmets.

"All right, first sim is just a simple movement program. You'll get the hang of it pretty quick, I'm sure."

The interior of the lab disappeared, and Cosmo found himself in an open field. The ground was covered with grass, but nothing looked real.

"This is the HAVOC view," Swift explained. "You'll notice it's different from what you normally see. We did that on purpose. Have a look around, and cycle through the weapons on board."

When Cosmo looked down, he could see the drone's strange body. The robotic drone had arms. Its right arm ended in a human-looking hand, albeit with only three fingers and one thumb. Its left arm ended in a mechanical pincer. The drone had a series of preprogramed movements that could be activated by voice commands.

"Double cross," Cosmo said.

The drone raised its arms and crossed them in front of its body, making an X shape. It was a defensive gesture.

"Right strike," Cosmo ordered.

The drone drove its right arm forward.

"Left chop," Cosmo said.

The left arm slashed down with the pincer in a karate-chop movement. It was simple and easy. Cosmo kept playing around.

"Combo, right hook, left upper cut, double smash!"

The drone responded instantly. The series of movements were quick, powerful, and smooth. It was almost graceful, despite the squatty, ape-like shape of the drone.

After putting the drone through its paces, Cosmo simulated the various weapons. On either side of its head, the drone had tracking lasers that moved independently of its body—and two more lasers at its shoulders that moved with its body and could target anything directly in front of the drone. Then there were the internal weapons. A variety of computer-fed ammunition could be loaded into the spinning barrels. The cannon at the center fired either a heavy laser or ground-to-air missiles that were guided using the lasers on its head. Finally, both arms had built-in flame-throwing nozzles.

All Cosmo had to do was glance at something and say the command—such as "Target lasers"—and the drone responded. Their second simulation was a targeting game. Disk-shaped targets popped up in the distance or rolled across the drone's field of view. Once Cosmo and Dyson got comfortable hitting the targets, the third simulation had them switching between their own vision and the drone's visual cameras. They could be positioned at any of the four corners of the MAL battle helmet's view screen, or in an overlay mode. Cosmo could adjust the opacity so that he could see what the drone saw while still having full view of what was around him.

"Getting the hang of switching views will take some time. Sort of like learning a new video game," Swift said. "But the more you play, the better you'll get. And then we'll take the drones into the field and test them in a real- world environment."

"It's pretty amazing," Cosmo said.

"Yeah, I'm starting to get a feel for this," Dyson said.

"Your data is amazing," Swift said. "I couldn't have asked for better partners in this experiment. Do you want to take a break?"

Cosmo glanced at Dyson, who shrugged.

"No way," Cosmo said. "Let's keep going."

"Yeah, this is pretty cool, man. Load the next sim," Dyson added.

"You've got it," Captain Swift said. "Next up, Ma'Tis Incursion One. Good luck gentlemen. This one isn't difficult. Go ahead and kill a few crabs hand to hand. I've programmed the sims to be exact. I think you'll be impressed."

"Bring 'em on," Dyson said.

"We're ready," Cosmo said.

"Initiating simulation," Captain Swift said. "Here we go!"

CHAPTER 27

AT FIRST, the difference between what Cosmo saw and what his drone counterpart saw was difficult to deal with. The simulated aliens were coming up out of the ocean. To his right were sand dunes. Cosmo had to keep track of the enemies. Some were on the hills, and some were charging straight toward him. It was tempting to just put all his attention on what the drone was seeing, but occasionally one of the aliens got past the robot and threatened Cosmo. But after an hour of running the incursion simulation, he was starting to get the hang of things.

"That's enough for today," Captain Swift said. "I've had all your belongings moved here. As you can imagine, this entire operation is strictly classified. You'll have your meals here and do all of your training here."

"We're not going back to the barracks?" Dyson asked as he and Cosmo removed their battle helmets.

"No, you can't," Swift said. "Is that a problem?"

"It's not a problem," Cosmo explained. "But people will think we washed out."

"Let them think whatever they want," the captain said. "What we're doing here is going to change warfare forever. Not just on Fiona Grand, but all across the galaxy."

"I have a question about that," Cosmo said. "Drones have been used before. They don't work inside the Ma'Tis haze that scrambles electronics, right? How is this going to be different?"

"It's different on two levels," Swift said, coming out of the control room at the top of a metal staircase. "First, the haze affects electronics when the signals pass through it. So a drone controlled by a pilot hundreds of miles away loses control. Secondly, the haze is meant to protect the Ma'Tis from above. It's projected upward, not at ground level."

"You sure about that?" Dyson asked.

"You proved it," Swift said. "The MAL armor wasn't affected by the haze when you went into their ranks to check the effects of the first bomb. It wasn't affected when they came after you or when their bio-bots attacked you. That's how I know."

"Are you saying we were in experimental armor that might not have worked?" Cosmo asked. "We might have been killed if the armor had failed."

"I knew it wouldn't," Swift said.

"How exactly did you know?" Dyson asked.

"Because the data doesn't lie," he said. "The HAVOC and MAL armor technology is built on the observed data of the enemy."

"But I read that the bombers can't use computer targeting because of the haze," Cosmo insisted.

"That's right. In the air, the haze is very potent. But on the ground, it is weak. And proximity combined with a simultaneous, multi-frequency command stream ensures that the HAVOC platforms will work."

"In theory," Dyson said.

"Yes, yes, in theory," Swift said. "But I'm betting my reputation as a scientist and an officer that it will."

"It's your reputation, but it's our lives on the line," Dyson said. "We didn't volunteer for this."

"Do you want out?" Swift asked, clearly incredulous that anyone would choose not to be involved in his research.

"No," Cosmo said. "We're not saying that."

"Well then, trust me," Captain Swift said. "This is going to turn the tide in our struggle with the Ma'Tis."

Their quarters were an improvement over their barracks. They shared living quarters and the bathroom, but they each had their own small bedrooms. Meals were brought into the R&D building. And they had a small exercise space in the corner of the workshop laboratory. The next day they practiced actually moving the HAVOC drones around. For the most part, the robots stayed in a given position behind their controls. Cosmo and Dyson walked the robots around the lab like pet owners at a park. Then they sent the robots around using their helmet controls. Moving the robot was more difficult than it sounded, requiring well-timed voice controls.

"Forward, half speed," Cosmo ordered, sending his drone, through a narrow obstacle. "Halt. Half turn right... forward half speed."

Dyson called his drone Nut, and Cosmo named his Bolt. They were looking forward to getting their counterparts out of the lab and into the field. During their downtime, Cosmo tried to connect with Allura, but she wasn't returning his messages. He couldn't help but feel worried that something was wrong until Dyson got his attention the night before they scheduled for their first field exercise.

"Hey, Cos, ain't this your lady?" He said, casting a video from his MACS to the display wall in their shared living space.

On the wall, a news reporter was with Allura on a stage. There were people all around. Allura looked different. She had on fancy makeup, and she wore a dress uniform with medals dangling from her smock. Cosmo was shocked.

"Yeah, that's her," he said. "Turn it up."

The volume came on and the reporter smiled.

"So you gave up a full scholarship to the Triton Technical Institute to join the Air Training Academy?" the interviewer asked. He was a handsome man with a dazzling smile and dimples in both cheeks. The crowd seemed enthralled with him. Cosmo felt a stab of fear. Perhaps Allura wasn't messaging him back because she had fallen in love with someone else.

"That's right," Allura said. "Bombardier training allowed me to use my intellect to really make a difference right here on Fiona Grand. And with the Service First plan, I'll be able to continue my education when the time is right."

"She's hot, man, I'll give you that," Dyson said.

"She's not acting normal," Cosmo replied.

"Dude, she's on stage in front of all those people. You'd be nervous too."

The reporter smiled, and said, "That is truly amazing. You are a modern-day hero, Allura Presley. And there are thousands of people here who want to show you their love and appreciation."

"In that case, I'm calling out the men and women like me who have the chance to make a difference. Don't wait to be drafted or rule out a career in the armed forces. Join me in fighting the Ma'Tis. Nothing is more important."

A website flashed across the bottom of the screen. The reporter called out Allura's name as if she were a celebrity, and the crowd went wild. A voice off screen said, "Now we go to Saint Stevens where Elizabeth Steel is with Allura Presley's proud parents, Eugene and Victoria Presley."

The picture changed to the high school football stadium. There were hundreds of people there, and Allura's parents were on a stage. A woman in a long gown held a microphone and began to interview the Presleys.

"This is surreal," Cosmo said.

"Yeah, seems like your lady is a big celebrity. There's a story about the bombing of the Ma'Tis vehicles. They ain't said nothing about us though. Not even about Nash."

"Of course not," Cosmo said. "They have to spin it as if the war is just a wild adventure. They can't have people reminded that it's a deadly enterprise, can they? What's the word on the offensive against the Ma'Tis?"

"It's happening," Dyson said. "There's stories of troops being mobilized, but no actual details. I think they must be using the bombing to distract from the real fighting. Apparently, hitting a target from that high up is really hard. Lots of math and stuff since they can't use computer-guided missiles."

"And she took out five of them," Cosmo said. "At least that's what this story says."

"Yeah, she's the only bombardier from ATA in the Air Force right now. The rest are recruited from the rank and file but don't have the same training."

"So they're using her to keep the public distracted," Cosmo said.

"And drum up more recruits," Dyson said. "They want more college types, I suppose."

"I was on my way to business school when they drafted me."

"You mad, bro?"

"Not anymore," Cosmo said. "I want to be here. I want to fight, but what are the odds we make it out alive?"

"Who knows?" Dyson said. "But they need to get us out of here soon. I'm about to lose my mind up in this place."

"Me too," Cosmo said, looking at a news story that had a big close-up of Allura in her dress uniform.

He found it hard to sleep that night and wrote Allura a long message. He didn't know if his messages were even getting through to her. Maybe Captain Swift was blocking their messages to make sure they didn't tell anyone about the HAVOC program. But that didn't make sense because he had a dozen messages from his mother. She had volunteered to help with the wounded and had struck up a friendship with Sergeant Reed. Cosmo didn't care who his mother made friends with, and he certainly wanted her to be happy, but he couldn't fathom his gruff, never-happy drill sergeant being friendly with anyone. So he tried not to think about it.

The next day, they were loaded into a big cargo truck and taken off base. They drove for over an hour, and when the truck finally stopped, they were in the middle of nowhere. It was actually a beautiful mountain valley. Boulders were set up long one side of a wide, grassy meadow between two towering mountains. And at the far end of the meadow was a beautiful lake.

"All right, gentlemen, you can activate the HAVOC drones," Captain Swift said.

He was in the control compartment that was set up in the front of the cargo truck's long bed. The rear hatch was open, and with a command, the drones activated. Cosmo and Dyson used voice commands to guide them out. The big robots made their way down the ramp and followed the battle troopers out into the field.

"All right, start with a quick run to the end of the valley," Swift ordered.

They ran and the drones followed, keeping up, step for step. In tracking mode, the huge drones followed behind the two troopers, with Cosmo's slightly to the right and Dyson's slightly to his left. The two battle troopers on their own were formidable, but with the drones they made a really scary group. The HAVOC platforms packed major firepower.

"All right, come back one at a time, moving through the stone monoliths," Swift ordered.

Dyson went first, sprinting around the boulders that were as tall as he was. Nut followed. The drones had object recognition that kept them from running into things. The robot followed right at Dyson's heels, and when they reached the end of the line of stones, it moved back to the side, bringing all its weapons to bear. Cosmo followed. He loved running in the MAL armor. It was a little like being on a fast vehicle. The suit compensated so much and propelled him along faster than he would have thought possible. As he ran, the drone thumped along behind him. Cosmo sped up and slowed down, just testing the robot. If it had stepped on him, he would have been hurt, maybe killed, but testing the drones was the purpose of the exercise. After their run, Swift ordered Cosmo and Dyson to get weapons.

"I've modified the X-cal laser rifles," Swift said. "We swapped out the grenade launcher for plasma rounds. That should keep the bio-bots at bay. And the superheated gel will also burn through the crab shells. Try them out."

Cosmo checked his safety, then popped out the magazine on the bulky rifle. It was filled with silver shells. He reinserted the magazine, worked the loading lever to feed the first round into the breech, then flicked off the safety.

"All right, here we go," Cosmo said.

"Let it rip," Dyson said.

They fired at the same time, shooting a single round at the nearest boulder. The shells hit and popped apart. The chemicals inside reacted to the oxygen in the air, heating so fast they turned red and made the rock smoke.

"What's the range, Lt.?" Dyson asked.

"Forty meters under normal conditions," Swift replied.

"You take the third boulder; I'll take the first," Cosmo said.

"You got it, sharpshooter," Dyson agreed.

They fired again, both hitting their marks. The shells were heavier than bullets and reacted more like the grenades. But the splatter of the superheated gel was wide, and it was obvious they would be much more effective than the grenades against the swarming bio-bots.

"All right, let's test the weapons on the drones," Swift ordered.

It didn't take long before most of the boulders were little more than piles of rubble. The HAVOCs were walking arsenals. And the sim training was paying off. Cosmo and Dyson could move freely, firing their rifles and directing the fire of the drones. They even climbed halfway up one of the mountains together. All in all, the test was a complete success.

When they were back on the truck and headed to Mammoth, Captain Swift leaned back in his seat and crossed his hands behind his head.

"Tell me you couldn't take out a platoon of crabs with the HAVOC drones," he said. "This is a total game changer."

"If they work as well in battle as they did on the test today, I'd agree," Dyson said.

"And there's only one way to know if you're right," Swift said. "Which is why tomorrow we're joining the fight."

"What?" Cosmo asked. "We're going to fight the Ma'Tis tomorrow?"

"There's no reason not to," Swift said.

"Spoken like a true officer," Dyson said.

"You guys know what I mean," the captain said. "The infantry is dug in at strategic locations around the Ma'Tis forces. They still have three of their cannon vehicles, but they haven't pressed inland yet."

"What are they doing?" Cosmo asked.

"Just congregating together," Swift said. "No one knows why for sure. But we'll be switching from defense to offense tomorrow, and you two are the tip of the spear."

Cosmo looked at Dyson, who raised his eyebrows. They had trained and worked for the opportunity to fight the Ma'Tis. But they both understood the stakes. The aliens were dangerous. Still, they were itching for a chance to get out of the lab and actually do something for real. Cosmo just hoped it wouldn't be the last thing they ever did.

CHAPTER 28

"I JUST THINK this isn't the best use of my skills," Allura said. "I should be with my division, running missions."

"No one is running missions," Major Reece said. "The Ma'Tis are consolidating. The Army, as usual, is dragging its feet. And even if they were in the midst of a major offensive, there's nothing more important than keeping the public on our side. That's the job, or mission if you like that vernacular better. You're doing more good here than you ever could on a battlefield."

Allura thought the Major's attitude was way out of line. Some people thought of themselves or their work as more important than anything else. That much of the Major's point of view was at least understandable, but thinking that public relations was more valuable than saving lives was absurd to Allura. Still, she was smart enough not to voice her contrary opinions to her superior directly.

"You're killing it across all our target demographics," Lieutenant Tessa said. "Girls, fifteen to eighteen are tuning in. You're a celebrity."

That compliment didn't have the effect the young officer was expecting. Allura had never been eager for the popularity of her peers. It's not that she felt like she was better than anyone else, but she simply had too many interests to spend her time trying to fit in. Her mind was curious and her intellect such that she enjoyed learning a wide variety of things. And what other people thought about her wasn't really all that important to her.

"We have a duty to maximize this opportunity," Major Reece said as she looked at herself in the reflection of the mirror in what was supposed to be Allura's dressing room. But the PR officers used it more like a prison. They had taken her PIP and closely guarded any communications she was getting. Perhaps it was for the good of the Air Force, but Allura had her doubts.

"It feels like I'm just doing the same thing over and over," Allura said. "They ask the same questions; I give the same answers."

"It's called staying on topic," Tessa said, trying to brush a little more makeup onto Allura's face.

"You stick to the scripted responses," Reece said. "We're strengthening the brand message here. I hope you can see that. It's all about communicating to the masses and getting people interested in what the Air Force is all about."

Allura understood, but she just wasn't enjoying her work. Not that she expected to have fun all the time, but she had enlisted to be a bombardier. It was the one place she felt like her unique skills could really make a difference. Getting interviewed on TV and webcasts was not.

"Recruiting numbers are up," Tessa said, checking the information on a large data slate she kept in a designer flip case. "Your media campaign is working."

Allura sighed. Over the past week she had gotten used to being the third wheel on the PR team. Reece and her subordinates often left her completely out of their conversations and sometimes talked about her like she wasn't even part of the media blitz. At first it had made her angry, but it didn't take long to see that nearly everyone on the PR team was focused solely on their career. Allura understood the importance of being good at one's job and wanting to maximize a person's career opportunities, but she couldn't see how the entire team, from Major Reece down to Lieutenant Tessa, had no concern for the war effort at all.

"General Saville will be pleased," Reece said. "The old goat better not try to steal the credit."

"You'll be promoted," Tessa said. "There's no way they deny you a promotion at this point."

The door to the dressing room opened. The staff of the television show seemed unconcerned about privacy. Allura was glad she was fully dressed when the producer stepped in and said, "We're going live in sixty seconds. You're first up on today's show. It's best if you move to the set now."

"We're ready," Major Reece said, speaking for Allura.

Tessa held the door as Major Reece followed the producer. Allura fell into line behind her, and they made their way through the dirty, unglamorous bowels of the television studio. At first, Allura had been curious about the major networks she had watched growing up. But the shine of show business quickly faded when she experienced it for herself. It was all glaring lights and constant primping. The sets were fake. Behind the scenes seemed like chaos, and all she really wanted was to get back to Condor Squadron.

"Here we are," the producer whispered.

When the host called her name, Allura actually had to step around Major Reece to get past her in the narrow passageway that led onto the stage. The audience applauded. Allura wasn't the first female to make a splash in the military, but she was the darling of the moment. She walked out onto the stage, gave a short wave to the audience, then shook hands with her host.

"Bombardier Presley, welcome to the McClaire Show," the host said. She was a middle-aged woman with blonde hair. The crowd continued, to clap as Allura sat down on one of the uncomfortable chairs. She sat up straight in the dress uniform Tessa had picked out for her and kept her hands in her lap.

"It's good to be here," she lied with a smile.

"It's so exciting and, dare I say, refreshing, to have a young, intelligent woman volunteering for the Air Force. What made you sign up?"

She had been asked the question at every interview she had done. Not once had she told the truth—that she wanted to be involved because Cosmo had been drafted. Instead, the scripted answer was all about the intellectual challenge and helping the war effort on Fiona Grand.

Allura gave the scripted answer, remembering to smile the way

Tessa had emphasized when prepping her. The host couldn't help but interrupt her before Allura had even finished. The older woman obviously loved to talk. And just like every other show Allura had been on, they didn't care about her accomplishments in the Air Force. It was only about what would get their show more viewers. Allura couldn't wait for her story to become old news. Then she could go back to Hawkstone Air Base and rejoin her squadron.

The questions were easy, and before she knew it, the interview was over. The audience clapped as she left the stage. Allura passed the next guest, an author whose book was being promoted by the television host.

"All right, we've got a photo shoot in half an hour," Tessa said, reading from her data pad. "Then three web interviews and an appearance at the Cosmopolitan Society gala."

"The red-carpet shoot will be picked up by everyone," Reece said. "Tell me the gown is ready."

"They have it back at the hotel now," Tessa said. "We've got hair and makeup scheduled for seven."

They continued to talk about their jobs as if Allura were just a commodity. It seemed like the PR tour would never end. All Allura could do was follow along and try to make the best of it.

"Oh, my gosh!" Tessa suddenly declared grabbing the Major's arm as they neared the elevators. "Check your messages!"

"What?" Reece asked.

Allura thought they sounded like teenagers who just got asked to prom.

"This is fabulous," Major Reece said. "We'll announce tonight at the gala."

"We can extend the tour," Tessa said. "I'll make plans for more media events. We'll smash every recruiting record they've got."

"What's going on?" Allura asked.

They both turned as if they were surprised to see that she was even there.

"The PM has decided to give you the Gold Star for Meritorious Service," Reece said.

The Major turned back to her associate, and they made plans. Allura knew what the Gold Star Medal was. It was issued by the government and was the highest award a member of the military could get. She felt a sour twist in her stomach. She didn't deserve the award, she knew. Having been on the media tour, she understood that so much of what happened in the military was as much about political maneuvering as it was about achieving military goals. The prime minister was going to use Allura as a way of putting a positive spin on his military draft mandate. As the other officers talked about extending the media tour and making plans for the award ceremony, Allura felt the dark funk of depression descending over her. Somewhere, Cosmo was making a difference, and she had become a poster girl for the Air Force. It didn't seem right. And yet she had no say in the matter. She couldn't even message to share her frustrations with the person she cared about most in the galaxy. She was a prisoner to her own success, and there didn't seem to be an easy way out of the obligations that went with it.

CHAPTER 29

"WE KNOW what they're doing because it's exactly what we'd do in that same situation," General Sanjay said. "They're digging in. Building a defensive perimeter."

"How do they expect to survive aerial attacks if they hold one position," Major Zukov asked.

"They've still got three tanks," the General said. "They've essentially circled the wagons. There's no way for our birds to get in behind them to drop ordnance."

"They're learning from their mistakes," Captain Swift said.

Cosmo and Dyson were standing at the back wall of the command tent. They had spent the day traveling with their HAVOC drones to the battlefield. The Ma'Tis were gathered together in one place. The crab-like aliens were busy building defensive bulwarks around their position. The army was gathered too, but neither side was ready to launch an offensive.

"Yes," the General agreed. "And we can't let them stay here for long. Any day they might send more up from the ocean, and we've essentially lost the ability to push them back."

"They can land as many troops as they like?" Swift asked.

"More or less," the General said. "From this base, they can mount raids to more populated areas. They can also bring in reinforcements."

"But we could flank them, sir," Zukov said. "Hit anything new they bring up."

"With this group here," General Sanjay said, pointing at the hologram that showed the Ma'Tis on a map of the surrounding area, "they can strike at us from both sides. They're claiming this ground, gentlemen, and there's not much we can about it without losing a lot of soldiers in the process."

"Sir," Zukov said. "Send me in. I volunteer to take the fight to the Ma'Tis."

"That's noble, Major, but a direct assault is suicide. Even Mechs won't be able to scale their defenses or make a difference," the General said. "We need to lure them out into the open."

"The HAVOCs can do that," Captain Swift volunteered. "We're fast, sir. Send my squad in and we'll make them so uncomfortable they'll have to come out after us."

Cosmo didn't like Captain Swift's train of thought. He was volunteering the HAVOC drones, but that meant Cosmo and Dyson would be in the line of fire too. And if Swift was right, it meant having an army of aliens chasing after them.

"It's untested tech, General," Zukov said. "Mechs are the only proven division to have success in offensive encounters with the Ma'Tis. Sir, my battalion stands ready to engage the enemy. We'll destroy their position and force them to move out."

"Unless they obliterate your forces with their heavy laser cannons," Swift said. "Mechs can move fast enough for evasive maneuvering."

"They have to keep those cannons pointed at the sky," Zukov said.

"The problem is we can't guarantee what their tanks are capable of. The after-action reports from their initial invasion showed those tanks to be deadly," The General said. "That, combined with their defensive posture and their numbers, gives them an edge over us."

"All the more reason to test the HAVOCs, sir," Swift persisted. "Two special operators are all you are risking."

Cosmo looked at Dyson. The big man's jaw was flexing, but he didn't speak. Cosmo understood that they were battle troopers trained to fight the Ma'Tis, but he didn't like the idea of taking on an army of aliens with just two humans and their drones. It didn't matter that they were fast in the MAL armor or that the HAVOCs had more fire-power than a platoon of battle troopers.

"It would be a good test," General Sanjay said.

"Or we might just be kicking the hornets' nest," Major Zukov declared.

"In which case I want your Mechs standing by in a support role," the General said. "We'll have infantry in position to ensure the crabs don't advance. We need to shake things up, Malcom. Get the bugs out of their lair so we can hit them. The Air Force has strike teams sitting on go. But first we have to take down their laser batteries. Can your drones do that?"

"Yes, sir," Swift said. "The HAVOC drones have enough fire-power to disable their tanks."

Cosmo knew that Captain Swift was making a claim they couldn't yet prove. The Ma'Tis tanks were huge vehicles with multiple high-power cannons. Cosmo had been close enough to one during the battle for Lois Station to see that they were armored. It would take more than small arms to bring one down.

"Then get it done, Captain," General Sanjay said. "You make this happen and I don't have to promise you the funding for your new creations. The government will throw the money at your feet. But only if your drones can deliver."

The General turned to Cosmo and Dyson. Both of them snapped to attention.

"You pilots do your best out there," General Sanjay said. "Give 'em hell, but don't be heroes. Is that understood?"

"Yes, General!" Cosmo and Dyson replied in perfect unison.

"Very good. Let's get everyone ready. We may only get one shot at this," the General said.

Captain Swift led the way out of the command tent. They went to the big hover-truck where the HAVOC drones were kept. As Cosmo and Dyson suited up in their MAL armor, Captain Swift laid out his plan.

"I'm loading thermite mortars," he said. "They've got a range of two hundred meters. You drop a few on their tanks. The thermite will burn through the armor and give you target points."

"What about the thousands of Ma'Tis?" Dyson said. "You think they'll really just sit back and let us take down their artillery?"

"No, but you'll have two advantages. Your weapons have a greater range, and you are faster."

"We can't win a war all by ourselves," Cosmo said. "There's too many of them."

"Your job isn't to win the war. It's to take down at least one tank. You do that, and they can't cover every direction with their heavy lasers."

"Any chance the General calls in the bombers?" Dyson asked.

"Exactly. You take out one tank, we've got a shot at hitting them from the air. You take out two, and we'll slaughter them from above."

"Two tanks," Cosmo said sarcastically, "piece of cake."

"No one said it would be easy," Captain Swift said. "Just keep in mind that all eyes are on us right now. Go show them what you're made of."

Cosmo strapped on a belt around his armor. It had fifteen loops. Six he stuffed with battery packs for the laser rifle. And the other seven were filled with magazines full of plasma rounds. He and Dyson slung rocket launchers over their shoulders and used the magnetic clamps to fasten the rocket-propelled grenade rounds to their chests.

The HAVOC drones, Nut and Bolt, were armed both internally and with large rail guns that looked like rifles. They were too big for battle troopers and were normally carried by Mechs. The big robotic drones looked deadly.

"I think it's time," Dyson said. "Let's see what these bad boys can really do."

Cosmo laid his bulky LA6 over/under tactical rifle on one shoulder and marched out of the hover-truck's long cargo bay. People were watching. They tried to look casual, but it seemed obvious to Cosmo that they all wanted to see what was in the truck. He and Dyson in their MAL armor weren't really new. The armor had been seen, and even used, by other battle troopers. It was a serious upgrade to infantry plate armor but a full step down from Mech hardware.

And then the HAVOCs were activated. Cosmo brought Bolt out of the cargo area. The wide robot moved easily down the ramp. It should have stomped, but its thick legs had powerful struts that allowed the drone to move with a mechanical grace that was unexpected. The huge rifle it carried and the variety of mounted hardware, on the other hand, were exactly what one expected to see. The HAVOC was the very definition of a killing machine. And it got the attention of the crowds. Everyone in sight was military; many were veterans who had seen combat. But they hadn't seen anything like the HAVOC drones. They were tall and wide like the Ma'Tis but heavy with defensive armor and bristling with weapons.

"Don't make a scene," Captain Swift said from the control center in their cargo truck. His voice in their helmets made it seem like he was standing right beside them. "Save that for your triumphant return. The enemy is fifteen kilometers due east."

"Roger that," Dyson said. "Just a quick jog."

"Only you would call fifteen klicks a quick jog," Cosmo said.

"Hey, in this armor, it is. Time to put these gizmos to the test."

They set out at a steady jog. The MAL armor made running easy. There was no impact on Cosmo's knees or hips, and the legs of the armor seemed to almost spring up. He was in motion, fully in control of his body, but the armor negated almost all of the resistance. It was like jogging in zero gravity, if that were possible.

They passed a platoon of Mechs marching out from the main body of troops gathered on the grassy plain around the temporary forward operating base. They came out in formation, carrying big rifles just like the HAVOC drones. To Cosmo, they looked like mechanized skeletons. There was something dangerous about the Mechs, and their pilots were tough individuals. Each one had the pilot's call sign printed down one leg, and they had huge fighting knives as part of their weapon supply. The blades were bigger than swords, and so heavy a regular battle trooper could hardly lift one.

A new voice sounded in Cosmo's com-link on the command channel. "Good luck, HAVOC Squad. Mech Platoon Delta has your back."

"Thanks Delta," Cosmo said. "See you downrange."

"Copy that. Give 'em hell," the speaker from Delta platoon said.

"Cut that chatter," the stern voice of Major Zukov demanded.

Cosmo and Dyson pressed on, quickly leaving the FOB behind. The plain wasn't as flat as it seemed. There were soft, rolling hills, like swells in the ocean. The grass waved in the breeze. It had turned a light gold color. The soil was soft underfoot, and they made good time. It didn't take long for the Ma'Tis to come into view. From the prairie they couldn't see as far as they could from the hill overlooking the sea, but after the first ten kilometers, the big tanks and the brown hills of dirt the aliens had built up came into view.

"Would you look at that?" Dyson said. "The bugs have been busy."

"Wild to think they could do so much in such a short time," Cosmo said.

"I have a question. Why are we attacking them in broad daylight?"

"I suppose it's because the bombers can't hit them at night."

"It would be better if we were doing this just before dawn then," Dyson suggested. "There's no cover out here."

"What's the range on those rifles the drones are carrying?"

Captain Swift's voice broke into their conversation. "The HC8s are loaded with thermite mortar rounds. They can reach as far as three hundred meters under the right conditions."

"What are those conditions?" Dyson asked.

"Good weather, no wind, and downhill," Swift said. "I would push the drones in to about one hundred fifty meters and hammer those tanks."

"At one fifty, won't they be in range of the Ma'Tis?" Cosmo asked.

"Negative. Their laser arms are only effective up to a hundred meters. You should be fine."

"Unless they shoot those pointed projectiles they use to take down aircraft," Dyson said. "They're known to use them against the Mechs."

"That's because Mechs and most aircraft can't move like you can," Swift said. "If they fire those projectiles at you, just move back."

"Easy for him to say," Cosmo claimed. "This could be a total disaster."

"Yeah, that's the right attitude," Dyson said.

"Sorry, bro, but you have to admit this is a little crazy."

"It is, and that's why I like it. Give me an audacious plan any day of the week."

"Weren't you just saying it would be better to attack in the dark?"

"Well, yeah, but it's too late for that. If we can see them..."

"They can see us," Cosmo said, instinctively checking his rifle. He flicked off the safety and used voice commands to ensure that Bolt had all weapons ready to fire.

"Bolt is ready. All weapons hot."

"Nut too," Dyson said. "Ready to get this party started."

"Yeah, send 'em."

The two battle troopers slowed, but their counterparts sped up and spread apart. Cosmo zoomed his helmet's telephoto view in on the tank that was nestled behind a sloping wall of dirt. There were crabs on the ramparts of their fortress, and more on the tank between the big laser turrets that were pointed up toward the sky.

"Keep an eye on those guns," Cosmo said. "Distance is three kilometers."

"We should have brought long-range rifles," Dyson said. "We could sit out here and ping those bastards all day."

"Distance twenty-five hundred meters. The Ma'Tis are on the move."

"Getting close enough to use the rifles won't be easy."

"Spin up your rotating machine guns," Captain Swift said, his communication signal starting to break up as they approached the Ma'Tis. "Load the armor-piercing rounds and push the enemy back as you approach."

"You heard the man, and you know the plan," Dyson said. "Time to bring the heat."

"Fifteen hundred meters to the tanks," Cosmo called out. "Approaching units are eight hundred meters."

"They hive is on alert," Dyson said. "There's hundreds of them coming to the top of the wall."

"I hope they stay up there," Cosmo said. "They make easy targets. Approaching bugs are five hundred meters."

"I've got movement on the tank," Dyson said. "They're swiveling one of the laser turrets toward us."

"Three hundred meters," Cosmo said. "Time to fire."

They both gave the order, and the HAVOC drones began to spew armor-piercing bullets. They blew apart the hard shells of the Ma'Tis charging out to fight them. It was a short, one-sided massacre. The drones fired at such a high rate of speed that it was obvious the slow-moving aliens couldn't get within range to use their laser weapons. They began to fall back, but as Cosmo jogged in behind the drones, he could see blobs of bio-bots seeping from the aliens.

"We've got trouble," Cosmo said. "They've released the bio-bots."

"I see them. We can't really get much closer."

"Can't stay still long either. That cannon will target us any minute."

They gave their drones the order to fire their mortar rifles. The robotic drones held up the weapons and fired. Dark projectiles launched upward, curved in the air, then fell. Cosmo emptied his drone's load of mortars in quick succession. Most fell onto the bulwarks of their makeshift fortress, but a few dropped onto the tank. The thermite exploded and burned with intense heat, melting the metal plates almost like acid. Where they hit the ground they threw up clouds of dirt and turned the ground into molten sludge. Cosmo couldn't see much through the debris clouds, and what he did see wavered from the heat, refracting the light.

Dyson targeted the laser turret that was turning toward them. The bombs hit the rotating base and one even hit the laser barrel itself, which turned bright red and then bent in the middle.

"Time to rock!" Dyson shouted.

They both had rocket-propelled grenade launchers strapped to their backs. They were simple devices. The grenades were loaded with rocket fuel, and the nose was a grenade. The launchers were basically hollow tubes that directed the flight of the projectiles, but they were notoriously easy to knock off course. Even a strong breeze or dust in the air could alter their flight path. Still, the low-tech weapons were perfect for use against the Ma'Tis haze.

Cosmo dropped to one knee, pulled the launcher from his back, and took aim at one of the holes in the side of the alien tank. The grenade shot out like a spit wad being launched from a straw. It left a contrail in its wake as it streaked up over the dirt-works and into the side of the tank. It missed the hole and blew up on the side, hardly damaging the thick metal armor.

"That was a bust," Cosmo said.

"Close but no cigar," Dyson said.

As he loaded another rocket-fueled grenade, he ordered Bolt to fall back and dialed up the drone's thermobaric rounds. It fired in a sweeping spray across the growing blob of bio-bots. The thermobaric rounds were low-impact cartridges that sprayed chemicals around them when they hit the target. The chemicals burned in the air, expanding and spreading heat. They didn't burn hot like the phosphorus in the thermite mortars or even the plasma in the LA6 rifles. But it did get hot enough to cause the bio-bots to pull back.

"Gotta get closer," Cosmo said, getting to his feet and starting to run.

"We got movement on both sides, bro. We need to pull back or we run the risk of getting surrounded."

"Nothing else matters if we don't disable that tank," Cosmo insisted.

"But we'll be surrounded."

Cosmo looked over his shoulder. He could see a group of Ma'Tis crabs moving toward him. There were easily a hundred, probably more. He looked the other way and saw even more crabs pouring over the bulwarks to flank them from the other direction. What they needed was time, and it was quickly running out.

"Dyson, I've got a plan. Pull back."

"What are you doing?" Dyson cried.

"Trust me," Cosmo said, hoping he wasn't just fooling himself.

The Ma'Tis tank was a massive object. He was over a couple hundred meters away, and yet even at that range it was huge, dominating the landscape. Even the towering earthworks, which were twenty meters tall, seemed small in comparison. The tank was easily a hundred meters wide and close to thirty meters high. The treads were huge, the laser turrets like something one would find on a battleship. Cosmo remembered what one blast had done to the upper floors of the admin building at Lois Station. In a fraction of a second, tons of metal and concrete were vaporized, not to mention the people who had been on the upper floors.

"This will work," Cosmo insisted. Then to himself he said, *it has to work or I'm going to die.*

CHAPTER 30

HE HAD SEEN it in a movie. A western set on a rural planet. The scene in the movie hadn't been all that different from where Cosmo was at that moment, a grassy plain. In the movie, a fire had caught on the dry grasses and was racing toward a group of settlers. It had seemed they would all be burned alive, but the leader of the group did something Cosmo had never seen before, and it stuck with him.

Running, he shot with the laser blaster of his LA8 one handed, pointing up the dirt mound as he closed in on it.

"Cosmo!" Dyson said. "Get out of there!"

There was no time to look at what the Ma'Tis were doing. Or even to focus Bolt on a new target. Instead, he pressed his bulky rifle onto his armor, which held it fast like magnets on the door of a refrigerator. Then brought up the grenade launcher. Out of the corner of his eye he saw the bio-bots as they swarmed over the crest of the hill the aliens had built up. But there was no time to fight them. He steadied his body, aimed at the gaping hole near the top of the tank, and fired. The rocket-propelled grenade shot out, flying so fast it was hard to track. But it was well aimed and didn't get knocked off course. Instead, it shot into the alien vehicle and exploded.

For a moment, everything slowed down for Cosmo. The grenade's explosion was loud and immediately followed by a series of blasts inside the armored vehicle. In that moment, nothing else mattered. The tank shuddered and then smoke belched from the gaps in the plate armor. It came shooting from the barrels of the massive guns. Finally, the entire vehicle crashed down on one side. It was, as far as Cosmo could tell, completely out of commission.

"You got it!" Dyson shouted.

Cosmo had already dropped the grenade launcher and was sprinting back from the hill with a swarm of bio-bots on his heels.

"Get back in comms range!" Cosmo ordered his friend. "Call in the Air Force."

"What about you?"

"No time," Cosmo said. "Keep Nut working though."

Cosmo wasted no time in pulling out his bulky rifle and activating the plasma shooter. He fired quickly as he spun around, but not at the swarm. Instead, he fired in front of them, laying down a line of plasma that blocked their progress. The bio-bots were resourceful. They could link together and rise up over an obstacle, but the heat from the plasma was rising upward too. The bio-bots tried to build a bridge over the obstacle, but the heat was too much, and they withered.

Moving quickly, Cosmo kept firing. He made a circle around himself and Bolt, emptying four magazines in the process. It didn't take long for the swarm of bio-bots to surround him, but the tiny mechanical organism couldn't find a way through the plasma. He hadn't connected the superheated gel all the way around him in an unbroken line, but the heat killed the bio-bots that tried to sneak through. And then the Ma'Tis came down en masse. They were furious that he had wrecked their tank, and while they didn't have faces he could read, their antennae waved furiously, and their massive claws cracked as they snapped them closed over and over again.

His control of Bolt wasn't perfect either. They weren't moving, but he would pause for a second to adjust the big drone's aim. It was firing laser blasts. The big laser tore through the throng of aliens. Even their exoskeletons couldn't stop the concentrated energy beams. And the lasers on the drone's shoulders fired in rapid succession, taking down any enemies directly in front of the big drone. Cosmo would fire with his rifle, back on laser mode to hold back the enemy on his side of the circle, but he had to stop every few seconds to adjust the aim of the drone.

As effective as the pair were, they wouldn't have survived without Dyson's drone, Nut. He had run back to report in just as Cosmo had told him to do, but that left him free to fully control his counterpart. Nut ran past the circle of superheated ground where Cosmo was fighting and fired at the oncoming aliens. Lasers and armor-piercing rounds filled the air. The Ma'Tis were shooting too, but they couldn't get close enough for their laser blasts to be effective. The impact-absorbing fibers of the MAL armor turned the weakened energy into power for the suit.

There were bodies falling everywhere, but despite the massive advantage in firepower, it was clear to Cosmo that they couldn't hold out forever. The plasma on the ground was cooling with every second. The bio-bots huddled back, waiting for the chance to strike again. If help didn't come soon, he wasn't going to make it.

"I'm running low on ammo," Cosmo called out as he ejected a spent battery and shoved his fourth one from his belt into the LA6. "Bolt's down to one-third power."

"Hang on. Help's on the way," Dyson said.

Cosmo shot a crab, then stepped back between Bolt's massive legs. He flipped the switch on his rifle to activate the plasma and started shooting the ground again. In the movie, the leader of the group of settlers had taken a torch and burned the grass all around their live-stock and hovercraft. He burned a big circle around the group, and when the grass fire came rushing toward them there was no fuel left to burn. The fire essentially hit the burned area and split like water around a boulder in a river.

The same concept was working with the swarm of bio-bots, but the plasma cooled when exposed to the air. What started as a few thousand degrees cooled quickly. Cosmo had just enough plasma rounds to reheat his circle, but once it cooled again he would be exposed. And while he was firing at the ground, the Ma'Tis warriors moved closer. One laser beam hit with so much force it felt like someone had punched Cosmo. He looked up and fired a plasma round at a bold crab who was scrabbling toward him. The cartridge hit the creature in the middle of its body, which was the thickest part of the shell. Cosmo had no idea if the plasma would burn through, but it did burn. Smoke boiled up into the alien's face and caused it to stumble backward.

"Incoming, incoming!" Dyson shouted. "Brace for impact."

All that Cosmo could do was to grab onto Bolt's massive leg. He didn't hear the bomber, but he heard the bombs. There were several ships flying in formation. They dropped several napalm bombs, which sent fire boiling through the ranks of Ma'Tis and spewing from the fortress. The bombers were in low altitude. The two leading ships dropped high-yield warheads onto the tanks that were still operational. For a while, it seemed like the world was about to split open. The ground actually rolled with waves, like the oceans. Dirt, debris from the tanks, and body parts from the desiccated aliens flew into the air and rained down on Cosmo. The drone took the brunt of the impacts. Smoke, clouds of dust, and walls of flame surrounded them. Even with the enhanced vision capabilities of his battle helmet, Cosmo couldn't see. One bomb landed so close that the shock wave knocked Cosmo backward. It also toppled Bolt, who fell directly onto Cosmo. The crushing impact would have killed him if not for the MAL armor that locked together at the last possible second to form a protective shell.

Another bomb exploded in the earthworks near their position and nearly buried them in dirt. By the time Cosmo crawled free, the battle was over. The Ma'Tis were in full retreat back toward the ocean, and the Mechs were stomping past to clean up the stragglers.

"You dang fool!" Dyson said as he approached with Nut right behind. "I thought you were dead for sure."

"Me too," Cosmo said. "Bolt's pretty jacked."

"Yeah, some of those bombs were off the mark," Dyson said. "But you did it."

"We did it," Cosmo insisted. "You called in the big guns."

"Yeah, and next time do that together."

"Had to take down that tank," Cosmo said. "Bolt paid the price though."

They both looked at the HAVOC drone. It was dented, dirty, and damaged. The lasers on the top of its robot head were missing, one of the lasers at its shoulder was hanging by wires, and there was dirt in the big main gun that protruded from its chest.

"Yeah, I don't think it's going to work right for a while," Dyson said. "Good first test though."

Unfortunately, not everyone agreed with Henry Dyson.

"It was too much risk," Captain Swift said. "These machines aren't mass produced at the local factory, Private Frost. Your job is to use the HAVOC to achieve mission outcomes, but not at the expense of the hardware."

"It wasn't his fault," Dyson said. "Bolt didn't get damaged until the bombs were dropped."

"He shouldn't have been so close to their fortress," Swift insisted.

"Tell me about it," Cosmo said. "I won't make that mistake again."

"You're lucky to be alive."

"But it worked. The HAVOC drones did what they were supposed to do," Cosmo insisted, and again, not everyone agreed.

Major Zukov was irate when Cosmo was brought into to General Sanjay's command tent at the FOB for the mission debriefing. "What did they do that our Mechs couldn't do?"

"No one was killed," Captain Swift said. "Statistically, that's a perfect mission outcome."

"Your toy was wrecked," Zukov argued.

"We sustained damage in the bombing, but it's repairable," Swift said. "I'll have it running in a few days."

"Why were you so close to the fortress?" General Sanjay asked.

"We had to be," Swift answered.

"I wasn't asking you, Captain," Sanjay replied. "Private Frost, why were you so close to their bulwarks."

"Sir, the mortars worked well against the tanks, but getting explosives inside them was more difficult. We had to get close to make the shot."

"Rocket-propelled grenades are notoriously poor at hitting their targets," Swift pointed out.

"Why not send in the drone?"

"I had the RPGs sir."

"But isn't that what the drones are for?" the General asked. "To keep you out of harm's way? And correct me if I'm wrong, but what happens when the operator gets hurt or killed."

Cosmo looked at Captain Swift. "In that instance, the HAVOC drone can be slaved to another operator, or if the drone is in range, by the controller at the base."

"It's a risk, isn't it?" General Sanjay said. "I don't want to belittle your contribution to the battle, Private Frost. But money and time has been invested in this experimental unit, and I don't want setbacks. Not when we're dealing with a threat of this magnitude."

"Yes, sir!" Cosmo said.

"My Mechs could have done just as well," Zukov snapped.

"Could two of them have accomplished the same result?" General Sanjay asked.

Zukov bristled, but he knew he couldn't claim that two Mechs could have done the same thing that Cosmo and Dyson did.

"Could even four?" General Sanjay pressed the Major.

"I think it is possible," Zukov said.

"I think it highly unlikely," the General said. "Frost and Dyson have proven themselves enough that we should give them what they need to continue on with this program. But at this stage, I think it's best that you do that back at Mammoth. That is all."

"Yes, sir," Captain Swift said. "Thank you, sir."

He and Cosmo left the tent. They were halfway back to the hover-truck when Zukov caught up with them.

"Malcom, your science experiment is a complete failure and a waste of resources," the Major said.

Cosmo and Captain Swift stopped walking and turned to face their superior officer.

"The brass disagrees," Swift said.

"The brass don't know you the way I do," Zukov said. He turned to face Cosmo. "He'll get you killed. Mark my words. If you know what's good for you, find a way to get transferred out of his command."

Cosmo didn't reply but just stood back, at ease, but trying to be respectful. Swift stepped closer to Zukov. "This isn't what you think it is, Nigel. Please, just give it a chance."

"You're a fool. There's a reason they outlawed killer robots. You may have found a loophole, but you're playing with fire. All of you."

He stormed away. Captain Swift looked embarrassed, and uncertain what to say.

"Home then, sir?" Cosmo said.

"Yes, home," the captain said, looking relieved.

But Cosmo wondered just what Zukov was talking about and if something about the HAVOC drones was dangerous. They seemed as benign as any tool that is used for war. A gun is deadly, but when handled correctly, it is a powerful tool. The drones seemed to be the same, but maybe Capt Swift wasn't telling them everything.

CHAPTER 31

ALLURA WAS KEPT in a little tent on the capitol grounds while Fiona Grand's prime minister schmoozed his way through the throng of guests. At times, she peeked out to see what was happening. The award ceremony was being held on the wide lawn between the capitol building and the PM's mansion. It was to be followed by a state dinner, which in turn would be followed by a ball. The award ceremony was full of media reporters, which Allura had been told would be excluded from the dinner and only allowed to take part in the red-carpet event leading up to the ball. Each segment required a special invitation.

"Who's out there now?" a man in an army dress uniform asked. He was in a hover-chair and had only one arm and no legs. Most of his hair was missing, and there were surgical scars crisscrossing his scalp.

"Lots of news people and a few politicians," Allura said. "And senior officers too."

"All out to see the freak show," the man in the chair said. "Wish I could see it."

"Who's the freaks?" an older woman asked.

"The politicians of course," the man in the chair joked.

Allura wasn't sure she could keep up a positive attitude if she were in the man's situation. His name was Vernon Riley, a former staff sergeant in the army where he had served until his platoon was overrun by the Ma'Tis. Vernon was the only survivor, but Allura wasn't sure she would even say that he survived. He had lost his legs, one arm, most of his memory, and his sight after being torn apart by the aliens and left for dead. He suffered brain trauma and was in constant pain, which he tried to quell with pain pills that Allura knew would eventually kill him.

The older woman was there to receive the Medal of Remembrance after having lost both her sons in the war. It was obvious to Allura that no medal would ever heal the woman's broken heart. Nor did she seem to want to be there. The woman had unveiled hostility toward the government and all politicians.

Allura tried to sit down, but she was nervous. News of a major victory had broken, but without a PIP or access to an information terminal she had no idea what was happening in the war. Allura had never tried to keep up with news about the war when she was growing up. But since becoming a bombardier and having Cosmo on the front lines, she was desperate for information. Unfortunately, her handlers didn't care what she wanted. Major Reece and Lieutenant Tessa were busy working the crowd along with the prime minister.

"How much longer do you think this is going to last?" Vernon asked.

"Who can say?" Allura said.

"Politicians never get in a hurry," the older woman said.

Allura paced. She wasn't nervous or fearful of the crowds. Being in front of people had stopped giving her anxiety pretty early on in her media tour. But she felt like she was needed elsewhere, and instead she was stuck pretending to be honored by all the attention. What she really wanted was to go back to Condor Squadron at Hawkstone Air Base and rejoin the fight.

Eventually Major Reece returned to the tent where the ceremony's *guests* were being kept secluded. It felt more like she was a prisoner than a guest of honor. There was no honor in the smelly tent or uncomfortable folding chairs they had been given as they waited for the ceremony to begin.

"Almost time," Reece said. "Remember, every news agency on the planet and many from around the galaxy are here for this. Smile, stick to the script, and don't do anything that might distract from our branding."

"Of course," Allura said.

"That's my girl," the Major said.

Allura bristled at the condescending nature of Reece's reply. She hated all the attention. At first, she could almost believe that her actions on the bombing runs had been special. She had in fact done something that no one else in the military was able to do. Not that they couldn't do it, but they weren't trained. And high-altitude bombing took knowledge, experience, and a certain touch that Allura had learned from her friend at ATA, Celeste Sha'Andar. But any honor for her accomplishment was quickly overshadowed by the unveiled desires of everyone around her. The news media wanted a story. Talk shows wanted viewers, and network interviews were all about getting clicks. They all saw Allura as a tool to get what they wanted. No one cared about her or the war effort or what she had accomplished. She was a springboard to something else. Even Major Reece was using Allura to enhance her career and get a promotion. And the Air Force as an organization was using her to increase their recruiting efforts.

"Tessa will come for you and lead you all onto the stage. Good luck," the Major said, as if the outcome of the ceremony were in question.

Allura had learned that nothing in politics or the media was ever left to chance. Everything was staged—from what a person wore to where they stood. And certainly every word spoken was written beforehand. In every interview Allura had been told what questions would be asked and had been given a script of approved answers. She wasn't being interviewed; she was playing a role. She was a trained monkey with a job to do, but not the job she had enlisted for.

Another half hour passed before the group of medal recipients were called up onstage. When Tessa came to the tent, she seemed almost giddy.

"It's time," she said, beaming.

"What's with you?" Allura asked.

"I just met Carlos Santana from Triton Galactic," she said. "He gave me his card and told me to keep in touch. Can you imagine? I've met more people at this event than the rest of my career combined."

"How great for you," Allura said, but Tessa didn't realize she was being sarcastic.

"I know, right! And he's so handsome. He'll be at the ball, and if I play my cards right... well... who knows."

"Everyone knows what you're saying, honey," the older woman said with a frown.

Tessa looked distressed for a split second, then her grin returned, and she led the trio from the tent. Vernon went first. His hover-chair moved gracefully over the capitol lawn. The older woman went next. Allura felt bad for her. They hadn't even exchanged names. The poor woman was so distraught when they first brought her into the tent that Allura gave her space. Bringing up the rear, Allura could hear the military band playing a triumphant song as they marched up on stage. There were a few politicians there waiting. One tried to take Vernon's hand to shake it, but the exchange was awkward. The older woman's scowl kept the others away. Instead they flocked to Allura.

"Welcome to the capital," one woman in an expensive suit said.

"Congratulations," a white-haired man said. "We are watching your career with excitement young lady."

"Thank you," Allura mumbled.

From the crowd came the sound of cameras snapping pictures and a few people clapping. The prime minister was then brought out to great applause. He was surrounded by his cabinet of advisers, who tried to crowd onto the small stage with the guests. Allura looked out over the faces. She was shocked when she saw her parents there. They were basking in the moment, surrounded by politicians all looking to land a photo op with the proud parents. In the distance were the towering buildings that she had seen on television all her life. It was Allura's first visit to Hallsberg, or what many people called "Capital City," and she had spent the entire time in a musty old tent.

"Welcome," the prime minister said from the podium that was at center stage. "It's an honor to be here today with the people who have sacrificed so much for our freedom. For decades, the Ma'Tis have threatened our liberty and demanded our constant attention. As many of you know, a recent invasion was thwarted by the selfless deeds of our valiant military forces. Today we honor just a representative few of the people who stand in the gap for us day after day. And as a world in the Union of Human Planets, we say thank you."

There was more polite applause. Every word was being recorded —every gesture and expression captured on video and broadcast around the world and through the galaxy. Allura stood on her spot, which was marked with tape that actually had her name printed on it. She tried to remember to smile and not lock her knees or fidget as Lieutenant Tessa had repeatedly instructed. She didn't want to draw any more attention to herself than necessary or do something embarrassing that might be caught on video.

"First, we as a grateful planet, present the Silver Star for Valor to Staff Sergeant Vernon Riley, sole survivor from Infantry Platoon Echo, Marshal Company, Fifth Battalion, of the Fiona Grand Army."

An aid to the PM stepped forward and hung a medal around Vernon's neck. The maimed soldier tried to smile and waved with his remaining hand as the crowd clapped. His chair moved him back to his spot, and the older woman stepped forward.

"Miss Anita Lewis, it is an honor to share this award with you," the PM said.

Allura guessed that sharing was exactly what the PM had in mind. He didn't want the sadness or suffering caused by losing two children to the war, but he very much wanted to share in the acclaim and perceived honor of the older woman's sacrifice.

"We are each called to make sacrifices in life, but none are as great as losing our children in service to our planet. For that sacrifice, we are eternally grateful and award you the Plantary Medal of Remembrance. May this small token be a reminder that your children did not die in vain."

More applause, but with a bit of reserve. Anita Lewis didn't smile or respond. Allura saw tears on her cheeks as she returned to her spot in the line.

And finally it was Allura's turn. It felt strange to be getting the highest award in the military. She had only done her job and was anxious to return to it. Walking to the designated spot on the stage, Allura did her best to keep smiling. Unlike in most media events where spotlights made it difficult to see the crowds of people, in the bright daylight of the award ceremony she could see the faces. There were around three hundred reporters and as many politicians in the crowd along with a handful of senior military officers. Allura didn't look at her parents. Perhaps there would be time to see them and talk to them later, but at that moment all her attention was on standing still and trying not to look nervous.

"Finally, we award the Gold Star for Meritorious Service, the highest honor in the military, to Airman First Class Allura Presley. When the call went out in our time of need, Ms. Presley answered that call. Having spoken with her parents today, I know where that selfless sense of service comes from. I also know they are extremely proud of their daughter.

"Ms. Presley walked away from a full scholarship to the Triton Technical Institute to join the FGAF and take up bombardier training at the Air Training Academy on Triton. After graduating at the top of her class, she came home and immediately put her skills to use. Many of you know that she was able to make high-altitude heavy ordnance drops with such precision that it crippled the Ma'Tis advance on Hillsdale and saved thousands of lives. Bombardiering is both dangerous and extremely difficult. Without the aid of computers or outside guidance, our bombers put their lives on the line to give air support to our ground forces. It takes courage, intelligence, and nerves of steel, which Airman First Class Presley has demonstrated for us all. But what you may not know is that on her first bombing mission, she survived when her bomber was forced to make an emergency landing that crippled the aircraft and trapped the copilot. Her fellow bombardier, Senior Airman Tony Makinsey was gravely injured. Airman Presley pulled her compatriot free from the wreckage, secured him to a gurney, and moved him over five kilometers to safety. And Airman MaKinsey is alive today because of her heroic efforts."

The prime minister, a master orator, paused while the crowd cheered. Allura wondered about T-Mac. She had asked Major Reece and Lieutenant Tessa to check on his progress, but they were always too busy. It was a relief to know he was alive and recovering.

"That's the kind of heroism we are honoring today," the PM continued. "Self-sacrifice, commitment to our great planet, intelligence, and courage under fire. These are the hallmarks of our military, and Airman First Class Allura Presley has and continues to demonstrate them all. It is my pleasure to award her with the Fiona Grand Gold Star for Meritorious Service."

An aid stepped forward to hang the medal around Allura's neck. But the prime minister stepped in, took the medal, and put it over Allura's head himself. They shook hands and the politician smiled. Allura felt like she was gazing into the eyes of a large, predatory animal. Then the PM leaned forward as the crowd applauded. He whispered in her ear, his hot breath puffing against her neck.

"Great work, darling. I'll be seeing you tonight."

He straightened, still smiling. If there is an opposite of flushing with embarrassment, that is what Allura felt. Her blood seemed to run cold, and she felt small, weak, and vulnerable next to the lifelong politician. He was a powerful man, and she wasn't sure what he meant by the remark, but it didn't feel right.

There were questions for the PM, and Allura moved back to her spot. After a few moments as the PM talked about the route of the Ma'Tis forces outside Hillsdale, Anita Lewis leaned over and whispered to Allura.

"Be careful," she said. "I've seen that look before."

"What?" Allura asked.

"Men like that, they don't respect you as a person. They see us as playthings, just pawns that exist for their enjoyment. I wouldn't get caught alone with him."

Allura looked at the older woman. There was compassion in her gaze, but Allura didn't know if Anita Lewis was right or if her disdain for the government that had claimed her children was behind the warning. Either way, Allura didn't feel comfortable. And it seemed like the award ceremony was never going to end.

CHAPTER 32

"FINALLY, A NIGHT OUT!" Dyson said. "I was beginning to think we'd never get a night off."

"I think we've earned it," Cosmo said. "What do you want to do?"

"Get a drink and see if this place has any pretty girls, bro. You know?"

Cosmo did know. He knew he wasn't old enough to drink and that he had a girlfriend who was on every talk show and newscast. On the way back from the battle, he had discovered that she was even getting the Gold Star for Meritorious Service, the highest honor bestowed on a member of the military. He was happy for her but frustrated that she wasn't answering his messages. Of all the people he knew, Allura was the last person he would have thought that would ghost him. Still, until he knew with absolute certainty that their relationship was over, he wouldn't risk it by flirting with other women.

"I got your back, man," Cosmo said.

They were both in civilian clothes for the first time since getting drafted. Captain Swift was busy with repairs to Bolt, and that left the pair of battle troopers with nothing to do but celebrate their victory on the battlefield. They left R&D building six and headed off base. They didn't get far before trouble found them.

After catching a hover-cab to a bar they had heard about before even arriving at Mammoth Base, they found themselves in an older building. The walls were covered with pictures of platoons and banners from different battalions. There were even old weapons on the walls. Some of the photos showed battle troopers standing over the bodies of slain Ma'Tis warriors.

Dyson went straight to the bar, ordered a beer, then looked around. There were other people hanging around. Most were at tables, but a few lingered near the bar. A jukebox in the corner belted out music. The big man leaned against the bar and looked around.

"Some place, huh?" he said.

"Yeah," Cosmo said after ordering a soda. "This is amazing."

"Not many honeys though," Dyson said. "We'll have to cross over to the civilian side of town I suspect."

"You have it all planned out?"

"Gotta make the most of this time off," Dyson said.

"We could be called back into action tomorrow."

"I doubt that. Seems like it'll take the Captain at least a few days to get Bolt back in working order. We should be good."

"Should be... but we better not get too crazy."

"I didn't take you for an uptight prude, Frosty. Come on, man, we gotta let our hair down."

When his beer came, Dyson drank half of it in one long pull.

"Oh, man, yeah," the big man said. "I been missing this."

"First liberty?" the bartender asked.

"Since we were drafted," Cosmo said, taking a sip of his soda.

"The draft is a real shame," the bartender said. "In my day, the FGA was an all-volunteer fighting force."

"How long ago?" Dyson asked.

"Enlisted in twenty-nine, served my twenty and retired with full benefits. Now I run this place."

"It looks older," Cosmo said.

"Yeah, it's been around a long time. I bought it from an old veteran who bought it from another. Same decor though. Same drinks, same atmosphere. It's an institution, you know. Welcome to the service, fellas."

"Thanks," Dyson said.

"You missed the big fight 'eh? I bet that was something. Haven't seen the bugs push so far inland before."

"We didn't miss it," Cosmo said.

"We were there," Dyson said. "Your boy here turned the tide."

"It was a team effort," Cosmo argued. "I just carried the ball over the goal line."

"You two are the robot jockeys I heard about?" the bartender asked.

"HAVOC operator is the official job description," Dyson said. "But yeah, that's us."

"Outstanding. Some people don't like change, but I say as long as it works, I'm for it. Great job out there. First drinks after an official engagement are always free. Drink up."

"Hey, thanks," Cosmo said.

"In that case, I'll take another," Dyson said.

They stayed for half an hour. Most of the time they wandered around, looking at the memorabilia on the walls. Neither of them noticed the group of four men watching their every move. When they decided to move on, the group of four followed them outside.

"Hey," a big man with massive biceps called out.

Cosmo turned and saw the four men hurrying toward him. It didn't occur to him that they were looking for trouble. He smiled, just as the big armed man threw a looping haymaker. The punch didn't really land. Cosmo saw it coming and tried to avoid the blow, but couldn't get out of the way in time. The big armed man's knuckles scraped across Cosmo's cheekbone and ear. The punch, barely landing, still hurt and ignited a fury in Cosmo who lashed out with a fast kick to the big-armed man's groin.

Beside him, a tall, lanky man hit Dyson. The man's T-shirt had the name Cephas stenciled on the chest. Beside him was a shorter man with a barrel chest and hairy forearms. The punch caught Dyson's cheek and caused him to stagger back several steps. The shorter man charged in after him.

Dyson had broad shoulders and long arms, which he raised to defend himself. As the short man rushed in, Dyson threw out a quick jab. The punch hit the short man in the nose and sent blood flying, but he didn't slow down. Diving forward, the short man wrapped his arms around Henry's legs, lifted him into the air, and slammed him down.

Four on two was a difficult fight. Cosmo grabbed the hair of the man who had hit him and was about to smash his knee into the big armed man's face, but the fourth man charged into him. The shoulder charge sent Cosmo staggering sideways, straight into the lanky man named Cephas, who grabbed him. Cosmo tried to pull away, but the lanky man held him fast.

As the fourth man came at Cosmo, he reared back with one fist. The fourth man was older than the others, with a mustache and wrinkles around his eyes. Cosmo saw the punch coming but couldn't escape. Instead, he lifted his legs and kicked out. One boot missed, but the other caught the mustached man in the face. The older man's legs flew out from under him, and he landed hard, just as Cosmo sank to the ground and out of the lanky man's grip.

Beside them, the stocky man who had slammed Dyson to the ground dropped onto one knee on top of Cosmo's friend. He punched Dyson in the face. Blood poured from the black man's nose and stained his teeth as Dyson's lips pulled back in a snarl. He bucked his hips so hard the short man flew over Dyson's head. He scrambled to get back to his feet, but Dyson was faster. He rolled over, gathered his feet under him and tackled the short man, who was face down.

Fights weren't rare in the army as recruits tested one another. And fights outside bars were common all over the galaxy. The patrons in the bar heard the commotion and moved to the windows and doors to watch. The bartender called the cops. Soon sirens could be heard, but not by Dyson, who was in a rage. He hammered his elbow straight down into the side of the short man's head. The blow knocked the man unconscious, but Dyson hit him again just before the man with big biceps grabbed him.

"Get off!" the man shouted at Dyson, who turned, grabbed a fistful of the big-armed man's shirt and got punched in the jaw for his trouble.

Dyson staggered sideways and tripped over the legs of the short man who lay unconscious. Nearby, Cosmo was yanked up by Cephas who drove a punch into the younger man's kidney. Pain shot through Cosmo's body. His back arched and he staggered forward. Cephas grabbed his arm, spun him around, and then pulled his fist back, intending on hitting him again.

"Cops!" someone shouted.

Cephas glanced toward the hover-car that was speeding toward them. They were right on the outskirts of Mammoth Base, and MPs were running toward the fight too. The split second of hesitation was enough for Cosmo to grab the lanky man's wrist and give it a savage twist. Bones snapped and Cephas screamed in pain. Cosmo was in a blind rage. He yanked the lanky man toward him and drove his palm up into the man's chin. The lanky man's head snapped back, and his feet flew up. He crashed hard on the ground, knocked senseless by the palm strike.

The man with big arms and his companion with a bloody mustache bolted away from the scene, but not before kicking Dyson hard in the ribs. Cosmo was still in a rage and started to chase after them but got hit with a taser by a police officer rushing to the scene of the fight. One moment he was completely focused on chasing down the two runners, and the next his lights just switched off. He fell to his knees and then toppled to the ground, his body convulsing from the sudden surge of electrical current.

The next thing Cosmo knew, he was waking up in the back of a patrol car. His hands were in restraints, and he was slumped against the door. Beside him, Dyson groaned.

"What happened?" Cosmo asked.

"They tased you, bro," Dyson said in a weak voice.

"Oh," Cosmo said, drawing the word out as he straightened up. "Where are they taking us?"

"Back to base," the police officer in the driver's seat said. "The Army can sort you two out."

"I think that punk broke my ribs," Dyson said.

"Why'd they attack us like that?" Cosmo asked.

"Beats me," Dyson said. "But I hope I see 'em again. They won't get the jump on me twice."

The patrol car hovered near a building that Cosmo didn't recognize. It was an ugly square block with a tall fence around the back. The car settled onto the ground with a thump that made the passengers wince. Then the policeman got out and came around to Cosmo's side of the vehicle. He opened the door.

"Last stop," he said. "Everybody out."

It wasn't easy getting out with his hands bound by plastic restraints. Cosmo's entire body ached and his muscles felt weak as he stood up. The policeman turned him around and removed the restraints as Dyson climbed out of the car. His hands were bound too, and he was hunched to his right, favoring that side of his body.

"Did you get the bastards who jumped us?" Cosmo asked.

The two you assaulted are headed to the hospital," the policeman said as he led them into the building.

"What's this?" the desk sergeant asked.

"These two idiots were fighting outside the Liberty Bar," the policeman said.

"That's off base, not our problem."

"They're military, and that bar is in the overlap," the policeman said. "You can book them or send them to the brig or whatever you do."

"You've seen too many war movies, bub."

"Not me, I'm too busy doing paperwork and breaking up the fights you yahoos cause. Good luck with these two. They put two men in the hospital."

"Civilians?"

"No, they're your people too."

"Fine, I've got them, but you owe me one."

"You catch civilians fighting on base, you can bring 'em to me."

"Like that will ever happen," the desk sergeant complained as he walked around the counter.

"Not my problem," the policeman said, pushing out the double doors and hurrying to his squad car.

"Tell me what happened," the military police sergeant said.

"We had a couple drinks," Dyson said. "Then we were headed to town. As soon as we were out of the bar, four guys jumped us."

"What'd you do to piss them off?"

"Nothing," Cosmo said. "Never even noticed them inside."

"And they just attacked you for no reason?"

"That's what happened, Sergeant," Cosmo said. "We were just defending ourselves."

"Four against two and you sent *them* to the hospital?" the sergeant asked, clearly not believing a word Cosmo and Dyson were saying.

"Scout's honor," Dyson said, holding up a three-finger salute and wincing in the process.

"How bad are you hurt?" the sergeant said, leading them around the desk and into a holding area.

"Busted a rib, maybe," Dyson said. "I'll live."

There were benches in the open and a heavy-duty cage in the corner. Cosmo didn't want to be locked up, but he had no say in the matter. Fortunately, the sergeant directed them to the benches, not the cage.

"How much were you drinking?" he asked.

"I had two beers," Dyson said. "My boy wasn't even drinking."

"I'm not old enough to drink, Sergeant," Cosmo said.

"New recruit?"

"Drafted, both of us," Cosmo explained.

"I knew it. We've be lousy with discontents after the prime minister ordered up the draft."

Cosmo didn't reply, and the sergeant walked over to his computer. On the screen a window popped up with various video feeds from different places around the base. The sergeant tapped one and it enlarged. He backed up the feed to see the fight, which was caught by the security cameras at the gate where Cosmo and Dyson had left the base.

It was tempting to say, *see, I told you*, when the sergeant watched the fight. Instead, he kept his mouth shut hoping the sergeant would see things from their side. He opened a file, typed in some information, then asked their names.

"Private Cosmo Frost, Armor Brigade, 87114."

"Private Henry Dyson, Armor Brigade, 87159."

The sergeant typed it all in. Copied the security footage of the fight. Then put them both in a booth to get a full body med scan. Dyson's ribs were bruised, but not broken. Cosmo had no lasting damage other than two slight burns from the taser darts and some bruises from the fight.

"All right, I'm filing a report," the sergeant said. "We'll have to get the names of the men you fought from the hospital. If they won't give up their friends, we'll run them through facial recognition. It's going down as an open investigation and there could be charges, but at this time I'm sending you back to your unit. Any questions?"

"No, Sergeant," both said.

"Try and stay out of trouble, okay?"

They both nodded as he opened the door. They walked slowly past the big desk and out of the building.

"Man, what the hell was that?" Dyson said. "We didn't do a damned thing."

"I don't know," Cosmo said.

"Those guys had to have a reason for giving us a beatdown."

"Can't say what it was. Glad we're not in trouble though."

"Not in trouble yet," Dyson said. "You heard the sergeant. It's an open investigation. That kind of thing follows you around, bro."

They hobbled back to their quarters in R&D six. Dyson climbed into bed with an ice pack on his face and another on his ribs. Cosmo cleaned himself up and then checked his MACS. There were still no messages from Allura. He got into bed, wondering what she was doing at that same moment.

CHAPTER 33

ALLURA DIDN'T SEE Vernon or Anita again. Tessa informed her that they were staying at the PM's mansion. It was a great honor, she was told, but they were too busy for Allura to think much about it.

After the award ceremony, the trio of medal recipients formed a line. Reporters came by, shaking hands and handing out cards. They all asked for interviews and Allura was thankful she could point them to Lieutenant Tessa. Afterward, she was whisked away by Major Reece and taken inside the mansion, which was a massive building. She was going to stay in the Cushner bedroom, named after the first person to set foot on Fiona Grand. It was a big room full of antique furnishings and gilded fixtures. Allura thought it was the type of place her grandmother would have enjoyed. But there wasn't enough time to relax. Makeup and hair stylists came in and went to work. Allura would attend the state dinner in her dress uniform with the navy-blue jacket and matching skirt. She had never worn the skirt before, and she didn't like being tugged and painted by the stylists. When they were done, she looked completely different, as if she were playing dress-up or attending a cosplay event.

"You can eat," Major Reece told her. "But there will be several courses. It's better to take small bites and go slow."

"Put your fork down between bites," Tessa suggested.

"I know how to eat," Allura said.

"Yes," Major Reece said. "We've seen that."

"Hey, don't blame me if you only give me sixty seconds to have a meal after doing interviews for hours," Allura said.

"Just remember, everyone will be watching you," Tessa told her.

The truth was, very few people noticed her at all. Allura was seated at the PM's table along with seven other diners. The PM was joined by several powerful politicians and two well-known actors. They were all focused completely on themselves, at least to Allura's point of view. After the first few minutes, no one even spoke to her again. They talked about politics and complained about the opposing parties. It was dreary and depressing. The food was good, but Allura took the advice of her handlers, who sat across the room at a table full of senior officers from the command staff. In between, there were celebrities, government officials, and more politicians. A jazz band played in one corner, and once the final course was served, people began to move around from table to table, talking. Allura stayed in her seat. Occasionally, someone came over and congratulated her. One by one, the senior officers all stopped and saluted Allura, which she found unnerving. It was a privilege that came with receiving the military's highest honor, but it only made Allura uncomfortable.

Her parents were there too. Her father wore a tuxedo and her mother a fancy dress. They spoke to every celebrity in the room before finally coming to her table.

"Hello, dear," her mother said.

"Mom," Allura replied.

"Isn't this amazing?" her father said, looking around to make sure he hadn't missed introducing himself to anyone he thought was important.

"It is," Allura replied.

"We're so proud of you, honey," her mother continued. "You know we weren't happy when you enlisted, but you've really made us proud."

"Couldn't be more proud," her father said.

"So you don't think I'm throwing my life away?" Allura said, using the words they had used when she told them she had enlisted.

"No, of course not," her mother said.

Allura would have pulled out her PIP and showed them the message they had sent her, but she didn't have it.

"How are things at home?"

"Oh, you know," her father said, still looking around the room. "Just the usual."

"But people are talking about you," her mother said. "I've saved every article and interview. I've got a special data drive just full of them."

"That's great," Allura said without much enthusiasm.

"Look, that's Byron Taggert," her father said, pointing across the room at a tall man in a custom suit that was clearly twice as old as the woman in the skintight dress who was clinging to his arm.

"From the *Galaxy Files*?" Allura's mother asked. "I love that show."

"And he was in that movie, *Traitor's Destiny*," her father said. "Come on, we've got to get a picture with him."

Allura's parents hurried off without even saying goodbye. The dinner was a who's who of entertainment and politics. Fortunately, it didn't last long, and Lieutenant Tessa hurried Allura back to her room for a change of clothes before the grand ball began. It was mind numbing, and Allura was getting tired. She had been paraded like a prize animal at a county fair. Awarded the highest prize, yet little more than an oddity to gawk at before she was sent to the slaughterhouse. Allura didn't like to think of the danger in being a bombardier, but she couldn't deny it, not after seeing T-Mac's bloody body. Still, she would rather risk the dangers of a bombing run than be at the capital. When they got to her room, Tessa brought out a sequined evening gown.

"No way," Allura said. "That's not happening."

"It's a black-tie event," Tessa argued. "You can't show up in uniform."

"Then I won't go," Allura insisted.

"You have to go; you're the guest of honor."

"No one will even miss me."

"You're going. Don't make me pull rank," Tessa said. "Now hurry up and get dressed. You're not the only one who has to get ready, you know."

Allura looked at the gown. It was stunning, but she wasn't the evening gown type. She preferred comfortable clothes, something baggy that concealed more than revealed her figure. Not that Allura was unattractive, but she was a naturally modest person. Unlike most of her classmates, she hadn't sought surgical enhancements of her body. She might have, but Cosmo thought she was perfect just the way she was. It had seemed like a blessing at the time, but faced with the reality of wearing an evening gown to a celebrity ball, she began to rethink her decisions.

The dress fit, which was no surprise. Major Reece had brought in tailors who took all her measurements and fashioned her dress uniforms to custom fit Allura's body. The gown hugged every curve, but to Allura's eye it revealed every flaw. She didn't have an hourglass shape. Her body was more of a rectangle, but there was nothing she could do about it. The low-cut front was made with extra padding to accentuate her natural size, and the waist area had a hidden band that cinched tight to make her seem thinner than she was. The slit in the side of the dress came up high on her right thigh, and the back of the gown was cut so low it reached her lower back. It felt a little like being stuffed into a mold of what her body should be.

The hair and makeup stylists returned. The foundation they applied covered every flaw and even made her skin look darker. They used strategic contouring and highlighting to make her face seem more angular and less round. They lined her eyelids with dark lines and painted the areas around her eyes with a rich purple with flecks of silver. They drew her lips on around her mouth, then filled in the space with thick gloss. Her hair was braided into a dozen strands that were then wound up and pinned into place on top of her head. When she saw herself in the mirror she didn't just look different, she wasn't even sure she looked human anymore.

"This isn't me," Allura said.

"We aren't trying to present you to the world," Major Reece said. "You reflect the brand messaging. This is your role, and you will go to the ball. The red carpet entrance is the most important thing you'll do. Take your time. Pose for pictures. Be friendly to the reporters and any other guests that come along. Again, there is no hurry. We need as much publicity as we can get from this. Think of it as your crowning achievement in an already stellar career."

Allura wanted to argue that her career had just begun, and walking a red carpet wasn't what she joined the Air Force to do. But there was no arguing with the PR officers who, for the moment, had complete control of her. They were both in dazzling gowns as well. Their excitement about the event was undeniable and Allura sincerely wished that she shared their enthusiasm, but she didn't.

After getting dressed and worked on by the stylists, they made their way to the lounge just down the hall from the grand staircase that wound down to the reception room. A long corridor from there led to the ballroom, and the entire walk from the top of the staircase to the ballroom would be recorded. She could hear the reporters and photographers in the reception room and beyond.

"Now, take your time at the top of the stairs," Reece said. "You can look around but keep smiling. You're a modern woman in a modern military. You kick ass on the battlefield and break hearts in the ballroom. Do you understand?"

"I'll do my best," she said without much enthusiasm.

"Do you know how many people around the world would kill to be here tonight?" Tessa chided her. "You're at the center of the most exciting event on Fiona Grand. You're wearing a designer dress that cost half a million credits. Downstairs there are, actors, athletes, musicians, artists, and most of them are single and ready to mingle."

"Take advantage of the moment, Airman," Major Reece told her. "Odds are good that you'll never be in a position like this again for the rest of your life."

That was such a relief to Allura that she actually smiled.

"That's it, girl," Tessa said.

"You'll be great. Just take your time, be nice, and stick to the script," Reece insisted.

Allura didn't hurry, even though she wanted to. She wanted to blow through the red carpet, make a token appearance, and then slip away before she had to do anything that might really embarrass her. The evening gown was bad enough. She had never worn anything so revealing in her life. When her friends had pool parties, she and Cosmo would sneak off to the movies. Her idea of a good time was perusing a bookstore and sipping a fancy coffee, or ordering in while she binged watched television with Cosmo at her side. She wondered where he was and what he was doing at that moment. It had to be better than parading around for strangers who saw her as something she wasn't.

When she reached the top of the stairs, she paused and looked down. The wide, curved staircase was beautiful, but in the reception room below were dozens of reporters, every one of them with some type of camera. The bottom of the stairs led to a walkway with velvet ropes to keep the reporters at bay. Allura held her smile in place and raised a hand. The reporters began to shout her name and call out questions. She didn't reply. With one hand on the banister and one holding her dress so she didn't trip and tumble down the stairs, she descended. The sounds buzzed in the back of her mind as she focused on not falling. Her feet had been strapped into high-heeled, designer shoes. She could walk in them, but it felt a little like being on stilts.

At the bottom of the stairs, she stopped and breathed a sigh of relief while the photographers and videographers did their job. Some had microphones and called out questions.

"Airman Presley, what do you think about winning the gold star?" someone shouted at her.

"Airman Presley, how does it feel to be a hero?" another reporter called out.

She didn't ignore them, but she was selective in who she wanted to answer.

"Allura," a woman in a little black dress called out. "Who are you wearing?"

That was the one Allura wanted, the safe question that had a solid answer that wouldn't get her into trouble.

"Federico Salazar," Allura replied, before bending her leg at the knee to show off the designer shoe. "And Kelton shoes."

"Fabulous," the reporter said in a loud voice. "You look gorgeous."

That statement hit Allura in an unexpected way. She didn't feel pretty. In fact, she felt like she was in a costume, playing pretend. She wasn't famous, yet there she was in a designer gown being told she was gorgeous by someone who was probably viewed as an expert on fashion and beauty. It was a surreal moment. If Cosmo had been at her side, she might have even enjoyed herself.

Someone else called out for her to turn around. It felt silly, but she turned and looked over her shoulder. The pose caused the photographers to surge forward.

"Who are you looking forward to meeting the most?" someone else called out.

"Are you single?" another reporter asked.

"No," Allura said, her smile slipping a little. "I'm not single. I have a boyfriend. He was drafted. Cosmo Frost—his name is Cosmo Frost."

As if she had known that Allura might go off script, Major Reece appeared. She took Allura by the arm and led her down the corridor.

"Stick to the script," the Major hissed under her breath.

"Yes, ma'am," Allura said. But it felt good to assert herself in the midst of the chaos. She hadn't been allowed to check her messages or reach out to friends. But maybe, just maybe, Cosmo would hear that she was thinking about him.

CHAPTER 34

COSMO COULDN'T SLEEP. He lay in bed staring at the ceiling for a while, then checking the messages on his MACS. There were a few from his mother—just updates and questions. He had answered them all. A few friends from high school had sent messages when they heard he was drafted. But there was nothing new, nothing he hadn't already replied to, and most importantly, nothing from Allura.

It didn't make sense. She wrote him messages the entire time she was at the ATA. And when he had connected with her before the bombing run, she had seemed glad to hear him. But maybe he was projecting his feelings onto her. She hadn't messaged him since that day. His doubts and fears plagued him, like a terrible itch that he couldn't reach. When he closed his eyes, he saw Allura, or worse still, he saw Sid Nash being overwhelmed by bio-bots. Laying alone in his little room, he alternated between feeling sorry for himself and feeling survivor's guilt.

Eventually, he got up and left the small quarters that he shared with Dyson. His partner was snoring softly, but had left his bedroom door open. Cosmo slipped out and walked the halls of the Research and Development Building. It was essentially a big laboratory and workshop, but there were offices and smaller labs on the upper floors. Cosmo had no thoughts about where he was going. His mind was focused on his problems. He knew they were really inconsequential, but they seemed overwhelming to him. It didn't take long to stumble into the main workshop area where Captain Swift and a couple of maintenance droids were hard at work repairing Bolt.

"Hey, what are you doing here?" Swift asked. "I thought you and Henry would be out making a splash."

"We... well... things didn't work out," Cosmo said, before changing the subject. "I'm sorry for the damage."

"Oh, well, you know, this is a military platform. It's going to take damage if it's doing what it was created to do. Besides, this gives me a chance to make some improvements."

Captain Swift stepped back and let the droid take over the delicate work. The main cannon had been removed, and the droids were cleaning out the internal mechanisms that had been damaged when the drone was nearly buried in dirt during the battle with the Ma'Tis.

"What's really on your mind, Cosmo?" Swift asked.

They leaned back on one of the work benches. In that moment, rank was set aside. Captain Swift wasn't a superior officer, he was just an older friend, and Cosmo felt very young at that moment.

"Do you know who my girlfriend is, sir?"

"Everyone knows," Swift said with a chuckle.

"How's that, sir?"

"You don't know?"

"I know she's been on the news and stuff."

"More than that," Swift said, powering up a computer display. "She was awarded the Gold Star for Meritorious Service."

"Oh, really?" Cosmo said. He had heard of the medal being awarded but didn't know much about what it meant.

"Yes, really," Swift said. "That's the highest honor we get, and she's been at the capital as the guest of honor."

He brought up a list of newsfeeds, found the one he wanted and played the video. Allura was there, coming down the stairs at the prime minister's mansion. Cosmo's heart was in his throat. Allura looked like a movie star, only she didn't look exactly like herself. There were cameras flashing and reporters shouting her name. Cosmo got the feeling she was nervous, and he couldn't blame her. In all the years he had known her, she rarely wore dresses. They just weren't her style. She was more of a sweatshirt and jeans kind of girl, but things had changed so much so fast. He was a battle trooper, she had become a bombardier and then a celebrity, and as he looked at the computer screen, he thought she had become a fashion model too. Would they even have anything to talk about if she decided to message him? He knew nothing about fancy clothes.

The reporter whose stream they were watching asked Allura about her dress. Cosmo felt dumbfounded. Allura didn't care about fashion or keep up with trends. She didn't know dress designers, and yet she answered without hesitation. Cosmo felt a sense of cold deep inside, and his heart seemed to shrivel in his chest. Tears stung his eyes. It was as if his worst fears were coming true.

Allura turned around, revealing the low hem of her gown. Cosmo gawked. His instinct was to cover her up, but she clearly didn't mind how much of her body the dress showed. She looked over her shoulder and smiled. He felt a sense of hollow despair, and simultaneously a sense of pride. She was beautiful, and his heart ached to be with her.

"Who are you looking forward to meeting the most?" a reporter called out.

"Are you single?" another member of the paparazzi asked.

"No," Allura said, her smile slipping a little. For just an instant her persona on the red carpet cracked, and Cosmo saw the woman he knew, the girl he loved. "I'm not single. I have a boyfriend. He was drafted. Cosmo Frost, his name is Cosmo Frost."

There are times when a person feels such an incredible sense of euphoria that everything else around them seems to disappear. Cosmo didn't know how long he sat there, his mind spinning. Allura had said his name. She hadn't forgotten him. She still loved him. It was everything he wanted and everything he didn't know he needed. Her confirmation in that moment, at that place, looking the way she did, meant more to him than anything in his life up to that point.

"Looks like things aren't as bad as they seem," Captain Swift assured him.

"No," Cosmo said, feeling numb all over.

"Good. Now, why aren't you out enjoying yourself with Henry?"

"We tried, sir," Cosmo admitted. "We went to the Liberty. That place is awesome. Then we were going into town and... well, sir... we were jumped by some guys."

"Jumped?" Swift asked.

Cosmo suddenly had a lump in his throat that was hard to swallow. "Four guys. They followed us out of the bar and just attacked us for no reason."

"There's always a reason, Frost," Captain Swift said. "What did they say?"

"Nothing."

"What did you say to them?"

"Nothing, sir. I promise. I can't even say for sure they were in the bar. I think I saw them at a table, but we were checking out the memorabilia. We had zero interaction with them. But once we got outside, they came right at us."

"And what happened?"

Cosmo looked down. "We defended ourselves, sir. We took two down, and the other two ran when the police showed up."

"The police?"

"Yes, sir. I got tased, sir."

"That's just great. Wonderful. They give me two battle troopers, just two of you, and now you get into trouble."

"What were we supposed to do, sir?" Cosmo asked.

"Was anyone seriously hurt?"

"I don't know for certain," Cosmo said. "Things are a little fuzzy."

"How much did you have to drink, Private?"

"I didn't, no, sir," Cosmo said. "Soda pop for me, that's all. And Dyson only had two beers. We were fine, sir, I swear it."

"Then why is your memory fuzzy?"

"It all happened so fast," Cosmo said. "And maybe getting tased scrambled things. I don't know. But it was all on security video. The policemen took us to the MPs on base, and when we told the sergeant what happened, he found video and checked out our story. That's why he let us go, sir. We didn't instigate anything. They attacked us."

"How's Dyson?"

"Bruised ribs, sir. A bloody nose, but he'll be okay."

"Your liberty is canceled," Captain Swift said. "Until we get this sorted out, I don't want you leaving the base. We have work to do and I can't have my operators getting locked up. What if—"

Before he could finish, their MACS sounded a strange tone. Cosmo had never heard it before, but the alarm was ominous sounding.

"What's that?"

"Action alert," Swift said. "Get back to your quarters and stand by for orders. Something is going down, and we have to be ready."

An alert icon filled the screens of their MACS devices, but there was no indication of orders.

"Ready for what?" Cosmo asked.

"There's only one thing we get summoned for, Frost. War."

"Yes, sir, we'll be ready," Cosmo said.

He gave a quick salute and ran out of the laboratory and back to his quarters.

CHAPTER 35

THE BALL WAS nothing like Allura expected. And it didn't take long to realize she was in way over her head. She made her way past the red carpet and into a grand ballroom where a string ensemble was playing music. There were tables at one side of the room near a bar where people were getting drinks. There were a few photographers as well, but they were members of the government's PR team.

Allura felt uncomfortable in her dress and did her best to just blend in with the surroundings. A few people were dancing, but most lingered with drinks. It was obvious that the people at the ball weren't interested in the pomp and circumstance of the event. Allura only recognized a few faces. They were the ultrawealthy, and from the snatches of conversations that she heard, they were making deals.

"This is it," Reece said as she brought Allura a glass of champagne.

"This is what?" Allura asked.

"The real government," the Major said. "Knowing these people will be of more benefit than anything you could possibly achieve."

She was flushed with excitement, but Allura felt uncomfortable. There were only a handful of politicians in the room. Likewise, the celebrities were nearly all gone. Her parents weren't there, nor were the senior officers from the military. As Major Reece and Lieutenant

Tessa mingled with the rich and powerful, Allura looked for a way out.

She tasted the champagne but thought it was awful. Still, she liked having something to hold in her hands and a reason to keep her arms in front of her body. Once the PR team put their cameras away, it didn't take long for some of the people to get drunk or high. She saw more than one couple making out as if they were alone somewhere, their bodies entwined as they feverishly sought to fulfill their pent-up desires. Drugs were evident too, laid out on tables for people to use freely. The laughter was loud, and people were acting in a brazen manner that shocked Allura.

"And there she is," the prime minister said as he strolled up to her.

Allura had taken refuge by a wall in the back of the room. She nodded, but didn't speak to the most powerful man on the planet.

"Are you enjoying yourself?" he asked.

"It's a little outside my comfort zone," she replied.

"Oh, don't worry. The cameras are gone. You can let your hair down."

He leaned in close and Allura felt trapped between him and the wall. She was reminded of the college party at the dorm on Triton, only the rich and powerful people in the prime minister's mansion were more sinister.

"I think I'm ready to call it a night," Allura said, sidestepping to put some distance between herself and the much older politician.

"The night is young, Airman," the prime minister said, following her. "We can enjoy ourselves. Maybe you need something a little stronger than that champagne."

He reached into his jacket, brought out a silver container and opened it. Inside were dozens of pills in little slots.

"This," he said, taking a blue pill and holding it up in front of Allura, "will help you let go and really enjoy yourself."

Before she could object, he dropped the pill into her flute of champagne. It immediately began to dissolve.

"Now you drink that honey, and we'll have us a real good time," he said with a smirk.

Allura's fear was suddenly replaced with anger. She couldn't believe the head of Fiona Grand's government, who preached acceptance, tolerance, and respect at every event and in every speech, was suggesting that she take drugs and do things with him that she certainly did not want to do.

"No, sir," Allura said, finding a well of strength and courage that up until that point she hadn't realized she had.

"Now, don't be that way," he said, moving closer. "Think of it as your duty to our great planet."

He reached out and put his hand on her shoulder. She started to move away but he gripped her upper arm tight and grinned. Allura dropped her champagne flute. It shattered on the floor. The prime minister laughed and puller her close to his body. He was larger than she was, taller and much heavier. She could smell the alcohol on his breath and see that his pupils were dilated. Looking around for help, she realized no one was watching them. No one cared—not Major Reece or Lieutenant Tessa, and certainly not the rich and powerful guests at the ball.

"Let me go," Allura said.

"Let's have a little fun first," he said and actually bent down to kiss her.

At that moment, Allura was thankful for the slit in her evening gown as she rammed her knee into the prime minister's groin. His face contorted in pain and he stumbled back a few steps, releasing his grip on her. Allura didn't hesitate. It wasn't her intention to make a scene; instead, she fled from the ballroom. No one could have changed her mind or convinced her to stay at the party. She didn't care if she was reprimanded by Major Reece or forced to scrub toilets for the next four years. She wouldn't be pawed over by the prime minister or anyone else.

She was on her way back to her room with the intention of gathering her belongings and getting out of the prime minister's mansion when she heard strange sounds, almost like miniature alarms going off. People began to hurry through the building. Not the people from the ball, but government staff workers and security professionals. Allura stopped at room with a long table and several display screens. There were four other people in the room, looking at their PIPs or watching the display on the screens.

"What's happening?" Allura asked.

"Who are you?" A man in a dark suit asked.

"Airman First Class Allura Presley," she replied.

"Oh, the bombardier," the man said with a nod. "You'll want to see this, then."

He pointed to the screen. She couldn't make out what she was seeing. It was a dark sky and some sort of object moving at speed.

"Recognize that?" he asked.

"No," Allura said.

"Yeah, that's the consensus right now. Damn thing just appeared out of nowhere. Strategic Command Services are tracking it visually, but it's not showing up on radar."

"How is that possible? Is it jamming us?"

"Maybe," he said. "I'm General Leon Fry, retired. This is my team. We advise the administration on military protocols."

"You live in the prime minister's mansion?"

"No," he said with a smile. "But we work here. The PM keeps offices in the south wing. We were at the dinner and came up to check on things. I'm damn glad we did too. This object is not one of ours."

"Is it from the Ma'Tis?"

"Not that we can tell," he replied. "Right now all we know is that it is alien. No one's been able to identify it yet. Emergency protocols are in place though. You'll need to cut your visit short, I'm afraid."

"No need to apologize to me, sir," Allura said.

"You can call me Leon or Mr. Fry. My military days are over. The party wasn't your cup of tea, I take it."

"No, sir," Allura replied. "I was on my way out when the alarms sounded."

"Well, good luck, Airman," he said, extending a hand. "Stay safe."

"Thank you," Allura said.

When she got back to her room, she pulled off the dress and put on her traveling clothes. Everything else was packed up in ten minutes. She was on her way to the door, not sure where to go but determined not to spend another minute in the PM's mansion when Major Reece came barging in. She looked furious, and at first Allura thought she was angry at what Allura had done to the prime minister.

"Can you believe it?" Reece said. "I was in the middle of a conversation with Ellis Ramsby. The man owns two television networks. Now he probably won't even remember my name."

Allura saw a rip on the shoulder of the Major's ball gown, and there was a dark splotch on her neck. There was no doubt in Allura's mind what sort of conversation Major Reece was having with the media tycoon, but she was pretty certain they weren't just talking.

"Do you know what's going on?" Allura asked.

"Emergency protocols," Reece said angrily. "Which means we have to return to Hawkstone ASAP. The timing couldn't be worse."

"So we're leaving the capital?"

"We don't have a choice," Reece snapped, obviously thinking that Allura was complaining. "Get your stuff together. We have to spend the night at the airport waiting for transport back to Hawkstone. Delightful."

Allura understood her superior's frustration, but after being pawed at by the PM, she was happy to be leaving no matter where they had to spend the night. A government shuttle took them to a private hangar at the Capital Air & Space Port. The hangar officially belonged to the Air Force but was empty at the moment. The three women went into a tiny office and waited for transportation that would take them back to the air base.

"Do you suppose this will disrupt the media tour?" Tessa asked.

"I'm already getting cancelations," Reece complained. "Four of the big eight networks have dropped us. We'll be lucky to get on a regional show if this emergency continues."

Allura was much more concerned about what was going on with the unidentified object than the media tour. She was anxious to get back to her squadron and hoped the media appearances would be forgotten altogether.

"The news cycle is already shifting," Reece continued. "And if the object they're tracking is a threat, we'll be forgotten. I hope you made some good contacts tonight. Odds are we'll never get a chance to be in the room with so many power brokers ever again."

"You would think the newscasters would want a military perspective on this UFO," Tessa complained.

They were both looking at their military-issued PIPs.

"Since it looks like you won't be needing me," Allura said. "Can I have access to my PIP now, please?"

Tessa looked up from her handheld communication device, and Reece waved at her as if she were swatting away a pesky fly.

"Whatever," Lieutenant Tessa said. She reached down, picked up a designer handbag and rummaged in it. After a moment, she brought out Allura's PIP and handed it over. "Just don't say anything that might get out to the media, please."

"Sure," Allura said, powering the slim device on. She was still using a commercial PIP that she had used through high school. It was worn and comfortable—a little out of date but still fully functional.

The first thing she saw were the dozens of messages from Cosmo. She was about to open them when Reece stiffened and said, "It's down!"

"Where?" Tessa asked.

"Near the coast," Reece replied, casting a video feed to a wall display.

Allura looked up. Some of the surveillance cameras that had been set up to monitor the coastal waters were still operational. One showed the strange object. To Allura it looked like a frisbee that was stuck in the ground edgewise. It was clearly metallic, with grooves and indented segments of varying sizes all around the outer edges. The middle looked to be made from hundreds of narrow spokes.

"What is that thing?" Tessa asked.

"Can't be a vessel," Reece said. "It's too small and has no flight capability."

"It just crashed?" Tessa asked.

"Obviously," Reece said.

"But it looks like it's standing on edge," the younger officer replied. "That would be like flipping a coin off the roof of a building and having it land on its edge."

It was, in Allura's opinion, the most intelligent thing that Lieutenant Tessa had ever said. And she was absolutely right. The thing, whatever it was, had come down as intended. It was the only explanation. Whether it had pilots inside or not, it hadn't just crashed by accident.

"Well," Major Reece said. "It doesn't look big enough to be a threat."

Allura felt a wave of relief. She had to agree the thing didn't look very big. Maybe it wasn't a threat at all. Perhaps the emergence protocols would be rescinded and things would go back to normal.

"Wait, what's that?" Allura said, pointing at the screen.

Out of the surf there came movement. One moment it was just foaming water, and the next it was obvious that the Ma'Tis were aware of the strange object.

"Ma'Tis," Reece said with contempt. "What are they up to now?"

"Not that," Allura said. "Look at the center of the object."

It was tiny, no bigger than a spark, but it was there. An orange light, almost like the glow of a candle. And it was slowly getting bigger.

CHAPTER 36

COSMO AND DYSON were in their MAL armor along with hundreds of other battle troopers. They were all watching the same video feed that was being simulcast to every military branch and division around the globe. With Bolt still inoperable, the two HAVOC operators had been called to join the other battle troopers from the various units that were stationed at Mammoth.

"We're closest," Dyson said. "I just checked, and Mammoth is the closest military base to that thing."

"Lucky us," Cosmo said.

They were watching the video being projected onto a large wall just outside the motor pool at the south side of the base. There were nearly four hundred battle troopers in various types of armor. Some were clearly in mech coveralls. Others were drivers and mobile artillery gunners. And there were plenty of regulation infantry in the group, but no one else that Cosmo could see in MAL armor.

"What do you think the bugs are going to do with that thing?" Dyson asked.

"I can't even imagine," Cosmo replied.

As they watched, the disk opened, and orange light shown out. The angle from the beach camera was wrong. They couldn't see directly into the disk, but in the darkness of night the light spilling forth was obvious. Cosmo was mesmerized. The Ma'Tis looked cautious as they approached.

"This is crazy, man," Dyson said.

"So they didn't can you two after all," a familiar voice behind them said.

Cosmo and Dyson turned. Their thick, bulky armor was a bit awkward even though the motion assist made movement easy. They shuffled around to see Todd Butler in mech coveralls.

"Butler!" Dyson said. "Hey, man, how you been?"

"It's all good, brother," Butler said. "They're fast tracking us through mech school. It's like learning to walk all over again, but man is it an amazing feeling to be in that armor. I feel like I could smash the world, it's so strong."

"That sounds awesome," Dyson said.

"What have they got you two doing? Latrine duty?"

"No, we got pulled into the Armor Brigade," Cosmo said.

"What's that?" Butler asked.

"HAVOC operators," Dyson explained. "You know, the units that turned the tide in the battle outside Hillsdale."

"Oh, yeah! I heard about that," Butler said. "The experimental units that nearly got blown to bits. I heard they had to dig you out of the rubble."

"After we blew up a Ma'Tis tank," Dyson argued.

"I'm glad to see you guys, and I hate to say anything, but the guy in charge of your unit is a bit of a pariah."

"Captain Swift?" Cosmo asked.

"Yeah, that's him. Word is he's crazy."

"Crazy like a fox, maybe," Dyson said.

"He invented the HAVOC drones," Cosmo said. "He isn't crazy."

"Hey, that's just what I heard," Butler said.

Cosmo felt his MACS vibrate. He wasn't wearing his battle helmet, and he had to open a compartment along the thigh portion of his armor to get to his device. He held it up and felt his heart skip a beat. The screen showed one new message... from Allura.

He left Dyson and Butler talking and focused on the message from Allura. It was short, but it made him feel so good.

Cosmo, they wouldn't give me access to my PIP until now. I got all your messages. I love you. Will write more soon. — Allura

It was the reassurance he had been longing for. And in that moment, it was all that he needed. She loved him, and she wasn't ghosting him. He didn't know who had taken her PIP or why they wouldn't let her communicate with him. But he had been without his PIP during basic training and had only gotten back online with his MACS when he graduated. Perhaps Allura had been in training. He didn't know, but she would explain it all in time, which was all he really wanted.

He started typing out a message to her when Dyson grabbed his arm and pointed at the screen.

"Something's coming out of that thing, man!"

Cosmo looked up and saw it. Something, not a man and not a Ma'Tis crab either. It was big and so thick in the body that it seemed to just keep coming and coming out of the orange light. Then, before they could identify what the thing was, their video feed dissolved into static. The crowd of battle troopers groaned. Cosmo looked around, but there was no one to see with any answers.

"Well, that figures," Butler said. "Somebody must have tripped over the video connection line."

"Sounds about right," Dyson said.

"They'll get it back up in a minute," Cosmo said.

But when he looked at his MACS there was no signal. His device had lost connection, which was odd since he was on base, but he didn't think much of it at the time. A minute later, a loudspeaker began to give orders. The battle troopers were told to arm up and get on transports. With video lost, they were being sent out to keep tabs on the device.

"Odds are it's some sort of Ma'Tis thing," Butler told them as they stood in line for the armory. "They've probably got dozens of them under the water—we just haven't seen them before. I'm guessing it's some type of 3D printer or robotic fabricator. That's probably how they made their tanks."

"Could be," Dyson said. "That one just came down off course, maybe."

"Then why haven't we tracked them before?" Cosmo asked. "We don't get put on emergency alert for stuff that happens all the time."

"Maybe they tracked this one and knew it was coming down on land," Butler suggested. "Which is why they're calling us out now."

"Comms are back up," someone else in line said.

Cosmo checked his MACS and saw that it was true. His device was connected, but when he looked toward the video feed it was still just static. He typed out a quick message to Allura: *Where are you?*

At the armory he was given the bulky LA6 rifle and a long-range spotting scope. He was tempted to tell the soldier in the armory that he didn't need the scope, since his battle helmet could zoom in and show him things in the distance, but he decided not to do anything that might slow down the process. He took the weapon and the scope before following Butler and Dyson toward a drop ship on the wide tarmac at the edge of the base.

"Looks like this is where we part ways," Butler said. "Good luck, fellas."

"You too," Dyson said.

"Stay sharp, Butler," Cosmo told him.

"Always. Catch you two on the flip side."

Cosmo put on his battle helmet and synced his MACS to the onscreen display as he walked up the ramp of a drop ship. There were thirty seats for battle troopers. Cosmo sat next to Dyson near the door. It only took a few moments for the transport to fill and the rear hatch to close.

"I could have used a few more hours sleep," Dyson said. "My ribs hurt like hell."

"Sorry, man. Bad luck, I suppose."

"Wake me when we land."

"You got it," Cosmo said, glad for the chance to read the message that had just come through from Allura. He brought it up on his view screen.

The capital. We're on our way back to Hawkstone. Looks like we'll be swinging out over the UFO to see what's happening. Can't wait to catch up. You'll never believe what's going on with me. Talk soon, love — A.

Cosmo replied as the drop ship launched. He felt its momentum pulling him sideways on the bench seat that lined the drop ship's passenger space. The seats were mesh fabric stretched between metal supports that stuck out from the walls of the ship. They weren't really comfortable chairs, but Cosmo didn't mind. He felt like everything in his world had clicked into place since reconnecting with Allura. They had a lot to catch up on, but she hadn't ghosted him. And that was what was important to Cosmo.

The flight took an hour. The drop ship set down ten kilometers from the beach. The battle troopers unloaded and began to spread out. Their assignment was clear. It came through as a message on the MACS. **Move within sight of the beach and report anything out of the ordinary.**

Cosmo knew that with hundreds of troopers being deployed, it was a long shot that he would be able to see the strange object or the Ma'Tis coming out of the ocean. But that was the way of the military. It was night watch all over again, just like in basic training. Hours of boredom, but at least he was doing something useful. The troopers spread out. Dyson was a kilometer to the right of Cosmo, and a trooper named Eldridge was to his left. They jogged toward the beach, the MAL armor making it easy for Cosmo. The grass plain along that part of the coast dropped down in a long, gradual slope. They could see the beach at five miles out with the spotter scopes, so they stopped there and began visual scans. They were far from the alien object, and there was no sign of the Ma'Tis in the water or along the beach. Whatever was going on around the object, other people would see it, not Cosmo. And that was just fine with him. His only desire was to see Allura again and get his life back in order. Little did he know things were about to get shaken up like never before.

CHAPTER 37

THE TRANSPORT CARRYING Allura back to Hawkstone was a small passenger shuttle. It had windows, which was nice in the daylight, but they were flying at night. While Major Reece and Lieutenant Tessa put on sleep masks and reclined their seats for the flight back to base, Allura went to the cockpit.

"Can't sleep?" the pilot asked.

"Just wondering what our ETA is."

"Four hours," the pilot responded. "We're supposed to fly over the object and get a better look at the situation."

"Can't they do that with satellites?"

"Too much cloud cover, and the bugs are jamming signals. We'll be getting visual confirmation if possible."

"Great," Allura said. "How can I help?"

"This shuttle has video cameras and thermal imaging, we should be good," the pilot replied.

"But you just said the Ma'Tis are projecting the haze," Allura said. "Will that stuff work?"

"It's what we've got," the pilot said.

"What about the tail section," Allura said. "You can fly with that rear hatch open, right?"

"Yeah, but you passengers won't be getting much sleep if we do."

"Sleep can wait," Allura said. "Once we're in the area we'll open the rear hatch. I'll do the visual myself."

"Might not see much in the dark," the pilot said. "There are flares in the emergency kit. Pop off a couple of those as we circle around, and we might be able to see what they're doing."

"Sounds like a plan," Allura said.

"I thought you PR people only cared about protecting your brand image," the copilot said.

"The officers are PR. I'm not," Allura said. "I'm Condor Squadron."

"The bombardier that just got the gold star?" the pilot asked.

"Yeah," Allura said.

"Well, hey, good to have a celebrity on board," the pilot said. "We're still a couple of hours out. You're welcome to take the nav seat here in the cockpit if you like."

Allura sat down and strapped in. The cockpit had large windows. She could see stars above them, and in places the lights from the cities below made the clouds beneath them glow. Her seat wasn't as comfortable as those back in the passenger cabin, but she had full use of the ship's navigation computer, which was linked into the planetary info networks via satellite.

She pulled up her message account and tapped out a quick note to Cosmo letting him know what was going on. It might not be military protocol to share what they were doing on the flight over a personal message system, but no one had given her anything else to work with. And she was so happy to be able to connect with Cosmo again that she wanted to share everything with him.

On a flight back to Hawkstone, she wrote. We'll be flying over the anomaly, doing visual recon. Feels good to be doing something useful again.

The hours passed quickly. Below the shuttle the clouds got thicker, and eventually the shuttle began to descend for their flyby over the strange object that had hit near the coast.

"Looks like we've got some weather moving in," the pilot said. "Be sure you tether in, Airman."

"Roger that," Allura said. "Is it too early to open up the back?"

"A little, but you could let the passengers know. And get your gear together. There's a lot of electrical interference, and we're not even over the site yet."

Lightning lit the clouds they were passing through. The shuttle shook in the choppy air.

"Yeah, okay," Allura said. "I'll let you know when I'm plugged in and ready."

She took the headset she was wearing and disconnected it from the navigation console. She got up slowly, holding on. The shuttle felt like it was bouncing. Most of the bounces were small, just little shudders or vibrations, but occasionally the vessel lurched hard enough to knock someone off their feet.

Coming out of the cockpit she found Major Reece and Lieutenant Tessa with their sleep masks pulled up on top of their heads.

"What's going on?" the Major asked.

"Bad weather," Allura said. "Lots of interference. The pilot is going to open the rear hatch so we can do a visual inspection of the anomaly."

"What? Why? We're supposed to be going to Hawkstone," Reece declared.

"We are, but we're passing over the object along the way," Allura said. "Better make sure you're buckled in tight and put away anything that might tumble through the cabin. We'll lose pressure when the door opens."

"We'll get sucked out!" Tessa shrieked.

"No, we're descending and the shuttle has depressurization capability. But it will get windy."

She moved on past them, holding onto the seats along either side. The back of the shuttle had a wide hatch that lowered into a ramp. Like most military vehicles, the shuttle was a variation built on a standard airframe. The shuttle was for passengers but was essentially the same vehicle as a drop ship, or a small cargo hauler. There were metal safety handles beside the hatch, and a communication nodule that she could plug her headset into, which she did. The emergency supplies were in a red box attached to the bulkhead. She unfastened the clasps and opened the case. Inside were a variety of items, most of which she had either studied about or learned to use in the survival course that was part of her bombardier training. She took a flare and the small gun used to launch it. After loading the flare, she stuck two more into the pocket of her fatigue pants and resealed the emergency supplies.

"I'm in position," Allura said, her voice carried to the pilots through the headset's mic. "Tether is attached."

"You find the flares?"

"Affirmative, right where you said they would be," she told the pilots.

"That's good. We've got a light rain and some lightning, but the real problem is the wind. She's whipping hard. You hold on back there."

"Yeah, good advice," Allura said.

"Okay, we're at one thousand meters," the pilot said. "Opening rear hatch now."

A light flashed for a couple of seconds, and Allura gripped the emergency handle tight. When the hatch began to open the wind wailed as it blew through the tiny gap. It sounded almost like a person being tortured. Allura felt chill bumps pop up all over her body. It only took seconds for the passenger compartment to pressurize. Still, it was a bit like stepping outside in the middle of a raging storm. The ground below them was pitch black, yet Allura could smell the salty sea air.

"Passing seven hundred meters," the pilot said. "Airman, you can launch your first flare."

"Copy that," Allura said, holding out the flare gun she had taken from the emergency supplies near the rear hatch.

She pulled the trigger and sent the flare shooting out of the back of the shuttle. It burned red, and once its propellent was spent, began to slowly descend, casting light down onto the ground. Allura would have preferred bright sunlight on a calm day, but the glare of red light from the flare made the ocean waves crashing onto the beach visible. She could see the coastline and the prairie too. Visibility wasn't great, but she could see all right. But what she saw was disturbing. Dark shapes lay on the sand and around the dunes, even up onto the grassy plain.

"We're coming up on the object," the pilot said.

"I've got Ma'Tis on the ground," Allura said.

"I think the brass were expecting as much. That thing down there must be theirs. Maybe a weapon of some kind."

"I don't think so. The Ma'Tis are all dead. No movement."

"Say again, Airman."

"There's no movement on the ground," Allura said. "They're just laying there."

"Maybe they're sleeping," the copilot suggested.

Allura fired her second flare. The dim, shadowy forms on the ground grew clearer, even though the wind was whipping the waves into a foam froth and sand was blowing across the beach head.

"Not sleeping," Allura said. "Dead. Something ripped them to pieces. I've never seen anything like it."

"The crabs?" the pilot asked. "I didn't think anything could break through their shells."

"Something did," Allura insisted, as the alien disk came into view. Light shown out from it on one side. The disk had come down on top of a sand dune. The tall grass around it was smashed flat, and there were strange grooves in the sand. More Ma'Tis body parts littered the area.

"You sure you're seeing clearly, Airman?" the pilot asked.

"One hundred percent," Allura said. "Something killed them. There must be over a hundred alien bodies. No sign of anything else though."

"All right, I'm calling it," the pilot said, as the warning light flashed and the rear hatch began to close. "We've seen enough. Sealing up the rear hatch now. Once it's closed Airman, I want you buckled into the—"

Allura couldn't tell if the headset lost signal or if he just stopped talking. Lightning flashed in the clouds again as Allura stared out. And for just an instant, she thought she saw something.

CHAPTER 38

"DID ANYONE ELSE SEE THAT?" the pilot asked.

"See what?" the copilot replied.

"I saw something," Allura said as the hatch closed and sealed. "Can't say what it was."

"Something big," the pilot said. "In the clouds."

Allura unhooked her safety tether from the wall and sat down in the rearmost chair so that her headset cable would reach. She looked out the windows, but it was hard to see out into the darkness with the cabin lights on.

"Can you shut down the lights in here?" Allura said.

They went off suddenly, and as she strained to see out the window on her side of the shuttle, she saw something. Only she couldn't believe what she was seeing. It was a massive snake, only it was flying beside the ship. She couldn't see it clearly. The glow from the shuttle's running lights weren't bright enough, and the window was spotted with waterdrops from the rain. But something huge was out there.

"I see it!" she called out.

Near the front of the cabin, Tessa was looking out her window on the same side of the ship. She screamed. Allura felt like screaming. Everything suddenly felt surreal. How could a snake fly? It couldn't. But there was something in the air. She had seen kites with similar shapes—long, curvy bodies that seemed to slither through the air. But the thing outside the window of the ship wasn't a kite. It was too big, too solid. In the dark it was impossible to make out clearly.

"What? Where?" the pilot asked.

"Portside," Allura said. "It's matching our speed."

"What is it?" the copilot said. "There's nothing on radar."

"We can't see it, Airman," the pilot said. "What's it doing?"

"Hard to tell," Allura replied. "But it's keeping pace."

"How big is it?" the copilot cried.

"Bigger than the shuttle," Allura said, just as the flying creature opened its mouth and billowed fire at the ship. "Look out!"

The flash of light from the fiery blast was enough to cause the pilot to veer away instinctively. But the shuttle was not like an attack ship. It had repulsor engines and twin main drives mounted on the wings. It was fast enough, but not very maneuverable. Flames licked along the belly of the shuttle, singeing the paint but not damaging the vessel.

"Mayday, Mayday, Mayday," the pilot shouted. "We are under attack by an unknown creature."

"We need altitude," the copilot said. "Climb! Climb!"

The ship started up. Allura felt the momentum shift and the g-forces pulled her back into her seat. Tessa screamed again. Major Reece was white as a sheet and gripping the armrests of her seat so hard her hands had turned red.

Allura had to strain to lean forward. She had the belt strap around her waist and the momentum of the ship's climb made the move difficult, but she got a look outside. The creature was nowhere in sight.

"It's gone," she said. "I can't see it."

"We outran it?" the pilot asked. He was an Air Force jockey but had spent his career flying high-ranking officers and special envoys, not dogfighting other ships. Allura could hear the fear in his voice.

"I don't know," she said.

The ship shook suddenly. Allura was thrown back in her seat, and this time both Reece and Tessa screamed together. A loud, metallic screech was heard. Allura knew it was metal under stress. There was shouting in the cockpit, which Allura heard over her headset.

"What the..."

"Starboard engine failure! We're losing cabin pressure too!"

"What happened? That wasn't turbulence."

"We're in a spin!"

"Get that engine back online."

"I can't. Nothing is responding."

Panic had set in, and it was contagious. Up to that point, Allura's fear had been tempered with curiosity. She like to discover new things and figure out how something worked or how a job was done. Mathematics came easily to her, and formulas made sense. She had no trouble thinking in three dimensions or visualizing something just by reading about it. At first, the creature in the clouds had fired her curiosity, but that had been overwhelmed by fear. And for the first time in her life, she thought she was going to die.

Her training kicked in. She bent low and covered her head, but she could still hear the pilots. Their frantic shouts were loud in her ears as she felt the ship falling. She was pulled back and up by the spin of the ship. Only her seatbelt held her in place. It was all she could do not to scream too, but Reece and Tessa were doing well on their own in that department.

The ship was hit again and went from a spin to a tumble. Even worse, the chatter from the pilots abruptly ended. The gravitational forces were so strong Allura was slammed back in her seat. The screams from the PR officers stopped too, and Allura felt like she could hardly breathe. There were times growing up when her brother would pin her down and put all his weight on her. It felt to Allura like that was happening even though no one was touching her. Sparks appeared in her vision, even though it was dark in the cabin. And then everything stopped. It felt like they had crashed into something. Fortunately, the seats around her were all padded, and even though she was flung sideways, it was away from the window. She lay over the armrest of her chair for a moment, panting to catch her breath.

"What is happening?" Tessa wailed.

Metal groaned again, and something rubbed across her window. Allura pushed herself to an upright position and looked out the window, but it was covered by something dark. She could perceive a sense of motion but couldn't tell if they were flying or falling. For nearly a minute, nothing happened other than the brushing sound of something rough moving over the hull.

Allura unfastened her seatbelt and got to her feet. It was dangerous, she knew. The plane was still shuddering and the sound of metal
creaking could be heard. But she had to check the cockpit. She pulled
off the headset and let it fall to the floor before heading up the aisle
between the passenger seats. She passed the weeping Tessa on one
side. Major Reece was passed out on the other side. At the flimsy door
to the cockpit, she stopped. She could hear the sound of air rushing on
the other side. In the middle of the door was a little window covered
with a flap of material. She pulled the flap free and looked into the
cockpit, but there wasn't much to see. The entire front of the ship had
been smashed. They weren't flying; they were falling.

"Grab onto something!" Allura shouted as she dove for the nearest
seat.

"We're all gonna die!" Tessa screamed.

Her hands shaking, Allura had barely gotten her belt fastened
when they hit the ground. It wasn't as horrible as she imagined. The
impact was startling and undeniable, but they weren't crushed. The
ship didn't explode or break apart. Allura looked around. They were
alive. The sense of motion had stopped, but something was still
moving on or around the ship. A wave of water crashed over them.
They heard the waterdrops pelted the hull. She looked out the
window and saw water surge back away from the crashed shuttle.
They were on the beach. She could see sand in the glare of lightning
in the clouds.

"We're okay," she said, mostly to herself as she unfastened her
safety belt and rushed to the other side of the ship.

What she saw defied understanding. It looked like a long, serpentine dragon, with wings on its back. It was slithering away from the
ship, leaving a trail in the sand. There were bodies on the ground too—
the fallen Ma'Tis. She could see bite marks on their exoskeletons in
some places and cracks in others. It reminded her of a man she had
once seen at the park, eating walnuts he cracked in his hand by
squeezing the shells together.

Then the shooting started and lit up the night.

CHAPTER 39

"ALL MECHANIZED UNITS, pull back and regroup at rally point Bravo," a voice ordered.

"You think that's us?" Dyson asked.

"Probably so," Cosmo replied. "I've got a positional beacon on my helmet's directional display."

"Yeah, I got it too. Last one there has to buy the beer."

"I can't buy beer," Cosmo complained as he turned and started to run.

"You better get moving then, skippy," Dyson said. "I ain't taking it easy on you just because your girlfriend's famous."

They ran through the darkness—the night vision on their helmets had no trouble displaying the terrain around them, and their suits made running easy. They reached the rally point at the same time, both laughing from the thrill of moving in the motion-assisted light armor suits. Around them, battle troopers in mechs were gathering.

"You two," a familiar voice said over their comm-link as a mech stomped toward Cosmo and Dyson. "Keep your science experiment out of our way."

"Yes, sir!" they both replied to Major Zukov. He pointed at them with one long, mechanical arm.

"You stay in reserve until called on. Is that understood?"

"Yes, sir!" they shouted.

He turned and stomped away, shouting orders at the other mechs. There were four platoons of mechanized troopers. They were put into battle formation and ordered to march. Dyson and Cosmo stood back, watching.

"Well, ain't this a bunch of malarkey," Dyson said.

"Major Zukov isn't a fan," Cosmo said.

"That's because we showed his ass up," Dyson said. "But we were just doing our jobs. Ain't no need to get nasty with us. We don't even have our HAVOC drones here."

"I guess he doesn't know that," Cosmo said.

"What should we do?"

"Follow, I suppose."

"Whatever," Dyson said.

They followed the mechs but kept their distance. The mechs marched in perfect order but moved at the pace of a slow walk. They were armed with big rifles that had heavy lasers or gas-projected explosive rounds. They also had huge knifes nearly two meters in length and massive sidearms Cosmo had never seen before.

Four kilometers from the coast they crested a hill. Below them was the ocean and the anomaly. It was just before dawn and Zukov gave his mechs a warmup speech.

"Rhino Company," Zukov shouted. "There's something down there on that beach. I don't know what it is, and I don't care. It took down one of our ships, and we are going to make it pay."

Cosmo felt a hollow sensation in his gut. The last message he had gotten from Allura said they were going to fly over the anomaly. Was it her ship that got taken out? He suddenly felt cold and shaky.

"Let's spread out. Attack formation Omaha," Zukov continued. "Watch the skies. We don't know what we're dealing with yet. But we ride the pale horse! We bring the thunder! Now, move out!"

The mechs stomped away down toward the coast. Cosmo noticed that Zukov lingered. He looked back. "You two watch the skies. I don't want anything catching us by surprise."

"Sir," Cosmo said. "What ship did we lose?"

"I have no idea and it doesn't matter. Get your head in the game,

Private, or return to base. We don't need you out here daydreaming in the middle of a battle."

Zukov stomped off after the other mechs.

"I see he ain't in no hurry to catch up," Dyson said over their private communications channel.

"Leading from behind," Cosmo said. "Go figure."

"Why you asking about the ship that went down?" Dyson asked.

"Because it's possible that Allura was on it."

"Oh, man, no way. The odds of that are astronomical."

"She said she was on her way to do a flyby. She called it aerial recon or something."

"They probably do that from forty thousand meters up, bro. It ain't her."

Cosmo activated the zoom feature on his battle helmet, but it could only see so far with night vision. The beach was too far away.

"I can't see anything," Cosmo complained.

"Be dawn soon, man," Dyson reassured him. "The mechs will deal with this. You'll hear from her soon."

Cosmo sent out a message, but there was no response. Not that there would be if she had gotten to the base and was sleeping. Still, he felt uneasy. He needed to know what ship had gone down.

An hour passed. The mechs scoured the area. Orange light continued to glow from the round disk that stood out to Cosmo and Dyson, but there was no sign of the enemy.

"Whatever came out of that thing was no friend to the Ma'Tis," Zukov said. "They were slaughtered down here."

"We need to find out what it was," General Sanjay said over the command channel of their communications system. "I've called in Captain Swift. He has more experience with this sort of thing."

"Sir, we're right here. We can handle whatever you need," Zukov said.

"Do you have a PhD in mechanical engineering, Major? I didn't think so," General Sanjay snapped. "We need eyes on the object by someone with a shot of telling us what it is."

"Copy that, sir. What would you have us do?"

"Just secure the area. Whatever killed those Ma'Tis has to be around here somewhere."

Shortly before dawn Captain Swift arrived. He was in MAL armor but had a scanner instead of a rifle. He joined Cosmo and Dyson.

"You two come with me," he said. "Let's go see what has everyone in such a tizzy."

"What do you think it is, sir?"

"At this stage I can't say," Swift replied. "Either a ship of some kind or..."

He didn't finish and Dyson just looked at Cosmo. The younger man couldn't see his friend's face, but he didn't have to. They were both curious, but frustrated by the way their superiors were treating them.

"Or what?" Cosmo asked.

"Like I said, I don't want to speculate," Swift said. "But it's possible, in theory anyway, that it's some kind of portal."

"Like what?" Dyson asked. "You mean magic?"

"Not magic, physics," Swift said. "A hyperlink, or a wormhole gate. It's possible for two places to be linked together, allowing a person to step between them. Again, it's just theory. We don't have anything like that, and I'm not saying that's what the anomaly is. But..."

"But something came out of it, or through it," Cosmo said. "Something bad enough to take out an entire company of Ma'Tis and bring down our ship."

"Those are the facts as we know them at this point," Swift said.

They were close enough to the object that they could see the details on one side. The disk was slightly buried in the sand at the top of a dune. The grass around it was pushed down, but from Cosmo's point of view it shouldn't have been able to stand on edge. A slight breeze would have toppled it over, and there had been plenty of strong weather through the night.

"It's weird," Dyson said. "How's it stand up like that?"

"Can't say until we get closer," Swift said.

"What do you know about the ship that went down?" Cosmo asked.

"Not a lot," Swift replied. "It was a shuttle, I believe. En route to Hawkstone."

Cosmo didn't say anything else. A feeling of cold fear had set in, and he brooded at the bottom of the sand dune while Captain Swift and Dyson went up to investigate.

"Yo, Cos, you gotta see this, man. It's amazing."

Cosmo looked up at his friend. The sky was slightly lighter than before. He flicked off his night vision. The gloom settled in, but the sky was slate gray. Thick clouds hung low. He couldn't see the ocean, but he could hear the waves crashing.

"What is it?"

"Can't say for certain, dude, but I think we're the first humans to ever see it," Dyson called back. "Come on."

Cosmo couldn't say why he felt so despondent, but he couldn't shake the feeling. Not even seeing alien technology seemed to move the needle on his emotions. He looked up at the object. The strange orange glow spilled out over the gloom. It felt mysterious and more than a little frightening. Cosmo started up the dune, his feet sinking into the sand. Thick clumps of sawgrass had been crushed down. A glance at the other dunes showed the grass standing out in spiny fans. He wondered briefly what had trampled down the tall grass on that dune.

And then he saw it. At first it was only a mere speck in the sky, and he didn't even pay attention to it. And then as he neared the top of the dune, he looked up again. The speck was bigger and looked like a dark squiggle against the sky.

"Look at these markings, man," Dyson said. "The captain thinks it's writing of some kind. Gotta be a portal though. It's not thick enough to be—"

"What is that?" Cosmo interrupted his friend. He lifted his free hand and pointed.

Dyson turned. "I don't know," he said.

"Captain," Cosmo said.

"What now?" Swift complained.

"There's something up there!" Cosmo said, switching over to the command frequency. "Major Zukov, I have movement. I think it might be the alien."

"Where?" the Major asked.

Cosmo was still pointing. "Over the ocean, sir. Due east of the object." He zoomed his vision in on the squiggle. There wasn't enough light to make it out clearly, but he could tell it was a solid object and that it was moving through the air the way a snake slithers through tall grass.

"Are you certain?" Zukov asked.

"It's organic, sir. Must be big," Cosmo replied. "It's headed straight toward us. And it is definitely a single organism."

"Rhino company, prepare for contact," Zukov ordered. "HAVOC squad, remain on that knoll and keep eyes on the enemy."

"Roger," Cosmo said as he took a knee beside the anomaly.

"Oh man, I got a bad feeling about this," Dyson said.

"Fascinating," Swift said, seemingly oblivious to the danger.

Cosmo could feel the disk pulsing with power. The orange light inside the circle seemed to dance like a candle flame. He put out his hand and touched the metal. It vibrated slightly, and it was almost as if Cosmo could feel the energy that powered the device flowing through it.

"Careful there, Frost," Swift said. "Even the touch of your hand could alter the artifact."

"Sorry," Cosmo said.

"Sir, you should get down," Dyson said. "Take cover."

"No time for that," Swift replied. "My scan is almost complete. The data is quite illuminating."

The sun was just beginning to rise. The clouds blocked it, filtering the light, but as Cosmo looked out to sea in search of the alien, his eyes spotted something else. It was half a kilometer out from the shore. In the dark he had thought it was a boulder, but with the light of dawn he could make out the semi-crushed hull of the ship, and the three people climbing out of it.

CHAPTER 40

IT TOOK a long time to get Major Reece and Lieutenant Tessa out of the ship. The rear hatch was too twisted to open properly, and as the tide came in, the shuttle was surrounded by water. The waves crashing into the ship were loud and frightening, but as the sun came up Allura could see enough to realize they could wrench open the upper portion of the hatch and climb out.

"Come help me," Allura said.

"Help with what?" Tessa said. "I don't want to be out there."

"We have to get out of the ship," Allura said. "You may feel safe in here, but it's not safe."

"And how do you know that?" Tessa demanded.

"Didn't you take survival training? The first priority in a downed aircraft is to get out of the vessel and survey your surroundings."

"Our surroundings are ocean. It's probably brimming with aliens," Tessa cried.

"Get it together, Lieutenant," Allura said, not bothering to hide how frustrated she was. "We have a duty to get out of this ship. Major Reece needs help."

"We all need help," Tessa said. "We should stay here until help arrives."

"Can't count on that," Allura said. "We have to help ourselves."

"Stop it! Why do you have to be so stubborn all the time?" Tessa said in a high-pitched voice. She was clearly on the verge of panic.

"Forgive me for wanting to live," Allura said. "Now, get over here and help."

"No! I won't do it."

"Go," Major Reece said, her voice ragged and weak. "Help her."

"This is so unfair," Tessa said.

Allura wondered how the woman had made it through basic training. She had done her own physical conditioning via an online correspondence course, but still, the way Lieutenant Tessa was acting it was doubtful she would have made it through the two weeks of exercise and safety training.

There were no real tools on board the shuttle. But with both of them pressing on the hatch, it opened half a meter at the top edge. It was enough for the three women to squeeze through one at a time. Climbing up and out would be difficult, but it would make getting on top of the shuttle easier. And with the water surging around the craft, getting as high as possible would be important.

"That's it," Allura said. "That's good enough."

"Now what?" Tessa said, just before a wave of cold water hit the shuttle and sprayed into the passenger cabin. "Ugh! This is terrible."

"Better than being dead," Allura said. "The pilots weren't so lucky."

She had checked the cockpit again, and the bodies of the pilots were both crushed. The big windows had shattered and cut both men to pieces before the controls were smashed into them.

"You call this lucky?" Tessa complained.

"We're walking away from a wreck, virtually unharmed," Allura said. "I call that lucky, yes."

They gathered what supplies they could. There was one more flare in Allura's pocket, along with the flare gun. In the emergency kit was food, shelter materials, and mylar blankets. Allura wished there was a real gun in the shuttle. Whatever had destroyed the shuttle was still out there, and she didn't like the idea of going out unarmed. But she knew that the shuttle would either be submerged in the rising tide or pulled out to sea when the tide receeded. Staying in the shuttle was a death sentence. At least on the outside they had a chance to survive.

"Come on, Major, we have to go," Allura told Major Reece.

She didn't resist. The Major was on her feet and moving on her own, but mentally she seemed to be in shock. Allura guessed that being a PR expert didn't prepare a person to survive a life-threatening situation.

"Who's going first?" Tessa asked.

"You," Allura said.

"Me? Why me?"

"Because we both need to help the Major get onto the roof of the shuttle," Allura said.

"Oh, rubbish! You just don't want to be the first to go outside in case that thing is still out there. You want me to get killed."

"Lieutenant, whoever is last in the shuttle will have no help getting out," Allura said. "If you want to go last, that's fine with me."

Tessa looked up at the opening of the hatch, then narrowed her eyes.

"Who put you in charge?" she demanded. "I'm the ranking officer with Major Reece out of commission."

"Yes, you are," Allura said.

"So why are you telling me what to do?"

"I'm not. I'm making a suggestion because frankly, I doubt you know what to do. And if you want to stay on the shuttle, go ahead. Just know you'll probably drown before long. Or you can help me get Major Reece to the beach."

"The beach? You mean through the water?"

"Yes," Allura said, wondering how someone could be as dense as Lieutenant Tessa was acting. Perhaps she was in shock too.

"That's crazy. I'm not going in the water. The aliens are in the water."

"The aliens are dead," Allura said. "I saw them. Bodies everywhere. Whatever was on the object that landed out there killed them. And then it nearly killed us."

"Well, that's it then," she said, her voice loud as she began to panic. "I'm not going out there. No way."

"Fine," Allura said. "Then help me up."

Tessa just looked at Allura, then turned her back. It was too much to hope for that the two women, who were her superiors in both rank and time of service, would be absolutely useless to Allura in a real emergency. She took the case full of supplies off the wall and used it as a step to get as high up as she could. Then she pulled herself up through the crack in the hatch. Water was surging around the ship, and a wave crashed against it. Cold spray soaked her short hair, but Allura kept climbing. She wiggled up until she could sit on the upper part of the hatch. Then she pulled herself up onto the roof of the ship. It was slick with water from the waves, but what was shocking was that the normally smooth hull was wrinkled like aluminum foil after it's used. There were rents in the outer air frame, and the wings were torn off.

As she looked around in the darkness, Allura wondered how they had survived. The only explanation was that the creature who attacked them had kept them from dropping out of the sky like a rock. Why it would do something like that was a mystery, and she had no time to figure it out. The tide was still coming in, which meant the water around the craft was getting deeper. She knew it wouldn't take much to float the ship and perhaps pull it out to sea. Better to get everyone out and then make their way to shore before it was too late.

Allura got on her knees and looked back down through the opening in the rear hatch. Tessa was there, looking up at her.

"It's clear. Help the Major up and I'll pull her through," Allura suggested.

"It's safe?"

"There's no aliens," Allura said.

It wasn't the answer to the question. The reality was they weren't safe. The ocean was dangerous, especially for people in shock. The water was cold and it was rough. They could easily be pulled out to sea if they weren't careful. And while she didn't see the alien, that didn't mean it wasn't there. It was very, very dark on the water. The only light was from the alien disk, but it was shining inland and served only as a marker. But Allura knew it was always darkest before dawn, and the pilot's flight time had them landing at Hawkstone right around dawn. Which meant the sunrise couldn't be far off.

"Okay," Tessa said.

She helped Major Reece step onto the emergency supply case. The older woman reached up and Allura grabbed her hand. Pulling her through the opening wasn't easy. Major Reece did nothing to help herself, but fortunately the woman was incredibly thin. Allura managed to get her pulled up and onto the roof of the shuttle.

"It's cold," Reece said, sounding like a scared child.

"I know. But we'll be okay," Allura told her, before turning her attention back to Tessa. "Hand me up the emergency supply case."

"How will I get out if I do that?" Tessa asked.

"I thought you were staying in the shuttle," Allura told her.

"Not by myself!"

"Well, we still have to have the case, and if you stand on it, we can't get it out," Allura said. "Hand it up and then I'll help you out."

"No, you won't," Tessa said in a desperate, shaky voice. "You'll leave me here. You never liked me. Don't you leave me here! Please!"

"I'm not going to leave you," Allura said. "I promise. Now hand up the case."

Allura had to climb back out over the tail end of the shuttle, but got the case pulled up and slid it toward Major Reece on the roof of the shuttle. It rattled across the rumpled metal. And when Allura turned back to Tessa, the Lieutenant was crying.

"Come on," Allura said. Get up here."

"I can't reach you," Tessa complained.

"So climb. Find a way, Lieutenant, or you'll die in there all alone."

"You'd like that, wouldn't you?"

"If I wanted you to die, I would have left you in there a while ago," Allura said. "Now, get up here. No one is dying on my watch."

"Why do you care about me?" Tessa asked, as she started scrambling up the hatch, trying to reach Allura's hand.

"You got me through the media tour," Allura said, although she really felt that both Tessa and Major Reece used her to further their own careers. But it wasn't the time to work through their hard feelings.

"You didn't need me," she cried, finally getting a grip on Allura's hand.

"You've got to help me, Lieutenant. I can't pull you out by myself."

They heaved and squirmed their way out of the ship. Allura helped Tessa onto the roof just as the sun began to rise. It was a cloudy day, the light a cold, gray color. The sea around them was choppy in the strong wind, and the breakers were rolling onto the beach. One hit the ship hard enough to rock it a little. The cold spray soaked them. While Allura was back in Air Force fatigues, Reece and Tessa were wearing lightweight sportswear—little more than pajamas.

"How are we going to get to shore?" Tessa asked.

"I don't know," Allura said.

The beach was still dark. The sun was coming up behind them, but its light was fighting a losing battle with the clouds. Allura looked up and saw movement. At first, her heart skipped a beat in fear. Perhaps the Ma'Tis weren't all dead. And then she saw the unmistakable form of a mech battle trooper. She had seen them on posters, in television shows, in commercials for the army, and even in movies. They were the unmistakable face of the Fiona Grand armed forces.

"There!" Allura said pointing. "Help! Help us!"

And then the shooting started. Allura dropped to her knees instinctively, pulling the other two women down with her.

"What's happening?" Tessa shouted. "Why are they shooting at us?"

The flashes of laser light in the dull gloom of dawn on the coast were unmistakable. But it was obvious that the mechs weren't shooting at Allura and her two companions. She turned and looked over her shoulder. Slithering along the underside of the clouds was the huge serpent she had seen out the shuttle windows.

"There," Allura said pointing back. "That's what they're shooting at."

"It's coming right for us," Tessa declared.

And we can't stay here," Allura said. "We have to move."

"Where?"

"Into the water. Come on!" Allura shouted as she shoved the last flare into the gun, raised it high, and fired the flaming signal straight up into the sky. Then she dropped down into the frigid water with Major Reece and Lieutenant Tessa, hoping that she hadn't called the alien creature right to them.

CHAPTER 41

"DID YOU SEE THAT?" Dyson asked.

The flare was bright, and Cosmo didn't know how he was supposed to miss it. His helmet view was zoomed all the way in. He saw Allura on top of the shuttle as she shot the flare and then dropped into the water beside the vessel as a wave hit, pouring water over the top of the aircraft and down on top of the three women.

"Yeah, that's Allura," Cosmo said, pulling his vision back to normal in the helmet.

"The lasers aren't penetrating," Captain Swift said, his vision locked on the alien creature. "See how they're ricocheting off its body. Fascinating. We've tried developing armor like that but failed."

"It's coming right for us," Dyson said. "This is going to be one hell of a fight."

As they watched, the flying serpentine creature flew wide of the flare and began zigzagging toward the beach.

"At least it didn't go after Allura," Cosmo said.

"You sure that it's her, dude?" Dyson said.

"I saw her. She's in the water with two other women."

"Probably safer than on the beach," Dyson declared.

Cosmo wasn't sure what to think of the alien creature. Was it a flying serpent? Did that make it a dragon? He had no clue and didn't know what to think about it. All his life the Ma'Tis had been a threat. They were frightening creatures but seemed real to him. The dragon was anything but. It looked like it was a creature from a fantasy film, not a living, breathing, sentient being. The only thing he could think was that it was a threat. It had slaughtered the Ma'Tis and then brought down the Air Force shuttle. Major Zukov was right to attack it, but they weren't having any luck.

The dragon roared. The sound was like metal dragged over concrete. And then came fire. It spewed greasy, orange flames from its maw.

"You have got to be kidding me," Dyson said.

The flames shot down across the beach and straight over a squad of mechs. They were heavily armored, but not completely encased. The flames found the weaknesses in their mechanical platforms. Screams could be heard as the dragon sailed back up into the sky.

"Switch to explosive rounds," Major Zukov shouted. "Don't let it get away."

The mechs with grenade launchers fired at the beast, but it was quickly out of range. Their munitions arced through the air, then dropped to the ground. The explosions were loud and the tension high as the dragon disappeared into the clouds.

"This could be bad," Dyson said. "Lasers don't work. And we can't get close enough to do any real damage."

"We need to draw it to us," Cosmo said. "Major Zukov, I have an idea."

"Who is this? Get off this channel," the Major barked.

"He won't listen," Swift said. "He hates me. Our feud goes back years. I'm sorry."

"Doesn't matter," Cosmo said. "Look, we need that creature down here. And the only thing that might draw it down is if we damage this."

Cosmo reached out with his rifle and tapped the large, upright ring.

"Damage it how?" Dyson asked.

"Wait, what?" Captain Swift said. "This is an artifact of incredible importance. The technology alone is worth more than you can imagine. We can't damage it."

"If we don't, that thing is going to kill us all," Cosmo said. "Look at the Ma'Tis."

It was impossible not to see the bodies. The morning light was dull, the sky gray, but there was more than enough light to see the blackened, cracked shells and tightly curled legs of the crab-like Ma'Tis.

"Not if we retreat," Captain Swift said.

"The Major is never going to do that," Cosmo said. "And I'm not taking any chances."

"You think lasers will do it?" Dyson asked.

"Probably not. Let's try plasma."

"No!" Captain Swift said. "That's an order."

The dragon dropped back through the clouds, diving straight toward the largest group of mechs.

"Fire! Give it everything you've got!" Major Zukov shouted.

The battle troopers fired their weapons—lasers, grenades, and even the depleted uranium rounds from their sidearms. But the dragon seemed impervious to all of it. It crashed into their ranks, knocking the mechs around like bowling pins. Some were crushed under the creature; others were flung through the air by the creature's lashing tail. Cosmo saw one get snatched into the dragon's mouth. Flames roiled.

"How does it do that?" Dyson asked. "I thought that kind of stuff was only in fairy tales."

"It's not uncommon," Swift said. "Take the bombardier beetle, for example. It has two pouches in its abdomen. One is filled with hydroquinone, the other with hydrogen peroxide. It shoots the chemicals through its body and out its hind quarters. The mixture of the chemicals creates a heat reaction that is almost as hot as boiling water and severely burns any insects attacking the beetle."

"Great zoology lesson, Captain," Cosmo said. "But we have to do something."

"We can't get close enough to use the plasma," Dyson said.

"Then use it on the device," Cosmo said.

He fired a single round at the base of the ring. Captain Swift waved his arms and shouted for him to stop, but he had to back away to keep from getting hit by the plasma that splattered when it hit the device. Smoke immediately boiled up and the metal around the plasma turned red.

"That works," Dyson declared, as he started firing.

They hit the ring nearly all the way around. The metal smoked and the light was cut off as the hundreds of spokes extended to the middle and sealed off the ring. The dragon, still fighting the mechs, roared. Cosmo saw it swivel its head toward them, the maw open wide. Cosmo saw the red fleshy tongue as it drew back, revealing a hidden tube underneath.

"Take cover!" he shouted, pushing Captain Swift down the ocean side of the sand dune.

The officer tripped and fell, rolling through the sand as Cosmo and Dyson dropped to their knees and bent low. Flames engulfed the hilltop.

"Fall back, fall back!" Major Zukov ordered. "All units, retreat."

Cosmo knew it was the wrong order. Rhino Company was devastated. Cosmo didn't want to think about Todd Butler being one of the injured or the dead, but a single glance showed that three quarters of the regiment was down. Only a few were still on their feet, and those were moving away from the dragon. But the perfect time to strike back was now while the creature was distracted.

"We gotta split up," Cosmo said as he and Dyson scampered down the sand dune.

"Hit it from both sides," Henry confirmed.

"And watch out for that tail," Cosmo added.

"Copy that. Don't die on me, Frosty."

"You either. Let's rock."

They ran around the wide dune and found the dragon slithering toward the disk. Cosmo let loose with the plasma cartridges. They hit the beast's scales and exploded, releasing the super-heated gel. The dragon wailed as the plasma burned through, searing the flesh beneath its tough outer skin. Oily black smoke erupted from the impact points, and the dragon whipped its tail toward him

Running in sand is normally difficult, but the motion assistance of his armor made it easy. He backpedaled, moving swiftly away between two dunes. A wave of sand was thrown up by the lashing tail, but it didn't strike him. On the far side, Dyson was repeating the attack. The dragon raced up the dune, its wounded body smoking and curled around the alien disk. Cosmo followed, still shooting. His rifle chugged in his hands as it emptied the first magazine. Cosmo hit the ejector switch, let the empty mag fall free, and rammed a fresh one into place.

"Keep hammering it," Cosmo shouted.

But the dragon had plans of its own. Fire from its open maw sprayed right toward Cosmo in a deadly wave. He dove backward, falling into the sand as the wave of fire surged over him. The sand was blackened in places, melted into glassy rocks in others. The projectile range of the bulky LA6 rifles was only thirty meters uphill, but it was enough that Cosmo continued to hit the beast. He could see long rents in the creature's scaly hide. Dark blood oozed from the wounds, and oily smoke rose from the burns as blisters began to form on the dragon's body.

They were winning because the creature was protecting the disk, but before they could kill the dragon it took to the air, carrying the alien disk with it. Cosmo stopped shooting and just stood back, looking up at the sky.

"It's running for the hills," Dyson shouted. "Yeah, baby. That's what I'm talking about. We did it."

"Major Swift!" Zukov's voice broke over their communication system. "Get your people to help with the injured. We are pulling out of this area now."

"Yes, of course," Swift said. "Dyson, Frost, help with the injured."

Cosmo felt a sense of anger bubble up in him. Why was the Major running away? And why hadn't he acknowledged that Cosmo and Dyson had saved his regiment? Instead, the commander sounded angry with them. It didn't make sense.

Looking out to the ocean, Cosmo could see that Allura and the two women with her were huddling in the lee of the downed shuttle. He ignored Major Zukov and started for the beach.

"Yo, Cos, where you going, man?" Dyson asked.

"To get Allura," Cosmo said. "And the people with her."

"We got orders, bro."

"That's right, and I'm helping those in need. Just because they aren't in a mech doesn't mean we can leave them."

"All right, I'm with you," Dyson said. "Cap?"

Malcom Swift set down his scanner on the sand and followed them into the surf without a word.

CHAPTER 42

"ALLURA!" Cosmo shouted.

The water was up to his waist. His boots sank into the sand, but his MAL armor had no trouble moving through the ocean. Cosmo doubted he could swim, but as long as his head was above water, he would be okay.

"We're here!" Allura shouted as she waved her hands.

It was high tide. The water around the shuttle was over two meters deep. Allura, Major Reece, and Lieutenant Tessa were perched on the broken wing.

"We're coming," Cosmo said. He hurried through the waves and reached them a moment later. "Are you hurt?"

"Shaken up," Allura admitted. "But we aren't injured."

"I'm freezing," Lieutenant Tessa said through chattering teeth.

"You have to get Major Reece out first," Allura said, just as Dyson and Captain Swift arrived at the mangled aircraft.

"Climb on," the captain said, backing up to where Major Reece was staring vacantly out toward the beach.

Allura had to help her. Captain Swift wasn't huge in the MAL armor. She wrapped one arm around the Major, and clung to the top of his body armor that ringed the low helmet.

"You're with me," Dyson said to Lieutenant Tessa.

He was taller than Cosmo, with wide shoulders. He still had his bulky rifle in one hand, but the other reached out to Tessa. She jumped to him, her legs wrapping around his waist and her arms clinging to his shoulders. He held her with his free arm and on their private channel said to Cosmo, "Yo, man, I could get used to this."

Cosmo reached out for Allura. "I'm so glad you're all right. It's so good to see you again."

"Cosmo?" Allura asked.

She couldn't see his face with his armor on. "Yeah, it's me."

She dropped into the water, and he lifted her out with one arm. She leaned in close, trying to see through his visor.

"It's me," he said.

"I can see you," she said, her voice cracking with emotion. "You came for me."

"Yeah," he said. "Of course I did. I love you."

"I love you too," she replied.

He began slogging back toward shore. His armor didn't make him immune to the strain, but it helped. He carried her back through the waves and was tempted to yank off his helmet, but his survival instincts told him not to.

"Captain Swift, get your people under control," Major Zukov said over the command channel. "This is no time to be dragging civilians into a battle zone."

"They're not civilians," Cosmo replied. "Air Force personnel. One is Major Reece. And the other is a Gold Star awardee, sir."

Before Zukov could think of a reply, there was an awful shriek from above, and the dragon returned. The disk was gone, and the beast was furious. It dove straight for Cosmo, who dove back into the waves with Allura in his arms. Fire spewed from its mouth over the water, which vaporized into steam. The blast only lasted a few seconds and Dyson hit the creature with several more plasma shots before it arced back up into the sky. When the light from the fiery attack dimmed, Cosmo rose out of the waves with Allura.

"You've got to get clear," he said.

"What about you?" she asked, breathlessly.

"I'll make sure it doesn't come after you."

"No," Allura said. "You'll get hurt. Come with us."

"Something has to stop that thing."

"The mechs," Allura said.

But Zukov was already ordering his people to fall back.

"It's just me," Cosmo said. "Dyson, get them out of here."

"Nah, man, you stay and I'm staying too."

"I've got them," Captain Swift said. "Good luck, gentlemen."

"I won't leave you," Allura said.

"You can't fight that thing without armor," Cosmo said. "You have to go."

She grabbed his collar, pulled herself up and planted a kiss right on his view screen, her eyes just inches from his. "Don't you die, Cosmo Frost. You hear me?"

"Yes," he said, his voice tight from making a promise he couldn't keep.

"Yo, man, I got an idea," Dyson said, rushing toward one of the fallen mechs.

Cosmo was tempted to turn and watch Allura running down the beach after Captain Swift. He was carrying Major Reece in his arms. Lieutenant Tessa was right behind him. They scrambled up the beach and between two sand dunes, while Cosmo brought his rifle to his shoulder.

"Emergency seal," he said.

The voice command sealed his suit. The only part of him that could move was his fingers. The rifle was at his shoulder as the dragon came charging down at him again. He flicked the control to the laser cannon and waited. The dragon was dark red, with black streaks and orange highlights on its scaly skin. If it charged into him Cosmo knew he would die. Instead it opened its mouth and spewed fire. Cosmo had no idea what the fire was made from. It was some sort of biological chemical mixture and was probably very hot, but he trusted the MAL armor to protect him and let the fire come. At the same time, he squeezed the trigger on his rifle. The weapon issued twelve beams a second on fully automatic fire. The battery waned as the high-energy output soared. The lasers had bounced harmlessly from the dragon's skin, but the inside of its mouth was vulnerable. Almost as soon as it spewed fire, the laser blasts hit and it jerked to the side.

Cosmo wanted to follow it, but his armor was locked in emergency mode, completely sealed to keep out the microscopic bio-bots of the Ma'Tis. The wave of fire poured over Cosmo. Warnings sounded from the heat, but it didn't reach him. The furious beast dove into the water, then surged up like a cobra and sent a wave of fire along the beach. Once again, the waves passed over him. But because it wasn't a sustained blast, they didn't wreck his armor. He unlocked it, rose to his feet and dashed ashore as the dragon dove toward him.

"I got it," Dyson shouted. He had retrieved one of the two-meter-thick knives carried by the mech units. The blade was as wide as Cosmo's hand from palm to fingertips. Normally, just lifting the weapon would take all his strength, but in the MAL armor Dyson could not only lift it but he threw the weapon toward Cosmo. It flipped end over end before landing tip down in the sand. The handle was up. Cosmo grabbed it.

"Look out!" his friend shouted.

Cosmo didn't have to look back to know what was coming. The dragon was right behind him. He tugged the sword from the sand, then jumped, locking his armor in safety mode again.

The dragon caught Cosmo in its mouth, just as he knew it would. Fury drove the beast's attack. Fire hadn't stopped the battle trooper, and so it did what any predator would do, it bit him. Only it hadn't counted on the sword. The dragon caught Cosmo in its mouth, but when the jaws came down to crush him, the point of the sword gouged the tender, unprotected flesh. Its tongue was severed, the roof of its mouth punctured by the sharp tip of the huge blade.

"Activate electric pulse!" Cosmo said.

He was caught between the serpent's teeth, his back laying right on the nozzle that spewed fire. His suit was equipped with an electric pulse that sent electricity all across the surface of the armor in emergency mode. The pulse was designed to kill bio-bots, but it also worked to burn the flesh inside the serpent's mouth. The beast roared and slung its head from side to side. Cosmo was sent flying. He would almost certainly have been killed if he had crashed into something solid, but instead, he skipped along the surface of the water, then plunged under the water as his momentum slowed.

"Cosmo!" Dyson shouted.

"I'm okay," Cosmo said, after unlocking his armor.

"What did you do?" Dyson said as Cosmo stood up, his head breaking the surface of the water in time to see the dragon flopping on its side and writhing along the beach.

"Gave it more than it could chew," Cosmo said. "We have to finish it. Target the wings."

Dyson still had his rifle and started shooting. Cosmo dashed to a fallen mech. The metal was mangled, the armor capsule dented. Cosmo wasn't expecting to recognize the bloody face, but as he bent over the large, mechanized battle trooper, he saw Butler staring up at him.

"Todd!" Cosmo shouted.

"Cos..." Butler said in a weak voice.

"Hang on, man. We'll get you out of here."

Butler tried to smile through the pain. Cosmo wanted to do more, but there wasn't time. He yanked Butler's huge knife free from the mech. In his hands, the long blade was like a sword, and it felt surreal to Cosmo as he charged through the surf back toward the dragon. He was an armored warrior with a sword, fighting a dragon. The irony actually made him laugh.

"I'm out!" Dyson shouted. "No more plasma."

Most of his shots had missed, but a few had found the dragon's wings. Cosmo didn't know if it was enough to keep the beast out of the sky, but he hoped it was. Still, there wasn't time to stand back and hit the dragon from a safe distance.

Cosmo screamed a battle cry as he ran, holding the blade out in front of him. The dragon was still writhing, unable to dislodge the blade wedged into its mouth. With the point of the blade held level, Cosmo ran straight into the dragon. The knife plunged deep—nearly the full length of the two-meter-long blade. The creature jerked away, knocking Cosmo off his feet. He fell into the water as the dragon reared in pain. When it crashed back down, the wave swept Cosmo away. It took him a moment to regain his feet. When he did, he saw Dyson charging at the dragon with a mech blade in hand. Cosmo rushed to help his friend. When the dragon reacted to Dyson's thrust, Cosmo managed to leap onto the creature's back. He grabbed the knife's long handle and tugged. The dragon reared again, but Cosmo held on, using the knife handle to keep his grip with one hand while the other latched onto Dyson's sword, which was dangling and on the verge of falling free.

"Watch out, Cos!" Dyson shouted. "Don't let it fall back on you."

Cosmo pulled out his friend's blade. The MAL armor made wielding the sword possible, but it wasn't easy to strike with a weapon that was as tall as he was. The blade came down onto the hard, scaly skin and glanced off. Cosmo realized that he must have hit a weak point in the dragon's hide, perhaps where plasma had burned through earlier. Even with his armor enhancing his strength, Cosmo couldn't hack into the dragon hide. It dropped back down suddenly and sent Cosmo tumbling toward its head. He was stopped when a short, curved horn located just behind the serpent's head, broke through the MAL armor, and punctured his thigh. Cosmo screamed in pain, and he felt the armor tighten around the wound. His first instinct was to pull free, but he realized that being impaled on the serpent's back—just behind its head—gave him an opportunity he might not get again. With both hands, he lifted the giant blade and then chopped it down across the dragon's eye on the left side of its wide head. The scaly skin protected the beast, but nothing protected its eyeball. Blood and fluid sprayed out, and once more the dragon reared. Only it didn't stop. It rose up and back until it flopped over, splashing into the deep water beyond the breakers.

"Cosmo!" Dyson shouted. "Cos!"

There was no time to reply. Cosmo screamed again as he was flung free of the dragon. His armor wasn't buoyant, and he sank beneath the surface. Weaponless, wounded, and sinking, he felt a sense of doom. Dark blood streamed from the wounds on the dragon. One eye was ruined—one long blade was still stuck fast in its side—but it wasn't dead. The salt water burned the gash on Cosmo's thigh like liquid fire. He couldn't fathom the pain the dragon was in. And then, out of the depths, he saw them.

White-shelled Ma'Tis came swimming upward, their big claws open wide. But they weren't coming for Cosmo. They attacked the dragon, dozens of them latching onto the beast and pulling it under. The dragon thrashed, but the water and perhaps its wounds made the beast slower, weaker. Not to mention the big Ma'Tis clinging to its body. The sight of them made Cosmo kick his feet. His leg throbbed with pain, but fear of death overrode his senses, and the MAL armor strengthened his movements. Soon he was moving toward the shore, the waves pushing him. When his feet hit the sand, he was able to trudge back.

"Dyson," Cosmo said. "You there?"

"Here! Cos! I'm here, bro. Where are you?"

"Coming out of the water."

His head broke the surface for a moment. Then a wave smashed him down to his hands and knees. Part of him wanted to quit, to just give up. On his view screen, warnings flashed. His blood pressure was low. His armor's emergency oxygen level was nearly spent. The power in the suit dipped below twenty percent. He thought about giving up —just closing his eyes and drifting away in the pain—but his training kicked in. Giving up wasn't an option, no matter how bad he hurt or how weak he felt. So he trudged on.

"Hang on, bro. I'm coming," Dyson said.

Before he knew strong hands grabbed Cosmo and lifted him up, half dragging him from the surf.

"What happened? Damn, look at your leg. We gotta get you to a medic."

"They got it," Cosmo said. "The Ma'Tis. They got the dragon."

"Oh, snap! That's some kind of justice right there, bro," Dyson said.

Cosmo collapsed on the beach. "Did Captain Swift get the Air Force people to safety?"

"We got medevacs inbound," Dyson said. "They're okay."

"Butler," Cosmo said. "I saw him. On the beach. Gotta help him."

"Yeah, okay," Dyson said. "You good?"

"I'm good, Dyson, thanks."

"Be right back, bro."

Dyson hurried off and Cosmo closed his eyes. He was surprised at how incredibly tired he felt. Every muscle ached, and there was a throbbing sound in his ears. His armor was tight around his thigh, acting like a tourniquet to staunch the blood flow. He wanted to drift off to sleep, but knew he needed help. If Drill Sergeant Reed had been there, he would have screamed for Cosmo to get off his keister, which is what he did.

While Dyson saved Butler, Cosmo managed to limp through the sand dunes and up onto the prairie just as a trio of medical hovercraft came on the scene. The battle was over, and Cosmo was glad.

"Cosmo?" Allura shouted as she rushed through the groups of mechs and wounded battle troopers in search of him.

"Over there," someone said, pointing to where Cosmo sat just inside a medical transport. A tech was busy working on his leg and she ran to him.

"Cosmo!"

"Allura," he said.

His helmet was off, but he looked pale. "You're hurt?"

"Just a scratch," he said.

The medical tech looked at Allura with a dark expression. "Remember your promise," she said.

"How could I forget."

"We're taking him to medical," the tech said.

"Hawkstone?"

"Yeah, that's closest. We got the bleeding stopped but..."

"They think I might have some poison, or maybe an alien germ in my leg," he said.

"Sorry, Airman, we've got to go," the med tech said, signaling the pilot to take off.

"I'll see you at the base," Allura said.

"Can't wait... to catch up," Cosmo shouted over the roar of the repulsor engines.

EPILOGUE

ALLURA WALKED into Cosmo's room. There was a plastic shroud around his bed, and machines were humming softly. The light was dim, and Cosmo's mother was on a chair on the far side.

"Is he..."

"Quarantine," Cosmo's mother Nicole said. "They patched up the wound. It was deep. Something punctured the muscle and scraped his bone, but they got it under control. The doctor said he should recover fully."

"Should?" Allura asked, joining her beside Cosmo's bed.

"As long as there was nothing injected into his blood stream," she said. "He'll be here a while, I guess. Until they decide he's not going to infect anyone."

"He saved us," Allura said as Nicole stood up and put her arm around the young Airman's shoulders.

"I shouldn't be surprised," Nicole said. "When he was little he was always pretending to be a superhero."

"He's my hero."

"Speaking of heroes," Nicole said. "Congratulations on getting the Gold Star. That's amazing, Allura. Your parents must be so proud."

"Oh, they are," she said. "Enjoying it more than me for sure."

"You should be proud too."

"I didn't do anything out of the ordinary—just what they taught me to do."

"From what I heard no one else could do it."

"Because the bombardiers here haven't had the same training."

"Maybe," Nicole said. "But you're talented. And you're making a difference in the world. That's something to be proud of. I know I'm proud of you."

"Thank you, Miss Nicole. I just... I feel kind of out of control."

"Things get hectic sometimes. But you'll land on your feet."

"How'd you get here so fast?"

"I've been volunteering ever since Cosmo's graduation," she said. "Sergeant Reed got me into a medical nursing program. I'll be here for as long as they need me."

"I'm so glad," Nicole said. "Has he been awake?"

"Not yet," she said.

They waited nearly two hours. When Cosmo finally came around, he was happy to see them, but frustrated by the quarantine.

"I kept my promise," he said, a little groggy from the pain medicine. He felt spacey and tired.

"You did," Allura replied. "Now keep on keeping it."

"I'm fine," he said with a goofy grin. "I feel great."

"That's good," she said. "Because we aren't through yet."

"Not by a long shot," Cosmo agreed.

A week passed before word of his friends reached Cosmo. Dyson was with Captain Swift, studying the anomaly that had been found on a hilltop eighty kilometers inland. The device had survived the plasma attack and either self-repaired or been fixed by someone else. Captain Swift was fairly certain that it was a transportation device that linked to either another part of the galaxy or a new dimension.

Butler survived too, but had sustained major injuries and wouldn't be returning to the field. Major Zukov was credited with slaying the alien creature despite having nothing to do with actually fighting it. The HAVOC program was still classified, which meant Cosmo couldn't talk about it and the Army couldn't credit him with having killed the beast. Instead, they were giving him a new assignment.

"That's the stupidest thing I've ever heard," Allura said as she paced on her side of the quarantine barrier in the room that Cosmo had been moved to a couple days after his leg had been stitched up.

"I don't know..." Cosmo said shrugging. "Beats twirling my thumbs in here."

"They want you to go through that thing? They don't even know where it goes?"

"So I'll find out," he said.

His orders had come through earlier that day. Cosmo had sent Allura a message that he needed to talk. She was serving with the other bombardiers at Hawkstone again and was enjoying the sense of camaraderie as well as the freedom to visit Cosmo in the hospital during her free time.

"Why you? You're barely on your feet," she pointed out.

"I'm fine," he said, even though it was an exaggeration.

"There have to be other people who could do this."

"There are other capable troopers," Cosmo said. "But I'm already exposed to whatever is on the other side of that portal. Sending me just makes sense."

"There could be more dragons out there," she said. "Or something worse."

"I imagine they're saying the same thing about me," Cosmo joked.

"I don't like it," she said.

"It's just a recon mission. I go through, take a look around, see what's there and come right back."

"If you can," she said.

"I will. I promise," he told her, stepping close to the plastic barrier.

He put his hands up, touching the plastic. She frowned but put her hands on his. She could feel the warmth through the barrier. They both wanted more, so much more, but they weren't allowed to touch or even breathe the same air.

"I'll be back before you know it," he said.

"And I'll be here, making sure the Ma'Tis don't run wild while you're gone," she said. "You'll need a world to come back to."

"I will," he agreed.

"And then your quarantine can end.

"Can't wait for that," he said with a smile.

"We've got to outlive this war, Cosmo."

"I wouldn't have it any other way."

An hour later he was on a special flight out to the anomaly. Suited up in MAL armor and fully armed with a variety of weapons, he stepped off the transport and into a plastic tunnel that led to the ring. It was still glowing with orange light.

"Yo, man, look who's walking?" Dyson said from outside the tunnel, his voice clear in Cosmo's battle helmet.

"Good as new," Cosmo said.

"Refurbished, maybe," the big man said. "You ready to make history that no one will ever know?"

"Sure am," Cosmo said. "Where's Bolt?"

"Cap's bringing him along. How was your vay-cay?"

"You mean a week in the hospital with a hole in my leg?"

"Tell me you didn't love it," Dyson said with a chuckle.

"I was bored out of my mind," Cosmo said.

"Yeah, but you got to see your lady. I got word your moms was there too. Couldn't have been all bad."

"It wasn't," Cosmo said. "But I'm ready to be done with quarantine."

"Better get used to it, bro. You're gonna be off limits for a while. The ring is open again and guess who drew the short straw?"

"Very funny," Cosmo said, looking toward the ring that was glowing from the orange light it produced. "What do you think's waiting for us on the other side of that portal?"

"I can't even imagine," Dyson said. "But they better be ready for us."

"You ever think you'd be an explorer, going where no human has ever been before?"

"Nope, thought I'd be playing ball in the big show. Now I'm here, backing you up."

"Who needs fame and fortune," Cosmo said. "That's nothing compared to being on the front lines."

"Sure, but I ain't ever heard of anybody getting killed playing baseball."

"A minor inconvenience," Cosmo said. They both laughed, but in the back of his mind Cosmo knew he was risking everything by going through the alien ring.

Captain Swift arrived in short order. A driver backed a hover truck to the quarantine gate. Cosmo synced his armor's control system to Bolt. The big HAVOC drone was led out of the truck by Cosmo's commands and into the tunnel.

"Remember," Captain Swift told him. "You go through, record as much as you can and come right back."

"I got it."

"If it's night," the officer said. "Record the sky. The stars could give us a clue as to where you are."

"And don't do nothing I wouldn't do," Dyson said with a laugh.

Cosmo walked to the ring. It was tall. Stairs had been built up beside it. The light glowed orange with swirls of red. The HAVOC drone followed behind Cosmo, pausing when he did. For a moment Cosmo stood at the threshold, wondering what lay beyond the portal.

"You okay, Private Frost?" Swift asked.

"Fine, sir."

"Very good. You are clear to proceed," the officer ordered.

"Here goes nothing," Cosmo said, as he stepped through the portal and into a different world.

AUTHOR'S NOTE

Thank you for reading Armor Brigade. I got the idea for the story listening to a Christmas song last year. What would it be like to suddenly be pulled away from your life and the people you loved to be sent into a world of fighting and dange?. And the second book is shaping up to be even more exciting from a creative point of view. I'm so excited about these books and can't wait to get the second one published. Look for Havoc Squad (Armor Brigade Book 2) in May, 2023. And don't forget to leave a rating/review on Amazon & Goodreads.

HAVOC SQUAD SAMPLE

Chapter 1

"Someone tell me what the devil we're dealing with here!" General Davina Song snapped.

The secured bunker for the MCS, the Military Command Staff, was called the War Room. It consisted of a long conference table with secure communications and computer interfaces at each seat that was built right into the tabletop. Generals Toliver and Ming, the top commanders of the Air and Space Forces were there, along with their support staffs. General Augustus McShay was head of the Fiona Grand Army's Infantry Division. General Julia Eclair was the highest ranking member of the FGA Artillery Division. And General Hugo Knots was the ranking member of the vaunted Armor Division, which included the Mechanized Battle Troopers.

"No one can say for sure," General Ming said. "Satellites can't penetrate the cloud cover. We're getting Haze from the Ma'Tis. The coastal surveillance cameras are down too. It's a mess."

"But something came out of that disk!" General Song insisted. "I want to know what the hell it is."

"Not human," General Toliver said.

"What happened to the bird you had doing a fly over?" General Eclair asked.

"It never made it back to base," General Toliver said. "Any broadcasts it made were lost in the Haze."

"Damn it!" Song said, banging her fist on the table.

"General, I've got Rino Company moving into position on the beach," General Knots said. "That's Major Zukov's people. Whatever is down there, he'll have it hand quickly enough."

Two hours passed while the most powerful people in the Fiona Grand armed forces waited. They were not patient people. Regular updates had to be sent to the government, including the PM. There were ugly rumors going around that the Prime Minister had been assaulted at his own party. Normally, General Davina Song wouldn't have cared. She knew the PM, and like most powerful men, he thought he could do whatever he wanted and get away with it. Only the rumor was the person responsible for assaulting him was the Airman he had awarded the Gold Star for Meritorious Service. The Grand Ball was being thrown in her honor, but General Song knew it was just a chance for the PM and his fat cat donors to indulge themselves. She had attended one such party herself and had been horrified at the lack of honor among the rich and powerful. Song had no doubt there was some truth to the rumor. The PM was in his mid-fifties, yet it was well known that he liked young girls. Airman Presley was barely nineteen years old, and no doubt had defended herself when the PM came on too strong. Still, the rumors might turn into more, and it was General Song's job to ensure that nothing stuck to the armed services that might damage the reputation of the Fiona Grand military. So, when she wasn't demanding answers from her staff of high ranking generals, she was finding out all she could about Airman First Class Allura Presley.

"I've got a report from the field!" General Knots said. "Word just reached General Senjay at the FOB. Rino Company was hit hard. They're requesting emergency medical assistance."

General Song looked to General Ming. "Send what ever they need."

"I've got a Flight of medical transports standing by," General Ming said.

"Send them," General Song ordered. "I want eyewitness reports as soon as they come in. General Knots, get me on video with Major Zukov ASAP."

"Yes, General," the head of the Army's Armor Division replied.

It was almost another hour before the reports were delivered to the War Room. There were descriptions of a giant snake, or dragon. The wounded were delirious it seemed. Some were claiming that the alien entity breathed fire. It seemed absurd, but eventually Major Zukov's video feed was piped into the War Room on the Military's encrypted server. A large video display on the wall showed the feed from the Major's MECH.

"It's true," General Toliver said.

"Unbelievable," General Eclair whispered.

As they watched the alien serpentine creature deflected the laser fire from the MECHs on the beach, then belched fire that poured over the battle troopers. They could hear Major Zukov's distraught voice calling his forces back, and ordering them to switch to explosives. The battle was one sided. The alien seemed invincible. General Song felt as if she might be sick.

The dragon pounced on a group of MECHs, using it's powerful tail to bat them around like a child swatting dolls to the floor. It was a military disaster, a massacre. But then the beast's focus changed. It ignored the MECHs and raced back to the disk. There were two Battle Troopers in experimental armor on the sand dune by the alien object. Smoke was rising from the disk, which was closed down.

"What's happening?" Song demanded. "Who are those two troopers?"

"General," Knots explained, "other than Rino Company, the only other troopers in the area are Captain's Swift experimental force. That has to be them."

"What experimental force?"

"He developed HAVOC drones that sync with Battle Troopers in Motion Assisted Light Armor. I don't see the drones, though."

"You're talking about the troopers who took out the Ma'Tis tank and called in the bombers outside Hillsdale?" General Ming asked.

"That's them," General Knots said. "Their HAVOC drones are being serviced though."

General Davina Song watched the two troopers fire what looked to her like plasma rounds at the dragon, which was coiling itself around the disk.

"Something is working," General McShay said. "That's smoke coming from the creature."

"Plasma rounds," General Eclair said. "That was quick thinking on the part of those troopers."

"Indeed," Song agreed. "Where the hell is that thing going?"

They watched the alien fly up into the air with the disk. It disappeared in the low, thick cloud bank.

"General, I've got Captain Swift on comms," General Knots said. "He's on screen now."

Captain Swift appeared. It was obvious that he was still in battle armor. All they could see was his face, and the helmet padding to the sides.

"Captain, what's the situation out there?" General Song demanded.

"General, I've got the passengers from the transport that flew over the area. The crew were killed, but Major Reece, Lieutenant Tessa, and Airman Presley survived. My squad is still engaged with the alien."

"What is it?" General Song asked. "And where did it come from, Captain?"

"My best guess at this stage is that the creature came through the device that landed on the beach."

"Through it?"

"Yes, General. It appears to be a wormhole generator or inter-dimensional gate of some type. I managed to get scans of the object. It's drawing energy from the ground. Very advanced technology, General. I'm certain it's nothing we've ever seen before."

"First contact," General Toliver said.

"A new, sentient race," General Ming added.

"What about the creature?" General Song said.

"My troopers are having some success it appears," Swift explained. "Plasma rounds managed to burn through the creature's scales. They've attacked with blades from the MECHs as well. They managed to drive the creature into the ocean."

"What about your troopers? Did they survive?"

"Private Henry Dyson is on the beach and appears unharmed. Private Cosmo Frost went into the water with the creature. I've lost sight of him."

"What else can you tell us?" the commander of Fiona Grand's military forces asked.

"Just that the creature isn't in league with the Ma'Tis. There are crab bodies all over the beach... hold on... I can't believe it."

"Believe what, Captain?"

"Frost! He's alive, General. I thought he was lost for sure," Swift said with a chuckle. "He's wounded, but alive. Dyson is helping him now. You want to know what the alien is, they've had the most contact, General."

Get them off that beach," General Song said. "I want them debriefed ASAP. General Ming, we need scans of that area."

"There's too much interference, General."

"If nothing else works I want eyes on the water," General Song demanded. "No excuses. We aren't getting caught off guard. General Toliver, you find that device. The creature couldn't have taken it far. General Eclair, I want high yield plasma cannons in place to stop whatever comes through that device next. This is what we exist for, people. Let's make sure that nothing can hurt the citizens of Fiona Grand. I'll brief the PM. Knots, get Captain Swift up here ASAP. I want to debrief him myself."

"Yes, General," Knots said, sending the orders through on the communications console at his spot of the table.

Davina Song turned her back on the rest of the room, which had burst into activity as she gave orders. There was a sweet sense of accomplishment to see others jump at her command, but that wasn't what had brought a smile to her face. She felt a thrill of excitement at the very idea of first contact with an advanced alien race. They hadn't come in peace, but that was fine by her. In fact, it made her role even more important than ever. History would remember that Davina Song, head of the Fiona Grand Military Command Staff, had been in charge with the aliens first arrived on their planet. And she was certain that no other world had been contacted by the strange aliens. Maybe they were all dragons, who knew, but she was staring at her legacy. The general who saved the people of Fiona Grand. That's how she would be remembered. It was the reason she had joined the military in the first place. It was what drove her to perform and had lifted her up through the ranks to the highest command position possible. She was at the pentacle of the military at the perfect time, and at long last her desire for fame and glory was coming true.

Chapter 2

Captain Malcom Swift was a genius. That wasn't just his ego either, intelligence testing had proven his mental superiority, as had the way he advanced through the levels of academia. He could have made a fortune in the private sector, but he didn't just want to make things, he wanted to make the greatest fighting creations known to man. And it wasn't enough just to build them either, he wanted to test them in the field. That meant the army was his path and so he had taken his place in the Armor Division creating all sorts of weapons for war.

None of that had caused him to be called to the Capital. His accomplishments were exciting, but it was the alien tech which had paved his way to the office of the high commander of the Fiona Grand military. Dyson and Frost had proven his ideas worked. They were valiant Battle Troopers and he had been lucky to find them in the first place. Somehow they had found a way to succeed in every test of military prowess that he threw at them. Even without his HAVOC drones they had defeated the alien creature. Unfortunately, the Ma'Tis had finished off the alien, dragging its serpentine body down into the depths of the sea, which meant he couldn't study the creature, but he had the first scans of it's device and the data was mesmerizing.

As he waited for General Song in her posh reception room, outside her private office on the fortieth floor of the Military Command Building just adjacent to the Capital Building in Hallsberg, he studied the information he had collected. Scans of the disk shaped device showed it to be an alloy made of elements humanity had yet to discover. He didn't know if it had some sort of protrusions that held upright, like the roots of tree, but it was drawing energy from the ground. And while he didn't yet understand how the device was doing it, he was certain that he could figure it out. Mankind had all sorts of technology to collect and harness energy, from sunlight to the power of the wind. Splitting atoms was still the most effective manner of energy production, but in every process there was waste, sometimes even toxic by-products that required expensive clean up and mediation. If Malcom could crack the code on the alien tech and learn how to derive energy from the planet, he would be the most famous man in the galaxy. Not to mention wealthy beyond his imagination. Not that Malcom craved wealth, or fame, but he longed to make his mark in the galaxy, to be remembered as a great man of science. And he was so close to greatness that he could taste it.

"General Song will see you now," a bored looking Lieutenant Colonel in his dress uniform said as he waved Malcom to the door.

The inner office was more austere, a simple, efficient work space. The General had a grand view of the capitol building, the PM's mansion, and the monuments that surrounded them. But her back was to the window, her focus on the modest computer display that was built into the top of the small standing desk. Captain Swift came to attention in front of her.

"At ease, Captain," General Song said. "Let's not waste time, shall we."

"No, General," Swift said.

"Good. You're work is cutting edge, but if I'm being honest, all things considered, I don't see HAVOC drones taking a primary role in the war."

"I'm sorry to hear that," Swift said, his mouth suddenly dry.

"Of course you are," she said. "Change in the military is slow and often a difficult process. But I'm not scraping the program. In fact, I think there's a place for your little squad. Now, what can you tell me about this alien disk."

"It's on the Montgomery Heights, just a little over thirty kilometers from where it first came down."

"I know where it is," the General said. "I'm more interested in what, it is."

Swift cleared his throat. "I took readings at the original site," he explained. "It's a mineral based alloy that consists of elements we have yet to find."

"On Fiona Grand?"

"Anywhere, General. It's a genuinely unknown substance. We've never seen anything like it."

"In what way?"

"Well, first of all, it's incredibly durable. Not many substances can withstand the heat of planetary atmospheric entry without showing any signs of damage."

"But your troopers damaged it with plasma rifles?"

"That was the idea, but from the photos I've seen the plasma didn't so much as leave a mark on the object."

"Alright, continue," the general ordered.

"Well, it's also a remarkable power conduit. The disk was drawing energy from the ground. And not just a little, but significant power."

"How?"

"I have no idea," Captain Swift said with a grin. "It's a truly remarkable object."

"Is it a ship?"

"I don't think so."

"What then?" the general asked.

"I can only speculate..."

"That's what you're here for."

"Well, it seems to me that it must be a portal of some kind."

"What are the possibilities?"

"The most likely would be that it is a wormhole generator. Although, that sort of device should require obscene amounts of energy to open."

"You said it was drawing significant energy from the ground."

"Yes, General, I did say that, but according to physics as we understand it, a wormhole would require more energy that most stars possess. We're talking about bending the fabric of space. That's no small feat. And we've not witnessed it anywhere in the natural universe."

"But the race that created the disk could have found a way," the general said. "Maybe even one that uses significantly less energy that we suppose."

"That's possible," Malcom said with a grin. "To be honest, I'm dying to find out."

"What are the other possibilities?" General Davina Song asked.

"Well, it's possible that it's a portal to a new dimension."

"Something outside the four dimensions we know about?"

"That's correct. We know there are others, but we've never found a way to look into them, much less cross over the boundaries that separate them from the four dimensions we live in."

"Anything else?"

"I suppose it's possible that it's a portal through time," Captain Swift said. "But that's not very likely."

"Why do you suppose that?"

"Because, that wouldn't explain the mystery elements," Malcom explained. "Or why the creature came through so quickly."

"You're supposing that the time portal theory only works to connect us to the past?"

Malcom shrugged. "It wasn't a sentient being that came through," he said. "We know that in the distant past there were massive animals roaming the goldilocks planets. I'd say that dragon thing was one. Plus, there's the fact that human mythology includes such creatures. The ancient tales including giant serpentine creatures that fly and breath fire. The past seems more likely than the future."

"What's your best guess?"

"Inter-dimensional portal would be my guess, but it's just that. Just a guess."

"How could we prove your hypothesis?"

"The easiest way would be to send someone though it," Captain Swift said.

"Yes, that was my thoughts exactly. But we don't know what's on the other side of that portal. Stepping through it could kill whoever tried."

"Yes, General."

"Or, perhaps trap them on the other side?"

"Yes."

She took a deep breath. "Was there any signs of radiation or biological agents from the creature? Say on your trooper who was in physical contact with it."

"PFC Cosmo Frost was wounded in the fight, but has no signs of any infection or exposure to a toxic or xenomorphic substance. He's in quarantine at Hawkstone, but I did the examination of his MAL Armor myself. It's clean."

"As far as we know," General Song pointed out. "It's possible that our scanners wouldn't even pick up an alien substance. The device wasn't picked up on radar. If it hadn't gone blazing across the sky we might never have known it was here."

"True," Malcom said.

"In that case, I think our only option is to send your man through the portal."

"Private Frost?"

"With his drone. He's proven himself to be a capable Battle Trooper. He's was responsible for taking down one of the Ma'Tis heave weapons vehicles outside Hillsdale, correct?"

"Yes, General, he did that."

"And he was heavily involved in stopping the creature," she continued. "His valor is unquestionable. Do you think he would have an issue going through the portal?"

"If it's even possible," Swift said. General Song just gave him a stern look. "No, General, he wouldn't hesitate."

"Then you have the ball, Captain. I'm putting you in charge of researching the anomaly. And if it opens again, we are sending your man through it."

"Yes, General," Captain Swift said, feeling a cold shiver run down his back.

"I know that command isn't your ultimate goal, Captain Swift, but let me give you a piece of advice. Don't hold onto the troops you command so tightly. Sending our Battle Troopers into harms way is what we are trained to do. Eventually, you'll have that responsibility. Sometimes they don't come back. And while it's only a last resort, sometimes we send them in knowing they will die. You should be prepared to make that sacrifice, Captain. Otherwise, you'll fail in the military and the decisions you have to make will haunt you for the rest of your life."

"Yes, General," Swift said. Her pep talk wasn't making Malcom feel any better.

"Besides, you and I both know this is an opportunity of a lifetime. So make the most of it, Captain."

"Yes, ma'am!" he said, returning to a rigid attention posture and saluting.

"That's all, Captain. But I want reports at least twice a day, and more frequently if you make breakthroughs."

"Yes, General. I'll make sure you are always aware of our study and preparations."

"Very good. You are dismissed."

He turned on his heel and left her office. Malcom Swift was both excited, and concerned. Sending Cosmo through the portal had huge potential for helping Malcom understand the alien object. But it was also incredibly dangerous. Still, it wasn't his order, and while he stood to benefit from it, he could tell himself that he was responsible for whatever happened. But the cold chill didn't leave him. Not even the warm sunshine and the beauty of the capital city could sweep away the feeling that he was meddling with things that were best left alone.